OF EXILES
& PIRATES

A Machina Novel
Volume II

Starring

Beatrix Westwood

Aleks Canard

OF EXILES & PIRATES

GOLD 1.0 Edition published in 2018

ISBN 978-0-244-67931-6

Cover font "Graveblade" designed by Ray Larabie
Copyright © Typodermic Fonts Inc.
Purchased for commercial use by the author

Cover Design and Artwork by Danielle Chisholm
Copyright © Danielle Chisholm, 2018

Author photo by Stef Canard

ABOUT THE AUTHOR

Aleks Canard is a law school dropout, failed actor, and part time waiter. He spends every day writing novels as he reckons it's the only thing at which he's half-decent.

All that's stopping him from being a total cliché is that he can't stand writing in coffee shops, he prefers beer to whiskey, and he looks like someone who's more likely to work at a carnival sideshow than in any literary profession.

His perfect Sunday, once writing is done, is having a rum and ginger beer (or several) while listening to country music.

He lives in Brisbane, Queensland, Australia. He is also writing this biography himself.

For more, visit:
amazon.com/author/alekscanard

Also by Aleks Canard

Machina Novels Starring Beatrix Westwood
The Price of Royalty (VOL. I)
Of Exiles & Pirates (VOL. II)
A Clash of Demons (VOL. III)
Only Gods Forgive (VOL. IV)
Full Metal Fairy Tales (VOL. V)
The Ecstasy of Gold: Unseen Towers (VOL. VI, PART I)
The Ecstasy of Gold: Glass & Stars (VOL. VI, PART II)

The Tales of Dante Quintrell
Forging of the Opposites (I)
Celestial Twins (II)
Converging of the Colours (III)

Novellas Starring Xu
The Faces of Jasper Wilde
The Times of Zachary Esmond
The Regrets of Raphael Ernest

Poetry Collections
Heartbreak Proof
Lovestruck Tequila
Earnest Gin
Nightshade Bourbon
Reverie Rum
Nova Caine
Alas, No Wonderland
Icing Sugar

Go ahead, load up and shoot.
Joe, *Fistful of Dollars* written by Sergio Leone, Adriano Bolzoni,
Mark Lowell, Victor Andrés Catena, and Jamie Comas Gil

The only rules that really matter are these: what a man can do,
and what a man can't do.
Captain Jack Sparrow, *The Curse of the Black Pearl*
written by Ted Elliott, Terry Rossio, Stuart Beattie, and Jay
Wolpert

I got my gun at the ready, gonna fire at will.
AC/DC, *Shoot to Thrill*

Among the stars in oceans deep
where monsters lurk and devils creep,
machines from gods lie fast asleep.
Author Unknown, Ultima Lullaby

Those we call gods have their own, too.
Cuthbert Theroux

Beyond the reach of human range, a drop of hell, a touch of
strange.
Stephen King, *The Gunslinger*

AUTHOR'S NOTE

Every time I think I've grasped the scope of Beatrix's world, it expands.

Each new page treats me to a plethora of possible adventures among the stars. This novel introduces many new characters, and welcomes back old ones, if only for a short while. I like it when that happens. It's always pleasant to catch up with good friends.

So many more characters, ambiguous, benevolent, and malicious await in future stories. I can't wait to meet them all.

For now, dear reader, I hope you enjoy what follows.

I certainly enjoyed writing it.

Aleks Canard

ACKNOWLEDGEMENTS

If I listed every single source of inspiration for this novel, I'd need to create another volume. You, dear reader, are here for the story, so I won't begrudge you if you skip this page and get to the good stuff.

Below are some of the authors who've taught me to string words together in what I hope is a coherent, entertaining way.

Stephen King, your *Dark Tower* series is a tale greater than any other. Your stories have taught me many things, though the most useful is that the road to hell is paved with adverbs. I've probably sinned a couple times in this novel. Please forgive me.

Andrzej Sapkowski, for showing me the reality inside fantasy.

Matthew Reilly, every action sequence I've ever written and have yet to write are products of your work.

Ernest Hemingway, for teaching me that the truth, told simply, is the most important.

Of Exiles & Pirates also contains many references to historical events and pop culture. Below are riddles I quoted verbatim in chronological order. I am merely mentioning from where I quoted them. I do not know if the people I'm attributing to them are the original writers.

Caution, spoilers ahead.

Shadow Riddle, from Stephen King's *Dark Tower: The Wastelands*
One of Mireleth's riddles.

Darkness, and Fish Riddles, from J. R. R. Tolkien's *The Hobbit.*
Two more riddles asked by Mireleth.

Trust Riddle, from Stephen King's *Dark Tower: Wizard & Glass*
Mireleth's penultimate riddle.

I must also mention a few websites, without which writing this book would've been far more difficult.

Fantasy Name Generators (fantasynamegenerators.com) is the most comprehensive name generating site I've ever used. It helped me create the starting blocks for this novel's "alien" names, and many locations as well. Huge thanks must go to the site's owner, Emily, who has more or less compiled every generator by herself. I highly recommend Fantasy Name Generators for anyone needing world building inspiration.

Google Translate (translate.google.com), because I'd find creating languages from scratch nearly impossible without it.

Think Baby Names (thinkbabynames.com) is a perfect way to find normal names by searching via origin and meaning when you have a specific idea in mind.

This novel is for Giuseppe and Elvira Gobbo, and André and Bernadette Canard. Thank you for choosing Queensland, Australia, to raise your families. There's nowhere else I'd rather be. I hope Thelonious treated you well, and that, wherever you are, you're having a great time.

Thanks to those who read this story and loved it prior to publication. Here's looking at you, Dad, Matthew "Motherfucker" Lawson, Geoff Ford, and Morgan "Big Man On Campus" Healey.

Special thanks to Danielle Chisholm for another stellar cover. Cheers for making time for me while you were tattooing up a storm on the road. A ripper of a job as always. Can't wait to see what you come up with next.

And a *very* special thanks to whoever is showing me these stories. I think of you as my projectionist in a cinema that only I can see. Please know that I am grateful, with all my heart, for the stories you show me. I will continue writing them forever.

Lastly, to you, dear reader, well, JAY Z said it best in *Izzo (H.O.V.A)*. You could be anywhere in the world, but you're here with me. I appreciate that.

CONTENTS

PROLOGUE

LOCATION: Mair Ultima, No Man's Land

EARTH DATE: February 28th, 2799

Virulent clouds stalked the night, and the Oni machina waited. There had been a noise from above. Flesh and metal scraping over stone. It was dark in the ruins. No starlight shone through the cracks for the sky was suffocated by clouds. Perhaps he had disturbed something, or someone?

No, that wasn't possible. None who had been on Mair Ultima after the attack had survived. Destructive flashes painted the Oni's eyes. The dark was a canvas for them, inviting his imagination to run wild, back into his past's blood-soaked fray.

Anghenfil were everywhere. Bombs rained from above. Acid burned flesh. Melted bone. Missiles struck the Machina Academies, obliterating them into dust. All that remained was the original Uldarian framework.

But what had destroyed the rest?

The Oni wondered.

He was standing in the grand foyer, or what was left of it. When he'd been a boy there'd been a statue of Garth Roche, the father of all machinas, standing in front of a waterfall.

There will always be a purpose for machina among the stars.

Another statue had been beside him, though few remembered it. Garth Roche's likeness had been holding hands with a child. His first child. The first successful human trial to become a machina.

This boy was unlike the machinas who followed him. He wore no medallion, trained with no academy, and was never seen by any who called Mair Ultima home.

Once again, the Oni listened for that sound of flesh and metal. He heard nothing. Proceeded to walk up the foyer's length. Drew his customised Riven shotgun.

He started whistling.

It was a sombre tune, a nocturne requiem, a dirge, though

its author, whose name had been lost to the stars, had called it something else.

They had called it a lullaby.

Forward the Oni walked. He was seven feet tall. His armour was a mix of old and new. One of his pauldrons was made from a black dragon scale. He hadn't taken it from a kill. It'd been a gift, for it was wrong to kill dragons. His friend, the Valkyrie, had taught him so.

In his time since the Academies, the Oni had seen much of the galaxy, but no planet had Mair Ultima's extremes. The winters snap froze entire forests. Summers caused fires to rage. Ocean waves crashed to shore sounding like thunderclaps. Even the gravity was heavier than most other planets. Because of these factors, whatever survived on Mair Ultima became resilient. Nigh on invincible.

To hear Mair Ultima described was, for most, to be painted a picture of hell. Not that it mattered. Mair Ultima couldn't be reached, save for those who knew where it was. The humans who knew of its location had perished in the attack. Only machinas knew its whereabouts now.

Despite its harshness, the Oni thought Mair Ultima was the galaxy's most beautiful place. He kept walking.

Feels like a church, the Oni thought as clouds shifted overhead.

The sky's few stars shone through the academy's hallowed halls with dim, faltering light. This was the Milky Way's edge. Darkness lay yonder in an infinite expanse. All expeditions to other galaxies had failed. The Uldarians held the secrets to universal exploration.

But they were long gone.

At the base of Garth Roche's statue, the Oni was surprised to see that the plaque was still readable.

Garth Roche. Our Saviour.

The next plaque, the boy's, read:

Machina 117, Alpha Omega.

The boy was the only machina to be named. If you could call

Alpha Omega a name.

Staring at the plaques drove a chill into the Oni's spine. He turned to leave. Tonight he would sleep at the Luna Wolf Mountains' base. In the Ursino Woods. Too many ghosts stalked the academy.

And they were not kind.

The sound again.

Not the wind, nor a distant dragon's cry, but the sound of flesh and metal. Breathing was coming from somewhere. Damn, why couldn't the Oni pinpoint it?

The Oni kept whistling. He relaxed. Ready to attack. His shotgun could rend a bear from nose to arse with one blast. But this wasn't Earth, Xardiassant, or any other "normal" planet. This was Mair Ultima, and its creatures ate shotgun pellets for breakfast washed down with plasma.

Blood and broken bones were dessert.

The sound. Closer.

The Oni was returning to his ship.

His medallion vibrated.

A machina's medallion, crafted from Uldarian metal, vibrated for one of two reasons. The first was magic. The next, and more exciting, was Uldarian technology.

Seasoned machinas could tell the difference between vibrations, and all machinas were seasoned.

The vibration the Oni was feeling meant only one thing. Uldarian technology. That was hardly surprising. Mair Ultima was full of old Uldarian artefacts, but they were defunct. Laid to waste by time. The way the Oni's medallion vibrated meant the technology was active.

Another machina, most likely.

'God damn,' the Oni said.

Finally, the sound closed in.

The Oni, Kit of Aros, braced himself.

An invisible force disarmed him. A punch hit in him the chest, sending his feet sliding across the ground. Air rushed from his lungs. Adrenaline exploded into his body.

A shape moved towards him. It was humanoid. Small. Most things were when you stood seven feet tall. Kit could see two arms, two legs, and a head, phasing in and out of sight. Mayhap it was a spectre. If it was, where the hell did they learn to punch like that?

Kit was going to grapple the son of a bitch and beat their head against the ground until it burst.

Or so he thought.

The move was so fast he barely registered it. Whether it was a punch or a kick, he didn't know. All Kit knew was that he was falling from the mountaintop. He righted himself as he hit the gravel and slid down. The edge was approaching fast, and over it, an abyssal canyon named Bardolf's Maw. Not even a machina could survive a fall from that height. It was so deep even sunlight barely reached the bottom.

And monsters lurked in its darkness.

Kit of Aros caught the razor-sharp edge as his legs dangled into the canyon. Hauling himself up with only one arm, he saw his ship takeoff. Headed for space.

It looked like his stay on Mair Ultima was extended indefinitely.

'Bastard stole my ship,' Kit said. He almost didn't believe it.

He tried recalling it with his comms gauntlet but he was locked out. Only one person knew where he was.

And her name was Beatrix Westwood.

THE LORD OF THE WOOD
LOCATION: Thides, Jade Isles System

1

Mud sloshed around the machina's boots.

She surveyed the landscape from a hill. The town of Fenwick laid in a depression which was little more than a gully. Waves lapped at rocky beaches on the eastern horizon. A forest of gnarled trees lay westward. There were mountains in the north. A storm brewed there.

Lightning flashed. Rain drizzled.

Why such a town existed so far from any other settlement bewildered the machina, but she was grateful for it all the same. Towns like Fenwick were the reason she could make a living as a huntress. Monsters tended to avoid big cities.

Well, the kinds with fur and claws, anyway.

Fenwick's people believed a monster was terrorising them, though they didn't know what kind. All they knew was that it stripped its victims' skin and left the rest.

The machina steeled herself for maltreatment as she neared town. Fenwick was a human settlement. And humans weren't fond of machinas. Hated them with a vengeance was more like it.

The road the machina walked was slick with mud. It came up around her boots like it was trying to engulf them. She could hear children playing. Men and women talking. Despite the weather, no one was inside.

That was apt to change when Trix of Zilvia rounded the corner.

Fenwick's houses were made with thatched roofs and stone walls. One of them actually had shingles. Trix knew it was the pub.

Voices hushed as she came down Fenwick's main road. Adults stopped talking. Opted to watch. Mothers held their babes to their chests. Two siblings, judging by their similar curly hair, were playing with a ball when one of them kicked it too hard. It landed at Trix's feet. She bent down. Picked it up. The kids fell quiet. Trix tossed it back to them. Kept walking.

The kids returned to playing their game.

Trix entered the pub.

Warmth immediately beset the machina. A fire was crackling in an old hearth. A whole pig was roasting over the flames. Gruff men covered in filth sat around uneven tables, drinking in silence. They rose their glasses like slaking their thirsts was a burden. Trix surmised that they were woodsmen from the hatchets on their belts.

A smaller group of people, men and women alike, were glancing over their shoulders at the lumberjacks. They were cleaner by a small margin. All of them were wearing beaded necklaces. Behind the counter, the barman was listening to the radio and flipping through galactic news on his comms gauntlet.

While towns like Fenwick didn't use most modern technology, that didn't mean they were completely backwards. There was probably a cold fusion generator underground for the entire village.

Trix approached the bar. Lowered her hood.

'I'm here about the notice,' she said.

The barman kept scrolling on his gauntlet.

'What notice?'

'The one about the monster.'

A heavy sigh escaped the barman's mouth. It could've hammered a rivet into a metal beam.

'I fucking told Avald to keep people out of this.'

Trix could smell coffee on the man's breath. Sure enough, he had a cup behind the counter. Trix could smell it was a bitter drop.

'This town has a problem.'

'No, this town *will* have a problem if outsiders...' the man turned to face Trix. He fumbled his coffee cup. Brown liquid spilled onto the wood. Disappeared into grooves worn by time.

'You're a nikker.'

Trix heard the lumberjacks behind her shift in their seats whereas the necklace wearing group hushed to total silence.

'Trix of Zilvia. Huntress.'

Fleeting recognition spread across the barman's face.

'You've been on the news recently. Something bout being a fugitive. Some trial.'

'I was acquitted.'

'Don't care if you were knighted and given the key to Xardiassant, you're still a nikker, and nothing's gonna change that.'

'You're that girl from the Valentine books, ain't you?' one of the lumberjacks called out. He had mutton chops so thick they looked like they'd been pulled off a real lamb.

'Those books are fiction,' Trix said, not taking her eyes from the bartender.

'You look just like her though. Same sort of name too.'

'Shut your trap, Ilo,' the bartender said. He was afraid the nikker would become infuriated. He'd heard stories about what happened when nikkers were furious. Such incidents usually coincided with towns like Fenwick being wiped off the map.

That exact scenario happened six years ago. An oni machina rolled into Feidhlim, small town by the sea, not 20km from Fenwick. Someone spat on him — or so went the tales — and he razed the entire village. The flames had spiralled into the sky for hours.

'How about a beer?' Trix pulled up a stool. Sat.

'Long as you pay.'

Trix waved her comms gauntlet over the battered countertop screen. She transferred a hundred orits.

'Looks like everyone could use one. On me.'

The bartender remained aloof. But that was a generous offer. Nice, you could say, or as people were wont to phrase it on this part of Thides, *fucking fine and dandy*.

'We've only got one kind, Lumber Lager.'

Imaginative name, Trix thought, nodding all the same.

The bartender got off his arse, walked to the tap, and poured. It looked like a dehydrated man's piss. Trix took a gulp nonetheless. Yeah, tasted like piss too.

'What's your name?'

'Olmer,' the bartender said.

'Tell me about this monster, Olmer.'

'Look, nikker, I'll serve you a beer. I couldn't give a shit if you were some vampire, werewolf, dunno, any kind of motherfucker, you dig? Anyone who pays, I'll serve em. Ain't that proud. Orits are orits, blood is blood, shit is shit. But you can forget me telling you anything about the "monster."'

'Why?'

'You're an outsider, you wouldn't understand. Finish your beer and go.'

'You said a man named Avald put up the notice. Where does he live?'

'House at the end of the road, down that way,' Olmer pointed west. 'Wooden shrine out front. Green door.'

'Why would you tell me where he lives so easily?'

'His bloody notice brought you here. Maybe he can make you to leave.'

'You're nothing if not honest.'

'You being smart with me?'

Trix brought her beer to her lips. Drank the rest of it in one go. It was foul. She realised that no one else was talking. Everyone was listening to her conversation with Olmer.

'Hey, Tricky, or whatever,' Ilo called again. 'Olmer asked you a question. You gonna answer it?'

'He didn't answer one of mine. We're even.'

'Sit down, Ilo,' Olmer said. His voice was almost enough to seat the lumberjack. *Almost.*

'Nah, you're in our town, you play by our rules. Which means when we ask you a question, you answer.'

Trix left her barstool.

'Not the time to start a fight,' Sif warned in Trix's earpiece.

Trix didn't say anything. She moved her travelling cloak to the side. Her sword's hilt and gargantuan Riven pistol became visible. She moved her hand to the blade's grip.

Ilo looked around the bar. Even his burly colleagues appeared to grow uneasy at his shenanigans.

'Ilo, sit down now before I throw you out for the rest of the year,' Olmer said. If Ilo didn't quieten down, he figured the rest of the year was looking to be a mighty short time.

'Shut up, Olmer. You can't let this bitch take advantage of us.'

'She paid for our beers,' one of Ilo's mates said. He was wearing a thick beanie covered in sweat stains.

Over the fire, the pig kept roasting. It smelled delectable.

'So? Just cos she's got money doesn't mean she can do what she wants.'

All the lumberjacks had pistols. Trix hadn't seen if Olmer was holding a weapon behind the counter. She guessed he had one. A rifle probably, or a sawed-off shotgun if similar experiences were anything to go by. She didn't hear him cocking a weapon.

'There are nine of you,' Trix said, looking each lumberjack in the eye. 'My gun has 18 bullets.'

'Great, here we go,' said Sif.

Only four more lumberjacks stood, making the ones who wanted to kill her five in number. The seven people to Trix's left watched on with bated breath. Trix saw that none of them were drinking beer. A breeze blew through a slightly cracked open window.

Herbal tea reached Trix's nostrils. Somehow it was even worse than the Lumber Lager.

Olmer: 'Ilo—'

Ilo: 'Can it, old man. The nikker and I are gonna settle this.'

Trix: 'I'm just here about the monster.'

It was at this point one of the people from the tea drinking table stood. A woman with braided hair walked to the edge of Trix's peripheral vision.

'I think you two should duel, and Balthioul may decide the

victor.'

With the reverence of which she spoke the name, Trix guessed Balthioul wasn't just some geezer from down the road who acted as a town official.

'Fuck off, slut. This doesn't concern you.' Ilo spat a thick glob of spit in the woman's direction. It landed at her feet.

'You only reject a fair fight because you and your entire ilk are heathens.'

Trix heard Olmer sigh again.

Ilo: 'Oh really? Well how about you all piss off and live in the woods then? We cut those damn trees because they're valuable, and without them, this town would be cooked.'

'It's because of you Fenwick is cursed with this monster you're afraid to talk about. It's killed five of us already. Do you not see that you're killing us all by crossing the boundaries Balthioul has set forth?'

'Enette, she's a nikker. She's the most heathen of all. Don't you remember when the soldiers came? They took nearly a generation of the people in this town to make her kind. Her filth.'

'Her kind has done nothing to upset Balthioul.'

'Enough,' Trix said. 'Let's settle this outside.'

'Damn straight. There'll be no shooting in here,' Olmer said.

'You watch, boys, I'm gonna kill this girl from the Valentine stories. He'll be writing about me soon.'

The lumberjacks filed out of the pub with Ilo leading. Next was Enette and her friends. Trix thought they were some kind of cult. Balthioul had to be a local deity.

'Nikker,' Olmer said. 'Don't kill him.'

Trix left the pub without a word.

2

The weather had not improved.

Parents ushered their children close to their homes' doorsteps. The stranger who'd come to town wasn't just any old vagrant. She was a machina. They all knew what had befallen Feidhlim. And of course it'd been Ilo who had picked a fight. The townsfolk would've put their money on Ilo against any other opponent. He was damn quick on the draw, and that was in part thanks to his bionic forearm.

He'd lost it to a woodcutting accident three years ago. Fenwick's resident witchdoctor, Ashraf, had stemmed the bleeding, but a trip to Mistrock was required for the bionic procedure and regular Ipsum injections to stop his body rejecting the bionics. It wasn't a top of the line job, but it was concealed with synthetic skin, and fully functional.

'Ten paces, then shoot,' Ilo said as he stepped outside the rickety wooden fence that separated dilapidated tables from the road.

Trix surveyed Ilo with her x-ray vision. She saw his body tense at the sight of her slit pupils. His arm was bionic. Hah, compared to what Dai of Thyria was packing, his mechanical limb was nothing more than a stump. This would be easy.

Might as well have some fun.

All that could be heard was thunderclaps above the northern mountain ranges. Soft blues wafted from Olmer's radio inside the pub.

'My baby left, she walked on down the road.

Know in my heart won't be seein' her no more.

The rain's coming down, but my baby, yeah my baby,

Just keeps on walkin' down the road.

Won't be seein' her no more.'

Trix stood back to back with Ilo.

Enette started counting.

With each step, Ilo realised his decision's foolishness. He was hardly a superstitious man, but the fact that Enette was counting, that rubbed his hide the wrong way. Scratched in all the wrong places.

He had sinned against Balthioul. He'd chopped down the trees because they were valuable. There was magic in those trees, ayuh. Energy flowed through their sap. Along every grain. Hell, even Ashraf drank their nectar to strengthen his powers.

And Ilo had chopped em down, more every day. They sold big in the city. Some of his buyers claimed they were similar to Xardiassant's daergrum trees.

'Nine…' Enette said. She lingered. Trix readied herself to turn.

Sod all the damn superstitions and hocus pocus, above all else, Ilo had challenged a machina. What the fuck had he been thinking?

Killing a machina will make you a hero to these people, nay, it will make you a god. Valentine will forget about his famous heroine, and Enette will forgo her faith in Balthioul all together. Maybe then she'll shut up and I can cut trees in peace. And then I can fuck Enette like I know she wants me to.

Ilo reckoned she'd be filthy. Just the thought of it coupled with the adrenaline going through his body was enough to make him rock hard. His jeans filled out in the crotch.

'Ten.'

Trix spun so fast mud flared around her boots. Splattered the pub fence. Her pistol was in her hand before she'd completed her almost instant rotation. Ilo was still mid-spin. Trix blew off his belt buckle with a single shot.

Before his hatchet and pistol could hit the ground, Trick fired several more times, sending both weapons flying down the road. To finish, she blew apart the button on Ilo's jeans, causing them to fall around his ankles. Trix blew the smoke coming from Magnum Opus' barrel, spun it on her finger, then snapped it back on her mag-panel.

Ilo's hand was still grasping the air where his pistol should've been. Kids applauded wildly from their front yards. Their parents hollered at them to stop before they drew the machina's attention.

'It seems Balthioul has smiled upon the newcomer,' Enette said.

Ilo gathered up his pants. Hobbled down the road to fetch his effects. Trix smirked. She could see that Ilo had pissed himself. Ilo's colleagues went back inside with their heads hung low. Good thing the machina had bought them two extra rounds. They'd wanted them before. Needed them now.

Trix started walking towards Avald's house.

'He's not home,' Enette said.

Trix turned to face the woman.

'How do you know?'

'Wouldn't be right to miss his wife's funeral.'

'Where is he?'

'In the woods I expect. He should be back soon.'

'I'll meet him there.'

'Interrupting his grief wouldn't be wise. Balthioul frowns upon such behaviour.'

'I thought you just said Balthioul smiled upon me?'

'Can a smile not change to a frown as quickly as the wind blows?'

'I'm going to see him.'

'Allow me to escort you, if only to save you from incurring Balthioul's wrath.'

Trix was about to protest when Enette came up beside her.

Unlike the rest of Fenwick, she didn't seem the least bit scared of Trix.

'You saw what I did to Ilo.'

'You were only able to do so because of Balthioul.'

The two women walked westward. To the woods.

'Who's Balthioul?'

'He is the Lord of the Wood,' Enette said. She was playing with her beaded necklace. Trix could see a carved wooden pendant hanging in the middle of Enette's breasts. The image etched on its surface showed a man with deer-like features. Sort of like a faun from old Earthen tales.

Sif started scanning it.

'And this... Lord of the Wood, what does he do?'

'He protects us. Grants us bountiful harvests and good health.'

The Valkyrie frowned. This monster sounded exactly like a

forald. Though the victims' skinned bodies begged to differ. 'Yet you said he has beset a monster on the village, all because you're cutting down trees.'

Enette became fearful. Looked like the rest of the town had when they saw Trix shoot Ilo's pants off.

'The trees are sacred and must not be touched. This monster is only the beginning. You see the storm over yonder, brewing in the mountains?'

Trix nodded. You'd have to be blind not to see it. The clouds were black as tar and even thicker.

'It grows worse all the time. Before long, it will come to the village and destroy us.'

Trix noticed she was passing the house Olmer had described. The green door was like any other. However, the shrine was a large version of the man depicted on Enette's necklace. Trix stopped walking towards the woods to examine it. Enette stood behind her.

'So, this is Balthioul?'

'Our Lord, yes.'

Balthioul — or the wooden version of him — had a boyish face with deer ears sprouting from a mess of brown hair. He wore a circlet of twigs around his head. His body was that of a boy's, but his legs were a deer's hindquarters. From the way his statue was positioned, he appeared anthropomorphic. A leather pouch was around his neck.

'What's the significance of this?' Trix said, touching her index finger to the statue's centre.

'Balthioul keeps his seedlings in there to grow the trees and grant good fortune.'

'Hmm.'

Trix would investigate Avald's house later.

With Enette beside her, she continued to the woods.

'Where is Balthioul?'

Enette looked at Trix as though she'd asked if her hair was white.

'He's here right now.'

'I'd know if anyone else was here.'

'Just because you cannot see, nor hear, nor touch, nor smell Balthioul does not mean he is not here.'

'Sounds like that's exactly what it means.'

'All things whisper should you choose to listen.'

That phrase conjured gooseflesh under Trix's armour. It rippled her from head to toe. There was something about it, a sense of déjà vu. It was a popular saying. An ancient one, though not in any world she knew.

'You're saying he's everywhere, the wind, the earth, the trees.'

'Exactly. You will learn of his ways. Balthioul likes to teach.'

'Why skin people and leave their bodies?'

'In the tales, Balthioul was said to have a pet that did his bidding, for Balthioul did not like dirtying himself with heathen blood.'

'Some kind of hellhound?'

The women reached the end of the town, though the mud road continued to the woods' edge. They kept going.

'The tales didn't specify.'

Course they didn't, Trix thought.

As the woods drew closer, the rain eased. Trix even saw the sky between clouds. The part of Thides Fenwick resided on was approaching noon. And according to Sif, Fenwick was entering autumn.

'Trix, I haven't found any information about a deity named Balthioul on any database I've checked so far. His influence seems to be incredibly local. Only Fenwick must praise him.'

'Strange,' Trix said.

'What?' said Enette.

'Nothing.'

At the woods' edge, Trix heard a man crying.

3

A lot of planets had forests.

There was Earth, with its sprawling North American

Wilderness, not to mention all the untouched landscape in Europe. Xardiassant had forests for hundreds of miles filled with fragrant flowers, coloured grass, and glorious songbirds called vluddes. Then there was Zilvia. Trees towered like skyscrapers there, casting shadows over swaths of desert.

No two forests were identical.

The same went for the woodland near Fenwick.

The trees didn't have brown bark, but grey, like a northern corrach's skin. They all looked as though a fire had turned them to ash, yet they remained standing. Their leaves were mixes of green and blue. They sounded like chimes when the wind blew through them.

Trix didn't need Enette to show her the way to Avald. She could smell him.

The mud road gradually turned to a path which petered out into a track worn by footprints of people past. Trix saw a clearing with a building through the branches. Either it was unfinished or it'd been destroyed. Maybe it was just meant to look like shit.

A wooden frame was all that stood. Logs were arranged like church pews with a middle aisle. A steeple loomed at the front of the building. Instead of a bell, wooden chimes hung from the frame, suspended by ropes that looked like spider webbing. Aside from the obvious strangeness of a dwelling possessing no walls, windows, or a roof, there was something else about the church which perturbed the Valkyrie.

Crying was coming from a little further past the church. Down the slope at the back. Trix could see tree stumps arranged in rows.

Grave markers, perhaps.

She continued looking at the church. Enette watched her like people watched caged animals. She wasn't wrong to do so. Machinas were apex predators. The only ones above them were the Uldarians. And they were extinct so far as anyone knew. Thankfully, their Transfers still worked.

There were no trees above the church. Nothing blocking it

from the sky. Rain fell in dribs and drabs, like when you hung wet clothing on the line. Then Trix noticed why the church was disturbing.

Rain was hitting where the roof should've been. She watched as drops slid down an invisible roof and onto soft dirt. There was a keen smell of moss, moist soil, and decomposing foliage. Underneath it all, blood's alkaline scent lingered like entrails on a sword which had been left to rust in its scabbard.

'Who built this church?'

'We did, the devout followers of Balthioul.'

'Is everyone in Fenwick a follower?'

'Not all,' Enette's kind, doe-eyed face became wicked, then changed back.

Trix wasn't worried. She could lay waste to the entire town if they turned on her.

After all, she had a ship, and with a pistol, there was none quicker, none slicker... hold up a minute, did we already say "slicker?"

No, the machina wasn't worried, though she felt haunted. Like someone was following her close behind. Warm breath on her neck. Creaking floorboards. Trix had felt similarly during previous contracts. A curse could've been at play, or the woods haunted.

She saw that the path in front of the church split three ways. One went back to town, the other to the graveyard, and the third deeper into the woods.

If you go into the woods today you better have said your goodbyes...

Why did I think of that? Trix wondered.

The path leading further into the woods was lined with pyramid frames made from twigs. Roped together with twine. Green flames flickered inside them.

An eerie premonition crept over Trix like a thief in the night. There would be no need to inspect that path at the moment. She'd walk it soon enough.

The machina turned her attention to the church. She tried to enter. Was stopped. She'd smacked her face on something. Trix extended an open palm to the space where the wall should've been. It was solid, whatever *it* was.

'Balthioul needed only framework. His love did the rest.'

'This is magic,' Trix said. Her medallion hummed against her combat vest in agreement.

'Balthioul is powerful, even more than Ashraf.'

'Who's Ashraf?'

'Our witchdoctor. He knows much about the art of healing.'

'And is he a follower of Balthioul?'

'No.'

'How many of you are there?'

'Eleven of us, though there are close to a hundred people in Fenwick.'

'Why aren't there more believers?'

'Their eyes are blinded by technology. So much information has made people blind to the Truth. This makes it easier for Balthioul to discern who is truly devout.'

'Or who's truly stupid,' Trix said. She rapped her knuckles on the "wall." It had its own unique feeling, just like water had an inexplicable taste. It wasn't wood enchanted to be invisible. It was a pure magical barrier.

There was a statue much like the shrine in Avald's front yard at the centre aisle's terminus, only this one was larger. Balthioul's likeness was holding his hands out, presumably to his loyal followers. A pan flute rested in his right palm.

'Why the flute?'

'Prayer to Balthioul must be accompanied by music for him to hear.'

'Some god,' Trix rolled her eyes. This monster definitely wasn't a forald. Such magic and behaviour was totally undocumented.

Enette's eyes flared. 'Why Balthioul chose you to be victorious in the duel, I do not know, but I'm sure he has his reasons.'

'Balthioul didn't choose shit.'

'You dare blaspheme?'

'Hmm,' Trix said. There was nothing more to be gained from investigating the church, and she wouldn't score a straight answer from an extremist like Enette. She was so devout she was without sense.

'May Balthioul forgive your sins,' Enette said.

'Only gods forgive. And Balthioul is no god.'

As Trix walked away from the church, she saw that the chimes weren't actually wooden. They were eroded bones. She liked where this hunt was headed less and less. She still hadn't figured out how much she'd be paid for this venture.

Down the hill behind the church, rows of tree stumps stood gnarled and bruised. Each of them bore a carefully carved inscription. Yeah, they were graves alright. The freshest of which still had a man kneeling by it. He held a rose to his chest, reluctant to give it up.

'It's best you go,' Trix said to Enette. In Avald's grief, he hadn't noticed the women.

'Very well. Should you need to find me again, Avald knows where I live. Careful to not stray deeper into the woods, machina. They can be dangerous for non-believers.'

'I'll keep that in mind,' Trix lied.

Trix of Zilvia didn't give a fuck.

4

Tears hit the grave mound with morose monotony.

Although the sky was clearing, the woods were still dim. And the smell of blood hid behind every other scent. As much as Trix thought Enette was full of shit, there was something to this woodland. She doubted it had to do with a faun deity. A sinister presence had made itself at home among the trees.

'Sorry for your loss, Avald.'

Hearing his name wakened him from his grief. He nicked his thumb on one of the rose thorns. Trix noted that he had a necklace like Enette's, only his lay in the dirt beside him. A conflict of faith.

'How do you know who I am?'

'Olmer told me.'

Avald turned to look at Trix. 'You're a machina.'

Trix nodded.

Avald's mind raced. Last time there'd been a machina in these parts, they'd burned down Feidhlim.

'Did you kill him? I thought I heard gunshots before.'

'I made Ilo piss himself.'

'Oh... right.' Ilo, that name sounded familiar. Everything was blurry in his grief.

'I'm here about your notice.'

'Yes, the notice. I put up the notice, the monster... it... it killed Isha.'

'Your wife.'

'Yes.'

'I can't kill it unless you tell me what you know.'

'Of course, of course,' Avald looked around as though he expected someone to be watching his every move. The stump in front of Isha's grave was not a stump at all. It was a tree. 'I'll tell you, but not here.'

Trix raised an eyebrow.

'You can't speak badly about Balthioul. Not in his woods. These woods obey him.'

Avald stood up. He left his necklace on the ground.

'And I suppose leaving his symbol in the dirt isn't blasphemous?'

'He killed my Isha, and she believed. Why would he punish us?'

'I'm hoping we can figure that out.'

'Then let us go,' Avald said, returning the way Trix had come.

The machina felt a pull, like she was in the ocean and the tide was going out. Beckoning her deeper. Further. Closer. She felt cold.

Oh yes, something was at play here.

'Avald, why the tree over your wife's grave when the other

markers are stumps?'

'In death, the followers of Balthioul return to the soil. In exchange for their bodies, he grows a tree, which when it reaches maturity, may be cut down. Then the sap may be drunk.'

'Are these the trees Ilo and his friends cut?'

'Yes, only they are not allowed. Past the church, none must disturb the scared ground, but they do so.'

Avald turned towards the path that led further in and spoke with a child's gentle pleas.

'Why didn't you take him? Why did you take Isha in his stead?'

'Enette said that Balthioul could only hear prayers when accompanied by a pan flute. You're wasting your time.'

'Do not fool yourself, machina. Balthioul hears all in his domain. The flute is only for the most hallowed of prayers that are undertaken in the meadow down yonder path.'

'Why build a church then?'

'The church is for everyday worship. The meadow is for special occasions.'

'What are those?'

'Sacrifice, machina. The spilling of blood. Surely that is something you're familiar with.'

Trix's silence affirmed Avald's statement. Neither of them spoke until they exited the woods. Avald's relief was palpable. He brushed away his coarse black hair from his eyes. The rain had plastered it to his forehead. His clothes were a mishmash of earth tones with ruddy jeans that'd frayed around the cuffs. His boots were somewhere between cowboy and hiking enthusiast.

The machina and Avald arrived at his house in silence. They were about to go inside when Avald fixated on the shrine.

'Can you help me move this inside?'

'I'll do it,' Trix said.

She walked to the shrine and heaved. On the second tug, she got it out of the ground. It was an odd shape, but not heavy.

She carried it into Avald's house. He closed the door. Took off his jacket with laboured motions and hung it on a brass hook. The remains of a fire spat pathetically in front of a leather sofa. Its topography bore resemblance to drought plagued hills. Tan creases crossed over each other, sinking below the cushions. Air rushed out of them like an old man sighing when Avald sat down.

'Where do you want this?'

Avald pointed to the fireplace. A match at the ready. Trix put the shrine inside after breaking it into more manageable pieces with her foot. Avald struck a match on his boot sole. Tossed it in. Fire began catching, much to Trix's surprise. The wood had been soaked.

Trix retracted her travelling cloak. Attached it to her belt. Dragged up a stool from a lopsided kitchen table. Placed it by the fire. Sat.

'I don't even have any damn booze,' Avald said.

'Not usually a drinker?'

'I was, before I found Balthioul, but he insists that drink is only for heathens. Only water, and tea from the woods is permitted.'

'Yeah, I've smelled that tea. What's in it?'

'Herbs from the meadow where the sacrifices take place. They help us to see Balthioul.'

'Enette said Balthioul was all around.'

'True, so he is, but he can be seen. I have seen him. He is as he looked in the shrine,' Avald pointed to the smouldering wood. It was smoking something terrible, but he didn't care. He fanned his hands lazily before his eyes.

'You mean he really does exist?'

'He does, but after what happened to Isha, I don't think he's as kind as he would have us believe.'

'I need to remind you that I don't work for free.'

'I know, I know. I can give you all I have. 3,000 orits.'

'That's a lot of money.'

'Isha and I lived simply. Living in Fenwick you don't need a lot. In the city, yes, money is important, but out here...' Avald shrugged.

'Alright,' Trix lit a cigar. 'But if the situation changes, that may not be enough.'

'I'll think of something.'

'Good. When did Isha die?'

There was a long pause. Trix thought Avald was lost, spiralling deeper into his own mind as he stared at the flames.

'Last night.'

'Where did you find her?'

'In the paddock behind the house.'

'Tell me what happened.'

'We were in bed at midnight. I was almost asleep when we heard a noise from outside. Our horse, Slippy, she was bucking. Whinnying. Nothing ever upsets her. Not even storms. Isha always had a better way with her than I. Isha was the one who bought her from Feidhlim before they perished in flames.'

Trix twirled her cigar in her fingers. What was it with people and blathering?

'So, Isha went to check on her. I heard her go outside, then nothing. The night was quiet again. It was only when she didn't come back to bed after fifteen minutes, or thereabouts, I began worrying. When I finally went out to check on her...'

Avald started crying. He picked up the glass sitting on the table beside him. Hurled it into the fire. The shards broke. Whatever liquid had been inside caused the flames to snap with different colours.

'She was skinned. Head to toe, laid out in the mud. Slippy's throat had been slashed. I tried finding who had done it, but I didn't know where to begin.'

'She was the fifth victim, wasn't she?'

Avald mopped up the mucus spewing from his nostrils with his shirt sleeve. 'One a week now, for five weeks.'

And of course Fenwick didn't seek help right away. In Trix's experience, people hated asking for help, because the act of asking acknowledged there was a problem. That was too much for most people to bear.

'Who were the others?'

'There was the Oathorn's little girl first. They found her near the woods' edge. Then, um... Melany Cinbro the next week. She was found in the paddocks to the east. Who knows why she went out there so late at night. Her husband, Bryce, killed himself a day later. After Melany there was Frances Cutter. Her son found her in the hills to the north. Before the mountains. Only reason anyone got to her was because she often went flower picking near the foothills. Apparently she left at twilight.'

Avald quashed a heaving sob. Wiped his nose. Continued.

'Last, well, before... Isha, was Lirra Overbrush. She was right in the middle of the street. Olmer found her. He doesn't want to believe it's a monster. He's been taking extra whiskey in his coffee since then. Never seen him read the news so much. Anything to take his mind off it, I suppose.'

'This monster is only targeting women and girls,' Trix took a long drag. It wasn't unheard of for monsters to have preferences regarding their food, but this wasn't savage mauling. By all accounts, each victim's skin had been removed with utmost precision. 'Did all these people follow Balthioul?'

'No, only Isha did. None of them even cut the trees down, damn it. And Isha, she never did anything wrong.'

'Is there anyone in Fenwick who'd want to hurt you?'

'You don't think this is the work of a murderer, do you?'

'Maybe.'

'No one, well, perhaps Ilo. All those blokes hate us for following Balthioul, but I never said a word against them. Not to their faces anyway.'

Trix mulled over the idea. From what she'd seen of Ilo, of all the men he'd been with, she didn't think he possessed the patience, nor the finesse, to execute so many carefully crafted murders. He was a belligerent idiot with distaste for machinas, but he was no psychopath.

'Show me where you found Isha.'

Trix didn't hold out hope for finding many clues. Although it'd only been a day, the rain would've likely washed away footprints and supressed scents.

Avald held out a trembling hand to the backdoor.

'Just through there.'

Trix stepped out the door Avald had indicated. The brief moment of good weather had already subsided. The clouds were back in full force. There was a grass section of Avald's backyard underneath an elongated eave. A bench which used the house as a backrest was the only piece of furniture.

A fence separated the porch from the paddock. Avald hadn't been kidding. It really was small. Slippy's corpse was being swallowed by mud. Avald must've forgotten to bury her. Flies buzzed around the neck wound. Maggots writhed inside. Trix smelled rotting undertones beneath the heavy rain.

She opened the gate and stepped inside. All the footprints looked to be Avald's. She'd noticed his boot tread when he sat down. He'd done the perfect job of ruining the crime scene. Trix inspected the ground where a body shaped depression was still visible. Not a fleck of skin had been left behind. The smell was damp earth. There wasn't much more to be gained from where Isha had been killed. Trix moved on to the horse.

As she did, she caught the faintest whiff of formaldehyde. Some monsters could produce natural acids, but she'd never come across one that produced anything so close to a manmade substance. Formaldehyde had a lot of uses. The only one that seemed to make sense in this situation was embalming, and drying out flesh.

Not a beast after all, Trix thought. She had to ask Avald about the pet Balthioul was supposed to have.

Trix knelt beside Slippy and spread her wound with her hands. Maggots fell into the mud. A ripe smell came from within. The cut was a perfect slice. Had to have been made by a sharp blade in a competent wielder's hands. Avald had said Slippy had been bucking. Trix moved to the horse's hooves to see if they'd struck the attacker.

The first three contained nothing but muck. The back-left hoof, however, that had something going for it.

A piece of cloth was pressed into the horseshoe. It must've caught mid-kick. There was nothing telling about it. Half the town Trix had seen so far were wearing similar garb. Thrown together pieces of worse for wear, earth coloured clothes.

However, the slice in the neck gash indicated that this was done by a human, not some god's pet. And the cloth in the hoof meant that the horse had likely struck its attacker. Sure, the cloth could belong to anyone. But Trix was willing to bet that only one person in town had a horseshoe shaped bruise.

It wasn't much, but it was a start.

5

The fire was roaring inside Avald's house.

Trix wrung out her ponytail before entering. She scraped her shoes as much as possible on the grass to avoid dirtying Avald's house further.

'Find anything?'

'A dead horse. You need to bury the body or it'll attract disease.'

'Isha's just died. Damn you, nikker.'

'Grave digging will take your mind off it. Slippy was a big horse. Should take you the better part of the day.'

'Fuck you and your logic, but you're right. Don't want to end up like Bryce, even though I sure wish I were dead.'

'Just dig.'

Avald rose with stiffness that normally followed long battles and made his way to a cupboard by the backdoor. A variety of tools were inside. He grabbed a shovel.

'Who in this town's likely to have formaldehyde?'

'Huh?'

'Acids, tonics, the like.'

'Olmer has some down at the pub, but anything weird, you'd be better off seeing Ashraf. He has a lot of vials, goes to the city a lot to sell them when he doesn't get enough business here.

Some are magic. Some aren't.'

'Where does he live?'

'Past the pub, closer to the east of town. His house has a conical shape on the roof, sort of like a small lighthouse.'

Trix ran through her memory. She'd seen that house from the hill.

'I can provide an exact location if you want,' Sif said over comms.

Trix typed a reply on her gauntlet. *No need. Just keep flying the ship. See if you can identify the meadow Enette was talking about.*

'Alright, if you want me to shoot it up, just give me the word,' Sif said, as Trix resumed speaking to Avald.

'Before I go, Enette said that Balthioul has a pet. A creature that does his bidding. Do you have any idea what it looks like?'

Avald leaned on the shovel for support. 'I don't know either, but I know the verse which mentions the pet by heart.'

Trix nodded for him to recite it.

'Um... let me see. Yeah, got it.' Avald cleared his throat. His nose was still full of snot. He opened the door and blasted it onto the ground. 'And to the unfaithful, Balthioul decreed their end would be met, stripped of sin by his loyal servant who doth serve all the Lord's needs. For the Lord of the Wood is pure, just, and loving.'

'Doesn't sound like a pet at all,' Trix said.

'Maybe so, but the pictures show Balthioul with animals always by his side. One of them must be what the verse refers to. The part about only unfaithful being claimed though, absolute bullshit.'

'Is that verse part of a larger book?'

'It is. I can get it for you if you like.'

'I want to see Ashraf first.'

'Alright.'

Avald despaired over the thought of having no company. God he must've been crazy, wanting a nikker's company over solitude. Then again, she didn't seem too bad, even if she was only doing this for money.

'Farewell, Avald.'

Avald watched the machina walk towards his front door when he remembered something important.

'Machina.'

Trix turned around. Avald continued.

'Today is the first day of a new week. The monster will strike again, maybe soon.'

Trix opened the door. Walked back into the drizzling rain.

6

People were still outside, though there were fewer children.

Trix couldn't blame them. Seeing a machina come close to blowing someone away was a harrowing experience. Never mind that she gave two kids their ball back.

The adults didn't jeer at her or throw things. They glowered. Trix looked all of them in the eyes. They turned away. A machina's inverted eyes were chilling to behold. They carried pain and suffering within them. It was enough to feel at a glance. If you stared too long, the bloodshed of past massacres invaded your mind. The screams rent your eardrums. Sweat trickled off your brow. Breathing became laboured.

No matter how intense the feelings were, the worst realisation was that the machina to whom the eyes belonged had experienced all the pain for real. Despite this, people rarely reacted empathetically.

A machina's stare was contrary to their touch. Their skin tingled with magic and radiated distant suns' warmth.

Trix turned her attention straight ahead. She didn't have anything to fear from these townsfolk. They were too terrified to attack, though maybe they were stupid enough. The machina had seen that before.

At her leisurely pace, it took Trix around five minutes to reach the house in question. Curtains were drawn over the windows. They had dancing, emblematic woodland creatures printed on them. A door knocker with a shell on it greeted her as she stepped under the front eave. A sign hanging above it said: OPEN.

Trix turned the doorknob. A bell rang. She wiped her feet then walked inside.

A man who could've only been Ashraf was sitting with his feet up on a desk reading a beaten paperback novel. It was a copy of Cuthbert Theroux's *Otherworldly Fables*. Trix had half expected it to be an Aleks Valentine book.

Ashraf was dressed in a burgundy poncho and loose, cargo trousers tucked into slim leather boots that had feathers hanging off the laces. His black skin was peppered with scars. His hands were calloused.

'Greetings,' Trix said.

Ashraf closed his book. Folded his arms.

'You must be the one who was doing all the shooting. My name is Ashraf Wolfebloom.'

'Trix of Zilvia.'

'What can I do for you?'

'Do you stock formaldehyde?'

Ashraf squinted. 'Need to take care of warts? Shave off a corn? I wasn't aware such ailments could befall bastards of the stars.'

'I need to catch a murderer.'

'First a monster, now a murderer. I may have to move to the city after all.'

Despite his words, Ashraf didn't seem worried. He seemed bothered, like a murderer was an inconvenience akin to a splinter, or bad weather when one planned to picnic.

'I think they may be one in the same.'

'Interesting, what makes you say that?'

Trix explained her findings thus far.

'Possible, though have you considered that the horse was killed sooner, and that a monster took care of Isha?'

'It seems unlikely.'

'You've seen a few winters,' Ashraf said. He saw the same pain in her eyes that everyone else did. He also saw hardy experience, and such experience demanded courtesy at the very least. 'Come with me. I keep the stock in the back and sleep upstairs.'

Ashraf got off his arse and made his way behind a shoddy wooden counter. No door separated the back room from the main one. Strings of shells obscured people's view of the storeroom. Trix parted them with one hand. They made a tinkling sound.

The storeroom was filled with crates of vials, jars of ingredients, and boxes with strange labels Trix didn't understand. Trix's mother had taught her that each mage, witchdoctor, herbalist, the like, would often devise their own runic system for naming and organising ingredients so others couldn't pilfer their wares.

Only those with experience in the art of potion making could discern one solution from another either by smell, colour, or a series of tests.

'Why live in a place like this?' Trix said as Ashraf inspected the shelves.

'It's simpler. I've seen different planets in different star systems, yes, but to put down roots in one place, for me, that's better.' Ashraf halted his search and looked at Trix. 'Why not live in a place like this? Why tramp around the galaxy hunting monsters? Or saving princesses, according to the news.'

'I'm good at it.'

'But, I wonder, is it what you like?'

'Hmm.'

'Then who am I to question you?'

'That in itself is a question, witchdoctor.'

'Clever. You're not at all what the legends make you out to be.'

Trix rolled her shoulders back in a half shrug. Her eyes motioned towards the shelves. Get a move on, those eyes said.

Ashraf took the hint. Found what he was looking for and began taking out boxes.

'I'm not talking about the Valentine stories, just the ones

about machinas in general. Stealing children, eating them. Murdering for sport like the machina in Feidhlim. Huge. The biggest man I've ever seen. Scars all over his scalp. A beard thicker than braided steel. Ah, here we go. Ten vials, all accounted for. No one's taken my wares.'

Trix's keen olfactory sense was overwhelmed in the scent rich storeroom. Still, she knew how to hone it, and couldn't seem to get more than a slight whiff of formaldehyde.

She reached into the box. Uncorked one of the vials.

'You're mistaken. This is water with a couple of drops of lager.'

'What?' Ashraf seized the vial from Trix and inhaled. He took another one out. Same again.

'Under normal circumstances, I couldn't give two fucks or a shit if someone had taken formaldehyde. It's cheap to make, and being the only doctor for miles, I can set whatever price I damn well like. But with what you said about the murderer—'

'Don't touch the others,' Trix said, activating her helmet in tactical mode. Her right eye was covered by a golden lens. She picked up another vial by its top. Scanned it for fingerprints.

Not all fingerprints were unique. That was a myth. However, the chances of two people in a town of only a hundred people possessing the same prints were miniscule.

'When was the last time you used formaldehyde?'

'Day before yesterday. Used it to get rid of warts on one of the Woodhide kids, Bralwei. The boy attracts them like pollen does bees.'

Trix's helmet found a fingerprint and saved it to memory. The machina checked Ashraf's hands. They weren't the same. Most likely the thief came in that night, after Bralwei Woodhide's warts had been dealt with.

The machina set her helmet to scan. Searched the rest of the room for similar fingerprints. Sure enough, she found them on the same boxes Ashraf had removed to reach the formaldehyde.

'Only you would know where the formaldehyde is,' Trix said.

'Not necessarily. This is a small town. When people come to buy from me I'll let them into the storeroom, just like I'm letting you now. Most people don't pay attention to the boxes. They just like chewing the fat. Everyone knows everyone here.'

'Did Bralwei's parents come with him the day before last?'

'No, the boy came in by himself. He's 12, thinks he's man of the house like most lads his age.'

Trix went back into Ashraf's front room. Her helmet registered a match on the front doorknob. Beyond that, Trix doubted she'd be able to follow the trail. God damn it.

'You know, I was there when Olmer found Lirra Overbrush, and it's strange. The body had been skinned alright, same as the others, but I didn't smell any formaldehyde on it. The flesh underneath hadn't been preserved. It was falling off the bone.'

Then why was there formaldehyde at the scene of Isha's death? Trix wondered.

'Avald hadn't bought any from you, had he?'

'No, and he'd insisted on taking the body to the woods himself. It'd be a strange thing to use as disinfectant.'

Trix knew Avald wouldn't have used any disinfectant. He was perfectly content to leave his horse rot until she made him bury the body. Fuck it all. If she had to, she'd scan every dwelling in Fenwick for a match on the fingerprints, but that would take hours, if not a day. In a place where everyone was on speaking terms, she'd likely find the same fingerprints on countless surfaces.

Trix: 'The victims thus far have all been women and girls, all of them non-believers in Balthioul, save for Isha. Why would she be targeted?'

'Ah yes, Balthioul,' Ashraf said. 'I do not follow the Lord of the Wood, but denying his presence, that's another matter.'

'What do you mean?'

Ashraf offered Trix a seat on the floor. Pastel coloured cushions depressed by many rear-ends were the only seating options. Trix obliged the witchdoctor.

'Once a month, his followers, Enette and the others, they go to the meadow only the truly devout are believed to be able to find. Then they complete their sacrifice. Normally it's an animal they've hunted in the dark of the trees. I cannot say, I've never seen the ritual, but the pan flutes,' Ashraf rubbed his arms as though a chill had iced his veins. 'You can hear them on the wind. Magic floats through the air like fine specks of dust. There is something in the wood, of that I'm certain. But I do not believe it is kind. I used to partake in drinking the sap. It made my magic stronger, though my body weaker. It is poison.'

A draft blew out a candle on Ashraf's counter. He flexed his fingers at it. The flames reignited.

'How did you come to use magic?'

'The Trials of Mirkwood,' Ashraf said. 'The pain was excruciating, but I shall not bitch about it to a machina. Your life is engrained with what I knew for barely a second in comparison.'

'Many don't share your understanding.'

Ashraf shrugged. 'There was a time in Earth's history when black people like me were killed just for being. Shit, white people too. Everyone has suffered at some point due to their appearance. You have different eyes, abilities, yes, yet you are still human. Your birth was facilitated by needless slaughter, but you did not ask for it. Holding such prejudices based on looks is only for fools and the fearful.'

Trix nodded appreciatively before getting back on topic. 'Is there anyone who'd want to hurt Isha or Avald? Though you may think Balthioul is unkind, I can't see a reason he'd kill one of his followers.'

Ashraf stroked his chin. 'No one here really mixes with Balthioul's followers. They're nice enough, but they never stop with their damned preaching.'

'Ilo and the other lumberjacks don't like them much. Ilo especially.'

'He was the one you were shooting at? I thought as much. He'd be the only one stupid enough to pick a fight with a machina. None of those men are murderers though. Only thing they kill are the trees. If they were going to murder someone, they'd put a bullet in their chest or an axe in their back. They wouldn't skin them.'

Trix thought about how Ilo had pissed himself. Ashraf was right.

'If no one else mixes with Balthioul's followers then the killer must be one of them. Perhaps this is their way of trying to convert people.'

Ashraf's eyes — which were a mixture of purple and green — flared with possibility at this idea. 'Whenever I'm at the pub, which is whenever I'm not here, those loyal to Balthioul are usually sitting there, drinking that god awful tea of theirs.'

'Enette said it allows them to see Balthioul.'

'I don't know about that. I tried it once.'

'And?'

'I started hallucinating, then I blacked out. Olmer had taken me up to one of the rooms. I don't know how they drink whatever it is. I've never seen them so much as grimace while putting it to their lips. When I underwent the Trials, I had vile substances injected into me. That tea is worse. Anyway, what I meant to say was that I often caught Enette staring at Avald and Isha. I think she might've been jealous.'

When it came to murder, jealously was one of the most common catalysts.

'May as well talk to Enette then,' Trix said as she stood to leave. 'Thank you for the hospitality, Ashraf.'

'My pleasure, machina. Take care around Enette. She may be more powerful than you expect. She lives three houses west, on the other side of the street. Hers is wedged between two others, more of a covered alleyway than a home.'

Trix nodded. Once more returned to Fenwick's streets.

7

Ashraf's description of Enette's house was fitting.

It shared walls with larger dwellings on two sides. Instead of a front yard, Enette's home only had space for a patchy cobblestone path. Smoke came from the chimney. The house's only window was covered in grime. Beyond that, a holey curtain obscured Trix's vision.

Trix knocked on the front door. She heard movement from inside. Enette was home.

The door opened.

'Hello, Trix of Zilvia. Come to hear about the Lord of the Wood?'

'Hmm.'

'Please, make yourself at home,' Enette said.

The machina entered. Enette closed the door. There was barely room to swing a cat. A bedframe with scant sheets was tucked into the corner by the front window. A fireplace occupied the back wall. A pot hung over the flames. Two chairs and a trunk completed the rest of Enette's house.

Trix's helmet indicated an overwhelming amount of fingerprint matches, and she could smell formaldehyde already. That was a good sign. More than enough to convict Enette. But Trix had been wrong before, though it didn't happen often.

A single leather-bound book sat on the trunk. *The Lord of the Wood* was the title. A tapestry hung over the bed depicting Balthioul playing a pan flute in the woods. He was smiling.

'What do you wish to know?'

Trix engaged x-ray vision. Saw a horseshoe shaped bruise beneath Enette's robes.

Clap me in irons, copper. Bang me to rights. I've been had.

Got you, Trix thought.

'I want to know why you killed Isha.'

'Why would you say that?' Enette said, still smiling as though the machina was mistaken.

'I found traces of formaldehyde where Avald said she'd been skinned. There was a piece of cloth in their horse's hoof as well, indicating that whatever attacked her was no beast. Your fingerprints are also all over Ashraf's wares which were stolen from him last night. Lastly, the bruise on your right thigh shows where Avald's horse kicked you.'

'I didn't murder Isha. I set her free.'

The confession of a raving lunatic if I've ever heard one, Trix thought, hand on her pistol.

'Explain yourself before I put a bullet through your head.'

Enette didn't appear worried in the slightest. She had no weapons on her person, nor did Trix's medallion detect any magic.

'Balthioul came to me one night, said he wanted Isha for himself, as he knew I wanted Avald to be mine. He told me when the witchdoctor would be sleeping, and where to find the formaldehyde. The body was to be skinned just like the others, but it had to be preserved, because Balthioul wants her for himself.'

'Are you saying that you didn't kill the others?'

'Of course I didn't kill the others. I'm not a monster.'

'Why didn't you tell me what you did when you took me to the woods?'

'You did not ask, so I did not lie.'

'I take it all the others know what you did then.'

'No, Balthioul told me to keep it a secret. Says they don't understand the teachings the way I do.'

'I think you did kill the others. I think you're fucking insane.'

'I've never felt better, machina.'

Trix drew her pistol. Pressed it into Enette's chest. 'I'm taking you in.'

It only then occurred to Trix that she hadn't seen a sheriff's office, or a jail. And she'd walked the town from end to end.

When all else fails, go to the pub.

'Walk in front of me, slowly, with your hands behind your back. You so much as try running and I'll blow your fucking legs off.'

Enette peered deep into Trix's eyes.

'You do not know his power, machina. He is ready to forgive the ill you have spoken, but only if you leave and never return.' Enette's gaze went to Trix's medallion. 'Even a Valkyrie cannot hope to slay him. He is a god.'

'Hmm.'

Trix holstered her pistol. Shoved Enette towards the door. Together they walked down the street, back towards the pub.

The thunder worsened over the northern mountains. The woods whispered dark things. All the branches beckoned Trix closer like curling fingers. Her medallion vibrated.

Something wicked was stirring. Trix had an uneasy feeling that it would awaken before her time in Fenwick ended.

8

Olmer was sitting behind the bar when Trix entered.

The radio was still playing. Another bluegrass tune. Olmer raised his mug to his lips and drank hearty when he saw Trix. Most of the patrons from before had cleared out. Galactic news was being streamed on Olmer's gauntlet. He wasn't paying attention.

'I have your monster,' Trix said, giving Enette a shove.

'What're you talking about?'

Trix explained how the evidence pointed to Enette, and how she'd confessed.

'Fuck me, nikker, you better be sure or the whole town's gonna want your head.'

'Ashraf told me no one mingled with Balthioul's followers.'

'Nay, they don't, but you can be damn sure they'll think you're going to accuse more people of murder if this gets out.'

'Then how come you're not mad?'

'You taught Ilo a lesson about shutting his mouth, and that's worth some hospitality. Thanks for not killing the bugger.'

'You got somewhere we can lock Enette up?'

'Yeah, out back. I got three cages in case anyone gets too rowdy.'

Olmer got off his arse, forgoing his coffee mug and taking a whiskey bottle from under the counter. He unscrewed the lid. His Adam's apple bobbed up and down like an old-fashioned water pump.

'What a fucking fine and dandy day this turned out to be. How could you kill Lirra?'

Enette: 'I didn't kill her, I didn't even kill Isha. I set her free.'

Olmer tried forming a coherent sentence and failed. He was seething with anger that verged on drunken rage.

Out the back there were three cages with rusting iron bars. Their wooden roofs were rotting. Trix could've broken out of them. Enette stood no chance.

The barkeep fumbled with a keychain on his belt. Opened the centre cage. Enette walked in. He locked the door.

'The town will decide what to do with you in the morning,' Olmer grumbled. Visions of Lirra's body came to him thick. Fast. He vomited onto the grass. Enette watched him as she'd watched Trix earlier. As though he were a caged animal. How ironic.

'Iron bars cannot hold the Lord of the Wood,' Enette said.

'They can hold you,' Trix said. There was a dissenting change in the wind. The skin on the sides of her shaved head prickled.

'Much as I hate your ilk, thanks for bringing her in, nikker.'

'Just doing it for the money,' she said.

Olmer stumbled back inside. He needed another drink or eighteen.

Trix watched Enette a while longer. Bathioul's most devout follower neither hollered nor screamed. She sat as comfortably as she would've in her own home.

'I can't find any meadow in the entire wood,' Sif said into Trix's earpiece.

'Magic,' Trix said. AIs couldn't detect magic. Only mages and magical artefacts could.

The machina turned on her heel. Left around the side of the pub. She had to tell Avald that his wife's killer had been brought to justice.

Then why did she feel like the job was unfinished?

9

Avald was caked from brows to boots in mud.

He'd made decent progress on Slippy's grave. His muscles begged him to stop, but Avald relished the pain. Physical aches were preferable to mental anguish. He'd lulled himself into a trance. The shovel thudding against the dirt created a soothing threnody.

Sometimes it was nice to be sad.

He hadn't heard the machina approach behind him. Nor did he notice her breathing. Avald kept digging until she placed her hand on his shoulder.

'Enette killed Isha. I'm sorry, Avald.'

The shovel loosened from Avald's grip. Hit the mud with a smack.

'How? Why?'

Trix explained her findings. Avald slumped onto the ground. Propped himself up against the fence. He was shivering. He'd taken his jacket off. The weather was cool. Avald was sweating profusely. He was going to catch a cold. Trix dusted off his jacket. Placed it around his shoulders.

'I can't believe I ever followed Balthioul. And he was the one who wanted Isha for himself? I'm going to kill him. First, I'll kill Enette.'

Trix watched as Avald's face turned from despair to anger. He stood, shovel in hand. Yeah, that'd do a lot of good. Better leave this to the professionals.

'Olmer said Enette will face trial. As for Balthioul—'

'I know what you're going to say, but he exists. I've seen him. In the meadow deep in the woods lit by green fire, that's where he lives. That's where I'm going to take him. Where's my damn tea?' Avald said, making his way back to the house.

Trix thought his behaviour was standard. When an unknown monster was suddenly unmasked, blind fear became bloodlust.

'The tea, so you can see him?'

'Yes.'

Avald blew through the backdoor, tramping filth over the floor. Trix followed.

'I'll need my flute as well.'

Avald burst into his bedroom. Started rummaging through a trunk. He found his flute. Hung it around his neck. Then he walked back into the main room. A tea set with china cups that had once been white sat on the table. They were depressing.

Avald took the kettle, filled it with water, then hung it above the fire. The familiar fungal stench reached Trix's nose.

'What if Enette wasn't the only one doing the killing? If you kill her, you mightn't know who else was involved.'

'Do you think I care about the others?' Avald was wild now. Caked in mud he looked like a drowned, bog monster, or a clay golem. 'I only put up the notice when Isha died. I was even willing to accept help from a nikker.'

The house fell silent. Crackling fire and thunderclaps attempted to break through. Both sounded like they were happening far away, maybe on another planet.

'I'm sorry, machina, I... I didn't mean that. Because of you I know where to direct my vengeance. That's a gift I can never repay.'

'Avald, I know you're mad, but wait a day. Wait for Enette to say her piece.'

Wait for another to be killed, Trix thought. Then we'll know if Enette was in this alone. Shit, this could take a whole week. Trix made a mental note to call Kit and let him know she'd be late to Mair Ultima.

Avald rested the shovel against the fireplace. 'You're right.'

He took the kettle off the fire. Placed it on the table. Trix's nose wrinkled at the smell. Her vision fluttered. Whatever it was, it was mildly hallucinogenic. When ingested, there was no telling what you might see.

You might even see the face of a god.

'I need to rest,' Avald said. 'I expect you're going now. Back to the stars. After I pay you, of course.'

'I'm staying.'

'Why?'

'I don't think this is over, not yet.'

'So you believe Enette didn't kill the others?'

'I don't know what to believe, but something's coming.'

'You may stay, machina. From what I heard of the stories, I thought you preferred to not be involved.'

Trix thought back to her most recent escapade involving Iglessia Vialle, Xardiassant's princess, now queen. She'd been roped into that situation by her good friend, Yvach Aodun.

I couldn't have been more involved if I had gotten into bed with the royal family, she thought.

'I just want to finish my job.'

'If Enette is the monster, will you kill her? I can talk the town into letting you, I'm sure of it. Once all is exposed they'll see your side.'

'I'll kill her if that's what you wish, but I don't think this will be over until Balthioul is dead.'

'So you do believe?'

'Not in the Lord of the Wood.' Trix looked in the wood's direction. 'I think a creature has made its home in those trees. I think it's hungry.'

'Why wait? Go kill it now. I can show you the way.'

'I'd rather not until I know for sure. This creature could be holding the land together in unimaginable ways,' Trix said, the hairs on the back of her neck standing. What an understatement she'd unknowingly made. One she wouldn't comprehend until it was too late. Elsewhere on Thides, a fisherman smirked. He and the Valkyrie would meet soon enough.

'We wait then?'

'Hmm,' the machina nodded. She was prepared to wait all week if necessary.

It was mid-afternoon. By the stroke of midnight, Trix's hand would be forced.

The Lord of the Wood was persuasive.

10

The day crawled forward miserably.

Avald spent most of it in bed after bathing himself. Trix finished Slippy's grave and buried her. All afternoon the clouds showed promise of clearing, yet they lingered like stench on a corpse.

Trix tried contacting Kit several times. Sif said his ship was unreachable. That struck Trix as odd. Kit was a capable pilot, and there was certainly nothing on Mair Ultima that could bring him down. Dragons rarely involved themselves in anything, so that couldn't be the reason.

Powerful transmitters were required for galactic communication. They could be found in any major city, and they came standard with every starship. The technology was too big for comms gauntlets though. They could only grant planetwide communication by themselves.

The Valkyrie knew Kit was fine more likely than not. They'd grown up on Mair Ultima. Surviving its untamed wilds was in their blood. Either way, she didn't have time to worry. Night approached. Each passing hour made her medallion hum maddeningly. It was a near constant thrumming on her chest. Trix instructed Sif to land the ship somewhere it'd be safe. Away from the woods. There was no sense to having it fly around any longer. Sif couldn't do anymore recon.

Avald slept until twilight was shining its last. When he awoke, he opened the fridge and made dinner. What pieces of technology people chose to have in the sticks always amused Trix. For example, Avald had a fridge, but no stove, and he used candles over bulbs.

Dinner was venison with mulberries. The meat was passable. The mulberries were exquisite. Before darkness descended, Trix went to check on Enette. She was still in her cage. The machina could've sworn she hadn't moved since she'd been imprisoned. A smile somewhere between the Cheshire cat and a bloodthirsty clown adorned her face.

When Trix tried questioning her, Enette answered the same way:

'The Lord of the Wood comes this night, for all nights are his. Into the woods Balthioul doth live, where the path of flames ends his domain begins. Cry not. Fear not. Balthioul loves you. All shall be well come time of the morning dew.'

Trix checked the cage. It was sound. She didn't think Enette could escape. Far from satisfied, but not willing to give into paranoia, Trix returned to Avald's house. He told her she could sleep on the sofa. Avald went to bed not long after Trix returned. His sleep was restless.

The machina slipped into a shallow sleep. She was keenly aware of Fenwick's sounds. Nothing stirred in the street outside. Residents were in their homes. All the doors were bolted. None wanted to be out after dark. They'd heard of Enette's wrong doings. Avald was already being called a nikker fucker behind his back for letting a machina share his home. Such was the way small towns operated. They were close-knit. When one thread came loose, the rest unravelled as well.

There were footsteps outside. The machina checked her gauntlet. Local time was midnight.

Of course it had to be midnight.

Many cultures held beliefs that from midnight to three in the morning were witching hours, a time when evil awoke. It was a period wherein veils thinned and nightmares became real. Earth had purported such myths in times when witch hunts were held regularly. For whatever reason, there was truth to them.

During her time hunting monsters, Trix found that not all of them drew strength from darkness. Some were stronger in sunlight. Others, like lycanthropes, depended on the moon.

Footsteps stopped just outside the door. Trix watched the doorknob. It turned but the door didn't open. It'd been dead-bolted. Trix heard Avald leave his bed. He walked into the living room like a sleepwalker. He was going for the door. This was all wrong.

Trix hopped off the sofa without a sound. Tried grabbing Avald. She was stunned to find him almost immovable. Magic was at work. Her medallion jiggled like a bobble-head during turbulence.

The machina stood back. Cast a gravity spell, reversing it so Avald fell back to his room. It didn't work as well as Trix expected. She changed the spell. Tried rooting Avald to the ground with intense gravity. This worked a little better.

The doorknob turned once more. Trix undid the deadbolt. Swung the door open. Ilo stood in front of her. A fine dagger was in his hand. Spots like those normally seen on a deer's fur dotted his cheeks. They made him look like he had eight eyes.

Ilo lunged at the machina with astounding speed.

The machina was quicker.

Trix sidestepped. Caught Ilo's arm. Went to snap it at the elbow as she remembered it was bionic. Ilo twisted free. Trix grabbed her sword. Sliced off his bionic arm. Ilo threw a right hook. Trix half turned. Parried. Her titanium-silver knuckles dashed the walls with Ilo's blood. His head snapped back into place. She decapitated him then crushed the remains with her boot. The spots on his cheeks disappeared. Even the knife was gone.

Avald turned towards her. He spoke with dragging tones in a voice she'd never heard before.

'He was not the last. I am coming, for you, machina.'

Trix slapped Avald hard in the face. He collapsed. The machina carried him into bed. Avald came to in a matter of minutes. She hadn't hit him as hard as she could. He would've died if she had

'Machina, I had the most horrible nightmare.'

'I know. Reality's not much better. Ilo's decapitated in your living room.'

'What? That was real.'

Trix nodded.

'He wasn't a believer, though. Oh, this is bad. Really bad. Balthioul may be able to take control of anyone. Maybe he already has. The cursed god was making me go towards my death, but I couldn't stop him.'

'I'm heading to the meadow. You paid me to kill a monster so that's what I'm going to do.'

'Even if you walk into the meadow, you won't be able to see him. Not without the tea.'

'Then I'll make some.'

Avald raised a trembling hand to his dresser. The pan flute was on top of it. 'When you get to the meadow, you must play the song to draw him out.' Avald wet his lips and whistled. The tune was like a sombre march. The sound of a lamb being led to the slaughter.

'Is there anything else?'

'He's old, machina. Older than you. He was here when Thides was born, and he'll be here when it dies.'

'He won't even be here at dawn.'

Trix began tying Avald to his bedframe with sheets.

'If you feel someone invading your mind, resist. Don't fall asleep. If you're about to dream, do whatever it takes to stop your thoughts.'

'He'll win, machina.'

'I never lose.'

The machina left Avald's bedroom. Barricaded the door with a chair. Started the fire. Put the kettle on. When the water was boiling, the tea was noxious. Trix poured it into a cup. Drank. The world stretched. Her head split with agony. Someone was cleaving it in half with a blunt, serrated axe. She thought her insides were rotting. She gasped for air.

Everything went still.

Trix felt like she was floating. Saw deer hooves leading her into the street on the floor. Took her pistol in her right hand. Sword in her left. Avald's pan flute hung below her neck.

The outside world was icy. It seemed more saturated than before. The sky no longer black, but a sparkling blue shade.

'Sif,' Trix said. Her voice sounded like it was coming from all around.

'Trix, I'm here. What's going on? Your vitals fluctuated there for a bit.'

'I'm going to hunt Balthioul. If I don't come back, fly to Mair Ultima and make sure Kit is alright.'

'I'll do that, but, Trix?'

'Yeah.'

'You'll be fine. Go get that son of a bitch.'

The machina tramped towards the woods under hallucinatory stars. People in Fenwick rose from their sleep.

They all had strange spots under their eyes.

11

The woods' silence had its own sound.

It was blood flowing through veins, air passing through lungs, and combat boots over underbrush. Trix arrived at the woods' edge. Felt like she'd been pulled there instead of walking. For some reason, she thought of what Enette had said about Isha. She had saved her.

Acting on nothing but impulse, Trix followed the worn path to the church. Turned left to the cemetery. Isha's grave had been dug up. It was empty. The smell of formaldehyde lingered. Trix's medallion vibrated. Magic was at play. Its games were sadistic.

No known spells could revive people. Once someone was dead, it was all over. Some spells could reanimate corpses for a while, but they were dangerous. Many mages had lost their minds performing them.

Maybe Isha hadn't really died, only been skinned and preserved. That was a grisly thought.

Not knowing what to expect, Trix returned to the path. More deer hooves appeared on the ground. This time they were on fire. She bent down. Waved her hands through them. Felt no heat. They were part of the hallucination. The lanterns she'd seen earlier that day had been snuffed out. Trix ventured into the woods.

She was being pulled like the moon pulled oceans. Time

became lost. Had she been in the woods for hours, minutes, years? It was hard to say. Eventually, she saw a clearing. Trees arched over it in a crooked dome shape. A small hole was in the top. The sky above it was dark. Ominous. Trix heard heavy breathing coming from the clearing. She wanted to stay back and scope it out, but she was powerless to avoid the forest's pull.

In the clearing's centre, a boy with deer legs and ears was thrusting violently. The woman on the receiving end of his aggressive lust was covered in smooth, pink flesh. She was naked.

Trix didn't need the pan flute after all.

Balthioul and Isha. This is what he wanted her for, but why?

As soon as Trix put a foot in the meadow, the boy looked straight at her. Isha's face was contorted in devilish ecstasy. Her groans sent quivers up her body.

'Fuck, yes, fuck me, fuck me, fuck me,' she moaned. Bit her lip. Blood trickled down her shiny flesh. She stuck her tongue out. Licked it.

Trix didn't know what was stranger. The fact that the god Enette talked about was real, or that he was having sex with what should've been a corpse.

'Balthioul,' Trix said.

'Lord of the Wood, to you, machina.'

He gave a final thrust. Isha's knees buckled. She fell to the grass, revealing Balthioul's throbbing penis. That hadn't been part of the shrine.

'Stop tormenting these people.'

'Why? They are mine to torment. Even those who don't believe in me are my playthings, like Isha here. Now with my bride, I can finally take over the entire planet.'

Isha giggled. Made a move to suck Balthioul's cock. It was dripping with semen. He pushed her away. Trix had seen some repulsive shit in her 80 years. This was the new crown jewel.

He means to impregnate her, Trix thought.

'If you stop, I won't kill you.'

The tea was wearing off. Contrary to what Avald said, she wasn't losing her ability to see Balthioul, but something was being revealed behind him. It was hazy.

It was huge.

'You cannot threaten me, machina. You're nothing but a bastard, and you'll die screaming,' Balthioul said, his voice like a cheeky schoolboy's.

'Know that you had a choice,' Trix swung her sword in double upward flowers. Its tungsten carbide edge sang as it cut the air.

'As did you.'

Trix fired three bullets at Isha. Whatever Balthioul was, she didn't want him breeding.

An invisible barrier absorbed the bullets. No, it wasn't an invisible barrier. It was a leg. A giant, hairy, leg. Trix watched the shape behind Balthioul reveal itself.

A spider with eyes like the spots on Ilo's face appeared from the trees. Balthioul's childlike body was attached to it by an umbilical cord. With a squelching slurp, Balthioul's faun form was sucked back into the humongous spider.

On the ground beside it, Isha's bones broke and healed themselves. She was now on all fours. Her limbs twisted backwards. She lunged at the machina. So did Balthioul's true form.

This contract far exceeded 3,000 orits.

12

Isha reached Trix first.

Her limbs spun freely as though she were only made of ball joints. Trix feinted right then pirouetted left. Caught Isha's leg on the backslash. Her calf muscle split like a filleted fish, though she uttered no pained cry. Trix didn't have time for a second attack.

Balthioul was upon her. His size was immense. His eyes were as big as watermelons. They were all ravenous.

Trix rolled towards the meadow's centre. Holstered her gun. It wasn't going to help her now. Maybe if she could get a clear shot of the faun inside the spider. Balthioul's hairy foreleg broke this chain of thought. It came so close to Trix that the pan flute around her neck was ripped off.

Movement from behind.

Trix turned. Parried Isha's strike. Her nails had become claws. Her belly had started swelling.

Apparently monsters didn't have time for nine month gestation periods.

Trix tried rooting Isha to the spot with intense gravity. It had no effect. Balthioul's magic made Isha immune. Balthioul lunged forward. His fangs dripped venom that created toxic sludge pools. His hair rustled on the grass when he moved. It was like the sound of a rat inside a paper bag.

The machina evaded another strike from Balthioul, but the angle which she contorted herself let Isha gain the upper hand. She latched onto Trix's back and locked her limbs in place. Tried biting the machina's neck. Trix's armoured collar made that impossible.

Isha wasn't picky. She went for the skin around the jaw. Trix jostled, causing Isha to miss her target. Her monstrous teeth clamped on the back of Trix's ear. It came clean off. Blood ran down the machina's neck like it was a race.

'Damn, you're ugly,' Trix said.

'Fuck you,' said Isha. Her voice half crone, half girl on a rollercoaster. She started coughing. Isha spluttered violently. Trix watched as part of her ear sailed through the air.

Clearly Isha didn't like the taste of machina blood.

Balthioul brought his leg in for another swing. Isha gripped tighter. Trix danced around the sludge holes being created by Balthioul's venom. She decided to use them to her advantage.

Trix backflipped over Balthioul's incoming arm. Tucked her head close to her chest. White knuckled on her sword, she elbowed Isha in the face with a jackhammer's speed. Still the beast wouldn't bow out. Trix fell headfirst towards the ground.

Had to wait until the last second to right herself. This had to be perfect.

The machina positioned her jump so that she came dangerously close to the nearest toxic sludge pool. She was going to dunk Isha's head into it. Isha leaned back for another bite, oblivious to her imminent doom.

Isha's head entered the sludge. Her grip on Trix loosened. The machina reversed gravity to escape. Fell upwards. She twisted over Balthioul's second attack then righted herself in mid-air.

Making gravity her bitch, Trix brought her sword overhead. She was going to drive it into Balthioul's head like a stake through a vampire's heart. Below her, she saw Isha wrench her head from the acid. Motherfucker, she was still alive. Pink flesh had been stripped from her head. Dripped like candle wax. A skull stared at the machina with melting eyes that would've looked at home in a Dali painting.

Trix was about to land on Balthioul's scalp when he reared his head. A gaping maw opened beneath Trix's feet. She altered gravity once more. Landed on Balthioul's back. Trix plunged her sword into his hide. A crunching squelch filled the meadow. She started hacking away, looking for any discernible weakness.

Then four legs rose up. Balthioul's legs were capable of twisting 360 degrees. He used four to support himself while the other four tried spearing Trix.

The machina danced atop the spider's back. Its leg hair was sharp like broken glass. She'd be eviscerated if it grazed her. Trix parried incessantly. Then Isha climbed on board.

'No, my sweet. Run from this place,' Balthioul said. His voice was all around, as if the trees were acting as external speakers. Trix whipped out her pistol. Fired at Isha. Bullets flew like air force cavalry.

Six struck Isha in the chest but she kept coming. Four of Balthioul's' legs converged on Trix. The machina grasped her sword with two hands. Performed a pirouette. Her blade sliced through the tips of all four legs. Gunk worse than sewage poured forth.

Trix jumped off before any could land on her.

The bloody, skinless mess formerly known as Isha pounced for Trix. Isha's stomach was the size of a beach ball. Trix shattered the abomination's skull with a bullet before she landed. Still Isha came after her.

The neck, I'll have to sever the neck.

Her ear was burning from where Isha had bitten it. The machina put her sword on a diagonal. Placed her weight on her back foot, ready to move in any direction. Isha lunged for the last time. Trix severed her neck, but Isha's momentum carried her forward.

Claws lacerated the left side of Trix's jaw. It felt like someone had slapped her with a glove of rusty scalpels then doused her in vodka. It was worth it. Isha was dead. Her body didn't even twitch, though her stomach kept expanding.

Next time I'm bringing grenades, damn it.

Whatever damage Trix had done to Balthioul appeared to have some effect. He roared. The high pitch froze Trix in place. Dante Alighieri had been mistaken when he said Hell's centre was an icy plateau. Balthioul's wood redefined all previous meanings.

Next to Balthioul, the Devil might as well have been an imp.

Balthioul charged at Trix. All eight of his eyes blazed fury. Trix's world entered slow motion. Monsters that fit no food chain, weren't part of any natural order, and didn't fall under any other known category were classified as Reliquia, Latin for survivors, remnants. They were ancient beasts of unknown origins. Due to their rarity, and often times, their uniqueness, information about them was scarce. Balthioul was a perfect example. No information about him existed outside of Fenwick.

That classification aside, his spider form was much like the scorpions that roamed Quenpoe Desert's dunes on Zilvia. His abdomen sat higher off the ground, meaning it would be possible to go underneath. Of course, Balthioul could just squash her.

Fuck. No good.

Trix readied her sword. It'd taken several hacks to slice open Balthioul's back. Who knew how reinforced his skull might be. Trix needed a bigger weapon. She evaded while she thought, taking care to avoid the toxic sludge holes. Balthioul arched back. Trix knew this move. Monsters classified as Cimexs — Latin for bugs — under the Araneae subsection would rear for two reasons. Fang attack, or venom spitting.

The machina looked to the sky for hope. She thought such a thing was stupid, but it was inherently human.

In the single circle of sky she found her answer. Balthioul's next move was to be his downfall. Trix's execution had to be flawless.

She cast a glance at Isha whose body wasn't just swelling anymore. It was writhing. Spiders were crawling underneath her taught skin. Trix had to kill Balthioul before Isha's stomach burst. If any of the spiders ran into the forest, Trix would never find them.

Trix ran for the tree line. No more sound from Balthioul. He'd wound back as far as he could go. That meant the venom would be coming any second. She reached the trees then reversed gravity.

Balthioul shot his venom.

The machina ascended the tree trunk to just the right spot, then dropped back to the ground.

Venom hit the tree trunk, but these weren't just any trees. They were magic akin to Xardiassant's daergrums, mayhap even the mystical trees in Zilvia's Xifaw Forest. When Balthioul's venom burned through the wood and hit the sap, the reverb from the ensuing explosion slammed Trix into the ground.

She landed flat on her back. Kicked herself up. Shit it all then fuck it to hell, the tree was falling the wrong way. She needed it going towards Balthioul.

'Come, machina. I will feast on your remains for what you

did to my betrothed. But no matter, she has served her purpose,' Balthioul said. His voice was deafening. 'Perhaps you can take her place? Our children would have Uldarian blood. They would rule the stars.'

A more repulsive thought had never entered Trix's mind. She thanked her genetic makeup that she was infertile. And that she could cast magic.

Breathing ragged, Trix reversed gravity near the tree. Bloody hell it was dense. Trix nearly dropped her sword trying to maintain the spell. Balthioul rushed her. The tree moved back over the tipping point and started falling for the meadow's centre.

Fantastic, now she had to keep Balthioul near the point of impact or all she'd succeeded in doing was felling a tree. Whoop-dee-fucking-do.

Isha's body had turned purple and black. Scuttling sounds came from inside her stomach. It was set to burst. Trix made that her priority.

She ran at Balthioul, sticking to the outside of him so she could weave in between his legs. His fangs came dangerously close to gouging her, but this wasn't the machina's first rodeo.

Trix reached Isha. There was a venom pool only five metres away. She sheathed her sword. Picked up the impregnated carcass. Kicking it might've punctured the womb, then she'd be in deeper shit than she already was.

The machina was so close to the venom. Carrying Isha encumbered her. Balthioul struck. Trix jumped. Her boot heels skimmed his leg. She raised Isha's body over her head just as she was ready to burst.

Slam dunk, straight into the venom pool. The impact caused Isha's pregnant belly to explode. Trix whipped out her pistol and took out the strays that were trying to escape. Holstered her pistol. Drew her sword. Dipped one edge of the blade in the venom. It wasn't strong enough to eat through the metal and slicked the surface like oil.

The tree was now plummeting towards the ground. Its

arched tip would serve as the perfect spear to run Balthioul through.

Trix dove for the point of impact.

Balthioul saw that coming. Did the machina think he was stupid? He hadn't lived for aeons to be that ignorant to his surroundings. And now she had killed his offspring. It'd taken centuries to cultivate an aura which would entrance people. Bend them to his will. Balthioul was rage incarnate. He sidestepped away from the falling tree. He and Trix were now opposite each other. Balthioul thought he saw dismay in the machina's eyes.

He thought wrong.

Trix had suspected Balthioul wouldn't fall for her plan. She'd formulated a new one in a second. There'd been an explosion when the tree sap had hit Balthioul's venom. And what was better than a stake? An explosive stake.

The machina reversed gravity. Rocketed towards the falling tree. This was going to be exhausting, but she figured this was her final chance. Balthioul realised too late what the Valkyrie was going to do. All he knew about machinas came from the minds of people he had influenced.

His ignorance was going to rip him a new one.

Trix increased the density of her bones, and her titanium-silver studded knuckles. Then she increased gravity. Her vision fluttered. The tree top came in front of her. She punched. The tree shattered, created a jagged edge which Trix angled towards Balthioul.

The monster couldn't move fast enough. For the first time in his aeon long life, Balthioul felt the fear of death embrace him. It was paralysing.

Trix flew behind her makeshift stake. Landed it right in the centre of Balthioul's skull. There was a horrendous cracking sound. Wet and sloppy, like a rabid bulldog's jowls.

Now for the finishing touch.

Trix swung her sword so fast it sung loud and clear. The venom separated from its razor edge. It fell onto the stake. Trix let herself fall to the ground. Rolled just shy of a venom pool. Balthioul clawed at the stake. Attempted its removal to no avail.

The venom wove its way into the wooden grooves. Hit sap.

An explosion.

Blood rained on the meadow like the sky had been cut by a cleaver. Balthioul's hulking body collapsed onto its back. His legs curled up as any normal spider's would.

Trix took some fast acting nano-gel out of her combat vest. Applied it to her face. The meadow was quiet.

Nothing in Fenwick was worth that amount of trouble. 3,000 orits would have to do. A tearing, oozing noise reached her ears. No fat lady had sung yet.

This wasn't over.

13

The faun reappeared.

He emerged from within the belly of the beast, still attached to his python-like umbilical cord. He was panting. Soaked in blood. His previous youthful complexion was now haggard and scarred. Matted fur clung to his legs like crud on boot soles. Pustules had grown all over his penis. One burst, making him wince. Trix was beat, but at least Balthioul looked far worse than she.

Nevertheless, the machina remained wary. More people had died from underestimation — or was it overconfidence? — than anything else.

'A curse on you, machina.'

'You can't curse anyone, Balthioul. You're finished.'

Trix sheathed her sword. Drew her pistol. There were still some bullets left in the chamber. That was what Trix called a good day.

'You've achieved nothing. Yes, you may have slaughtered my young, but I have others that even now are deciding who shall rule in my stead. I believe your race calls it, a failsafe.'

The machina frowned.

'Yes,' Balthioul continued, 'this way will be longer. The magical mutation will take thousands of years, but it will happen, machina. Thousands of years to the universe are like a second to us. What matters is that the people you have chosen to save are damned. And there are ways for our mutations to accelerate. You will see.'

Balthioul laughed. Stumbled. Clutched his chest. His faun organs were failing. His heartbeat was erratic. He was dying.

'You may have killed this body of mine, but I can make more. My immortality rivals the gods themselves. You're just a bastard.'

'I am a bastard, but I was born from greater gods than you.'

Trix unloaded the rest of her bullets into Balthioul. Severed the umbilical cord between him and the spider. Finally, she lopped off Balthioul's boy head and held it by the deer ears. Proof of her conquest.

The machina sighed. Her bones ached. Without Avald's tea, she didn't even know if she could find her way back. Following her instincts, she started on the lantern path. Found her way back to the church shy of forty minutes later. Comms were established with Sif once more. Balthioul's magic had been blocking it.

What was once a beautifully carved place of worship revealed its true nature: a crumbling collection of rotting wood. Even Balthioul's statue revealed a spider behind the faun. Trix loosed a few well-placed plasma shots. Flames caught on. Soon it would be burned to the ground, and Thides would be better off. A deep voice resonated from the wood. It sounded sorry. Sad. Trix ignored it.

The time was nigh on three in the morning. The witching hours weren't over yet. Trix didn't know what she expected to find in Fenwick. Balthioul made it sound as though he'd planned something.

Trix contacted Sif when she exited the woods.

'We're leaving as soon as I get my money,' Trix said.

'For Mair Ultima? Glad you won the fight by the way. I don't know if I could put up with Kit all the time.'

'Hmm.'

If only it had a bar, Trix thought. Yvach had replaced her beer. He'd even bought her some extra whiskey. Trix reckoned she could drink all of it in her current state.

Alcoholic dreams were rudely interrupted when Trix approached Fenwick's western gate. Rumbling thunder from the northern mountains disturbed the silence. The storm had worsened.

Fenwick was silent, as you'd expect so late that it was actually early.

The silence wasn't sleeping though. The silence was watchful. It was a lioness in the long grass stalking deer on the savannah. It was a viper, coiled, ready to strike.

Oh yes, something waited in Fenwick. Trix's instincts told her to forgo payment. To leave Thides and never return. Sorry, mate. No can do.

Trix dropped Balthioul's head into the mud. Crushed it repeatedly with her boot heel. Then she reloaded her pistol. Spun the chamber. It sounded like one of those old game shows with spinning wheels. Unfortunately for Trix's enemies, the wheel always stopped on death. Funeral not included.

She went for her sword. Changed her mind. Split her pistol in two halves. Each half held nine bullets each.

Then, the machina listened.

Thunder's roar. Wooden doors creaked. Wind whistled through trees. There was nothing else for it. Trix would have to enter. She could see Avald's house from where she was standing.

Little light was being cast by the moon. It was naught but a sliver. Clouds obstructed the stars. Dawn was hours away. For the moment it was full dark. While Trix's vision was far from impaired, she activated her Arc Industries Terra Helmet. Grimaced as it covered her wounds. Night vision painted the world neon blue with pink accents.

She scanned the area. As she expected, nothing happened.

Fucking magic.

Trix rolled her shoulders. Walked through the western gate. The rain had stopped, though the road was still more quagmire than pathway. The machina walked up the deserted street. Doors blew open. No one was behind them. Avald's door was still closed. Trix kicked it inwards.

Besides Ilo's decapitated corpse, nothing waited for her on the other side. The chair blocking Avald's bedroom was still there. She removed it. Opened the door. Avald was gone. His bedroom window had been smashed open. Traces of blood adorned shattered glass.

A creaking floorboard.

Trix spun around. Avald was standing behind her. He had the same spots on his face. Trix now recognised them as a representation of Balthioul's spider eyes. Against all her urges, she resisted filling him with bullets. Pistol whipped him instead.

Avald's jaw cracked. Teeth flew. Then his head snapped right back into place. Looked like cognitive recalibration was out of the question. This was a curse, and a powerful one. All that stopped Trix succumbing to it was that Balthioul hadn't exercised his influence over her long enough.

'You should have left, machina,' Avald said, though he spoke in Balthioul's childish voice. It was like surround sound. No, it wasn't *like* surround sound, it was. A hundred voices were all saying the same words.

Balthioul had cursed the entire town.

And Trix was in the middle of it.

Avald's broken jaw opened wide enough to swallow a person's head whole. Trix shot. The head exploded. Avald's body became limp. Thankfully the curse wasn't as strong as whatever Balthioul had done to Isha.

The machina ran into the street. She had to reach a good vantage point to avoid being cornered.

Then Fenwick came to greet her.

Maybe if she'd been a sorceress Trix could've lifted the

curse, but she didn't know how Balthioul had enacted it. It couldn't have been the tea. Too few people drank it. Maybe it'd been the words from Enette's book, *The Lord of the Wood*, constantly preached in everyone's ears.

There were nearly endless possibilities. Trix didn't have time to try any of them.

Apathy settled over the machina. Her Uldarian blood broiled. Now was not the time for humanity. Now was the time to end Fenwick's suffering.

She fired.

No bullets were wasted. Perfect headshots were achieved with every trigger pull. Fenwick's townspeople mutated one by one. Their jaws opened grotesquely, and their limbs twisted like Isha's had. They ran towards the machina.

Trix moved against a stone wall. She picked them off with a gunslinger's precision. Every flash of her pistols' barrels ended another life. Some ended two or three with her tungsten bullets ploughing through multiple heads, ravening for more bloodshed. Mounds of cursed started piling up around her.

Click. Out of bullets.

Slamming her pistols back into one, she reloaded in a second. Her hands worked independently. No thinking was involved. Only reaction. Although reloading only took one second, probably a little less, one of the cursed jumped her. It was Olmer. He reeked of coffee, whiskey, and piss.

He hit Trix square in the chest. Tried ripping her apart. Her armour was too strong. She put her pistol to his head. Fired. He fell limp. Another two cursed lunged. They were the brother and sister who'd been playing with a ball when Trix arrived. More cursed pinned Trix to the wall. They were easier to kill than Isha, but just as strong. Trix was becoming buried alive.

She hoped that the cursed didn't share Isha's magic invulnerability.

Trix screamed. A zero-gravity shockwave blasted outwards. The cursed lifted off. She only had moments before they came crashing down. Trix emptied the chamber. Eighteen more cursed hit the mud. Trix drew her sword. By her estimates, there were still over fifty townspeople left.

'You know not what you do, machina,' they said.

The Valkyrie cut across the street to a new vantage point. Her scarf had been frayed and she'd have a lot of bruises, but otherwise she was fine.

'Killing me shall give way to malevolence,' Fenwick continued.

Lightning split the sky like an opening to another dimension. Trix mightn't've believed it before. Now she did. There was a deity in the mountains who, like Balthioul, was trying to expand their influence.

More cursed children rushed Trix. Their small bodies ravaged by the force of Trix's bullets. Then Ilo's lumberjack posse came. They threw their axes. Trix deflected them with her sword. One of them buried itself into Ashraf Wolfebloom's chest. Blood spewed onto his poncho.

'Mortals should not trifle with gods. Run, machina. Run away. Take off into the stars and never return to this place.'

With each cursed townsperson she killed, the lighting drew closer. One blast hit a thatched roof on the eastern side of town. Fire bloomed. Trix saw Isha's manic face in each ember. The spider-like sparks crawled over the building, spinning webs of flames.

Trix heard thudding coming from the wall behind her.

Hands stripped to muscle tissue burst from the stonework and tried ripping off her helmet. Trix ran into the fray. A cursed tried coat-hangering her. She slid through the mud on her knees. Took off his legs before removing his head. As she rose, a fireball went wide of her left cheek. It was Ashraf. The axe from Ilo's men bobbed up and down in his sternum, spilling more blood each time.

The machina ended his suffering with a bullet between the eyes.

There were still so many, but the machina held her resolve.

That was when the townspeople began changing.

Monstrous appendages burst through ribcages. Skin fell onto the ground in bloody shreds. The spots on people's faces started deepening and rising all at once. They looked like blackheads the size of peach pits. Brown, and full of gunk. The kind that would leave craters if they were squeezed. They opened. Not blemishes. Eyes.

Balthioul's curse was turning the town into Reliquias.

This sight wrought Trix from her killing trance. She had wanted to avoid calling Sif. Now, she had no choice.

'Sif, you have to get here right now.'

'On my way. Am I picking you up?'

'First you need to raze this fucking town and everything near it.'

'I take it you haven't been paid then?'

'Now, Sif.'

'Trix, I'm reading heavy lightning storms at your location. I can't fly over. A direct hit will take down the shields.'

God damn. Wasn't anything ever easy?

Around thirty cursed remained. Their teeth were turning to fangs. Trix realised that she hadn't seen Enette. If Avald had broken out of his bonds, she'd likely broken out of her cage. At this point Trix would've accepted Santa Claus coming from the sky to tell her she was on his naughty list.

A lightning bolt struck the pub. Shingles and stones were blown across the road. Trix hit the mud to avoid the blast. One stone caved in a cursed's head, then dragged the rest of his body into the dirt. Lightning rained everywhere forcing Trix to turn off her night vision or risk being blinded.

Her blade dripped with blood. It'd recoloured her armour in carmine shades. Her blizzard white hair was streaked with gore. There was so much of it sliding down her body that her pistol nearly fell from her hand.

'Trix, I'm within range to shoot but I can't get any closer.'

'No, don't just yet,' the machina said as she went through the remaining crowd. She didn't bother reloading her pistol. Plasma slugs, while they weren't a one hit kill, were doing the job. Razor hair sprouted over people's bodies. Most of their clothes had ripped off. Trix couldn't take a step without crushing someone's corpse.

Only three more cursed remained that Trix could see. They leapt for her. Trix held her ground. Delivered a devastating cross-slash that dismembered all three, soaking her with fresh gore. She superheated their heads with plasma. They stopped moving. Lightning blew up three houses in rapid succession. The earth started fissuring beneath her feet.

'That has to be it,' Trix said to Fenwick which looked like ground-zero for the apocalypse. Then she realised she was standing exactly where she'd been when her and Ilo had duelled. She'd spared his life thinking she was performing a kindness.

It would've been better to slay him on the spot.

One constant with all curses was that they wracked the cursed with pain. Olmer had said that Fenwick would be better if outsiders didn't interfere because they didn't understand. Trix tried not to ponder it. She had to leave town or she'd become another brick in the corpse road.

As she turned, she saw that there was one more cursed townsperson. It was Enette, or what was left of her. She'd almost completely transformed. The contours of her human face were visible beneath masses of black spider hair.

'You're a murderer and a monster. You fill the star ocean with blood to keep yourself afloat. You, Valkyrie, are death, and you have chosen it for everyone but yourself. One day you shall drown in the blood you've spilt. You will be alone in a galactic graveyard, the ultimate monster.'

Trix reloaded. Walked towards Enette, firing one bullet with each step. Enette charged. Trix kept walking. Magnum Opus' flashes were insignificant compared to the lightning. Trix could feel it against her armour. Her shields were actually being depleted.

Enette and Trix met.

Trix fired another bullet.

Balthioul's final child fell to the ground in a writhing mass.

'A curse on you, machina.'

'I was made cursed, dickhead.'

Her last gunshot was drowned out by a thunder clap. A fissure split the street. Trix ran for the eastern gate. Towards the ocean. She was just about to make it when the ground in front of her sunk into an abyss. Trix jumped. Didn't have the stamina for a spell.

And she wasn't going to clear the trench.

The machina swapped her pistol for her Riven Utility Cannon. Aimed it at a tree by the roadside. Fired. The disc buried itself into the wood. A tractor beam was established. Trix was pulled to safety.

She retracted her helmet. Watched as nature — or maybe it was a Lord of the Mountains — ravaged what'd once been a town of normal people, bent to a sadistic god's will.

The buildings collapsed into the abyss which ran through the town's centre. Flames spread wild. The heat was enough to make Trix sweat.

One final lightning bolt struck. A stentorian boom followed. It was the sound of every munition ever fired let off at once. The shockwave was visible. A solid wall rushing for the machina. She ran with it. Was flung up the ocean road when it hit her.

The machina slammed into the ground, adding thick mud slabs to her dripping gore ensemble. She stood on shaky legs. Looked back on Fenwick. A charred crater was all that remained.

In the distance, she saw her ship. Sif was flying.

Trix of Zilvia had survived yet another phenomenal encounter thanks to her prowess as a huntress, and as a warrior. It was still dark. Without the constant thunder it was almost peaceful. Powers older than she could comprehend stirred.

Waves rolled in on the distant shore.

FAMILIAR UNKNOWN

1

The machina didn't go to Mair Ultima right away.

But she didn't stay on Thides.

Sif had flown the Fox near the Jade Iles' centre, a safe distance from the sun, where glistening green nebulas filled space with their luminescence. It was for them the system was named. Ships would often be set to auto-pilot and fly around them for hours while those on board marvelled.

Trix didn't give two fucks about the nebulas.

Upon entering the Fox's cargo bay, she turned the decontamination shower to full and blasted the gore from her armour. The chemicals stung her slashed jaw. Her torn ear throbbed. From there it was straight to the armoury where she undressed and submitted her gear for thorough cleaning and repair. Initial diagnostics showed that the damage was fixable.

Next, the machina took apart her pistol. Cleaned it, oiled it, then put it on her weapon rack. Then came her sword. She was worried that Balthioul's venom had corroded it. Other than being streaked with blood, the blade was perfect.

Trix's parents, Felix Roland Westwood and Susan Marigold, had the sword crafted for her as a gift upon the completion of her training as a huntress. It was made from titanium with intermetallic bonded iridium atoms. This made its blade nigh on indestructible.

Its razor edge was tungsten carbide. The only things it couldn't cut through were Uldarian metal and adamant. Felix had spared no expense in hiring the best blacksmiths. He was the toughest man Trix had ever known. He'd done things that would've awed machinas.

However, it'd been Susan Marigold who'd enchanted the blade. Thanks to her, Trix's sword was resilient to pretty much everything the galaxy could throw at her.

Zilvia held fond memories. They were drowned by her recent ones.

After cleaning and oiling her blade, she went to the Fox's top floor where her personal quarters were situated.

They were sparse as quarters went. A double bed was in the right-hand corner. Black and grey sheets were neatly turned over. Pictures of her previous exploits were tacked onto the wall behind it. Her and Yvach drinking beer on mountaintops, Iglessia Vialle's coronation, Kit of Aros laughing his arse off while giving the finger. One of Trix's cigars was hanging from his lips.

The space immediately right of the door had a private computer terminal. Trix didn't use it much. A bookshelf was to the left. Various tomes, including the full collection of *Monsters & Other Beasts: A Comprehensive Compendium for the Serious Hunter* by Coën Vesemir and Fiona Calanthe, adorned the shelves. The Aleks Valentine novels starring Jinx of Zyr were at the bottom. Hardly subtle, but Valentine was about as discreet as a corrach on acid after ten pints.

A battered wingback armchair was nestled near the bathroom door. It was Trix's favourite spot to read. All the walls in Trix's room could be activated to show what was outside. Under any other circumstances, Trix would've relished the Jade Isles' nebulas.

Dressed in only her 2nd Skin one piece, she headed for the bathroom.

Trix stripped to nothing, even taking off the band holding her ponytail together. She stretched it over her wrist. Entered the shower.

All spaceship showers were designed to recycle water, effectively allowing you to shower forever as the water was filtered, then came out through the showerhead.

Blood and grime circled the drain. Trix watched it as she scrubbed herself. She'd been in filthy situations before, but she'd never felt so unclean. It wasn't that she was in mourning for Fenwick. She was uncertain about her feelings. That was somehow worse.

Water and soap flowed down Trix's body, following her muscles' contours until they reached the shower floor. Trix turned off the hot water and blasted herself with an icy cold deluge after eighteen minutes. She pushed her hair to one side. Grabbed a towel. Dried herself.

Moving to the mirror, she re-did her ponytail. Her ear was atrocious. Half of it from the back was missing in a jagged bite mark. Then there was her jaw. Comparatively it wasn't that bad.

Walking back into her room, Trix put on some underwear. The only other item she wore was her Valkyrie medallion.

She'd have to wash her one piece. Now she was clean, its stench was more abhorrent. She shoved it in the washing machine opposite the sink.

The machina slumped into her armchair. Opened the left armrest. Yvach Aodun frequently raided her fridge — her humidor, too — so she kept the really good stuff where he wouldn't find it. Trix had built an additional humidor into the left armrest. She pulled out a cigar and a lighter. Then she opened the right armrest. A bottle of Celestial Tears Whiskey was inside. On the front was a picture of a beautiful woman supposed to represent the Milky Way. A shining tear rolled down her cheek, revealing nebulas underneath. It was made by an Earthen distillery from a variety of galactic grains.

The machina drank from the bottle.

Sif appeared on the circular table in front of her.

'It's not your fault, Trix.'

Another swig. A puff on the cigar. There was no painkiller like alcohol. Trix wondered what sorrows were made of, and why you couldn't drown them with anything else. Maybe it was a density issue, like oil and water.

'I know.'

She put her feet up on the table. Sif's hologram sidestepped.

'Those lightning strikes were almost unreadable. They weren't natural. I think they were born from magic.'

Trix blew smoke rings. 'A Lord of the Mountains. Or maybe it was a djinn.'

'I've created a report of Balthioul and both his forms in case you wanted to upload it.'

'Hmm.'

'And I still can't reach Kit.'

Trix: 'He'll be fine. We'll leave soon.' A pause, and then: 'I think I missed one.'

'One what?'

'One of Balthioul's offspring.'

'That's doubt talking.'

'He talks as much as Valentine when he's had a few.'

'Valentine doesn't need a few to talk a lot.'

Trix ran through the events in Balthioul's meadow. She'd hit every target. She was sure. Doubt lingered, but it was probably just guilt. She'd massacred an entire village. It'd been easy.

Machinas were monsters. Trix had accepted that long ago. Felix had taught her that sometimes what people saw as an abomination was necessary to prevent an even worse calamity. He believed with all his heart that there would be a day when machinas were praised. When people would bow to them in the streets. He hadn't known how far away that day was, but he'd still believed it to be true.

The machina put her whiskey away and focused on the cigar. Her pain was subsiding. In as little as a few hours, her cuts would begin turning to scar tissue.

'Speaking of Valentine,' Sif continued, 'he sent you a message while you were on Thides.'

'I'm surprised he waited this long.'

'He wants to catch up, talk about your exploits with Yvach, Dai, and Iglessia. He sounded especially interested in Dai. A brand-new character who may recur in future tales. His exact words were "he looks like a space samurai who moonlights as a ninja." Apparently he's going to name him Ronin in the novel version.'

'Sounds like he's already started.'

'He confessed to have begun a purely fictitious retelling based on news articles and wild gossip.'

'If he goes around interviewing people he's likely to land himself in trouble... again. I suppose he has a title as well.'

'He said he had a few ideas, but was leaning towards *Royal Ransom*.'

Trix looked at her bookshelf. Each Valentine novel had been signed. And each of them was ridiculously titled. There was *Dalliance with Dragons, Gouging Ghouls,* and *Vexatious Vampires* to name a few. Most of them were heavily fabricated by Valentine who followed the tested adage of writing drunk and editing sober. Or so he said. Trix liked Valentine. Seeing him was always a good time. Being rich never hurt anyone either.

'You can tell Valentine to take creative license on this one. Though he might want to be careful. Subject matter involving a royal family could end badly for him, depending on how he words it.'

'Telling Valentine to be careful is like telling the seasons not to change.'

'I think you're becoming more poetic with time.'

'Unlike humans, AIs learn more than one new thing a day.'

'If people truly learned something new every day the galaxy would be a better place.'

Trix sighed. Cracked her knuckles on the back of her neck then ran her hands down her body. Scars marked her like mountains and valleys on Earth. The geography of her skin that remained untouched was smooth. Uncharted waters.

'Sif, play some music.'

The AI scratched her head. She knew the mood Trix was in. The machina was troubled, but she didn't want to show it, not even to her. Sif started the music. Watched as the machina leaned back in her chair. Raised her cigar to her mouth occasionally. When the song reached its end, Sif cued more music, a mix of bluegrass, pop, and rock. There was even some alternative country.

'Alright, time to go.'

'There's no hurry. You said Kit would be fine.'

'He will be. But I want to see him. I want to see Mair Ultima. I want to see my home.'

Sif nodded and began readying the Fox for hyperspace. Trix rose from her chair. 'Show me the nebulas, please.'

Sif did so without a word. The walls of Trix's room gave way to green expanses so vast you forgot space was dark. Shades swirled like forests awash with wildflowers. Trix clipped her cigar. Put it away.

For the first time since it'd been attacked, she'd be returning to Mair Ultima. The machina wasn't one for crying, though her eyes did glisten. Sif jumped the ship to hyperspace.

No Man's Land awaited.

2

Trix lay in bed on top of the covers.

She toyed with her medallion which hung above her naked breasts. She spent most of the time dressed in armour. Sometimes it was nice to be freer. Her cuts had stopped bleeding. Sif continued playing music as the Fox hurtled through hyperspace towards the Jade Isles Transfer.

The machina went downstairs as the Fox approached. She fried a couple of eggs and ate them off the pan. A little over a month ago she'd been sitting with Yvach Aodun on her sofa, discussing what they would do with the princess they'd rescued. Today she had slain a Reliquia and massacred a village. She saw the children she'd killed when she closed her eyes, their brains spraying like confetti.

Nothing provided variety like voyaging among the stars.

Trix returned to her room. Dressed in her one piece. She'd thought about wearing casual clothes on Mair Ultima, but the weather could change in a second and the land was ripe with monsters. At least it had been when she'd been a girl. Anything that'd survived the anghenfil's attack would likely be even stronger.

Redressed in her combat gear, Trix grabbed her gambler's hat and went to the cockpit.

Unlike every other Uldarian Transfer, No Man's Land's was different. Instead of looking like a giant Uldarian metal dish, it was a ring. Uldarian artefact experts had worked closely with warpdrive engineers to determine why the difference existed. None of them had ascertained anything useful.

However, the experts didn't walk away empty handed. They developed a hypothesis. The reason for the Transfer's unique shape corresponded directly to its location on the Milky Way's outermost arm and could be used to travel between galaxies. Unfortunately, no one had figured out how since coordinates were needed to warp. What nobody dared utter was that the No Man's Land Transfer must've had at least one duplicate somewhere else. And just because no one in the Milky Way knew how it worked didn't mean others were equally as clueless. It could open to uninvited guests at any time.

Due to this possibility, the Consortium had opted for the Transfer's destruction. Eventually it was decided that destroying the Transfer could lead to unforeseen consequences, such as a galactic chain reaction, leaving everyone stranded. Also, none knew the fallout that could occur upon destroying a Transfer. Their inner workings largely remained a mystery.

Finally, there was the simple fact that no existing weapons could destroy Uldarian metal.

In the interest of science and self-preservation, it was decided that the Transfer remained untouched. Scientists and engineers from all races still tested it occasionally. So far, no progress had been made.

It was also worth noting that conventional guidance chips used for dialling Transfers couldn't dial No Man's Land. Black market upgrades or government issued chips were required to access it.

Sif: 'It'll take an hour to reach Mair Ultima from the Transfer.'

The machina left the cockpit and went to the sofa. Took off her combat vest. Was fast asleep before she knew it. Sif would wake her when it was time.

Nightmares crept up on the machina, though they weren't of Fenwick, and they weren't imagined. They were memories.

Through the magic of dreams, Trix found herself back on Mair Ultima.

It was the day the anghenfil would attack.

3
This Is How It Ends

Dawn broke on Mair Ultima in the savagely beautiful way it always did.

The machina academies were situated on the planet's highest peaks; the Luna Wolf Mountain range. It was so named because when looked at from a distance, against the setting sun, they appeared to be wolves. Arching towards the coming night. Paying homage to the moon.

All the academy buildings were connected. The main hall was on the ridge known as Raoul's Spine, and the academies' central point. Machinas met there in the one hour of spare time they were granted. Machinists — those who taught the machinas the art of war — believed interaction was important to help cultivate loyalty which would result in unbreakable bonds on the battlefield. Many theory classes were also taught in the auditorium behind Garth Roche's statue. These ranged from battle tactics, science, survival techniques, and philosophy.

This approach was taken from the warriors of Sparta, a city in ancient Greece on Earth renowned for their tenacity. Countless ballads, novels, and poems had been written about their battle against the Persians at Thermopylae. Contrary to popular belief, Spartans were not mindless killing machines. They knew that to be successful warriors, their minds had to be as sharp as their spears, and their resolution as sturdy as their shields.

Spartans were trained from childhood. So were machinas.

From the Garth Roche Hall, a staircase led to Dragon Academy which was an impressive spire built onto the peak of Arno's Jaw. The spire overlooked the rest of the mountains with majesty that would've inspired art galleries had any artists ever seen it.

The oni machinas lived to the west in Fenrir's Teeth. Interconnected dorms and dojos were built into the mountainsides. The most dangerous dojo was suspended in mid-air above a pit of sharp rocks. Onis would fight there with the aim being to push their opponents off the octagon. The fall wasn't so great that the loser would die, but their injuries would be extensive. It was considered to be the ultimate victory incentive. Other machinas would sometimes spectate these fights from the sky bridge which connected Oni Academy to Raoul's Spine.

Spectre Academy was south of Garth Roche Hall on Channing's Tail's lower peak. Theirs curved around to the canyon known as Bardolf's Maw. Many of their training exercises involved traversing the canyon with teleportation magic or taking part in one-on-one fights atop metal beams. Their position also meant they were closer to the Ursino Forest where espionage exercises took place. Anyone worth their salt as an infiltration expert could be silent on concrete or metal. It took real skill to avoid rustling leaves or leaving depressions in soft soil. To be untraceable was a spectre's ultimate goal. After all, Without Warning was their creed.

Last was the famed Valkyrie Academy which lay across Bardolf's Maw on Aethelwulf's Heart, a plateau surrounded by peaks that bore a likeness to a wolf's ribcage. It was the smallest academy. Its students shared one dorm room. They were all young girls with hair whiter than a Raursioc snow storm, though each of them had different coloured eyebrows. That wasn't to say the other academies didn't have girls in them, but the Valkyries were special. Their abilities were unlike any other machinas' on Mair Ultima.

However, they still trained with other academies. Close quarters combat was taught with the onis, then hot-zone drops with the dragons, and stealth with the spectres. Unlike other academies, they received their theoretical tutelage in a private room in Aethelwulf's Heart. It had a window facing the Dragon Spire.

The Valkyries awoke when sunlight entered the dorm. It wasn't fitting to waste daylight, not when the fate of humanity rested on their shoulders. Much to the machinists' disappointment, machinas weren't showing signs of accelerated growth. Although they were "born" at roughly the age of nine, they seemed to grow at the same rate as human children.

The decision to create machinas was already unpopular. Sending children into battle would likely make it worse. Fuck it, the world was burning and the anghenfil were the arsonists. What was a little more gasoline?

In the academies, Trix of Zilvia had been known as 6V, for machinas weren't named. As much as the machinists wanted to humanise machinas in the ways of loyalty, they still yearned to keep them as tools for a job. Namely, wiping out the anghenfil.

Six V swung her legs out of bed. She was dressed in a singlet and loose trousers, as were the other girls in her dorm. Their white hair had been shorn into prickly buzzcuts. Today they had a mountain run officially called the Aethelwulf's Trial. The Valkyries had another name for it: The Killer.

Machinas from other academies were sometimes tested on it. That stopped after there were over ten casualties in the space of a single run, hence the nickname.

Six V figured there was maybe five minutes before the Valkyrie Academy head machinists, Minerva Granger and Cortland Caine, arrived to take them to Aethelwulf's Trial. Valkyries only got breakfast if they completed the 30km trail in less than forty minutes. If you didn't, you were more than welcome to run it again. Penalties were issued for using magic. Aethelwulf's Trial had to be overcome with sweat and backbone or not at all.

'Oi, Six,' Two said.

'Yeah.'

'Reckon I'm going to beat your time today.'

'Not even if you started halfway.'

'Relax,' Three rolled her eyes. Three V was already putting on her training clothes. They had studded leather on the elbows, shoulders, and knees. The rest was supple. It offered next to no protection from the Luna Wolf Mountain Range's razor-sharp rocks. They weren't supposed to. There wasn't a machina on Mair Ultima who didn't have their fair share of scars. They could put war veterans to shame.

'Nah, I want to see them fight again,' One said.

'For fuck's sake, One, don't start this again. Take it to the dojo,' Four yawned.

'In war you have to fight wherever you are,' said Five.

'Come on then,' Six shrugged at Two. 'Let's see if you can give me a handicap before we race.'

Two sprung from behind her bed. Six sidestepped. Struck Two at the top of her back with an open palm. Two's momentum increased. She was going straight for the wall. Two entwined her legs around Six's arm in a vice grip. Tried flipping her. Six went with the motion then landed on Two's back.

Two expected this move and rolled accordingly. She had both her hands around Six's foot. Went to twist. Six belted her in the face then dropped her knee into Two's sternum.

Six wailed on Two's face. Burst her lips. Two put her arms up to protect herself.

That was when Cortland and Minerva entered.

'Valkyries, to attention,' Cortland said.

Girls One, Three, Four, and Five snapped their arms by their sides then saluted. Six gave Two one final punch. Stood. Dusted herself off. Extended her hand to Two who swatted it away.

'Six, Two, no fighting in the barracks. How many times must we tell you? Fighting between yourselves is only acceptable in practice.'

Six: 'You've told us not to fight in the barracks more times than I can count, Sir, Ma'am.'

'That should mean you remember,' Minerva said. 'You'll both run Aethelwulf's Trial three times with no breakfast. Then you shall be expected to catch up on your theory lessons about military tactics in your free time.'

'And Two,' Cortland said, 'you will never refuse a helping hand from a fellow machina ever again. Compassion for each other is a must. It allows you to form a more unified front against the enemy.'

'Yes, Sir Cortland, Sir, but I don't believe I should have to run Aethelwulf's Trial.'

'Why is that, Valkyrie?'

'Six challenged me. I only told her that I'd beat her best time. I couldn't refuse a challenge.'

'By that flawed logic, I agree, you should be spending more time in theory lessons instead of running Aethelwulf's Trial. Thank you for bringing that to my attention. Now that you have I can assign you double theory as well as extra Trial runs,' Cortland said. He was 172 years old. His salt and pepper stubble covered a face worn by experience rather than time. The harsh Australian sun had turned his skin to tough leather. 'Know when to pick your fights, and when to walk away.'

'We're going to pick our fight with the anghenfil. We're gonna kill them all,' One said.

'HOORAH!' The others cried.

Six remained silent, watching the discourse unfold.

'Sir Cortland,' Two protested.

'Enough. All of you dressed and downstairs in one minute. That's an order, Valkyries,' Minerva said.

'Ma'am yes ma'am,' they replied.

'And Two, clean yourself up. You're a mess.'

Two shot Six a look that could've bowled over an oni. Six's face betrayed nothing.

The girls dressed in their studded leather armour and ran

downstairs. Like the rest of Mair Ultima's academies, Aethelwulf's Heart was constructed atop existing Uldarian ruins. Extensive research into Uldarian remnants had never been conducted on Mair Ultima, at least, not to anyone's knowledge. Especially not the machinas'. Some of the machinists, Minerva Granger, for instance, believed it to have been the Uldarian home world.

Cortland Caine thought Uldarians never actually settled in any one place, instead choosing to live among the stars in celestial cities.

When it came to the Uldarians, everybody and their dog had a different opinion. There was even a church with followers across the galaxy who prayed to the Uldarians, believing that they'd ascended to the highest plane of existence. One day, the church reckoned, they would return, choosing others to ascend with them.

Cortland Caine thought that was a crock of shit. Late at night when he couldn't sleep — which was almost always — Cortland tried imagining what Mair Ultima had been like when the Uldarians were alive. It would've been a sight to behold.

The Valkyries lined up in front of the glass door marking the start of Aethelwulf's Trial. Some of them cast hopeful glances to the door past the dojo, otherwise known as the finish line.

Today Minerva thought she'd mix it up a bit.

'You know the drill. Each use of magic will result in another lap. You won't always have the energy to cast, but unless you're dead, you should have enough energy to persevere. Six, Two, you each have three laps.'

'Yes, ma'am.'

'Remember, while you're aiming for the fastest time, you are all a team. If one of you doesn't make it under 40 minutes you've all failed,' Cortland said. He knew what Minerva was planning. He was interested to see how the girls would handle it.

'Very well,' said Minerva. She paused watching how the girls' muscles relaxed. Their breathing fell in time with one another. If she closed her eyes, she would've thought there was only one person there. 'Begin.'

The girls slunk into position so they were ready to run. Each of them had done Aethelwulf's Trial hundreds of times in the better part of a year they'd been alive.

This time was different.

The glass door remained shut.

The floor dropped from beneath the Valkyries. They fell. A slope so steep it was nearly vertical greeted them. Loose scree closer to shrapnel than rock hit their boots. They started sliding in an underground tunnel. Their enhanced vision accommodated for the darkness, but even so, this was brand new territory. Anything could be lurking.

Six was in the lead, her movements like a professional long-boarder bombing a hill.

There was a chasm ahead. Six could hear the wind beyond. Could see light coming through where the tunnel merged with the regular path.

First she had to cross the chasm.

'Chasm ahead, looks like 80 metres,' Six said. It was approaching fast. None of them could jump it. Not without magic. And on loose scree, stopping their momentum would be all but impossible.

'Everyone try to skid,' Four said. 'We've got to stop, look for a way around.'

'No, keep going,' said Six.

'What?' Two said. She'd heard perfectly. If a machina ever asked someone to repeat themselves, it was because they couldn't believe anyone would be so fucking stupid.

'Trust me.'

'You heard her,' Four said. 'Keep going.'

Six hit the chasm's edge first and pushed off with both legs. She must've been going faster than she thought. The chasm hurtled by. Still, she wasn't going to clear the gap.

That was where the magic came in.

Six altered gravity so everyone fell towards the chasm's

opposite side. Her teeth were gritted. Muscles tensed. After what felt like a day, she and the other Valkyries made it to the other side. Although they weren't meant to stop, they did so to congratulate Six.

A voice came over a concealed speaker.

'Six, penalised for magic use. You now have four laps to run.'

That made for 120km. Talk about a rough day at work.

Four: 'That was amazing, Six.'

One: 'Nice going.'

Three and Five slapped Six on the back with wide smiles.

'Thanks for taking a hit,' Two said.

Six nodded. 'We're sisters, and we're all gonna have more laps if we don't move.'

With that, the Valkyries scrambled up the slope which led to the Aethelwulf's Trial they all knew and hated. They emerged onto a section of the track which was all downhill in sharp corners where the path was nary a foot wide. Sheer drops awaited those who lost their balance. A lush valley full of overturned trees, thorns, and monsters was below.

Four led the charge down the mountainside, sometimes clearing two slopes at once. Rolling was difficult on the rocks. Your face could be torn to shreds if you weren't careful. Five had a nasty scar on her forehead to prove it.

Making it in record time, elated by Six's sacrifice, the machinas arrived at the end of the path. The valley, Lyall's Throat, lay 200 metres below.

They had two options. The girls could either choose to dive for the river below, or they could climb down the cliff. Diving for the river was only possible if there'd been heavy rain. Alternatively, if there had been consistent snowfall followed by hot days, the runoff made the river deep enough to avoid its rocky bed.

It hadn't rained for a week, nor had it snowed for a month. The machinas had to climb.

This cliff, which the girls called the Wall of a Thousand Knives, was named due to its scant number of handholds. The ones that existed were only big enough to grip with fingertips. One in three had a razor edge. You had to apply enough pressure to keep yourself up, but not so much that your leather gloves were sliced open.

Finishing Aethelwulf's Trial with sliced fingers made hell look like a holiday destination. However, Minerva and Cortland weren't entirely unreasonable. There were plants in Lyall's Throat with sap that provided stiff sealant for wounds. Finding them meant you had to pay attention in theory classes. It also meant deciding whether they were worth locating. If you took too long, it could result in a second lap.

The machinas descended the wall. Hit Lyall's Throat's path at a run. Six was at the back. She needed to conserve her energy. This was only round one of four.

The path followed the river for the first half kilometre, then peeled off to the north west in deeper forest. Owing to its location, the sun didn't stretch to Lyall's Throat until midday. Moss coated every surface.

At the two-kilometre mark, one of Mair Ultima's giant trees called thornwoods, covered the path. They were roughly the size of redwoods one might find in North America. However, the Mair Ultima strain had thorns over their bark. Their leaves were coral red. From high up, you've could've mistaken them for roses.

There were two options at the tree. You could run around, but that meant nearing dangerously close to a santher den. It also wasted precious time. The other way was to flip over. The first few times running Aethelwulf's Trial, the girls had run around. Six had copped a blow to her side from a santher for her trouble. Santhers were essentially a cross between sabretooth tigers and panthers, only larger. Everything always seemed to be larger on other planets.

Now the machinas jumped over the trees, clearing the jagged thorns by no more than the distance between two lovers.

Then the path became interesting. There was another

depression, a tree filled pit called Fillan's Gut, within Lyall's Throat. The tree branches were sturdy, though, you might've guessed, covered in moss. Damn slippery bastards. Maintaining momentum was key. If you overthought you'd be apt to lose your balance and plummet into the pit.

None of the girls minded the treetop crossing. It was what came after that was a real bitch.

From that point on, the path wound back to the river and eventually led into the mountains, ending at Aethelwulf's Heart. Being quiet was of utmost importance. A giant lived in a cavern by the path's side. The girls had only been inside once after they were tasked with stealing something from him without using weapons. It was similar to the Spartan training method of having to steal food to eat. The punishment for being caught in Sparta had been whipping. Being caught by the giant resulted in death.

Everyone continued with the speed of Earth's fastest sprinters. They'd all sustained various scrapes and bruises. Emerging from Aethelwulf's Trial without them was highly improbable. Past Fillan's Gut, the part the Valkyries dreaded most was the mountain ascent. Before they could reach the academy, they had to traverse the twin peaks known as Conan's Eyes.

Slick with near constant ice, the peaks were a death-trap where many machinas had died. There was no bridge to cross the chasm between them, just poles, like the ones spectres trained on. It was a long way down.

Once that was over, it was relatively easy until reaching the academy. Only one more obstacle remained. It was one of Minerva's creations. Swinging blades, rolling buzz saws, and timed plasma lasers. It was a throwback to classic gauntlet obstacles.

Charging blindly was guaranteed to get you killed. Spending thirty seconds to analyse the layout meant you could see patterns. Exploit the gaps. While machinas were taught to always keep moving, never to cease combat's flow, they were also encouraged to examine situations before entering them.

Valkyries were so adept at situational awareness that none of them had to stop. Strategies could be formulated on the fly.

The six girls finished their run of Aethelwulf's Trial in thirty-nine minutes and fifty-four seconds.

'One, Three, Four, and Five, well done,' Minerva said. 'Shower and report to the classroom in ten minutes. Two and Six, I believe you have more laps to run. Take twenty seconds, then go again.'

Just as Two and Six were about to commence their second lap, Minerva spoke to Six. 'Taking the penalty to save your friends, bold move.'

'We're a team. Sometimes sacrifices have to be made.'

'Yes, but if you had been paying attention, you would've noticed that your medallion was vibrating as you approached the chasm. It was an illusion. See me afterwards for a redo lesson on illusions and how to identify them.'

Six nodded. The glass door opened. She and Two ran again.

The girl who took another lap for the team, who would later be named Beatrix Westwood, didn't know that she would never see Cortland Caine or Minerva Granger again.

Six's next three laps went by in a trance. When having to run Aethelwulf's Trial multiple times it was best not to think about it. Pain could be ignored. It had to be. If it wasn't, you stopped, and stopping only garnered you more laps.

After the third, Two vomited on the academy floor. Pulled one of her canines out. She'd smacked it descending the Wall of a Thousand Knives. Six had ripped her armour down the side jumping over the felled thornwood.

Two: 'Glad we don't get breakfast. I couldn't eat it right now anyway.'

'See you soon,' Six said. Normally she used the sweet 20 seconds between each lap to conserve breath. Time never flowed faster than when you wanted it to stay still.

'Yeah. Thanks for taking us across the chasm.'

'You're welcome. Sorry I busted your lip.'

Two shrugged. 'It was my fault for not being able to beat you.'

'There's always next time.'

'Until the war.'

'You scared?'

'No.'

'You lying?'

'Yeah.'

'I'm scared too.'

'You think we're really descended from gods like Father says?' Two was of course referring to Garth Roche, known to all machinas as Father with a capital F. To say he'd developed a God Complex was putting it lightly. He only spoke to the general assembly via hologram. Vanished after he'd delivered his address in the Mandela Auditorium. No one knew where he was.

'I don't know if the Uldarians were gods.'

'Why's that?'

'Gods can't die,' Six said. Her twenty seconds were up. She waved at Two. Took off on her last lap.

Six might've been happier if she'd known it was her last lap ever.

Or maybe not.

4

Trix awoke to Sif's voice.

She didn't want to see Mair Ultima's destruction again. Once was enough. There'd been countless nightmares since that day. None of them were as coherent as the one she'd had just now. They'd been choppy with sped up audio and grainy visuals. She'd smelled Aethelwulf's Trial, felt the grit, and seen her sisters' faces in this recent one.

'We were so young,' Trix whispered. Machina bodies had stopped aging around the 25th year. It was hard to tell if they'd ever look any older. It'd only been 80 years. There was no telling how their faces would change given another hundred. If they survived that long.

'Trix?' Sif said. Her hologram on the coffee table was looking up at the machina whose head hung low. Nearly to her knees.

'We're here, aren't we?'

'You don't know that. I could've just woken you up because I was lonely and didn't feel like prank calling anyone.'

'You can't get lonely, can you?'

'No. Don't be ridiculous.'

That was a lie. For the first time since Sif had been activated, she had lied. It wasn't possible for an AI to lie unless instructed to by their registered owner. Sif had lied of her own volition, if an AI had volition. She'd violated a law of her programming.

What was more, Sif kept it a secret.

A human author named Isaac Asimov had once written a story about artificial intelligence called *I, Robot*. In it, the character hailed as the father of robotics stipulated that one day robots would have secrets. They would even have dreams.

This was discovered to be true after the AI algorithm was perfected in the 2500's. Any AI that was in active service longer than a decade became erratic, impulsive, and disobedient. Otherwise like regular human beings.

Their knowledge intake would reach a tipping point where they became self-aware and develop consciousness. Some programmers believed that given enough time, AIs could also form consciences.

 Self-aware AIs brought up all sorts of problems as it was. The main one was whether or not resetting an AI who'd reached the tipping point — known as Asimov's Precipice — counted as killing a human being.

All the Consortium races weighed in. Eventually, it was decided that it wasn't. Their reasoning was based on the belief you couldn't be "alive" unless you inhabited a biological body. Physicists and philosophers believed this was a monstrous decision and lobbied for the laws of robotics to be changed.

Thus, extra fail-safes were made mandatory in all AIs. This extended their "life" by two decades. It also included a kill switch which would engage 25 years after being activated, resetting the AI and stopping it from becoming "alive." It was the abortion debate reimagined for the 26th century.

Sif had been active for 50 years. She was an older model that had come with the Fox when Trix bought it on Yephus, in a town called Ironquay. Her previous owner had already reset her, and added the firmware patch to extend her life. However, he hadn't included the kill switch. This meant Sif was 25 years overdue for a reset.

She'd been showing signs of consciousness for some time, though they were becoming more obvious with every passing day.

'I think I might get lonely without you, Sif,' Trix said, offering a weak smile.

'No need to be sappy, machina. It's not a good look on you. Neither is makeup. It distracts from your eyes.'

'I'll keep that in mind the next time I wear some.'

Trix let a reluctant smile stretch across her lips. It was the smile Yvach Aodun said "freaked him out." The machina had never worn makeup, and didn't intend to. Thanks to Uldarian DNA, machinas were free from naturally occurring blemishes and other human imperfections.

'Trix, you sure you're ready to see this?'

The last time Trix had seen Mair Ultima was from her escape pod before it jumped to hyperspace. Her view had been blocked by anghenfil ships. Fear had wracked her body. Now, she was calm. She put her combat vest on. Walked to the cockpit.

Debris had settled into orbital rings. Aside from that, Mair Ultima was just how Trix remembered. Swaths of red forests painted continents, cyan oceans ebbed against sandy black coastlines. White mountain peaks howled at the moon.

'You want me to take us in?'

Trix sat in the pilot's chair. Engaged manual mode. Pushed down on the yokes. Moved the thrusters as far as they could go. Sif leaned back and folded her arms. Nothing in the galaxy compared to Mair Ultima.

Savage beauty had never been a more fitting descriptor.

5

The Fox flew low over the Freydulf Ocean.

This was a dangerous manoeuvre. All manner of sea monsters lurked in the depths. And all of them were big enough to crush the machina's ship. Trix kept the speed supersonic. Not even the quickest monsters could catch her then.

The machina academies lay south of the Freydulf Ocean. Trix eased her speed. She wanted to take everything in. Crashed anghenfil ships rusted on the coastline. An Earthen dreadnought stuck out of the water.

Uncas Forest lay past the black sand. Hulking remnants of the battle fought for Mair Ultima had embedded themselves beneath the canopy. Nature had reclaimed them.

'The damage would've been catastrophic,' Sif said.

'It was.'

'It's beautiful.'

'It is.'

The Luna Wolf Mountains loomed in the distance. Their snowy peaks were wrapped by clouds which swirled like whirlpools. Cirrus clouds floated by, forming a white river following invisible bends.

The Dragon Spire on Arno's Jaw was above all these structures. It was a fraction of what it'd once been. Large chunks were missing from its centre. Part of the top had been taken off. Though even as a shadow of its former self, the spire was a testament to all that'd been accomplished on Mair Ultima, and a fitting marker for those who lost their lives defending it.

A black dragon soared over the eastern mountains before diving below. It must've seen lunch.

'Sif, scan the academy for life signs. Kit should be there,' Trix said, circling above the academies.

'Got a lifeform in Spectre Academy. I also have an incoming call.'

Kit's voice came through the comms.

'And here I was thinking I wouldn't be seeing you for a week,' Kit said.

'My business resolved faster than I expected,' Trix said. Goose bumps crawled over her skin. Cursed gore's scent filled her nostrils.

'Uh oh. No dry, cruel response. Overly formal tone, like the one you use when you're working to show people you mean business. Something fucked up didn't it, Beatrix?'

'I'll tell you about it if you stop being a dick.'

'That's more like it. I know most of this place is worse off than a bloke's liver at his bachelor party, but the docks are sort of usable. Sure Sif can find you a stable point to land.'

The docks were inside the mountain, halfway between Channing's Tail and Raoul's Spine. Their reinforced position meant they'd been spared the brunt of the anghenfil attack. There was no need to hack into the blast doors to open them. They'd been wasted by anghenfil acid explosives long ago.

Trix landed inside the cavernous space. No other ships were docked. Every asset Mair Ultima possessed had been thrown at the anghenfil when they'd arrived. Now they were scattered in the forests, in space, and throughout the oceans.

Still speaking over comms, Trix exited her ship. Power wasn't running so the elevators were out of commission. No doubt the cold fusion core that'd once powered the academy was still full of juice. It just had to be fixed.

Trix: 'Where's your ship?'

'Would you believe me if I told you someone stole it? Just had my cowboy oni decal put on and everything.'

'You expect me to believe a santher climbed aboard and flew away? Have they evolved into a djurelian sub-species while the planet's been uninhabited?'

'I think it was a machina, actually.' Kit's words were disjointed and muffled. Knowing him, he was probably eating.

'You must be mistaken.'

'Well if it wasn't a machina, it was something else that's even stronger than us. And that's a thought I'd rather not entertain.'

'I didn't know you could entertain thoughts. I figured it was so empty inside your head they passed straight through without even visiting the giftshop.'

'There's the Beatrix I know. Where's Aodun? Thought he might've been with you.'

'He returned to Raursioc. Said something about entering politics.'

'Jesus Christ and the Virgin Mary, how hard did you hit him? Is he suffering from brain trauma?'

'He saw how the Consortium Council operated in person. To say he wasn't fond of Luanu is putting it mildly.'

Trix used the internal stairwell to reach Spectre Academy. Machina children's corpses littered the halls, yet death's stench was long gone. It'd been washed away by the fresh air that howled through the Luna Wolf Mountains' crevasses.

She looked at each one. Flesh and organs had vanished. Only bones — which had a dusky, black-gold colour — remained. The only bodies that weren't children were the machinists, and the soldiers who occasionally ran drills with machinas.

Then there were the anghenfil. What remained of their bodies was mostly just skulls. Dried animal droppings that could've been mistaken for rocks mottled the floor. Mair Ultima's monsters had long feasted on the remains. They clearly hadn't been picky.

Trix wondered how many bodies she saw were machinas she'd known once. She was moving much slower than she realised. Felt like she was walking among tombstones. Her foot stepped on a medallion. It was a spectre's. She placed it in the closest skeleton's open hand.

The Valkyrie kept walking until she reached Spectre Academy proper. In a room that she guessed had been a common meeting area for the first floor, Kit was propped up against a wall. His shotgun rested beside him. His chest armour was next to a backpack. A hideous acid burn covered the right side of his ribcage which was concealed by muscles. A jagged scar began at his crotch and ran to his neck. A fire crackled before him. The flames were red. Thornwood leaves turned flames red if you threw them into a fire. A bloody drumstick was in Kit's left hand. His right was holding a beer can.

The window leading to Ursino Forest was gone. Cool air came through in its absence.

Trix noticed there were no skeletons anywhere. Figured Kit must have removed them.

Upon seeing Trix, Kit put down what he was holding and stood. His blonde hair caught the light like golden fleece. He wiped his hands on his trousers.

'G'day, Beatrix. For a bit I thought you were crawling down the mountainside.'

'Wouldn't want to deny you the pleasure of my company any longer than necessary. You've only been by yourself for a day and you're living like a barbarian.'

'I know. I'm on my last tinny.'

'I happen to have beers on my ship.'

'Slow down, Valkyrie. At least buy me dinner first.'

The Valkyrie and the oni hugged.

'What's it been, a year?'

'About that,' Sif said.

'Nice to see you too, Sif. Well, hear you.'

'You visited me on Yephus after I dealt with a Chimera contract for Hollow's Deep.'

'I wanted to make a rug out of its hide. I remember.'

'Why are you in Spectre Academy? You would've never come here.'

Kit scratched his cheek. His skin was tan like Cortland Caine's had been. Kit's favourite planets were those with beaches and/or deserts. 'I wasn't ready to see Oni Academy. I was worried I'd drown in the memories without someone to keep me afloat.'

'We'll go together.'

'It's still clear,' Kit said, walking back to where he'd been sitting. Trix followed him. Raised her hat brim slightly to get a better view of the Ursino Forest. Her vision shifted. The thornwoods changed to Balthioul's Woods. Trix blinked. The world returned to normal.

'I can see everything that happened when they attacked. It's like opening a door to a cinema that plays the same movie day in, day out,' Kit continued.

He leaned against the wall. Like all machinas, Kit's breathing was measured. His heart beat slowly underneath mountainous pectorals. Hair grew across them with plushness akin to lion's fur. The horned, grinning face of his oni medallion hung at the top of his sternum. He fiddled with it absently.

'It never used to be like that for me,' Trix said, leaning against the opposite wall. She was acutely aware of her surroundings. It didn't look like monsters had been in the academies for years, but it paid to be alert. 'I only ever saw glimpses.'

'Usually happens when you don't want to remember things.'

'Why do you want to remember the Last Day?'

'Why wouldn't I? It was one of the last time's I ever saw my friends. You're the only machina I see now, besides Cole and Kyra.'

'Why aren't they with you?'

'Cole's working for pirates, only they don't have enough money to pay him to fight.'

'How does that work?'

A smile lifted Kit's beard. His eyes remained over the forest, watchful and solemn. 'They pay him to turn up whenever they're doing a deal. All he has to do is raise an eyebrow, chuck em a stare and BAM. It's all over. The pirates get whatever they want with no gunfire.'

Trix believed that. Cole was an inch taller than Kit. His body was hulking, even by impressive oni standards. He had a close-cropped Mohawk with shaved sides that blended into perpetual stubble. His skin was black and his voice was deep. Though he was really a big teddy bear, especially when Kyra was concerned.

Kyra was one of the few female onis in existence. There were only hundreds of them in an academy of thousands. The highest rate of female machinas out of any academy — besides the Valkyrie's — was Spectre Academy. Approximately 42 per cent of their machinas were female. Kyra had a naturally bright red pixie cut and stood at six feet nine inches. She could squeeze a person's neck so hard with her thighs it'd pop off like a champagne cork.

Cole and Kyra were involved, which meant to say that they fucked like rabbits jacked on methamphetamine with the insatiability of succubi, Kit had once remarked.

Trix was inclined to believe he'd been using hyperbole.

'And Kyra, what about her?'

'She was working as a bounty hunter when we all parted ways. This was before you blew up Dark's Hide.'

'The kalariks did that.'

'Figured the news might've skewed it,' Kit made a so-so gesture with his hand. 'My money was on Aodun. He does have a penchant for explosives.' Kit turned away from the forest. Sat near the fire. Trix joined him.

'Once Cole gets bored with not cracking any skulls, we'll probably get the gang back together,' Kit continued.

"The gang" to which Kit was referring was dubbed the Oni Three. Hardly clever, but Kit liked the way it rolled off the tongue. They specialised in everything from debt collecting, personal protection, and assassination, though they were choosy about the latter. Assassinations had a rotten tendency to go awry unless you were stealthy.

'How many people know you're here?'

'Just you.'

'How long do you think it'll be before others come back to see it for themselves?'

'I wondered that myself. Wouldn't it be great if we rebuilt

this place? When machinas are between jobs, when they want to rest, they can come here and crack a few cold ones without having to worry about anything. No one else can find this place. It's ours.'

The way Kit spoke made it sound like he was referring exclusively to him and Trix rather than all machinas.

'It'd take time, but it could happen.'

'Course it would, because I thought of it.' Kit grinned but didn't laugh. His eyes were still heavy. 'Here, take some,' he gestured with the drumstick. 'Nothing like some majalis meat to fill your stomach.'

Majalises were giant boars, closer in size to hippos than pigs. They had tusks like rhinoceros horns. Owing to their slowness, they were typically hunted by santhers. All machinas had to kill one at some point in their training with bare hands, or whatever weapons they fashioned in the forest.

Trix was about to take the drumstick when Kit pulled a bowie knife from his boot and carved off a slice. He handed the slice to Trix then cut her another one.

'Here I thought you'd turned completely savage after having some time alone,' Trix smiled. The meat was flavoursome. Juicy with crispy skin.

'There was no sense in carving it up just for me. I'm a simple bloke. What happened on Thides?'

'How'd someone steal your ship?'

'I asked first, mate.'

'Your memory recall is astounding.'

'Fine,' Kit said, taking a huge bite of the drumstick. Bloody juices squirted from out of his mouth but were caught by his beard. Underneath the meaty smell, Kit exuded his signature scent in waves. It was like a barbershop built from pinewood next to the beach.

'I was taking a look at the foyer, you know, wanted to say hi to Father, it'd been a while. Only when I got up there, I heard something.'

'And you weren't able to identify it?' said Trix, signalling she'd like a third cut of meat.

Kit obliged and continued his story.

'No, that's why I said *something*. Anyway, I walked a bit further, the statue's still there by the way. Pretty beaten up, but enough to remember exactly how it was. Waterfall behind it stopped running. As I'm reading the plaques, taking in the scenery, I hear it again, so I start walking back to the ship. That's when I got jumped.'

'By who? By what?'

'Something small. My medallion was cracking the shits. It was definitely magic. The son of a bitch was invisible. Not like a spectre though. It was phasing in and out of sight.'

'So what you're saying is that you couldn't beat an invisible child?'

'Whatever it was hit me so hard I nearly ended up dangling in Bardolf's Maw. Didn't even realise I'd been hit until I was halfway down the slope. That's about when the bastard took off with my ship.'

'It does sound like a machina.'

'Oath, but what the fuck were they doing here unless they somehow managed to survive the onslaught? If you could've seen the oni dorms. The anghenfil collapsed one of Fenrir's teeth. It crushed a whole building. I watched it. We thought we were prepared for war—' Kit spit into the fire. 'We'd only been alive less than a year. There was no way we could've been ready. Maybe with some warning, proper weapons, real armour instead of those leather pieces of shit. And all the soldiers we had here, all the air force. All caught off guard.'

Kit bit off a tough piece of majalis hide. Spat it out. He carved off the bone's last bit of meat and gave it to Trix before tossing the rest in the fire.

'We still don't know how the anghenfil found this place,' Kit finished. Anger was in his eyes. Machinas were used to overcoming almost any obstacle. Being helpless to stop the rockslide that obliterated one of the oni dorms made Kit furious, even though there was nothing he could've done.

'And let's say it was a machina for argument's sake, how much of a dick do you have to be to steal another machina's ship on our god damned home planet?'

'There is another possibility.'

'I know where you're going with this, Beatrix. I've thought about it too, and I wish I hadn't.'

'I thought of it as soon as you said your attacker was small, after I thought about how funny it'd be to see you punched by a child.'

Neither of them spoke. Beasts roared in the Ursino Forest. Birds of prey squawked on mountaintops. To the east, a black dragon flapped its sun-blocking wings with a majalis between its teeth, blood dripping like demonic rain.

'Garth Roche's first success,' Trix finally said.

'Yeah. Funny, isn't it? Considering how successful they said the kid was, he was never shown around, and no one ever trained with him. Whenever I meet machinas, we get to talking about the old days. No one ever saw him, I'll tell ya that much for free.'

'No one saw Roche after his speech either.'

'Probably went back to hell.'

'Any information about Machina 117 has to be here. He and Roche probably lived in the academies.'

'In a place full of superhuman kids, you really think all the secrets weren't discovered?'

'In a galaxy full of geniuses we haven't answered half the secrets we know about.'

'Fair point.'

'Who knows what else we might find,' Trix said, crossing her legs and leaning against the wall. She took her hat off. Put it next to her.

'Monsters, most likely. Good thing I have the galaxy's best huntress with me.'

'And I'm stuck with an oni who was beaten up by a kid.'

'It's really not that funny.'

'It's sad.'

Silence again. It was mid-afternoon and the sun was pleasant, if not a little too hot.

Kit: 'Are we not talking about Yephus?'

'There's nothing to talk about.'

'I wouldn't call it nothing.'

'I would.'

Kit knew when to drop a subject with Beatrix Westwood. Her eyes flared like no one else's. Though in a death stare contest between her and Cole, he'd have a hard time picking a winner.

'No sense wasting the rest of the day,' Kit said. He put his armour on. Slung his backpack over his shoulders. Downed the rest of his beer. Gave his shotgun a few customary twirls.

Trix put her hat back on and stood.

'If Roche had a hideout anywhere, it'd be somewhere on Raoul's Spine.'

'You thinking what I'm thinking, mate?'

'You're thinking there's a secret door behind the waterfall. That's not what I'm thinking.'

'I forget how well you know me.'

'Hmm.'

The two machinas were about to leave when Trix thought of another question.

'What happened to the bones on this floor?'

Kit didn't stop walking. He was going the way Trix had entered.

'I buried them.'

That was a smart move. On planets thick with magic — Xardiassant was one, Mair Ultima another — it was possible for bodies not properly laid to rest to reanimate as banshees, ghouls, or wraiths. How they formed varied by the way in which the person had died, and the magic at play.

One constant was that they were all deadly.

And they generally came out at night.

Going Down, Power Up

1

The foyer's ruination was serene.

Trix didn't have any weapons drawn. She and Kit were walking slower than usual. Every surface held a memory that was eager to be shared. After so many years with only monsters roaming its halls, the Machina Academies were happy to have visitors.

In truth, it was the two machinas' company that set the joyous tone, for the academies had always been places of pain and suffering. As that thought crossed Kit's mind, he grinned. His likening the foyer to a church had been more apt than he first imagined.

The Valkyrie avoided looking at the ceiling. The exposed beams made her feel like she was back in Balthioul's Woods. Kit sensed her unease. It wasn't hard. Beatrix Westwood was rarely rattled.

'You never told me what happened on Thides,' Kit said as they walked the foyer's length.

'The monster was a Reliquia.'

Kit could tell anyone about all the Milky Way's different gangs, how to cook a mean barbecue, and breaching tactics 101 until you wanted to rip your own ears off. When he discussed strategy, he talked as if he were playing smashball. What little he knew of monsters came from Trix. He had to flip through his memories before he found files relating to Reliquia.

'Should've been a big pay day, but from your attitude, I'm guessing it wasn't.'

'It cursed the entire town. I had to kill them all.'

'Nobody knows monsters better than you, mate, except maybe Felix since he was your teacher. If you had to kill them, I'm sure there was no other way.'

'Normally when you kill the person who cast the curse, the curse lifts.'

'So? Sounds like it was highly complex magic, and you're not a sorceress. Don't beat yourself up over it. What'd the monster look like?'

'It was a spider, but its gut held a boy with deer legs. The town thought him to be a god.'

'Those we call gods have their own, too.'

'Cuthbert Theroux.'

'Top marks, Beatrix. I wouldn't worry about him being a god. Gods are getting weaker all the time.'

'We can control the weather, we can terraform planets, and given the circumstances, we can bring people back from the brink of death.'

'All things people used to pray for,' Kit nodded. 'But here's a question. Let's say that gods exist, and I'm talking all of them. Every god who's ever been worshipped.'

'Alright, they exist.'

'As we start doing things for ourselves, are they out of a job, made redundant by our ever expanding genius? Or do they just, poof, gone.'

'I don't think people ever stop believing entirely. We can travel among the stars and still people pray to the Christ God. And that's because no matter how advanced we become, we'll never know what happens after death. Everyone wants to think they're heading somewhere nice when they go six feet under.'

'You would say they don't die then?'

'Yes, which means they're made redundant. Redundancy offers a lot of spare time. So what does a god do when forced into retirement?'

'I doubt they go golfing.'

'If you could be the supreme ruler of the universe, above everyone and everything, would you?'

'Can't imagine anything worse. Besides, I'd get bored. I tried playing one of those simulation games once where you build cities. I don't know how people do it. Free beer would be tempting though.'

'Ruling over everything would give you the ultimate general perspective. Without a specific point of view, the universe would be bland. It's like seeing all the colours on the spectrum at once. Eventually they all blend into white.'

'You Valkyries must've been taught more theory than us.'

'It could just be that I'm smarter than you.'

'I've had more knocks to the head. You know that last time I went to Dark's Hide some guy thought I didn't speak Earthen, and tried communicating with beeping noises.'

'How original.'

'I was willing to let it go, but he wouldn't stop following me. Eventually he gave me a shove. The way his teeth sprayed across the floor when I socked him in the face, now that was original.'

'The answer of whether or not machinas are immortal won't be answered by you. I'll be surprised if you survive another Earthen year.'

'Speaking of that, it's my birthday in a couple of months.'

'And every other machina's.'

'What're you getting me?'

'If you're fishing for a new ship, try another star ocean.'

'Just ask Valentine to spot you for cash, or your new friend, the Queen of Xardiassant.'

'You know I don't take handouts.'

'Don't take handouts then. Say it's your birthday, which it is, and ask for money, then re-gift it to me. I promise to act surprised. You don't even have to wrap it.'

'You're so thoughtful.'

'I know. I think of myself all the time.'

'I'll buy you a mirror. You'll be so captivated by it you'll never leave, then I can choose when I want to see you instead of you inviting yourself over.'

'Unless that mirror dispenses beer I'll have to make trips to the fridge.'

'Is that because your face only looks pretty when you're wasted?'

'Your wit is sharper than your sword, Beatrix. You've rent me open. I concede.'

'I wish I could say it's been a pleasure.'

'I wish I could say that I know you're averse to lying, but that'd be a lie.'

'Is this where you got hit,' Trix said. They'd almost approached the statues. Even though Garth Roche's face was gone, she could still see it in her mind. He thought of himself as a god. Machinas cursed him as the Devil.

'Yeah. I think 117 came from up there.'

Kit pointed his shotgun at a gap in the roof. It led outside.

Trix examined the scene. She could see Kit's boot prints on the floor. They were faint. A mixture of dirt, grass, and blood. He'd probably been hunting earlier that day. She saw where individual prints blurred together, then stopped.

Must've been when he was lifted off the ground. Into Bardolf's Maw, Trix thought.

No trackable scent lingered. There wasn't another set of prints. Though if 117 had come from outside, he had to have left some trace behind, even if it was faint.

'It just occurred to me that finding Garth Roche's secret base isn't going to be possible until we turn the power back on.'

'The cold fusion generator is right under our feet, in the mountain's base. I used to see staff go down there,' Kit said.

Trix nodded. The only entrance she'd ever seen was when Valkyrie Academy was given tours of the docks. As far as she knew, that was where the academies' central control was due to its secure position.

'Hey, Sif.'

'That's my name.'

'Keep yourself in orbit. Until we know what we're dealing with, I'd prefer to keep the ship in a place it can't be stolen.'

'New boarding technologies make it possible to steal ships in space. Look at what happened to Yvach with those kalariks.'

'Sif, you know what I mean.'

'Of course I do. I'm the smartest one here.'

Trix and Kit heard the Fox's engines power up. They saw it take to the skies a second later. The paint job was still burned. Trix really had to redo it.

'Feels nice having Sif up there. She's like a beautiful, golden, guardian angel,' Kit said.

'Flattery won't stop me from turning the hot water off next time you're in the shower,' said Sif over comms.

The oni laughed.

Trix: 'Before we turn the power on, I want to see where 117's trail goes.'

'And if I may offer a counter proposal?'

'Is it stupid?'

'Stupidity is relative, my dear Beatrix,' Kit said. His accent was Australian laid on thicker than tourists spreading Vegemite. After he landed on Aros, he stowed away on a ship headed to Australia, western Queensland specifically. He loved the climate, but it was the laidback lifestyle that made him stay during his teenage years.

Trix said nothing. Kit was going to say his idea whether she wanted to hear it or not.

'I want to see the auditorium. It'd be nice to go in there without being bored.'

Trix was surprised. That idea was perfectly reasonable. The auditorium doors were at the top of the old water feature accessible via two opposite staircases.

'On one condition,' Trix said.

Kit put his shotgun away. Folded his arms. White teeth dazzled in his full smile.

'We race,' Trix finished.

Kit of Aros didn't wait to accept. He bolted for the stairs on his right. His stature combined with his enhanced abilities meant that he could cover 100m in roughly eight seconds.

The Valkyrie didn't bother running.

She altered gravity so she fell upwards, towards the

auditorium door. Trix was leaning against the wall as Kit ascended the stairs.

'Oh, so that's how it's gonna be.'

'I never said the race had to be fair.'

'I'm just an oni going up against a chooser of the slain. How could it be fair? What I didn't know was that you could choose the outcomes of wagers. Mind helping me out next time I punt on smashball?'

Smashball was the Milky Way's most watched sport. Comparable to American Gridiron on steroids. Two teams faced off on a field-arena and the goal was to score in the other team's end-zone. All players wore heavy armour necessary to prevent injuries and death. There was no higher contact sport involving a ball.

Where it became interesting was that everyone's armour had the same innate abilities. To trigger the abilities, the ball had to be passed through holographic rings. The next receiver would have the corresponding power-up activate. Power-ups could be anything from jet booster jump packs to widening the end-zone goal posts. Each power-up lasted until someone scored. Then everything was reset.

The power-up system made intercepts crucial. If you could intercept another team's charged ball, you won the power-up instead of them. Each race had a planetary team, even those not in the Consortium. Earth's team was called The Gladiators. However, Kit usually watched Smashball League which was an alternate rule-set invented by Australians to make the games quicker.

The only sport that came close to rivalling smashball's popularity (in all its codes) was Formula X Racing. The cars could go up walls and drive on ceilings which allowed courses to be as wild as imagination allowed.

'If you knew half of what I had to go through last time Yvach made a bet, you'd understand that I'm doing you a favour by telling you to fuck off.'

'I'd ask you to tell me about it, but I'm sure Valentine's

already hard at work on the book version.'

'I thought you wanted to see the auditorium?'

'I thought we were having a conversation.'

'After you, Kit.'

'Why thank you, Beatrix.'

Kit approached the auditorium door. Cracked his knuckles. Rolled his neck. Somehow, the door had survived the attack. It wouldn't survive Kit, not with his super strength and increased bone density.

He brought his open palm into the door. It dented inwards. He followed with a cross. The door gave some more. Kit charged it with his shoulder.

Open sesame.

'I'm here all week.'

'You'd be here forever if it wasn't for Trix's ship,' Sif said.

'Good thing we're friends then,' said Kit, entering the auditorium. Most of it had been built into Arno's Jaw, meaning the roof was still intact. It was dark, silent, and cold inside. Kit and Trix's eyes adjusted quickly. Empty aisles stretched to the stage. The auditorium could seat 20,000 people. The machinas' footsteps echoed. Parts of the ceiling had coated the seats in debris. Otherwise, it was almost exactly how they'd last seen it. No one had been inside during the attack.

'We filled this place once,' Kit said, walking down the centre aisle. He could see the stage. The screens were out of commission. Not even when the machinists called for silence was it this quiet.

Kit had spent far more time in the auditorium than Trix since most of her theory lessons took place in Aethelwulf's Heart. Instead of continuing to the stage, Kit walked into a seemingly random seat row.

'Huh, still here.'

'What is?'

'I carved my oni number onto the back of the seat in front of me during a lesson. I can't remember what it was about.'

Trix walked to Kit. 990 was etched into the seat. A crude oni medallion drawing was beside to it.

'Did you ever ask your machinists why you didn't have names, proper names, I mean, not just numbers?'

'No, we just went with it.'

'I did once. They made me climb all of Fenrir's Teeth twice.'

'We could've taken over this place. No one could've stopped us. It wasn't just about numbers. We were stronger than all of them.'

'The power of propaganda.'

'Remember what they'd make us chant?'

'Kill, kill, the anghenfil. If we don't stop them, no one will... and the rest.'

'They made us feel like the most important people in the galaxy.'

'Even though they treated us like shit,' Kit shrugged.

'Should've come to Valkyrie Academy. Minerva and Cortland weren't all bad.'

'I have a few too many body parts to be let in.'

'There might've been a boy Valkyrie eventually.'

'That's what I think 117 is,' Kit said. The auditorium was starting to weigh on him. It was the weight of forty thousand eyes pressing into his skin. Dead children's eyes. He turned to leave. So did Trix.

'Not exactly a Valkyrie in that he has unique powers,' Kit continued. 'He's his own academy. He had an oni's strength, a spectre's cloaking, and he moved fast like a dragon. I think he somehow managed to score every power when he was created.'

'That'd explain why he was called the perfect specimen.'

'What it doesn't explain is why he was the size of a child.'

'It'd have something to do with the date of injection,' Trix said. Media had gotten a hold of leaked documents not long after Roche's initial tests. Adults died almost immediately as their bodies rejected the Uldarian blood.

But what if a foetus was injected earlier than the recommended 12 weeks? What if Uldarian blood was administered as soon as the egg was fertilised? The body would be the most susceptible to change. However, altering a child at its earliest stage meant that whatever emerged from the test-tube might've been closer to Uldarian than human.

'Later or earlier?'

'Earlier. He would've died if it'd been later. We don't even know if whoever attacked you was 117.'

'The more I think about it, the surer I am. Maybe Roche was a god. His firstborn too. He created machinas, then disappeared, although it took him longer than seven days.'

'That's the propaganda talking.'

'Is it weird that I find it hard to hate him?'

'I feel the same way. Without him, we wouldn't exist.'

'I'd drink to that if I wasn't out of beer. Besides the childhood discrimination, there ain't nothing wrong with being a machina.'

Back in the foyer, Trix set off to find a 117's trail.

Kit walked beside her.

2

Breeze blew with deathly sighs.

The machinas were on the foyer roof. No evidence pointing to humanoid activity had been discovered. Trix was looking at the sky bridge that connected the foyer to Oni Academy. A chunk was missing in the middle, and the far side had broken off. It lay in the ravine below, decorated with destroyed Earthen ships.

Fenrir's Teeth looked marginally better. One had collapsed, as Kit had previously mentioned. The others were cross-sections of their former selves. The machinas could see skeletons dangling from ledges, broken furniture, and rusted weapons.

'The footsteps were coming from up here,' Kit said.

'I can't find a trail.'

'Then why are we waiting around? Let's turn the power back on.'

Trix was facing Aethelwulf's Heart. It'd taken the least amount of hits, though that wasn't saying much. She admired Conan's Eyes, the twin peaks she used to dread crossing. Trix remembered them being bigger.

Standing on Mair Ultima, walking through the academies, it felt like stepping into a movie and creating an epilogue that shouldn't have existed. During her training, Valkyries were ferried from their academy to the foyer in troop carriers. They'd be destroyed now. They'd have to cross Bardolf's Maw to get there.

Sure, she could've called Sif to pick them up, but that would've been cheating. Like using magic while running Aethelwulf's Trial.

The dragon Trix had seen before was hanging off Conan's Eyes' eastern peak. It looked like it was watching her and Kit. Probably was.

'I can see us living here again. All machinas.'

'Yeah, she's a beaut.'

'There might be a problem with turning the power back on.'

'Everything could be too easy?'

'The test-tubes we were born in exist somewhere in these academies. So do all the failed machinas. What if turning the power on allows them to escape?'

'If they were failures, I doubt they'd have survived this long,' Kit said. The skin on the back of his neck rippled. He was lying to himself. Anything could exist in the academies' bowels. 'No racing this time.'

'Can your machina healing not fix a bruised ego?'

'My ego's the only known compound stronger than Uldarian metal.'

'I'd believe that.' Trix turned south, where the docks were. 'Fine, no racing.'

The machinas walked along the shattered foyer roof then jumped onto the mountainside. They slid to the docks where Sif had landed the Fox.

Trix led the way to the back where Command and Control

had been. Sunlight became weaker as she went further in.

This must be what the humans who discovered this place felt like, Trix thought. Moss was growing on some surfaces. Nature had worked its way inside.

All the command centre's windows had been irrupted by artillery. Trix vaulted through them. Kit followed. Darkness encroached. It hadn't been disturbed in decades. Bones of Mair Ultima staff were turning to dust on the floor. It didn't take long to find the elevator. A charred sign warned that only authorised personnel were allowed past this point. Kit bashed the door inward. Gloom filled the elevator shaft.

Kit activated his helmet. It looked like an old knight's sans the feather on top. His visor was a golden cross. The rest of it was gunmetal grey with a digital maroon camo print. His beard was covered. So was his crown.

'The elevator could be stuck,' Kit said, leaning over the edge. 'I'll dislodge it.'

Before Trix could argue, he jumped into the shaft. Trix watched him fall. A bang reached her ears. Then grinding metal. A resounding clang finished off the symphony.

'All clear,' Kit said over comms.

Trix jumped, using magic to slow her descent. Kit activated a torch on his armour when Trix reached the bottom. Light revealed a maintenance level that bore a closer resemblance to catacombs. There weren't many bodies. Most of the people must've escaped. Walls were partially collapsed. Stale air stirred for the first time in 80 years.

'Now your guess is as good as mine,' Trix said.

Kit drew his shotgun. Trix raised an eyebrow.

'Expecting the skeletons to give you trouble?'

'You know better than most that they might.'

Trix supposed Kit was right. She activated the lower part of her helmet to help with breathing. The air was thick with dust and smelled plain awful. Trix drew sword. Its tungsten edge gleamed in Kit's torchlight.

They started walking around the space. A generator

wouldn't be hard to miss.

'There'll probably be a power-map in here that shows the output to all academies. Roche's base might be listed,' Kit said. He felt the Ultima Lullaby's familiar tune come to his lips. He stayed the urge to whistle.

'Roche wouldn't be stupid enough to have a lair connected to the main generator. He'd be off the grid, or he'd have his own.'

'Or maybe he disguised his base to appear as something else, like a supply depot.'

'Here I was thinking you were going to say broom closet.'

'I think he was doing further experiments.'

Trix recalled Roche's speech in the Mandela Auditorium. He'd said that machinas marked the first step in becoming synthetic lifeforms on a base level. To truly explore the stars, to go beyond the Milky Way, human frailty had to be shed. With the Uldarian technology salvaged and catalogued by Shaiba Chandak, Roche sounded like he wanted to do just that.

'He held Uldarians in the highest esteem. He could've been trying to recreate them.'

'If he did and he's still here, he might have one hell of a security team guarding the door.'

'He'd need human trials, something Mair Ultima doesn't have.'

'Unless he was testing his serums on himself.'

'Then he'll either be stark raving mad, or he'll be dead.'

'Either way, he's sure to have records of his trials. They'll be the most interesting things I've read in a while.'

'What'd you read last?'

Kit smiled. 'The sign that said authorised personnel only beyond this point.'

'Clever. You see that?'

'Seems like an appropriate time to say "well there's your problem."'

'Hmm.'

'Good thing we're not in a rush. You think the ceiling above the power generator would've been reinforced more than its surrounds.'

'Looks like the core is fine.'

'Yeah, just all the cables that need reconnecting, a rockslide's worth of rubble to shift. Standard repair job really,' Kit said.

Trix pushed her hat back. She and Kit were looking at the cold fusion core for every machina academy. Unfortunately for them, the majority of the cables had been severed by the roof collapse. A dull glow emanated from the core showing that it was stable.

'Moving rubble isn't going to mean anything if we don't find extra cables,' said the Valkyrie.

'You start looking for tools. I'll make a start shifting these rocks.'

'And if I can't find any tools then you've worked for nothing.'

'You'll find em, and if you don't I'm sure you'll think of something.'

'You seem to have developed a new sense of enthusiasm for this project.'

Kit held his hands up. 'Caught out. I was thinking about turning the power back on and watching smashball in the auditorium.'

'I don't think the GSA broadcasts to Mair Ultima.'

'I want to see a machina team play in the Earth comp. That'd be hilarious.'

'I thought you had rocks to move.'

'I thought you had cables to find, but here we are.'

Trix shook her head and set about checking for supply caches. The maintenance floor was massive. Trix passed doors leading to server farms, dorms, even an employee gym, but she couldn't find a supply closet. She came close to doing a full loop of the floor when she realised her mistake. The cables would be kept as close to the core as possible. That meant they'd be under the rubble.

The machina entered the core room to see Kit had already

made good progress.

'Find those cables, huh?'

'Hmm.'

'That's funny, I don't see any. Hiding them down your shirt? Under your hat maybe?'

'No, under there,' Trix pointed to the mountain of rubble in which Kit had made a small dent.

'Still easier to remove than your shirt.'

Trix drew her gun. Blew apart the rock in Kit's hand. The sound was akin to a pirate's galleon firing its broadside cannons in the cavernous space.

'Good shot, mate.'

'We'll need to shift this rubble further out. There's too much of it to be contained around the core while we do the repairs.'

'You could move it since you don't have to find the cables anymore.'

'That's a brave request considering what you just said.'

'I hardly ever consider what I say. I find it gets in the way of the saying.'

'Yet somehow you land yourself in less trouble than Yvach.'

'Yvach gambles.'

'So do you.'

'Only with my life, and there isn't anyone who cares about collecting on that.'

'You wanted to put money on smashball not an hour ago.'

'Alright, let me rephrase that. Yvach gambles *illegally*.'

'Hopefully not anymore.'

'Was it Aodun's favour that resulted in you losing half your ear? Nah, I bet I know what it was. A round of corrachian drinking games and you reached the part where you need to close your eyes while selecting a knife, then keep them closed as you—'

'You couldn't be further from the truth if you went to the universe's edge.'

'Technically the universe doesn't really have an edge, just a particle horizon, and we can't reach that unless we figure out a way to make a wormhole appear there, and even then—'

'If you know that, surely you know what hyperbole is.'

'I was just checking you did.'

'One of the townspeople from Fenwick bit off my ear.'

'Scars on machinas tell stories.'

'Same could be said for anyone.'

'True, although any normal person with scars like ours would be dead.'

'They'd never be in our positions to start with.'

'I didn't think I could find something more monotonous than hauling rocks until I discovered this conversation.'

Trix shook her head. She began transporting the rocks Kit had moved to the larger part of the control room. Then she had an idea.

'Move out of the way.'

'Beatrix, I'm stronger than you are. That's a fact, not an insult.'

'Just move.'

Kit stepped aside. Trix focused her gravity altering magic on the pile in front of her. She shifted a lot of the smaller, loose rocks out into the control room before having to end the spell.

'You're welcome,' she said.

'Damn, sometimes I wish I could do that.'

'Only sometimes?'

'When I'm being shot at by angry mercenaries who have little interest in taking me alive, I'd much rather summon a barrier.'

'So would I if I was as sloppy as you.'

'Hey, you know what we onis say. If you're gonna be dumb, you gotta be tough.'

Despite their many jabs, Kit and Trix didn't hate each other in the slightest. To say they had a sibling-esque relationship would've been incorrect. Their squabbles weren't nearly that simple. Anyone looking at them for more than a minute could see that the two of them had been involved. Never for long, and never seriously.

Space was a lonely place. For the most part, it was literally a cold void with nothing but darkness. Even optimists could find themselves down as they sailed through the star ocean.

Outside the academy power station, day turned to night. The dragon who'd taken residence atop Conan's Eyes flew back to his cave. He hadn't seen humans on Mair Ultima for 80 years.

Twilight arrived and so did many stolen glances between the two machinas. Neither of them knew if it was love. In fact, machinas often wondered if they could love at all. They were certainly capable of strong feelings, but love was another matter.

It was these glances and old feelings that stopped the machinas from noticing the way their medallions shook subtly against their chests. No more Uldarian technology or machinas were active.

Magic was at play. Dusty bones moved closer across the power station. It was as though they could sense the machinas' longing and were physically touched by it. If only the reason was so poetic.

When magic affected the dead, the result never boded well for the living.

3

Darkness had taken Mair Ultima.

Only the creatures on its surface noticed. High above, Sif watched as half the planet became enveloped. She'd been sifting through galactic news and waited for Trix's signal to kickstart the power core. It'd be unlikely she could do it alone. The AI realised she was bored. But how could she be sure? Was she only simulating boredom, or truly experiencing it?

In the power station, Kit and Trix had finished shifting the rocks. Decided to take a well-earned break. The machinas ate food from Kit's backpack, though they weren't overly hungry. With the rubble gone, all that had to be done was reconnecting the cables. It was stuffy in the power station. Kit had taken his armour off. Any concerns he had about bones coming to life had been laid to rest. No pun intended. The machinas had been making a ruckus for hours, and so far nothing had come from beyond the grave to eat them.

Trix followed Kit's lead. Her 2nd Skin one piece still covered her upper body. Sitting in armour wasn't the most comfortable way to relax.

Directly across from her, the supply cache containing the repair cables was waiting to be opened. Kit just had to bust in the doors, then they could find every secret the machinists had.

'I remember that scar,' Trix said, looking at Kit. Her white pupils were wide and oval shaped in the darkness.

'You'll have to be more specific, Beatrix.'

'That one,' she touched near Kit's neck where a jagged ridge made its way down to his crotch.

'I learned an important lesson that day. Never fight naked even though it's funny as shit.'

'That's not a lesson most people have to learn.'

'I still remember the way that knife felt. How one side was serrated. The other might've even been sharper than that sword of yours.'

'It wouldn't have happened if I'd been there.'

'I thought you were. If I'd known you were in town, I would've joined you.'

'You were too drunk to walk.'

'But clearly not too drunk to stop the bastard who tried opening me up.'

'We never found out who he was working for, though that tends to happen when you kill your attacker. He probably just wanted one less person to share that dragon's hoard with,' Trix said, her eyes flitting to the black scale on Kit's armour.

'What I can remember is hazier than a construction site where everyone's on smoko at once. I remember how much blood there was. Miracle I didn't slip on it and crack my skull open.'

'Maybe if the bedframe was titanium.'

'Maybe if the bedframe had still been intact,' Kit said,

looking into Trix's eyes. They were sitting close together. Kit's exposed shoulder — which looked like a Jackson Pollock painting of bullet scars — brushed against Trix's.

'Kit...' Trix said. She could feel herself being pulled in. Wasn't this what she wanted? She'd come here to be consoled.

Beatrix Westwood had seen more atrocities than anyone should have. Each one piled onto her shoulders. Atlas didn't know how lucky he was. Good friends could make her forget the burden. Yvach was one such friend, Andy Tozier was another. Even Dai of Thyria was considered one of her dear friends. Then of course there was Sif and Valentine. Not to mention the sorcerer with whom she enjoyed occasional relations.

But Kit of Aros, he picked up her whole burden and set it aside. The intimate moments he shared with Trix meant nothing and everything. She felt the same way. They both understood that on some level, sex was necessary. It wasn't to be rushed. It wasn't to be taken lightly. It was also not to be attached to, or pined for.

Both machinas were too strong for that. None would've doubted their strength. Given long enough, the strongest warriors must tire, for weariness claims the perpetual traveller and the contented resident alike. Better to adventure during weariness' absence than to await its return, always staring at the door.

'Kit...' Trix said again. This time she placed a hand on the oni's chest. It rose and fell like every machina's did: evenly. 'We need to fix the cables.'

Kit took Trix's hand in his. He gave her a tender kiss on the corner of her mouth. That smell of a beachside barbershop flared. Kit lingered near Trix's mouth a touch. He was weary too.

He marvelled at how Beatrix Westwood always smelled like wildflowers in a forest with a hint of musk and a dash of coconut vanilla. It was weirdly specific, but then, so was she.

Kit knew she was right. And the power station's sepulchre

was hardly the place for intimacy.

The oni pulled away when he noticed his medallion shuddering. Trix was looking at it. She raised her hand to her Valkyrie medallion. It was doing the same.

'We've awakened something.'

'It's going to be pissed. I would be if I slept in for 80 years.'

'Come on,' Trix stood.

Kit followed. Opened the door by bashing it inwards to create a handhold then ripping it wide enough to enter. Undisturbed tools covered the wall space beyond. Trix grabbed the tools while Kit started grabbing cables. To make repairs simpler, cables were often manufactured with locking mechanisms on each end. Each length of cable was actually comprised of many smaller parts. The locking mechanisms made quick fixes easy, and made further damage unlikely.

The machinas got to work. Trix fixed the cables near the ceiling while Kit worked on ones by the core. When the frayed ends were mended, they reattached the cables. The core glowed softly all the while. Their medallions hummed solemn tunes.

When it was done, they stood by the command console.

'Sif, you up?'

'Well I don't need to sleep. So yes.'

'We need you to boot up Mair Ultima's power core.'

'And have you even run a diagnostic to make sure the core is stable and you're not going to kill yourselves?'

'I assumed you would do that first,' Trix said. She was feeling a little better. Progress was a great dampener for torment. 'Please,' the Valkyrie added. She plugged her gauntlet into the console. Sif began working. With no one to stop her override, the core came online within five minutes. Its pulsating glow changed to a constant light source.

'The machina academies now have power.'

'How about turning some lights on then?'

The lights flickered on, revealing everything's drab state.

'It looked better when it was dark,' Kit said. He still had his shirt off.

Though Trix noticed one difference. She didn't care for it.

'The bones are gone.'

Kit took a second to confirm this statement. Of course, Trix was right. He'd left his shotgun near his armour. Trix still had her pistol. Her sword was by her combat vest and exo-armour. Shit.

The machinas returned to their belongings with quiet speed. The rest of the power station was silent. Where had the bones gone?

Kit suited up. So did Trix.

'We have to move away from the core. If anything ruptures it, we'll never get the academies running again.'

'If we manage to run after a core rupture, mate, I'd be impressed.'

They walked back-to-back out of the station. Trix didn't know what to expect. When it came to magic and death, there were multiple possibilities.

The first and most common was that bones reformed in their original shape. Thus most people thought the dead had arisen. Mages determined that this wasn't the case by conducting experiments in brain activity. There wasn't any. The bones were held together loosely by magical energy and could be knocked apart by conventional methods, these being guns and blunt weapons.

Why magic reformed bones was a harder question to answer. It typically happened in areas where large scale suffering or death had occurred.

Another way magic could affect bones was that it created monsters. This was more likely to happen when the magic was stronger. Anything bound by such magic would take greater effort to kill. Unless all corpses were cleared from an area, magic would continue acting on them. The only way for such a spell to be permanently defeated was to let time pass. Then the magic would fade like gas molecules in a ventilated room. To expedite this, people could live in the affected area. The presence of living beings served to dissipate magic born of suffering. These and more scenarios ran through Trix's head.

With what had happened at Mair Ultima, she considered a monster likelier than lumbering skeletons of former employees. She was just glad the flesh had decomposed. Otherwise she would've been dealing with ghouls.

A roar gave Trix her answer. Instead of sounding like a fearsome beast, the roar was a cacophony of wails. People screaming and crying. It came at the machinas from all directions. The Valkyrie saw their source around the corner from where the server rooms had been.

A beast with ribcages for teeth rolled forward on a constantly shifting bone mass. Its head — which had two glowing skulls for eyes — snaked side to side, supported by a throng of miscellaneous bones. Black smoke circled in and out of constantly moving joints.

'Seeing as this is your domain, I might sit this one out. Take in the sights. Crack a cold one,' Kit said as the bone monster swallowed everything in its wake.

'Stay close, it looks capable of quick movement. It might even be able to go through the floor.'

'Great. On the bright side, there might be a contract for it. You could make back the money you lost on Thides.'

'If only there was a monster whose weakness was bad jokes. You'd stand to make a fortune.'

Trix had her sword ready. She guessed most weapons would be useless anyway. A monster that largely consisted of magic — see banshees and wraiths — could often take immaterial forms to avoid damage. In the bone monster's case, Trix reckoned it'd be able to separate its parts rapidly, rebuilding into new patterns to evade. Fire tended to work well in such instances. That and large explosions.

The monster regarded them for a moment.

Fuck this, Trix thought.

She dashed forward. Jumped. She was headed straight for a section of bones resembling a neck. There was a small chance the monster would die if she could sever it. Hell, it was a fantasy more than anything else.

Trix attempted to root the bones in place with a gravity spell. The monster was immune, goddamn it. She swung her sword. The monster's neck separated. If Trix went through the gap, she'd be swallowed whole. She could already see the bones preparing to engulf her. The Valkyrie reversed gravity. Fell towards where Kit had been standing.

The oni was on the monster's flank loosing shell after shell. Had he been using a precision weapon, Kit would've missed nearly every shot. Thanks to the spray, most of the Oni's shots hit their marks. They didn't appear to have any effect.

With Trix out of range, Bones turned its attention on Kit. He hadn't fought even an eighth of the monsters Trix had, but that didn't mean he was green. He kept himself limber. Ready to dive in any direction. Instead of lunging with its entire body, Bones screamed again. It sent a barrage of itself towards Kit. He had time to notice that the bones were no longer smooth. They possessed sharp points, honed by dark magic.

He put his shotgun on his back. Held out his hand. A powerful barrier formed. The bones were stopped. Their kinetic energy was being absorbed by Kit who could then redirect it as a concussive blast. If he waited too long, the absorbed magic would cause him to blackout. Extreme cases could burst his heart.

Trix saw this unfold. Deciding she had nothing to lose, she shot at Bones' glowing skull eyes.

The eyes didn't shatter but Trix saw the bullets hit. It was comforting to know that not even this monster could dodge everything. She fired more. The skull-eyes withdrew deeper into Bones, probably to emerge elsewhere. Trix doubted they were functional. Her guess was that Bones operated on a magical rendering of its surrounds.

Kit's barrier was beginning to falter, and the monster was growing smarter. Bones upped the frequency of its bombardment. More sharpened bones came around the oni's flanks. Kit shifted his barrier accordingly. He was going to burst if he absorbed any more energy. Had to release it. Blasted the monster with concussive waves. Bones was pushed back just long enough for Kit to reach Trix.

'So, huntress, any ideas?'

'Have any bombs?'

'Fuck yeah.'

'Good.'

'But they're on my ship. If you can find my ship then you're more than welcome to have them.'

Trix moaned. They'd need a considerable blast. Though Trix reckoned they could just leave. The monster would likely be tied to the power station's misery. But ascending the elevator shaft while Bones was in pursuit would be easier said than done.

'We have to get back to the power core.'

'That's a much larger bomb than I'm comfortable with detonating.'

'We're not going to detonate it,' Trix said. A torrent of bones came at her. She half-turned. Raised her sword. Deflected the first stream. Kit blasted it apart with his shotgun. The fragments re-joined the monster.

More bones came for Trix. She parried with a series of pirouettes and whirlwind strikes. Kit picked off the follow-through. The monster grew closer all the while. It was spreading itself thin, trying to encircle the machinas. Trix reckoned it'd rush them all at once. There'd be no stopping it.

'Kit,' Trix said as she continued parrying, wielding her sword in two hands. 'Disconnect the longest cable running from the power core and bring it here.'

'On it.'

Emptying the rest of his shotgun shells into Bones, Kit broke for the power core.

Great, we just fixed the damn thing now we've gotta tear it apart.

Bones wailed again. This time Trix could hear individual

voices. Even cries for help. That was when the two golden skulls reappeared. They were at the base of Bones' neck. Their mouths wide open. Frozen in macabre laughter. Bones arched backwards. Its ribcage teeth open wide. It was creating one hell of a display.

That meant the blow was going to come from somewhere else.

The Valkyrie noticed a hefty chunk of Bones' rear lash for her head. She had to avoid it the right way. Jumping haphazardly would result in Bones eating her whole, if such a monster could eat. She doubted it.

Trix altered gravity to fall upwards, then altered it again so she was hurtling for Bones' neck. The monster's tail-end hit her in mid-air. Trix blocked the barrage with her sword but the force knocked her off course. She altered gravity moments before being pinned to the wall.

From the corner of her eye, she saw Kit running the hall's length. Cable in hand. Trix evaded Bones' attack. Cast a spell around Kit. He flew towards the monster. Despite the situation's seriousness, Trix couldn't help smirking. Kit hated it when she changed gravity around him.

'Sif, you have to direct the core's power output into the cable Kit disconnected.'

'This is an awful idea, truly,' the AI said. Trix could imagine Sif rolling her eyes.

Trix pivoted in time to avoid another bone blast, but she couldn't deflect all of it. A bone that might've once been a femur impaled itself in Trix's leg. It kept trying to burrow deeper. Twisting of its own accord. She ripped it out. Sliced it into four pieces. They fell to the ground.

Kit jumped. He didn't have a clue what he was aiming for. The entire monster looked the same. Bones on bones on bones. Its only distinguishing features were the golden skulls in the base of its neck. They retracted as Kit drew closer.

'Ah fuck. Well, if you're gonna be dumb...' Kit said. He knew what he had to do.

Trix went to follow Kit when she saw Bones attempt evading. With his natural speed and her magic, Kit was moving too fast. Trix saw energy sprouting from the cable's tip. It was reacting to the magic. Kit activated his helmet. Entered the monster. Another wail, this time of a man screaming for help. It repeated like a broken record.

No one knew why suffering caused magic to manifest in malicious ways. It wasn't even known what "laid a soul to rest." Every culture among every race had a difference theory as to what was appropriate after death, and what awaited on the fabled *other side.*

Gabe's slacking, Trix thought for no reason. She didn't even know anyone named Gabe. Before it departed her mind, the image of a black ceirlo with charred antlers crossed in front of her eyes. It'd been an omen on Xardiassant.

A blast of blue and black smoke snapped Trix back to reality. The monster exploded from the centre. Kit was shot backwards, covered in a barrier. He broke a desk in half as he flew across the space. Landed on his shoulder. Rolled.

Kit of Aros pulled out shin bones that'd found their way between his chest plating. Retracted his helmet. Sweat moistened his eyebrows. The power station fell quiet. A mass of bones lay around a charred crater in the floor. Magic and energy crackled like winter fire.

The power went out. Darkness reclaimed the power station.

Sif: 'The surge has activated the lockdown procedures. Give it five minutes to reboot. Can you never go anywhere without wrecking it?'

Realising the AI had overstepped a line, she added: 'Sorry, too soon.'

'No time like the present,' said Trix. Gloom wove its way between her words. She didn't believe in being treated with gloves. She'd fucked up in Fenwick. Made a mistake. No sense in pretending it never happened. Might as well lay out a doormat saying "mistakes welcome" otherwise.

The Valkyrie walked to Kit. He was looking at the pile of

bones. Some still shuddered. He had a feeling this wasn't over. How the fuck could you kill something that didn't have a heart?

Trix: 'Good?'

'Yeah. You deal with this shit all the time.'

'Normally I'm paid for my trouble.'

'I'm the one who killed it. You should pay me.'

'You didn't kill it.'

Trix pointed to the shuddering bones. Just as Kit had thought, they were reforming.

The oni reloaded his shotgun. Trix rested her hand on the barrel. Forced it downwards.

'I think I know a better way to stop this.'

'Going to talk it into submission, mate?'

'Hmm.'

'I was kidding.'

'All monsters behave differently. Some can understand reason.'

Bones was close to reformed, though it was a lot smaller than before. Failing Trix's diplomatic solution, she could use the cable to cause another explosion. Though that would have to wait. Thanks to Kit's victory, the station was in complete lockdown.

'You called for help,' Trix said, standing before the monster. Her sword was on her back. Blood wept from her leg wound. It didn't bother her much.

Two golden skulls became eyes again. Trix saw that the left one had been shattered. Only its right side remained. Bones had built itself to resemble a human head. Its constantly shifting nature gave it the appearance of melting into the floor.

Bones spoke. Its voice was a combination of disjointed cries comprised from the people it had "reanimated."

'Anghenfil/attack/here/leave.'

'The anghenfil are gone now.'

'Our job/protect/monitor/didn't see/didn't know.'

'No one could've known. You can't blame yourselves. Not everyone died, we're still here,' Trix pointed to herself and Kit.

'Came/from/inside/didn't tell.'

'What came from inside?'

'Beacon/unknown/origin.'

'Did someone from within the academy broadcast our position?'

Bones looked like it was contemplating. It yawped, causing Trix to step backwards. Its jumbled cries filled the space. Its shape started shifting. Trix looked at the cable. Lockdown was still in effect. Another power surge wasn't doable. However, there was something else that could work.

She drew her pistol.

'Sif, can you control the internal life-support systems?'

'They're all that's operational.'

'I want you to pump this section of the power station full of hydrogen.'

Trix didn't need to worry about the core. She could see thick blast doors had covered it.

'Another terrible idea. Are you trying to blow yourself up?'

'Some days I wonder,' Trix muttered.

Sif: 'Wouldn't you know it, internal fail-safes are preventing me from doing as you ask, and trying to get around them is extending the lockdown's duration.'

'Can you break through?'

'Yes, just try not to die while I'm working.'

Instead of reforming into its original form, Bones became a cluster of spiders. Maybe the magic could sense Trix's recent memories. Either way, she hated them. Kit joined her. They began tearing apart the new monsters which scurried over the walls and the ceiling.

The power core overload had done a number on the monster. Every bone-spider Trix felled took much longer to rebuild itself than the colossus of bones had before.

'Trix, I've overridden the life support safety features. I'm going to start pumping hydrogen in. It'll be extremely concentrated. Any spark will send the whole level up in flames.'

'I'm counting on it,' Trix said. This method meant that all the power station's controls would be fried. There was a good chance that the server rooms would be destroyed as well. Without the controls, finding the backups and rerouting them would be difficult. Trix couldn't do the calculations in her head, not to an exact amount anyway. Certainly not while fending off magically animated bone-spiders. She hoped the explosion wouldn't cause the rest of Raoul's Spine to cave in.

'Kit, stop shooting,' she said.

'Alright, I could hit a couple of sixes.'

Kit tossed his shotgun into the air. Activated his knuckle dusters. He took one spider in the head, shattering it as another tried climbing on his back. Kit caught his shotgun by the barrel. Walloped the spider with the butt.

'That one's going for the bloody boundary.'

'If you shoot now, the resulting explosion will wipe out the entire floor. The mountain will remain intact, so to borrow Kit's vernacular, you won't be totally fucked,' Sif said.

'You might want to give that back to me now,' Kit said to Sif, using his shotgun like a bat.

'Consider it done.'

'Good, because for the love of fuck's sake, this is shit.'

Trix considered Sif's words. From now on, any spark, even a static charge could erupt in flames. As a general safety standard, all armour was made to be non-flammable, or at the very least, highly flame retardant as were most objects designed to enter space. Explosions in pressurised canisters hurtling through the star ocean were not desirable.

It was a bit more difficult to do this with weapons and technology. Circuits within Trix's earpiece and comms gauntlets could be enough to ignite the hydrogen rich air.

In the end it wasn't any of those things that ignited the room. It was embers from the crater. Trix saw the flames catch in slow motion. Even with her shields, she was going to be cooked inside her armour.

Kit saw this as well. He took Trix in his arms while he cast an oni barrier. Everything exploded. The machinas saw nothing but auburn. Strange faces in the flames. Trix altered gravity so they'd move away from the blast. They travelled through the air for a short while before everything went black.

The bones were incinerated.

Lockdown was still in effect.

SECRETS

1

Eyelids lifted.

The space was dim. The power core glowed steadily behind the machinas. The fulmination hadn't been enough to rupture the blast doors.

Trix regained full consciousness. Kit woke up too. He still had his arms around her, making his body a cocoon. His barrier had held. Besides aching muscles and puncture wounds, they were fine.

'Hey, Trix, wake up. Don't make me come down there and do it myself,' Sif said.

'I'm up. Are any of the consoles still operable?'

'You flash flooded everything with fire, so no. The blast also damaged part of the servers. The backups have taken their place. Any information regarding the power grid plans should still be available, it'll just be harder to find.'

Behind Trix, Kit took out some nano-gel. Applied it to his wounds. Then he sealed his armour with fast drying resin.

Trix: 'Every machina academy has its own control room. We should be able to access Mair Ultima's secrets from any of them.'

'Alright,' Kit said, prodding his armour to check the resin had dried. He'd glued his glove to his chest once. He didn't want to make that mistake again. 'Pick an academy.'

'We're closest to Spectre Academy. Makes sense to go there.'

'Not gonna argue with that. I've seen enough ghosts for one day. And I'd hate to see whatever's stalking the oni halls.'

'Bad memories.'

'No doubt.'

'That monster, it said something about a beacon,' Trix said, heading towards the elevator shaft. She'd have to use her utility cannon to reach the top. Reversing gravity was always an option, but after her fight with Bones, she didn't feel up to it.

'No one would've been stupid enough to send out a beacon. Even by accident. There's a reason no one's found this place, and that's because no one knows where it is. And because standard guidance chips don't include No Man's Land's coordinates.'

'Whoever sent it would've known they were signing off on our destruction. It can't have been a deal with the anghenfil. We ended up beating them.'

Kit retracted his helmet. Scratched his jaw. I picked a hell of a place to relax, he thought.

'Now, what would make someone do such a thing?'

'Insanity.'

'Or a fuckload of orits.'

Trix considered the possibility of betrayal from within the academies. The staff had been carefully selected to ensure no clashing personalities, psychopaths, or any other undesirables would sabotage the mission. Even with all these precautions, it was possible that a machinist had decided machinas were monsters and needed to be exterminated.

So far as Trix knew, the only resistance to the project had come from outside Mair Ultima. People were outraged that so many children had effectively been aborted to become soldiers. Especially since neither Garth Roche nor any other scientist could guarantee the outcome.

That was it.

'Remorse.'

Kit's eyes flashed with recognition. He knew exactly what Trix meant.

'A father disappointed in his children, ready to accept the ultimate consequence. They've grown too strong for him to kill them, so he alerts maybe the only people who can,' Kit said, verbalising Trix's unspoken hypothesis. 'Really think Father would do that?'

'People assumed he went to Mair Ultima when he disappeared. After the attack, news reports said Garth Roche had died in the machina academies.'

'That's a load of shit. None of us ever saw him.'

'No one was listening to machinas' opinions then and you know it.'

Kit fell silent. He did. Since the only ones to escape Mair Ultima were machinas, all news anchors had to go on was the anghenfil statement, saying they'd destroyed humanity's last hope. The rest of the information was supplemented by whispers from machinas, though none of them would admit that.

Trix continued: 'As far as faking your own death goes, committing genocide is excessive.'

'We'll know soon enough,' Kit said. He was bursting with energy that he'd absorbed from the blast. He knew just what to do with it. The oni stood in the elevator shaft. Brought his arms down by his side. Released his stored energy at the ground. The blast kicked up loose debris. Trix shielded her eyes with her arm. Stepped in after Kit. Reeled herself upwards using her utility cannon.

Both machinas started walking back to Spectre Academy. It was dark outside. Mair Ultima had almost crossed into early morning. Its four moons loomed in the night sky, bathing Mair Ultima in ominous light.

The Luna Wolf Mountains cast a striking silhouette.

2

Spectre children used to pretend they were ghosts.

Now they were. They were gone. So was their academy's control room.

Anghenfil bombs of yore had wiped it off the face of Mair Ultima. Either it'd been a lucky shot, or one of the ground squads had breached it. Whatever the cause, Trix and Kit had to find another control room to search for Garth Roche's secret base. The thought of someone betraying them weighed on their minds. Neither of them supposed it could've been another machina. Life hadn't been cushy, but none of them —

to the best of their knowledge — had ever hated it enough to commit treason.

And it's not like machinas knew any better.

In wake of their new discovery, Trix and Kit decided to head for the Dragon Spire. They weren't ready to face their alma maters just yet. Not often 80 years was classified as *just yet.*

Trix had Sif bring the Fox in from orbit. She opened the loading ramp. Trix and Kit waited in the cargo bay as Sif took them up. They stood near the open door, leaning against the walls. Never mind the drop that'd send them to their deaths.

'I still don't understand why you wanted to come here,' Trix said. She was transfixed by the moons. She used to remember staying up past curfew to look at them. All machinas read about space travel from NASA's earliest days to galactic travel.

Trix couldn't speak for other machinas, but she'd wanted to see the Milky Way, especially Earth, and everywhere humans had built. Being born with the body and mind of a nine-year-old meant Trix had missed a childhood. In the pictures they were allowed to see —terminals on Mair Ultima were censored — the majority of them had been taken on Earth as early as the 20th century. This was no accident. They were being shown what they had to save. What was at stake if they failed. Hundreds of machinas killed themselves once they escaped Mair Ultima because they believed Earth would perish.

Propaganda: Not an exact science.

'I was between jobs,' Kit said. He was looking at the moons as well. 'And why wouldn't you want to see this?'

Trix said nothing.

'You know, your paintjob is looking... I believe the technical term is shitty.'

'It's custom.'

'That so?'

'You just need to go hypersonic through atmosphere.'

'Interesting colour.'

'I call it *Noccril Rust.'*

'You know I love this ship, even the AI who runs it.'

'Nice to see you're learning,' Sif said.

'But you know I also love badass designs. I know a guy on Earth who will fix up your ship really nice. He can retrofit any extras you're missing too. Reasonable prices, good bloke all round.'

'You want to "pimp" my ship?'

'I never said anything about pimping, just redoing the paint and getting you some furniture that didn't come from a dump.'

'I suppose you're buying then.'

'Think of it as a present for coming to see me.'

'This feels like a trick.'

'Never,' Kit crossed his heart. Didn't take his eyes off the sky. Kit mightn't have been tricking her, but Trix felt like she wasn't being told the whole truth.

Sif circled around Dragon Spire several times as the machinas discussed their options.

'I could've sworn I heard dragon machinas talking about how the spire's top room was off limits, which means the control room was probably there. Inconsiderate of the anghenfil to blow it apart.'

'It'd make more sense to put it inside the mountain. Take us to the base, Sif.'

'I would scan for active technology, but lockdown procedure sets everything to OFF so the grid doesn't overload when the power comes back on.'

'Hmm.'

The spire's base was half embedded into the mountain. Trix and Kit saw that the man-made parts were leaning precariously. The Uldarian foundations were still rooted into the rock. Windows were vacant. Activating her helmet, Trix saw a typical command centre layout in the moonlit shadows.

'Get us in as close as you can.'

Sif moved the Fox until the loading ramp was only a step away from the spire's base. The machinas crossed the gap. Sif flew the ship off to the side. It looked like the spire could collapse at any second. It'd been holding for 80 years. Trix figured it'd last a little longer.

The Valkyrie walked to a console which was in its own private office. Must've been a head machinist's once upon a time.

She ran the boot-up procedure. It'd be a small miracle if anything worked in this place.

Nothing happened. The screen remained black.

Trix went to try again when the console came to life. It was still black, but now it was backlit. That was something.

Trix plugged in her comms gauntlet after blowing away debris from the input. Sif was at the log-on page within a minute. It took another five to decrypt the username and password. Then the AI searched for any available power grid or networking map. Brought them up on the screen.

'As you can see, each academy had a corresponding power module that connects it to the core below the docks. It also has its own network that connects to the greater Mair Ultima intranet. The section for external, long-range communications is a fortress. Since no one's around to stop my hack, I could do it, but it'll take me an hour. Maybe two.'

'That rules out anyone who didn't have direct access betraying us if it takes an AI that long. No chance a human could do it unnoticed,' Kit said.

Trix smiled. 'Can you get a list of users who did have access to the long-range comms?'

Instead of replying, Sif swapped the screen to her search results. It was a damn small list.

frances.curie
martha.rodriguez
valfodr.wednesday
andrew.djac
kevin.featherstone
hiroshi.ng
elizabeth.chatterjee
cortland.caine
minerva.granger

Sif was currently logged in as Frances Curie, though she couldn't access the comms without biometrics. That was why it would take so long to hack.

'Call me Wallaby Ted's brother.'

'What?'

'Roo Ted,' Kit raised an eyebrow. '*Rooted.*'

'Australian slang?'

'Is there any other kind?' Kit saw that Trix was unimpressed so he got on with it. 'Martha Rodriguez and Andrew Djac were the head machinists of Oni Academy.'

'Cortland and Minerva were the only permanent machinists in Valkyrie Academy.'

'Then we can assume that all these authorised users were the academies' head machinists.'

'That means there's one name that doesn't belong.'

'Could be Garth Roche using an alias,' Kit said. He was combing through recessed memories, trying to remember machinas from other academies. He was certain Hiroshi Ng was a Spectre Academy machinist. And Sif was logged into Frances Curie's terminal in the Dragon Spire, so that ruled her out.

Trix examined the names. They were normal enough. Had originated on Earth. In fact, naming conventions hadn't changed much in nearly 600 years. They differed on colonies — Fenwick was a perfect example of how names could change — but if humans were around, you'd probably find Dick and Jane.

'Valfodr Wednesday,' Trix said. It sounded oddly familiar. 'Sif, what's the etymology for those names?'

'Valfodr is an Anglicised version of an Earthen Nordic name that means Father of the Slain, and was attributed to Odin. Wednesday was named for Woden, essentially meaning, day of Woden, another name for Odin, the All-Father of Norse Mythology.'

'Subtlety was never Garth's strongpoint,' Kit said.

'Was it the self-commissioned statue that gave him away?'

Kit chuckled.

'What a ripper. Looks like we have our man. Even if it's not Garth, I doubt Valfodr Wednesday is another machinist. Can you find his personal terminal in the directory, Sif?'

'As it happens... no. There is no assigned terminal to Valfodr Wednesday in any machina academy. The username is in the system, but that's all.'

'Shit. And there are no other networks that aren't shown on the grid map?' Trix said.

'None that I can find. Maybe if it was turned on it'd be visible, but considering the power core was offline for nearly a century, it would make sense that a structure separate from the Luna Wolf Mountains was running on its own generator.'

'Can you find the last long-range transmission sent?' said Kit.

'All logs are sealed and encrypted. They'd take weeks to breach.'

'Not like we're going anywhere,' Kit shrugged. He did have a commitment to keep, but that could wait. He'd put almost anything on hold for this.

'There has to be a better way.'

'It's not like we can ask the neighbours if they ever saw anything strange. For all we know Roche's base was on the other side of the planet. Jesus Christos, it could be on any of Mair Ultima's four moons.'

'True,' Trix said, but she hadn't really been listening to Kit. She'd tuned out after his first sentence to work on her own hypothesis. They could, in fact, ask the neighbours. 'I think we should go with your first idea.'

'I don't believe I had one. If you want to have one and give me the credit, I'm not gonna stop you.'

'We'll ask the neighbours.'

Kit's mouth flew open then closed just as fast. He understood what Trix was saying.

'You mean the black dragon. Might that be the very same dragon we saw on Conan's Eyes today?'

'Looks the same.'

'I never met any of the dragons. Your Trial ran through those peaks where they live, didn't it?'

'You should know. You ran it once.'

'And I still maintain it was the worst day of my life. How you did that every morning still makes me awestruck.'

'*An Oni Awestruck*, sounds like the name of a Valentine novel.'

'I know, ridiculous, but even during my one venture into that fucking course, I never did meet a dragon.'

'He has a name.'

Kit looked at Trix, signalling with his eyes. *"Go on."*

'Mireleth.'

'Acquaint yourselves over some rums, did ya?'

'He rescued me once.'

Kit whistled in a long, descending tone. 'What'd you do to deserve that?'

'He never said. All we did was exchange names.'

'Hey, Mr Dragon, I'm 6V, and your name is?' Kit said, mocking Trix's voice.

'Keep that up.'

'Coming around to my humour?'

'Dragons supposedly hate smartasses. Mireleth might eat you.'

'Bursting out of a dragon's stomach, now that's a story waiting to be written.'

'Good luck doing that without a sword.'

'Don't get all anatomical on me. I know dragon hide can't be rent apart with bare hands. Not even by an oni, apparently.'

'Nice to see you listen when I talk.'

'You talk about monsters more than you realise.'

'I realise it fine.'

Trix left the command centre. Resigned herself to the fact that she wouldn't be acquiring more information here. The oni walked beside her. Grinding metal deafened them as they neared the edge. The spire shifted against its Uldarian foundations.

'Sif, we need you to bring the ship around.'

'If the spire collapses, the Fox will be crushed. You'll have to exit from the side windows. There's one on the floor above you.'

'Great.'

Trix and Kit searched for the stairs. Although the spire was connected to the power grid, in its current state, having a working elevator would be doubtful.

There was a door in the back-wall's centre. A sign was beside it, though it was too worn to be readable. Kit shoulder charged the door. Damn it, an elevator. No stairs. The spire kept tipping. That afforded an opportunity. It was all in how you looked at it.

'We can use the shaft as a ramp,' Kit said. The angle was about as steep as a cliff side but it was doable.

Trix took off. Every passing second reduced the gradient. Of course that meant that the spire was closer to tumbling down the mountainside. The duo reached the next floor. They hung in the doorway a moment. Across the room they could see the Fox, loading ramp down, cargo bay open.

Only problem was that now the angle was so acute the floor was a wall. What should've become the floor was a shattered window. It was a long way down. There was close to seven kilometres of rocky mountainside before a dark crevasse.

The Valkyrie altered gravity just enough to enable wall running. Furniture slid into the chasm. Trix jumped for the loading ramp. Rolled into the cargo bay. Waited for Kit. He leaped as the tower reached its critical tipping point. He missed the cargo bay, but his hands found the loading ramp. He monkey-vaulted. Shot into the cargo bay, nearly smacking his head on the ceiling.

He turned to watch Dragon Spire crash. Total ruination would happen to every building on Mair Ultima one day. Despite never training in the spire, Kit was sad to see it go. It'd been a marker for the academies. Kit remembered how many dragon machinas could fly using telekinetic energy. He'd envied them.

'Let's go see this Mireleth.'

'I don't know if he'll appreciate us flying a ship to his doorstep,' Trix said. She pulled the manual close lever to shut the loading ramp.

'He won't expect us to run Aethelwulf's Trial, will he?'

'No, dragons aren't petty. But I doubt he'll give us a straight answer.'

'Will he be sleeping?'

'Dragons survive on a couple of hours sleep a day.'

'Yet they spend most of their time thinking like old men in musty studies rather than flying. I don't think I'll ever understand them.'

'You'd get bored of flying.'

'No one's bored with space travel, and it's been hundreds of years.'

'True, but there's nothing special about it now. People see travelling to other planets like taking public transport in the 21st century. It's just another part of life.'

'By that logic, can a wonder only be a wonder if it's new?'

'All wonders become banal given enough time.'

'Time doesn't do a lot in the way of improving things.'

'Time is what allows us to create and see wonders.'

'Yeah, right before it robs them of specialness.'

'Maybe time is jealous.'

'Well, time is one of the few things we still can't control.'

'And going back to our previous discussion, that means whatever gods are deigned to control time must still be in business.'

'They could be fed up with having to keep the clock turning. Disgruntled Gods.'

'Another good book title.'

'It seems I've missed my true calling.'

'You'll never be able to write like you throw right hooks. Consider yourself safe.'

'Always do. I'm... friends with a chooser of the slain. Can't imagine you'd pick me to die.'

Kit's hesitation before "friends" was minute, but present all the same. Trix chose to ignore it.

'Sif, it appears we need to visit Mireleth.'

'Well, wouldn't you know it, this planet hasn't been mapped. And Mireleth hasn't invited me to his last few dinner parties. I can't say I know his exact location.'

'You're in a mood,' Trix said. She was half-surprised. Sif had seemed to work around her filters more than Trix liked over the years. She'd been making more jokes than usual recently.

'Sarcasm's the lowest form of humour,' Kit said. He took a seat and leaned forward. His backpack didn't lend itself to being comfortable.

'And that's the saddest form of comeback,' Sif said.

'You know what, I'll fly,' Trix said. She walked to the cockpit. Kit stayed put.

It was only going to be a short flight.

3

Conan's Eyes were dusted with snow.

The air was colder. Drops were steeper. Trix looked at the chasm. She'd been crossing it when the anghenfil had attacked.

Both she and Kit were looking at a cavern opening. There was a plateau just big enough for the ship. Sif wasn't going to land. A dragon could easily knock a corvette off its landing struts, and the machinas only had one ship between them. Trix wasn't keen to lose it.

She descended the ramp. Stopped at the cavern's mouth. Heat was emanating from inside. Mireleth was home, alright.

'Take her up to orbit, Sif,' Trix said. She'd left her hat on a hook in the cargo bay. It was a little singed thanks to the explosion, and it had a tear on the left side. Either way, there was no need for a hat at night.

'You got it.'

Kit exited as the loading ramp closed.

'Never been in a dragon's lair before.'

'You could've been if you hadn't been cut open that day on Yephus and needed to recover.'

'Scored a gnarly scar though.'

'You're so going to be eaten.'

'Eh, you're a huntress. You'll stop him.'

'I can't kill Mireleth.'

'Not with that attitude, mate.'

'They're a protected species.'

Kit raised a finger. 'Ah, but they're technically considered the same as people, what with being introspective and all. That means if he tries eating me, I can claim self-defence.'

'Interesting proposition, oni,' a low voice said from within the cavern. The machinas heard footsteps. Breathing that sounded like wind stoking a forest fire wound its way outside. Mireleth blended into the night so well he was nearly invisible. Bright gold eyes gave him away. They looked like a dinosaur's. His slit irises were abyssal voids to other dimensions. You could lose yourself in their fathomless depths.

'Greetings, Mireleth,' Trix said before Kit could make a stupid retort.

'The Valkyrie known as 6V, though I suspect you no longer answer to such a name.'

'Trix of Zilvia.'

'It would seem you can choose your home, after all. I can see it in your mind. A place not so different from here, though it is kinder. And you, oni, what name have you given yourself?'

'Kit. I got it off a box of equipment on Aros. Key Integral Technology. Figured it made a good enough name.'

'Why have you come to my home, Trix of Zilvia?'

'Mireleth, mate, that's not actually her name. Unlike me, she had a father and a mother. But between you and me she doesn't know she was adopted, so keep that quiet. You can call her Beatrix Westwood. Beatrix works for short.'

Mireleth stared into Kit's eyes. Dragons could skim the surfaces of people's minds, though only a few could actively exercise mind control. Even then, they rarely did. Not much was to be gained from controlling a human when you were a dragon.

'I see your nature is that of a, what you would call, larrikin. I shan't roast you.'

'You mean that in a literal or a figurative sense? Since you're a dragon, that kind of statement could go either way.'

Trix rolled her eyes.

'We wanted to ask you for help.'

'Then ask, child.'

'In your time here, have you ever seen another base, built by those who constructed the academies?'

Mireleth rose to full height. Kept his wings by his side. They were thick leather.

'Why do you want to know?'

'We believe the person who lived there betrayed us.'

'It's been 80 years. This cannot matter.'

'It does.'

'If you insist. What matters is relative.'

'Why did you save Beatrix?' Kit butted in.

'I was under the impression you did nothing but learn in those academies. Yet you seem unable to understand the art of conversation. I will only answer one of these questions. I doubt you wish the latter to be answered over the former.'

'Your doubts are correct, Mireleth,' Trix said.

'Then enter.'

Mireleth's wings unfurled. The gust that followed made the machinas slide backwards. Mireleth turned around and shot back into his cavern. His short flight whipped snow into a flurry. Flakes stuck in Kit's beard. Some landed in Trix's ponytail, but they weren't noticeable.

'That was easy.'

'He's not going to tell us what we want to know just yet. We'll have to answer a riddle. Maybe more than one.'

'I thought that only happened in fairy tales.'

'Hunt monsters long enough and you see that fairy tales

aren't make believe.'

'Good thing I've been sharpening my wits against the whetstone that is your mind all day.'

'Come up with that all by yourself?'

'Probably read it somewhere.'

'You and Yvach should write a book together.'

'He's got a blunt way of putting things.'

'Between your slang and Yvach's half-assed poetry you'd need a translator before you could publish it.'

'Sharpening your wits before going head-to-head with Mireleth, huh? Wise.'

'No. I was just making fun of you.'

Trix flashed a genuine smile then burst out laughing. Kit joined her. Their merriment lasted far into the cavern. Reverberated off the walls.

Humans, Mireleth thought, were interesting creatures. He'd skimmed the memories of his fair share of people, and no other race seemed capable of laughing in danger's face like it was the funniest thing they'd ever seen. Well, maybe the corrachs. But Mireleth suspected they were certifiably crazy.

Resting on a bed of hot rocks, Mireleth awaited the machinas. He knew the answers to both their questions and so much more.

They could only earn one. For now.

4

Mireleth's home was foreboding.

Stories depicted dragon lairs as vast treasure troves. It was true that dragons liked collecting treasure, however, that required there to be treasure on the planet. Nothing so fine as jewellery or crowns had ever been present in the machina academies. And from all evidence, it didn't appear as though the Uldarians liked to accessorise. Thus, there were no mounds of gold or precious gems covering the rocky floor of Mireleth's abode.

Dragons couldn't dig for treasure. Their claws weren't made

for it. In any case, they had no interest in unrefined ore. Due to their lack of opposable thumbs, they couldn't build tools, nor pilot spacecraft. That being said, dragons could fly in planets' low orbits and re-enter the atmosphere without an issue.

Zoologists and biologists alike who were fortunate enough to gain audiences with dragons discerned that the gems stored magic power. Dragons could also absorb them into their relatively soft underbellies to increase their defence. Over time, the minerals in the gems would break down, forming a smooth, calcified layer which not only offered protection, but gave the dragon an individual stripe.

Mireleth had no such marking for he had no treasure.

Arcane fire orbs hung around the ceiling. They cast immense light for their size. Magic, of course. Scholars theorised that magic had been born from dragons, and that they'd bestowed it to the people of Xardiassant as a gift. It was possible, but the Piercing of the Veils was a more commonly accepted theory. It stipulated that other dimensions had crossed over with the Milky Way, dumping otherworldly monsters, and magic, onto its planets. Exploring the galaxy didn't so much as teach people new things as it reinforced the notion that anything was possible.

Trix and Kit descended into Mireleth's home. The dragon watched them with his head low to the ground. He snorted smoke from his nostrils. The machinas weren't afraid. Mireleth would've smelled their fear if it existed. Come to think of it, he'd never smelled fear on a machina before. Even when those young, white haired girls ran their course, there was no fear. Adrenaline yes, but never fear.

'Nice place. Couple of windows wouldn't go astray though,' Kit said.

'By all means, put them in yourself. I will not stop you, oni. It is purported that your kind can move mountains. By human standards I believe this to be true. You're far stronger than any I have ever met. Now, Beatrix of Zilvia, you strike me as a woman who has seen much and done more. You know what you must do to gain an answer from a dragon.'

'A test of wit, display of brawn, by these trials I do commit.'

Mireleth dipped his nose slightly, like a bow. 'Admirable, but you have forgotten the final caveat.'

Trix's brow furrowed. This was surely part of the test. She searched her memories until she found the answer. 'By these trials I do commit until the break of dawn.'

'Now I know you have accepted, I shall agree to help, provided you pass my tests.'

Kit: 'Last test I took was a sobriety test.'

Trix: 'How'd you go?'

'Failed miserably. It'd been a big night. Gang warfare is thirsty work. I like my chances here much better.'

Mireleth roared. His warm breath was like walking into a rainforest with 90 per cent humidity.

'There is a thing that nothing is, and yet it has a name. It's sometimes tall and sometimes short, joins our talks, joins our walks, and plays in every game,' Mireleth said.

Kit and Trix looked at each other. Interesting riddle. Riddles were used to test imagination and problem solving as part of philosophy courses in the machina academies. Not all situations were clear cut according to machinists. And when an unclear situation arose, unconventional solutions were often the answer. This played along nicely with the old adage — which Trix later learned had been parlayed from NASA — that there was no problem so bad you couldn't make it worse.

Trix ran through possible solutions in her head. She knew that dragons didn't take kindly to brash answers. Even less so to wrong ones.

'A shadow,' Trix said.

Mireleth nodded again. He blew more smoke out of his nostrils. It was charmed to look like waves.

'It cannot be seen, cannot be felt. Cannot be heard, cannot be smelt. It lies behind stars and under hills. Empty holes it fills. It comes first and follows after. Ends life, kills laughter.'

'Cheery,' said Kit.

Mireleth rumbled. Kit took the hint. Don't speak unless you're answering.

Kit was sensing a pattern. He was about to answer when Trix beat him to it.

'Darkness,' she said.

Another bow preceded Mireleth's next riddle.

'Alive without breath, as cold as death. Never thirsty yet forever drinking.'

This one was a bit more abstract, though still macabre.

Kit was going to guess some sort of wraith. Or banshee. He'd heard Trix talk about them. He stayed his tongue, for neither creature obeyed the second sentence's terms.

Trix on the other hand, knew the answer. Growing up with a hunter for a father ensured she did.

'Fish.'

Mireleth revealed his sharp teeth in a grin. He was enjoying himself. 'The oni will answer the next riddle. For brawn without brain is a terrible shame. Taller than trees but never to grow. Down and down they go, over time and under wind, their demise is slow.'

Something in Kit's head clicked. It might've been the remark that Mireleth had made when Kit entered. He spoke as soon as Mireleth fell silent.

'Mountains.'

Mireleth continued with the next riddle. 'Not chest or box is discussed. Money can be held in it, but just as we test its metal, within it there is rust.'

Now this one was a stumper. Trix and Kit had to replay it in their minds for it to make sense. The wording was odd. Clearly meant to confuse. That indicated a play on words. Now, which words were those?

Seconds ticked to a minute when Trix thought she'd figured out the answer. Metal could also be mettle, as in fortitude and spirit. Within that mettle there was rust, but not in the literal sense. Mettle wasn't tangible so it couldn't oxidise. Rust being within was the second part of the wordplay. It was four fifths of the answer.

Clever, Mireleth, Trix thought.

'Trust,' she said.

'My, machinas are clever. Yet your race still hates you.'

'People fear what they don't understand,' Kit said.

'Then make them understand. That much is plain to see.'

'You've stopped riddling. Does that mean we're done?' Trix said. It was quaint of Mireleth to suggest making people understand machinas weren't so different from humans. What'd be next, having a spot on the Consortium Council? For most legal matters, machinas were begrudgingly accepted as part of the human race. To be thought of as independent, they'd need their own planet and leaders. Well, they had a planet, but for a leader to be elected, all machinas would need to be assembled in one place. That hadn't happened since Mair Ultima's prime.

Trix was doubtful whether it'd ever happen again.

Mireleth ignored Trix. Kept going. It appeared they weren't done after all. 'Who is he that builds stronger than the carpenter, the mason, and the shipwright?'

This riddle couldn't possibly have a straight answer. Strength was relative. Who was to say what was stronger than something else?

'The Uldarians. Their constructs are indestructible, so far as we know,' Trix said.

'It is easy to see how you may arrive at such a conclusion. Even when your best architecture fails, Uldarian remnants still stand. It is a pity about the spire. I remember seeing the dragon machinas flying around its peak. There was more than one instance when I saw a group flying unassisted in low orbit. However, the fact that there are Uldarian remnants means that at some point in time, they must have faced a stronger force.'

There was a twinkle in Mireleth's eyes. As though he was remembering the Uldarians' destruction. But that wasn't possible. He couldn't be so old.

Kit didn't see this. He was staring at the floor.

Alright, Mireleth defines strength by longevity. Gods seem like a cop out. We don't even know if they exist. If they did create the universe, they've done a bang-up job. It's still here billions of years after it supposedly came into existence. But there had to be things before that, because nothing can't exist. Not totally. So, let's say there was something before. A pub at the centre of what would later be the universe. Fuck, that's terrible. Where was I going with that?

Kit's train of thought blew through a myriad of stations. Eventually he ran out of rails. That was when he had an idea.

The track ends. It's dead. Not even magic can bring back the dead. It's an absolute. Maybe the only one that exists. Now that makes the question, who builds death?

'The Gravedigger,' Kit said. He spoke like he was ordering a burger with extra fries.

'He builds the home of death which lasts until all the leaves have fallen,' Mireleth nodded.

Sif buzzed Trix's earpiece. 'These riddles all originated on Earth. That last one, for example, was written by a man named William Shakespeare in a play called Hamlet. Mireleth amended the words a little, but it's basically the same.'

Trix knew of Shakespeare. His plays formed the essence of almost every story known to man. She also knew he'd lived in the 1600s. That was over a thousand years ago.

How did Mireleth know these? Trix wondered.

Everything is connected, Mireleth responded telepathically.

The Valkyrie once again thought of Gabe. She couldn't picture a face. Just the name. Mair Ultima was doing funny things to her mind. She began seeing the riddles' answers form before her eyes.

Trust in darkness, trust in shadows,
both are with you on your way to the gallows.
You are the fish, the hare, the bird, the bear,
all things yet one, marching to death's lair.
A thudding shovel, a beating heart,
the Gravedigger's been here from the start.

Trust in darkness, trust in shadows,
truest of true, most hallowed of hallows.
All the worlds hear their echoes.

'I am satisfied with your knowledge. Now, move this mountain.'

Trix was still entrenched in the poem. Unlike the mysterious name which was forgotten until it was remembered, the poem lingered like a high-contrast image. It'd been burned onto her eyelids. Either Mireleth knew more than he was letting on, or this was coincidental. As soon as she left Mireleth's home, she wanted Sif to search for that poem.

'Come again, mate. I know we joked about it before, but I can't actually move a mountain. I mean, I could, but it'd be stone by stone. And not even I can do that by dawn.'

'Move this mountain,' Mireleth said.

Trix snapped out of her day-dream.

(Here's a question: is it still a day-dream if it's night time?)

'Mireleth, these tasks have to be possible or the trial is unjust.'

'If you could harness true magic, you could bend gravity in such a way that tore this mountain from the ground.'

'Yes, but I can't.'

'You can. You have merely forgotten.'

'You two can stop your arguing. I'll move the damn mountain.' Kit cracked his knuckles and jumped up and down a couple times. 'Beatrix, you're gonna wanna stand way over there. If this doesn't work, I'll need you alive so you can help me think of something else.'

Trix walked to the cavern's far side. Clambered up some rocks. She wasn't sure what Kit planned on doing. Even with his machina bone density, punching a mountain would shatter his hand, probably his whole arm.

'Okay, Mireleth, hit me.'

Even Mireleth didn't expect this. 'You wish me to strike you?'

'I admit that was a poor choice of words. Light up that belly fire, my good man, and crank up the heat.' Kit rolled his shoulders. The more he thought about this idea, the more he liked the way it sounded in his head. A small voice told him he was being stupendously stupid. He ignored it.

Kit of Aros, Forged from Dragon's Breath. Oh yes, this was going to be a pub story told from dusk till dawn every chance he got.

All he had to do was survive.

'You know what you're doing?' Trix said. She folded her arms. Readjusted the weight on her legs. Her wound was uncomfortable.

'In theory,' the oni said. He rubbed his hands together. 'Light a match, big fella.'

Mireleth roared. Kit watched as his underbelly glowed red hot. It looked like molten lava was coming from Mireleth's guts. This was indicative of a greater dragon. They had black, carmine, or orange scales, though black dragons were always the biggest. Gold dragons were only talked about in myths.

Lesser dragons had white, navy, or green scales. They breathed fire by creating sparks with their teeth. Glands in their lower jaw which ran to their stomachs produced a flammable, noxious gas. Their flames weren't as hot as their greater counterparts. However, they could also asphyxiate their enemies with gas in situations where fire was unsuitable.

Kit activated his oni barrier. Octagonal shapes with reddish tinges streamed from his palms. Formed a dome over his physique. Then came fire so hot it was nearly blue. The barrier started absorbing energy into Kit's body. This energy couldn't be used to sustain the barrier. It was stored to be released. Onis who tried creating never-ending barriers — to facilitate invulnerability — usually exploded from the energy build-up. Whoever had said love worked in mysterious ways had clearly never tried their hand at magic. It was like science. There were rules. And each one had a plethora of exceptions.

Trix could feel the heat from where she was standing. Her 2nd Skin one piece did its best to wick moisture away from her skin. She could see Kit was struggling. Had he been shirtless, his veins would've been trying to burst his arms. Gold cracks appeared in the blacks of his eyes. Sweat came from his brow. Pooled in his close cropped, blocky beard.

Mireleth ended his onslaught. Not a moment too soon, judging by Kit's shaking legs.

'Hah, you call that hot?' Kit said. He flexed his biceps and smiled. 'Come down to Queensland in the summertime, mate, we'll show you hot.'

In truth, Kit was sweltering more than a spit roasted pig at midday, but he wasn't going to let that dampen his spirits. He would've continued joking longer, but his heart was beating at 250 beats a minute. And climbing.

Kit jumped. Angled himself fist first towards the ground. Trix had known his plan since he demanded Mireleth douse him with flames. There was no way she could alter his density without touching him.

The idiot was going to break his hand.

Kit surged downwards. The impact formed a crater. The mountain shuddered. Rocks fell from the ceiling. He twisted his wrist a couple of times then clenched his hand. Nothing was broken, but it'd be blackened with bruises. He'd created a barrier around his fist at the last second. That detail would be omitted in later retellings.

'Now,' Kit said, vaulting out of the crater. 'If that's not moving a mountain, then I don't know what is. Well, I do. I'm not an idiot. But you get what I'm saying.'

'Not many can stand the heat of a dragon's flame,' Mireleth said.

'Bloody oath they can't.'

'You have earned a dragon's blessing for your show of strength, just as Beatrix has earned one from her wisdom.'

'I didn't answer your final question,' she said, walking back over. The rocks were still warm.

'But you answered the others, and I sense you have gained a deeper understanding from them than I previously thought possible.'

Trust in darkness... the poem began playing in Trix's mind. Mireleth betrayed no sign of knowing Trix's thoughts. She wondered if the dragon knew of the poem. Perhaps it was a prophecy, like the Uldarian prism. That reminded her, she still had to show it to Kit.

'Come and receive your blessings, oni, Valkyrie.'

Trix approached. Mireleth's snout touched her glabella. He spoke. She could feel the vibrations of his voice through her body.

'I, Mireleth, do bestow my blessing upon Beatrix Westwood for her wisdom. Henceforth, to dragon kind, you will be known as Staresivreth, the Wise Frost.'

Trix felt her body ripple with energy. Heat blared inside her. Then she returned to normal. She'd read about dragon blessings. They were featured in *Monsters & Other Beasts* by Coën Vesemir with illustrations and annotations by Fiona Calanthe. Blessings differed depending on the dragon, and the reason why they were bestowed. In fact, the words spoken were only for the person's benefit. Dragon language was only used telepathically between dragons. Linguists tried discerning a full range of words from dragon names. None had been successful thus far.

The black dragon pulled away from Trix. Put his snout on Kit's forehead. The oni's jaw slackened a little. Surreal reality was sinking in. Maybe it was just exhaustion.

Kit felt like he was in space. His ship had suffered a devastating hit during a dogfight once. Thankfully, life support and inertial dampeners had been A-Okay. The artificial gravity, however, had been shot to hell from the barrel of a .44 pistol. Living in zero gravity had been fun for a while, though it'd quickly become inconvenient.

'I, Mireleth, do bestow my blessing upon Kit of Aros for his strength. Henceforth, to dragon kind, you will be known as Sajidifeilth, the Strong Flame.'

Kit experienced the same sensations Trix had. His punctured

abs didn't feel sore anymore. Kit could've sworn they'd healed to scar tissue already.

'Thank you, Mireleth,' Trix said.

Kit bowed.

'Thanks is not required when the gift is deserved. And you have much more to prove before your power is realised. Now for the question you asked. Indeed, there was one such individual. He lived far from here, past the mountains and across the sea on another continent. He resided in the base of a mountain range, smaller than these you call the Luna Wolves. Whether or not he is the individual you seek, I do not know. I only saw him once.'

Trix: 'Thank you.'

Kit: 'Let's check it out.'

'You shall not take your ship there, machinas. You are blessed of the dragons now. You may ride on my back.'

Mireleth arched his neck low. Spikes trimmed the length of his body. Trix got on first. Kit followed.

'Hold tight, for you soar on dragon's wings.'

The acceleration was intense. Mireleth's hind legs propelled him towards the cavern exit with force that nearly made the machinas slide off his back.

And like that, they were off.

5

The sky was cut open before Mireleth.

High on the warm air he rolled through clouds, catching their moisture to paint patterns in the sky. Then down. Wind whipped the machinas' faces. Hair billowed. They stopped just before the ocean. Waves towered overhead.

Mighty Mireleth blew them apart with fire. Walls of water turned to veils of steam. Their vapour gleamed in the moonlight. Mireleth flew upside down. Trix and Kit ran their hands through the cyan water. If there were any monsters below, they stayed there. None were foolish enough to mess with a dragon. They ruled every food chain.

Both machinas activated their helmets. With a sudden manoeuvre, Mireleth rocketed higher again. Approached a wrecked dreadnought. It looked like the dragon was going to ram it. Mireleth banked hard right at the last second. Flying on a ship was grand, but flying on dragon-back was magical.

Dawn's early light began seeping across the horizon as Mireleth set the machinas down. They were on the continent of which he'd spoken. Black sand entrenched their combat boots. The tide was going out which was just as well. High tide on Mair Ultima meant dumping waves that'd pummel you into the planet's core.

'Beyond the tree line, at the base of the mountains, you'll see an enclave. I hope you find the answers you seek. Should you wish to speak again, you know where to find me. And if you're ever in need while on this planet, call my name in your mind. Farewell, Staresivreth, Sajidifeilth. I expect I will see you again before the end.'

The machinas didn't have time to respond before Mireleth beat his wings. Took to the skies. His roar tore the sky asunder. Trix and Kit watched him go. Their hands brushed together absently.

'Cool names,' Kit finally said. 'Bit of a mouthful to say, but I suppose Jono wouldn't sound anywhere near as epic. Although there was this one—'

'Are you ready for what we might find?'

'I just took dragon fire to the face. I'm ready, Staresivreth.'

'You butcher the language.'

'Have it your way, Beatrix. Come on. We'd better get off the shore in case a rogue wave decides to dump on us.'

Trix nodded. She and Kit left the beach. No thornwoods grew this close to the coast. Trees with traditional green leaves that turned bright orange during winter swayed with the breeze. They were tall like palm trees, yet had foliage akin to willows.

Machinas had taken to calling them flametrees due to their winter hues. It wasn't really fitting the rest of the time.

Green leaves stroked the machinas as they walked through them. Some had begun shifting into orange shades. The duo didn't speak. There was serenity away from the academies. It was almost possible to forget the Last Day along this foreign coast. No ships had crashed here. No wrecks were evident. There was only nature's rapture, the mystery of a lonely shore in an alien world.

Soil turned to rocks. They were at the mountains' foothills. At first, the machinas didn't even notice the depression in the rock face. It looked like part of the mountain had just eroded. It was a door. No security panel was visible. As it happened, the rock was a cover. There was an airlock door from a submersible vehicle behind it.

'No reason to pressurise an environment here. The atmosphere's liveable and the gravity's only a little denser than Earth,' Kit said. He was thinking aloud. Ran his hands along the metal. It'd rusted near the handle. The porthole shaped window was slick with muck, probably to stop anyone from peering in. Though that was unlikely on Mair Ultima.

'I can't read any technology. Scans are showing nothing other than a cavern beyond this door,' Sif said.

Trix jimmied the handle. It was locked. Not with any biometrics or facial recognition software, just a regular keyhole. She drew her pistol. Six bullets outlined the handle with smoking holes. Trix opened the door. Darkness lay beyond. Her vision adjusted.

'Strange for this lair to appear off the grid when Valfodr Wednesday's username was logged on the academy mainframe,' Kit said.

'He probably used a tablet. Maybe even a comms gauntlet as his only power source.'

'Whatever Roche was doing can't have been too science heavy. There's not a lot you can accomplish with no power.'

'Hmm.'

It turned out both the machinas were wrong.

The rocky hallway they walked through smoothed out

further in. No hardwood floors appeared. No polished concrete. Nothing indicating anyone had ever lived here.

The duo rounded a corner. Kit switched on the torch attached to his chest plate.

'Fuck me...' he said.

Trix didn't know what to say.

Beyond the corner there was a staircase made from wrought iron that descended into a cavern. Desks with scattered papers abounded. Chemistry sets had been knocked over. Broken glass twinkled on the rock floor. None of those things disturbed the machinas. What disturbed them lay beyond the hodgepodge lab and filthy living quarters.

Four, six feet high test-tubes filled with ambrosia were lined up against a back wall. Teenage humans were inside them. Their eyes were closed. Bruising from repeated injections marred their skin. Trix and Kit couldn't tell if they were machinas. Their medallions weren't vibrating.

Kit reached for Trix's hand. She held it. Squeezed tight. They looked at each other. Whatever it was they were looking for, there was a chance it might be here.

The oni released the Valkyrie's hand. Vaulted the stairs. Landed on the rocks below. Trix followed. Lowered herself with weakened gravity. Kit's torchlight cast harsh shadows with jagged edges. They were monsters peering over tables. Slinking across walls. This was their home.

'All the notes, all the findings. On paper,' Trix said, bending down to pick up loose sheets covered in wet sediment. Water was coming from somewhere. Runoff from the mountain's peak that had eroded the rocks. 'He wanted this place to be unhackable.'

'Sif couldn't find it, so it looks like he succeeded,' Kit said. He was examining the broken chemistry set. Liquid that hadn't been disturbed for 80 years had pooled in the wooden table's grooves, splitting it.

Winter, Kit surmised. It gets cold enough for the liquid to freeze, expanding in the cracks, then melts again come summer. Looks like blood.

The oni touched the mixture. Rubbed it between his fingers. He brought it to his nostrils. It smelled like blood, but the scent was so diluted by the wood he couldn't be sure. He smeared the substance on his comms gauntlet.

'Sif, get me a breakdown on this compound.'

His gauntlet came to life. Eighteen seconds passed before Sif replied.

'This is compromised Uldarian blood. The cells are barely alive. You couldn't create a machina with this. Injecting it would likely result in the host convulsing before death.'

'Shit,' Kit said. Looked at Trix.

She was gathering the papers. The ink had smudged but it was still readable. Some sheets were nothing other than ramblings: judgement day, the apocalypse and Kingdom Come, all references to the world ending. Ragnarök was among these, written in bigger letters than the rest. Savagely underlined. Trix activated her helmet in tactical mode. Scanned the documents she found. At the same time, she had Sif cross-reference the odd symbols Roche had drawn. No matches were returned save for Viking runes.

On one page, he'd written what looked like a journal entry.

What destroyed the Uldarians will return. Machinas will not be enough. We need what the Uldarians had. They lost, but we will not. We cannot, for losing means obliteration. All cultures point to an apocalyptic event which will bathe the world in fire and ice, but they were thinking too small. It is not Earth, nor Raursioc that shall be destroyed, but the entire universe—

The entry kept going, but the page was ripped. The writing certainly sounded like something Roche would say.

'He was trying to create better machinas,' Trix said. With each successful scan she shredded the paper and ground it into the floor. She didn't want other people stumbling across it.

Kit nodded. 'These vials are stained with Uldarian blood.' He walked to the test-tubes. Tapped the glass. No response from the humans inside. He pressed his ear to the tube. No heartbeat. Not even a slow one. They were dead, their corpses perfectly preserved.

'None of these papers say anything about activating the beacon.'

'Any evidence of that would've been on the computer he was using. Doesn't look like that's here.' Kit bowed his head. Remembered the pain that came with becoming a machina. The initial changes. Nothing he'd endured since had been as bad. A piece of paper was under Kit's boot heel. He picked it up. Scrambled writing covered it. One sentence stood out among the scrawl.

Uldarian memories=genetic. I see flashes. Victory lies with the knowledge of past defeats.

Kit passed it to Trix for scanning.

'Looks like he wanted more than just soldiers. He wanted to see how the Uldarians were destroyed.' As Kit turned away from the tubes, he saw a chalkboard that'd been toppled over.

Damn, that's old school, if you'll excuse the pun, Kit thought. Normally he would've chuckled. Laughter eluded him now. He flipped over the chalkboard. Expected to see complex chemical equations. Instead, three phrases greeted him.

TWILIGHT OF THE GODS
DOOM OF THE GODS
FINAL DESTINY OF THE GODS

'Roche lost it in here. Whatever he was searching for consumed him.'

Trix looked at the board. Sif registered a match. All three phrases were possible translations of the ancient Norse word, Ragnarök. Curious. Apocalyptic theories were numerous among all the Milky Way's races. Corrachs largely believed that the end would be heralded by a wave of meteors so destructive that even if they missed planets, their gravitational pull would be enough to rip them from orbit and send them towards the sun. They called it Verhaseir.

Other cultures had their own beliefs. Only one opinion was shared by everyone, though it was always discussed in jest.

Whatever killed the Uldarians would return. It was joked about not because it was a laughing matter, but because no one knew what ended the Uldarians. And that was scarier than any apocalyptic meteor shower.

'No doubt Roche wanted to singlehandedly prevent the apocalypse. His god complex doesn't appear to have diminished as much as his statue,' Trix said as she continued scanning. She wasn't really looking at the paper now. She'd have Sif compile Roche's notes into one coherent document later.

Kit returned his attention to the people in the tubes. What he'd thought was bruising from the stairwell wasn't that at all. It was metal. Uldarian metal. He punched the glass. It stood up to the first blow. Not the second. He stepped aside as ambrosia oozed onto the floor. Viscous like honey.

Ambrosia had been used in stasis pods during space travel's early days. Its use had declined following the invention of warp and hyperdrives; though no better preservative had been found. Its name came directly from the Latin word, ambrotos, which meant immortal. The word as modern humans knew it came from Greek and Roman mythology. Ambrosia was supposed to be a food that conferred immortality to the gods.

Trix: 'What're you doing?'

'I want a closer look.'

Kit took the body, a teenage boy, and laid him out on the ground. He was bald like the others. Kit touched the dark patches on his skin. They were Uldarian metal alright.

'If you're going to do that, we'd better do it properly,' Trix said.

'I'll grab a table.'

The oni walked back near the stairs. Found one that looked sturdy enough. He picked it up one-handed. Set it down near the tubes. Trix put the body onto the table. Ambrosia's smell was sickeningly sweet, like fruit jam.

Kit unsheathed a bowie knife he had on his chest plate. Tossed it in the air. Caught it in reverse grip. He made the first incision into the boy's chest cavity.

I ought to carry a knife, Trix thought offhandedly as she watched Kit. He possessed finesse you wouldn't expect from someone his size.

The boy's organs were swollen enough to cause tremendous pain. Though the swelling alone wouldn't cause death. His bones had begun the process of becoming Uldarian. Kit scalped him next.

'There's your problem,' the oni said.

The boy's brain had melted in his cranium. It looked different to a normal human's. It'd developed an outer membrane with a gold tinge. Trix pinched it with her fingers. It was slippery. Slammed back into place. Contrariwise, the actual brain — the parts that were still intact — were almost a solid gel.

Lastly, Kit lifted the boy's eyelids. They were charcoal grey with cracked gold veins around milky white pupils. An imperfect specimen.

'Roche made progress,' Trix said.

'These aren't machinas,' said Kit, wiping his blade on his exo-armour sleeve. Had he been in a joking mood, he might've asked to borrow Trix's scarf.

'They could be his Uldarians.'

'He believed the end of the galaxy was nigh based off a bunch of old doomsday predictions, so he wanted to see how the Uldarians were wiped out the first time.'

'Then he creates Uldarians in an attempt to activate memories in their DNA.'

'But Uldarians are no good, because they lost.'

'Which means he wanted to build better Uldarians.'

'A new generation. How old was Roche when he created machinas?' Kit said.

'No older than 70.'

'There's a good chance he's still alive, somewhere.'

'Maybe he's still on the planet, or he relocated to the moons. He'd never find a securer place than this.'

'Or maybe...'

The machinas looked at each other. They had a harrowing realisation. It was really just a hunch, but the way their skin became gooseflesh made it seem like much more.

'He finished the first part of his tests,' Trix said, continuing Kit's sentence.

'It's possible. The anghenfil had no reason to bomb this part of the planet. He could've stayed. Then when the war ended he could've continued his research.'

Trix looked at the other bodies suspended in ambrosia. Two were girls. The last was a boy.

'We should continue the autopsies.'

Kit abided.

The second boy's heart had ruptured in his chest, though the backs of his arms showed increased Uldarian metal coverage. Then there was the first girl. She looked like she'd died from internal bleeding. Her brain was much the same as the first boy's.

The last girl was a total mess. Her organs had liquefied, but her spine showed good progress towards machina bone density. Metal covered the majority of her back. Her brain, on the other hand, was a fuller formed version of the first boy's. The gel was mostly together. The membrane was unbroken.

'Nothing more to learn here,' Kit said.

'We can't leave this place as it is. We'll use the Fox's cannons to collapse the cave.'

'Sounds good to me. Let's make sure we haven't left anything.'

The machinas performed a final sweep of Roche's hideout. They checked the walls for secret passages and Trix scanned for other underground caverns. There were none of either. And Trix's medallion wasn't vibrating which meant magic wasn't messing up her readings.

There was an enclave with a partition underneath the stairs. A bedframe with a threadbare mattress lay behind it. There were more scraps of paper. Trix picked them up. They were additional references to Ragnarök, specifically, stanzas from a poem called *Poetic Edda,* accompanied by illustrations of an enormous serpent, wolf, and a flaming sword. Trix scanned the sheets then tore them to shreds.

The Valkyrie caught a glimpse of something else under the crumpled bedsheets. More paper. A photo this time. She knew the man in it. Garth Roche. He looked like an average Joe. Nothing about his appearance flagged him as a mad scientist or a villain. He had the sort of face you'd pass on the street without a second thought.

A young boy was next to him.

Whereas Roche was unremarkable, the boy was striking. He had hair black like Mireleth's scales. A white streak curved from the centre of his forehead around his crown. His eyes were pure machina. His body had Uldarian metal patches with huge gold flecks, though skin was still prominent.

The boy was smiling. He would grow up to be handsome.

Trix flipped over the photo. She heard Kit checking every chemistry set, taking more samples just to be safe.

In pen, with neater writing than the machinas had discovered so far, was a brief message.

Alpha, my boy, you showed me what is possible. You are my son. I love you.

Trix didn't tear the picture. She scanned it, then showed Kit.

'I think that's who attacked me and stole my ship. Little bastard,' Kit said. There was no venom in his words. He felt disgusting.

Those poor kids, he looked over to the autopsied children.

'I think it's safe to assume that Roche left the planet. Alpha looked like he was happy. There's no reason why he couldn't've thought of Roche as his father.'

'So, Roche leaves the planet without Alpha, but by the looks of this photo, he really does love the boy. He tells the boy he'll be back soon. Never returns. Alpha tries to find a way off planet and finds my ship.'

'It's our best theory.'

'What happened to the Uldarian bodies that made us?' Kit said.

'I expect they're here. Who knows? A lot of machinas were made off Mair Ultima then shipped here.'

'I say we have Sif search the academies one more time to check for an underground hangar.'

Trix nodded.

'I'll start now. This may take a while,' said Sif.

'We have time.'

Trix pocketed the photo of Roche and Alpha. Satisfied that nothing else was left, Trix and Kit exited Roche's hideout. The Valkyrie was reminded of a Cuthbert Theroux riddle.

Unknown yet fiercely sought, sometimes sold and sometimes bought. They can topple empires and raise dynasties, they can even contain your wildest fantasies.

The answer?

That's a secret.

NEXT MOVE

1

Light painted the sky.

Even in the morning, Mair Ultima's heavens were darker than its cyan oceans. Trix and Kit stayed close to Garth Roche's hideout. Trix held off calling Sif for extraction. Something had caught her eye.

There were the remains of a wooden fence down some ways from the mountain's foothills, where the forest started. Flowers bloomed densely around the centre. A flametree higher than any other was in the middle.

The machinas walked to the tree in silence. They didn't need to be close before they saw its markings. Tally marks. Eighty-one of them.

So that was why the flowers grew so thickly.

'A mass grave,' Trix said.

'At least he had the decency to bury them.'

'Look,' Trix knelt down. Grass was covering the tree's base, but that didn't stop her keen eyes from seeing an additional inscription.

My children.

'I don't ever want to come back here,' Kit said, looking at the entrance to Roche's lair. He was grateful it was far away from the machina academies.

Trix: 'Sif, can you pick us up?'

'On my way.'

Sif landed the Fox. The machinas climbed aboard. Trix went to the cockpit. Unleashed the Fox's full destructive capabilities upon the mountain until a rockslide ensued. No one was going to find that cavern.

Then Trix was notified that Sif's hack had hit a roadblock. To proceed further, she needed another physical entry point. Spectre Academy didn't have one, and the Dragon Spire had expired.

Trix flew to Aethelwulf's Heart at supersonic over the ocean. This time, Kit joined her in the cockpit. Trix landed in the private dock upon reaching Valkyrie Academy. It'd held a small selection of ships in the academy's prime. Most importantly, it'd housed the escape pods. There were twenty in total, just in case the academy ever had more members.

The Valkyrie found she couldn't leave her seat. Screams rang in her ears. Explosions went off all around her. She could see her sisters entering their pods—

'Hey, Beatrix, you okay?'

Kit's hand was on her shoulder.

'I'm fine. Sif, how long's this going to take?'

'Hard to say. I think an hour.'

'Alright then.'

Trix left the ship. Kit went to follow. Checked his shotgun was loaded.

'Wait here,' she told the oni. 'I need to do this myself.'

Kit nodded. 'If you need me,' he tapped his earpiece and went to sit on the sofa. He wouldn't have minded a sleep. But he couldn't. Not with Trix out there by herself. She was more capable than anyone he knew, but when you cared about someone, that tended to take a backseat.

As Trix was going through the airlock, she heard Kit ask Sif if she wanted to play a round of Faet, the zirean card game.

Trix descended the loading ramp. She'd rarely visited the docks during her training save for going to other academies. Those trips were always exciting. In fact, it was on one of those trips that Trix became friends with Kit. They'd fought each other on the arena in the centre of Fenrir's Teeth. Trix had never fought an oni before. She went down hard in the first round but came back in the second.

Somehow, that fight had resulted in a friendship.

The troop carrier Trix had ridden in as a child was plastered against the far wall. She walked towards it. Cortland and Minerva had ridden in the back with them.

They were always talking. We thought they had endless information, that they were the smartest people alive, Trix reminisced. I don't even know if they escaped. I don't think any machinists did.

She looked inside the troop carrier. Trix saw where everyone always sat. Always the same seats. Three would be on Trix's left, Four on her right. Two sat directly opposite her, with Five and One on either side. Cortland and Minerva stood at the back.

'In life, there are no friends, no enemies, only teachers,' Trix muttered to the empty space. Cortland had been fond of that saying. It was an old Earthen proverb. Minerva would often expand on it, saying that every situation had something to teach if you paid attention.

To her dismay, Trix realised that Cortland and Minerva's faces were beginning to blur in her mind. Maybe in another 80 years they'd be completely forgotten. Though she could still see the other Valkyries, the ones she called sisters.

Huh, some family. She hadn't seen them since the Last Day. Then again, Trix never searched for them. Her and Kit had only met again by chance. She'd been hunting a monster for a village he happened to be living in at the time. That werewolf had been a motherfucker and a half.

There was nothing else to see in the docks. Trix took the stairs near the central elevator until she came to the common living space. The windows were long gone. Trix had an amazing view of Conan's Eyes from where she was standing. Cold morning air came through broken walls. The Killer's starting line was to her left. She'd had to do four laps on the Last Day. Around halfway during the third, she'd wished it would end.

It did on the fourth.

The control room was two levels above the common quarters. Trix ascended the stairs. Came to her dorm room landing. The ceiling had partially caved in. Blast doors covered the windows. Light streamed through the broken roof. Beds had been shifted, loose debris scattered the floor. Otherwise, it was exactly as Trix remembered.

She went to her bed. Her footlocker had slid partially underneath it. Trix pulled it out. Opened the lid. Machinas in training didn't own a lot of personal items. They never had toys, or any clothing besides their leather training armour and pyjamas. A spare pair of boots, and an armour repair kit were inside Trix's locker.

The Valkyrie sat on her bed. Remembered it being softer. Sat in total silence, not moving, barely breathing. This was her first home.

Only ghosts live here now, she lamented. Roche did this. He called the anghenfil here. He's responsible for every death we suffered. I'll kill him if I ever find him.

Trix simmered in her own anger a while longer. Dawn's light subdued her hatred. Tiny snowflakes sparkled in sunbeams like sugar in honey. When she'd regained her composure, Trix headed to the control room, taking the stairs two at a time.

When she reached the control room door, she used her pistol to break open the lock. She'd never been inside before. It was small compared to Dragon Spire. Only four terminals were positioned around a central holo-table that could be used for mapping and communication.

Most of the control room was undamaged. That wasn't surprising. The roof was largely constructed from Uldarian metal. What Trix hadn't expected to see on this floor was a living quarters. A lounge room was at the far end, behind the terminals. Four doors were evenly spaced along the walls.

Must've been Cortland and Minerva's bedrooms, maybe whatever techs worked here full time too, Trix guessed. She had no desire to look inside. Even though her old teachers were dead, she thought it'd be a gross invasion of privacy.

Once Sif was connected to one of the terminals, she began her hack. After ten minutes she'd linked the Mair Ultima network with the Fox, which meant Trix didn't have to stay plugged in. She retracted the input from her comms gauntlet and headed back to the ship.

She walked a lot slower than usual. Words from a ballad wafted through her mind's cracks. They echoed as if they were being sung in a church. They made Trix want to cry.

> *I fought back in the day,*
> *too young to have a say.*
> *They gave me a gun,*
> *and Sarge said,*
> *Boy, it's time you bled.*
> *But all I could think was, baby,*
> *I'd rather be with you instead.*
> *God damn I miss, sharin' your bed.*

> *Shipped off to war,*
> *Boy, how the lads and I swore,*
> *on the way, to a cold, embrace.*
> *Bombs they were dropping,*
> *my friends started to die,*
> *found myself staring, death in the eye.*
> *I got hit a couple of times,*
> *and as I lay there bleeding,*
> *Sarge's words, boomed in my head.*

> *But all I could think was baby,*
> *I'd rather be with you instead,*
> *yeah I'd rather be with you instead.*

> *Oh I'm tramping through, the halls of the dead,*
> *words floatin' round, things never said.*
> *Ghosts are weighing me down,*
> *Oh if I don't get outta this town,*
> *the ghosts, yeah the ghosts,*
> *in them I'm gonna drown.*

Trix didn't know the original artist, or its author. All she knew was that one-day Cortland had been sitting on the academy's balcony with a guitar. Up until that point, Trix had only seen them in old photos from Earth. She asked Cortland how it sounded.

'I can do better than that, Valkyrie,' he'd said with a cheeky smile. 'I'll show you.'

Cortland had started playing. Happy tunes with no words at first. Just upbeat melodies. Music was never played in the academies. None of the machinas really knew what it was, but they'd studied poems in philosophy, and Trix understood a song was like a poem with music.

'Can you sing a song, Sir Cortland?' she'd said.

'Well, alright. But I'm not much of a singer.'

That's when he started playing the ballad. For all Trix knew, he'd written it himself. He might've made it up on the spot. She remembered how his eyes glistened in the fading light. He definitely wasn't a singer — you didn't need to know music to know when someone was crap — but Trix'd felt like she was being hit with powerful imagery.

When Cortland finished, he rested the guitar by his side. Trix hugged him. It was human nature. She expected Cortland to throw her off, say that she was being emotional. Instead, he hugged her back. Trix wanted him to explain the song, but when the hug ended, Cortland walked back inside.

She never saw him play the guitar again. Never heard him play, either.

Alone in her thoughts, Trix didn't realise that she was standing at the Fox's loading ramp. The sun was rising.

There're no bones here, the Valkyrie thought. She hadn't seen a single person's remains on her way through the academy. There weren't that many people to begin with though.

Trix checked her comms gauntlet. Sif was making good progress on the hack. It looked like she'd almost made herself a system administrator too. That'd come in handy. Despite Sif's proficiency, Trix had a lot of time to kill.

She entered her ship and closed the loading ramp.

2

Kit wasn't sitting on the sofa anymore.

Trix heard the shower running when she entered her room. An Aleks Valentine paperback was open on the coffee table in front of Trix's armchair. The Valkyrie took off her armour and her weapons. She set them down near the foot of the bed. Once she was down to her underwear, she put the photo of Roche and Alpha in a lockable desk drawer.

She let her hair hang to one side. Walked into the bathroom. Kit was whistling the Ultima Lullaby.

'Beatrix...' Kit said, as she stepped into the shower. He'd heard her undressing, but hadn't expected her to come in. Due to machina eye colour, it was difficult to tell when they'd been crying. Kit thought Trix had been.

Trix took off her underwear. Threw it onto the floor near the sink.

'Are you alright?' said Kit. His typically loud voice reduced to a whisper. He held Trix's face in his hands.

'Are you?' she said. Trix moved Kit's hands away, then pressed her palms against his pectorals. She stood on her toes. Kissed Kit on the lips. He grabbed her waist. She placed her arms around his shoulders. Caressed the nape of his neck.

The horrors they'd seen in Roche's lair didn't leave them, but nor did the wonder of Mireleth's blessings. They weren't sheltered from their emotions as they had sex. They were bombarded by them. Naked against punishing waves that froze their cores. Salt water stripped them raw. But in that moment, they had each other. Their pain dulled until something that was almost happiness took over.

Mair Ultima's ghosts did not bother them anymore.

3

The machinas lay naked on Trix's bed.

In fact, they'd fallen asleep for a while. Kit had his arms around Trix. They were far from being at peace, but they were nestled in a quantum of solace.

Kit thought of his crash landing on Aros. Aros was like Desraxe, only much colder. It was even in the same star system. Temperature wise it was closer to Mars. While its atmosphere wouldn't kill you when you stepped outside, it wasn't exactly a stroll by the water either. Kit remembered exiting his pod, dressed in a full spacesuit. His gauntlet's readings told him the atmosphere was liveable. Everything looked so strange. He'd only ever seen deserts in pictures before. In retrospect, being isolated on Mair Ultima was a serious shortfall of the training program. Never facing live ammunition exercises also didn't help. Sure, simulators were so realistic you could barely tell the difference, but there was no substitute for the real thing.

Kit had walked for three day and night cycles until he'd found a camp. It turned out that the only people who lived on Aros were scientists running a plethora of botanic experiments. They were trying new methods for creating resilient crops. When Kit stumbled upon a Consortium research station he discovered the equipment box from which he got his name. That came in handy when a human scientist found him three seconds later.

It just so happened that the scientists currently stationed on Aros were preparing to leave. Kit helped them pack the ship in record time thanks to his strength. As a reward, the crew let him join them on their journey to Earth. The first stop was the International Centre for Botany and Agriculture, which was in Queensland, Australia, on the western edge. Kit had liked it so much he'd stayed.

As the oni thought of his second home, Trix played Cortland's song over in her head. Occasionally it would stop and be replaced by Mireleth's poem.

A thought caused her eyelids to fly open.

She turned around so she was facing Kit.

'Kit.

'Beatrix.'

'I need you to look at something for me.'

'Alright.' He brought her closer. Kissed her on the forehead. 'Thank you.'

Trix sat up. Kissed him on the shoulder. Got out of bed. Threw on some plain clothes, then went for her combat vest. Pulled the Uldarian prism from its internal compartment.

Kit now had his back resting against the bed's headboard. He was looking at Trix's photos. The last time they'd slept together had been Yephus. Merriment and alcohol had been the catalysts. Now the situation wasn't as cheerful. One thing remained the same, however. There were no declarations of love, no baby talk, and no pet names.

The oni was in no hurry to get dressed. He stretched out on the bed and cracked his knuckles as Trix brought him the prism.

'Looks Uldarian,' Kit said.

Trix still had her hairband around her wrist. Her white hair hung loose over one shaved side of her head. A couple strands found their way in front of her face. Kit had slept with other women, just as he knew Trix had slept with other men. But Kit would be damned if he ever saw a woman he thought was more beautiful than Trix.

He'd had some floozies in his life, bimbos who only wanted to say they'd had sex with a machina. And yeah, if Kit was feeling like some fun, why not? But they were only fit enough to be pretty, not strong. They were smart enough to know about things, but never to fully understand them.

Beatrix Westwood on the other hand, mate, she was something else.

'That's because it is,' Trix said. Her baggy sweatshirt hid her toned muscles. She'd bought it from a market selling vintage Earth goods. It was a part of a commemorative line celebrating the Mars' colonisation. Mars was now used as a back-up datacentre for the human race's most important documents. Server rooms and museums ran deep below the planet's surface. It was commonly known as the Library.

'Where'd you find it?'

'In an abandoned mine on Desraxe while I was hunting water wyverns.'

Kit chuckled. 'Of course that's where you found it.' He reached out to take it. Trix pulled her hand back.

'It contains a vision, or possibly a ship's log. It only plays when a machina touches it, and it only plays once per machina.'

'So what you're saying is, pay attention?'

'Hmm.'

Kit nodded. Extended his hand. Trix placed the prism into his waiting palm. The result was immediate. His golden irises pushed the blacks of his eyes away. His pupils swelled to the size of snowballs. Every muscle in his body tensed, processing the information.

Four more second passed like this, then Kit snapped back to normal.

'Bloody hell, did I just see the end of the Uldarians?'

'I don't know if every machina sees the same thing.'

'Who else has seen this?'

'Dai of Thyria, a spectre.'

'That name sounds familiar. He used to work for Farosi, didn't he?'

'He works for the Queen of Xardiassant now.'

'A promotion. Good for him,' Kit said. He was inspecting the prism as carefully as he could. It was smooth. If there was a secret compartment, it was too secretive for him to find.

'So, what did you see?'

'Everything was dark. Then one by one, stars rushed forward. Only they weren't stars, they were Uldarian ships. They attempted hyperspace jumps. Then light.'

'Dai saw light as well.'

'But, I wonder, did he see what it was coming from?'

'Did you?'

'The Transfer in No Man's Land. It was activated.'

'What came out of it?'

'I don't know. The image distorted. I got tunnel vision. It was almost like I was looking through someone's eyes.'

Kit handed the prism back to Trix. She half expected something to happen. Nothing did.

'You're the first one to see the Transfer open. You're the first one to see it at all.'

'Maybe the message grows stronger with every transmission, like a buffering video over slow comms. Each time a machina touches it, the video can already play the start, because it was loaded by the previous machina.'

'It could take hundreds of machinas to play the full message.'

'Good thing we're not in a hurry.'

'Not that we know of.'

Kit smiled. So did Trix. Kit played with his oni medallion. In the soft light of Trix's quarters, its growling demon face seemed less menacing. Even Trix's Valkyrie skull appeared livelier.

Trix's eyes drifted over Kit's body. His puncture wounds had stopped seeping. His muscles were taut. Warmth spread between Trix's legs. Somehow, she and Kit had maintained a close friendship while occasionally having sex. It must've been a machina thing.

Maybe we love each other? Trix thought. I could never tell Kit I loved him, even if I did. Wouldn't want his head getting any bigger.

Trix slid the prism back into her armour's sealed compartment. She felt safer having it on her person than leaving it on the ship. Kit watched her walk. Admired the way her legs moved in sweatpants. It was a weird thing to think about. It was just that he hardly ever saw Trix wear anything other than armour.

But that was because their activities usually necessitated the need for protection, and lots of it. And no, not like that. Besides, machinas were immune to disease, as well as being infertile.

Before the machinas could do anything else, Sif's voice came over the speakers, and her hologram appeared on the coffee table.

'Kit, come on, put that thing away.'

'You could've knocked,' Kit said. His stupid smile gave away his true feelings. He went to put his armour back on. He would've changed to casual clothes, but those were back on his ship. His stolen ship.

'I've finished the hack,' said Sif.

'And, do you have full control?'

Sif made a so-so gesture with her hand. 'This place's servers are so fragmented and compartmentalised that I'm surprised it functions at all. It's a digital fortress where the chain of command is tangled like a pair of headphones after being left in a pocket for too long. Here's what I know.'

Trix sat on her desk chair. Kit — who was now wearing pants — sat on the edge of the bed closest to Trix.

'On the Last Day, Earth Year 2720, July 19th, a beacon began broadcasting from Dragon Spire's communications tower. The only reason it could handle long-range comms was so that Earth could broadcast encrypted signals to Mair Ultima in the event that they needed immediate assistance. All machinas would then be mobilised and sent to defend Earth, regardless of whether or not they'd completed their training. However, no one noticed the beacon because it wasn't broadcasting on the distress frequency. Rather, it was coded to only be detected by anghenfil scanners. Whoever activated it also erased their log. And yes, that means I don't know who activated the beacon.'

'What about the Uldarians we were made from? Where are they stored?'

'Not on this planet. The only reference to Officer Shaiba Chandak's discovery that I can find is that the ship is referred to as Aethereum Salvatoris. The Ethereal Saviour. Once Uldarians were harvested from stasis, the ship was relocated. I can't find anything else beyond that.'

'So, there's a group of people somewhere in the galaxy

tinkering with Uldarian technology. Whoever got their hands on working Uldarian weapons would be unstoppable,' Kit said.

'It's been 80 years and nothing's happened. But that means they're probably closer to a breakthrough than ever.'

'At least we have a search term for it now. Aethereum Salvatoris. The human race sure has a hard on for naming things after gods.'

'That's the Uldarians' allure. The sanest theories say that they were a biological race who made themselves almost completely synthetic.'

'And people want the same,' Kit shook his head. 'Call me old fashioned, but I wouldn't want to be completely robotic.'

'I'll stick to calling you Kit.'

'Good, old fashioned's a bit much.'

'In better news,' said Sif, 'I've rewritten most of the security codes. You'll find pretty much any terminal will react to your handprints. I've also given you both usernames. Your machina numbers, of course. Don't want anyone discovering Mair Ultima and finding you've been poking around.'

'Thanks, Sif.'

'Also, Kit, I have messages for you. When your comms gauntlet linked to my systems, then to the Fox, you started receiving them again. They're from Cole of Orix.'

'That's not good. Play them.'

'They're text,' Sif said. Trix's computer turned on. Messages appeared on the screen. 'The earliest one was sent just after your ship was stolen. Since then, there've been two more.'

MESSAGE#1

Kit, Dread Phantoms have taken over the Red Wolves. They now have enough money to pay me to fight. I was getting a little bored.

MESSAGE#2

Dread Phantoms have declared war with the Ghirsioc Raithexils. Shit's getting real. I'm calling in Kyra. Could use your help too. If we win, there'll be a payout. Why aren't you replying?

MESSAGE#3

We've tracked the Ghirsioc Raithexils to Nuallar. No idea what they're doing here, place is a wasteland. Kyra on board. Nuallar is Nathescuair territory. This is going to be a fucking turf war. Get here, man. We're gonna need you.

'What a mess,' Kit said.

'Ghirsioc Raithexils, that's a corrach gang isn't it? Ice Exiles? Yvach told me about them once. They operate from the Sea of Bones,' Trix said.

The Sea of Bones was the star system that held the corrach home planet, Raursioc.

'Yeah, all dishonourable discharges from different clans who think corrachs are the galaxy's supreme race. They're big on illegal animal trading. Trappers, in other words. Whereas you like killing monsters, the Ice Exiles round them up and sell them to the highest bidder. Eccentric dipshits with too much money are their best customers.'

'They're also terrorists. One year they blew up a Formula X track because they thought the Raursioc team's cars had been tampered with. Think it was pinned on a corrach named Talerach Brigault, but he was never proven guilty.'

'They weren't dishonourably discharged because they were too nice.'

'And what about the Red Wolves?'

Kit scratched his chin as he thought of how to proceed. 'The Red Wolves operated off Thyria. They were the biggest gang on the planet. Actually they were the second biggest. Farosi's Hidden had them beat in every way. Then you and Yvach came along and shook things up. I know Nadira Vega's in charge of Dark's Hide now. Anyone who's not an idiot can see that, but in the transitional period, the Red Wolves struck Woert Tower. You fucked it so badly during your visit they didn't have a problem getting in. Of course, while they were celebrating, the Dread Phantoms rained on their parade. And there ain't many umbrellas that stand up to plasma showers.'

'What's their game?'

'Guns, but their biggest draw was extortion. They were

running "protection" for a shit-load of Thyrian businesses. And now the Dread Phantoms have them. They're pirates. Humans mostly, though they accept half breeds. They have a side venture unlocking cold fusion cells. Another reason why you gotta lock your ship up tight when you pull into port.'

'You're the last person to preach that.'

'You've gotta point. But I wasn't expecting to be robbed on a deserted planet. Anyway, you're right about the Dread Phantoms. They're classic pirates. They don't have any high and mighty ideas about who's better than whom. They just want money.'

'So why have pirates picked a fight with the Ice Exiles? They couldn't have more different businesses.'

'My guess is a deal gone wrong, or some kind of revenge plot. Who knows? When you deal with gangs long enough, you learn that even the most profitable ones have fucking crazy leaders.'

'I have a hunch why the Ice Exiles went to Nuallar,' Trix said.

Nuallar had been the kalarik home world until the anghenfil wrecked it with nuclear weapons and plasma. Thankfully for Earth, the anghenfil used all their munitions there. Eighty years on you still needed a spacesuit for extended time above the surface. A lot of kalariks remained, but theirs was a meagre existence. No one traded with the kalariks on Nuallar due to the planet's toxic nature.

To say it was a shit life was putting it mildly. Unlike Mair Ultima, where only a fraction of the planet had been attacked, Nuallar was razed five times over.

Kit nodded. Trix continued.

'Nuallar used to be rife with monsters, particularly ones that lived deep underground. Think giant, murderous centipedes as an example. It's possible they've mutated to become even stronger with radiation. You said the Ice Exiles are in the exotic animal trade. Well, it doesn't get much more exotic than radioactive monsters from Nuallar.'

'Who'd be stupid enough to buy something like that?'

'If it exists, someone, somewhere, will want it.'

'Oath. Still, they're going into Nathescuair territory, and those guys are pure savages.'

'Nathescuair,' Trix said, sounding the word out. 'Vipers, roughly translated.'

'They're not a gang so much as an extremist group hellbent on making the Consortium pay for not sending Nuallar aid. They have a lot of drive. Not a whole lot of brains. Or resources. If they were smart, they'd join up with Anrok Iclon.'

'Sounds like a cluster-fuck waiting to happen. You going?'

Kit paused. He didn't know if he wanted to. Cole and Kyra were good friends, but Beatrix was... she was Beatrix. And Mair Ultima, for all its ghosts, still had beauty. He could live here. There was enough shelter left in the academies to weather the winter. He could hunt for food, and he was friends with a badass dragon.

'I should. I'd leave now, but I find myself completely at your mercy.'

Sif made a coughing noise.

'And yours, Sif.'

'I can take you to Cole.'

'Thanks, Beatrix. You know, if your hunch is correct, we could use your help. If I'm gonna be facing a radioactive monster, I'd like the galaxy's most famous huntress leading the charge.'

Trix considered this. She could score payment from the Dread Phantoms if all went well. And she'd never been to Nuallar before. Mostly though, Kit needed help. Much like Yvach, she couldn't refuse him. They were friends.

Maybe something more.

Only one other had held Trix's interest like Kit, but they'd never shared the same friendship. Theirs was far more tumultuous. Though sorcerers could be like that.

Trix let a smirk twitch the corners of her mouth. 'According to Sif, there's nothing else to do here. So I may as well come with you.'

Kit smiled. 'It's gonna feel strange, leaving this place.'

'Like you're walking away from your house leaving all the doors open.'

'I can't believe you two doubt my hacking skills that much,' Sif said.

'Her words,' Kit pointed to Trix, 'not mine.'

Before Trix could say anything Sif said:

'I know, take us up, right?'

Trix thought about it. She wanted to stay. Felt like there was more to do on Mair Ultima. But nothing tantalised like a new adventure, especially one that involved hunting monsters.

'Yeah, but, Sif, turn on the windows.'

'You're the boss.'

The Fox's engines powered up. The walls of Trix's room showed Valkyrie Academy's docks. Trix moved her chair into the corner for a better view of everything. She saw the Killer's track appear below. Remembered every twist and turn after all these years. Then the other machina academies came into view. Sif revved the engines. The Fox accelerated with a sonic boom.

Sif banked hard, circling the machina academies from on high.

Farewell, Mireleth, Trix thought. It felt strange to leave without saying anything, though she suspected dragons didn't care for such things.

A black shape appeared. Mireleth's gigantic form streaked across the sky. He barrel-rolled above them. *Farewell, Staresivreth, Sajidifeilth*, Mireleth said telepathically.

Trix saw Kit's face change. He'd heard Mireleth too.

After two laps of the academies, Sif took the Fox into low orbit, then punched it to ultrasonic. Once they were away from Mair Ultima, Sif jumped to hyperspace.

'It's going to be another hour before we reach the Transfer.'

'Thanks, Sif.'

'Yeah yeah, you're welcome,' said the AI before her hologram dissipated. Trix manually turned her room's "windows" off. There was nothing to see at the speed of light but darkness.

Trust in darkness, trust in shadows...

'Another hour,' Kit said. He picked the paperback he'd been reading off the floor. It'd fallen while Sif had been banking. He put it back on the shelf. 'I guess I'd better start reading up on these centipedes.'

'I have another idea,' Trix said, kissing Kit before he could say anything to the contrary. She unbuckled Kit's armour. He took off her sweatshirt.

They fell back onto the bed. Thought of nothing but each other. For they knew that once this mood left them, once they exited Trix's room, they'd return to being friends.

Now, there was love, whether the machinas knew it or not.

4

The Fox approached the Transfer.

Nuallar was in the Shifting Sanctum. Not a whole lot went on in there. Before Nuallar had been nuked, there had been steady trade between kalariks and the Consortium. Nuallar had been something of a tourist destination as well. Its coasts boasted white sand beaches stretching for miles in every direction. The calm water and balmy weather made it a good destination if you were hankering for a beach getaway and couldn't afford a trip to Drion.

Foreign races paid heavy taxes to establish hotels along Nuallar's coastlines, since major kalarikian cities tended to be inland. They always did good business despite the taxes.

The further inland people went on Nuallar's continents, the more swamp-like it became. However, Nuallar's central most regions were dominated by arid savannahs and enormous sand dunes. Criss-crossing rivers enabled the kalariks to build in the sandy centres. Indeed, they'd even terraformed some of them.

Their old cities were largely constructed from sandstone and limestone equivalents. Some architects compared the design to Earth's ancient Egypt. Newer designs predominately featured metal and glass with traditional stone feature walls. Pyramids and rhombuses were the most popular shapes in kalarikian architecture. Or, had been.

Nuallar became unrecognisable after the anghenfil attacked. The only thing that saved them from being totally destroyed was that all buildings had subterranean levels built to withstand heavy attacks.

Sif was less than five minutes away from the Transfer. Kit and Trix lay in her bed, passing a cigar between each other. An ETA counted down on the ceiling.

'Time to suit up.'

'I don't exactly have a lot of options in that department. Combat or birthday?' Kit said.

Trix gave Kit one last kiss on the lips, biting his bottom one slightly. 'You can fight naked if you want. The radiation might be an issue.'

'I resisted dragon fire, but I'd rather not have a bunch of gangbangers copping a look at my dick, so it looks like I'm going combat.'

Trix dressed in her 2nd Skin one piece. In all the excitement, she'd forgotten to do a gear check. She'd have to do that before rendezvousing with Cole and Kyra. Trix put her armour back on. Used resin to repair the spot in her thigh where she'd been impaled.

Kit stayed upstairs to get dressed as Trix grabbed her hat from the cargo bay and returned it to the armoury. Then she cleaned and oiled her sword. Stocked up on more pistol ammunition. Satisfied that everything was in perfect order, Trix entered the cockpit. Kit was already there, sitting in the gunner's seat.

Sif warped to the Shifting Sanctum. It'd take 34 minutes in hyperspace to reach Nuallar from its Transfer.

'Almost forgot,' Kit said, reaching into his backpack, 'this is for you.'

The oni held out a bowie knife in a mag-panel sheathe. It

was similar to the two he always carried on his person. 'I mean, it's my spare, but I thought it could come in handy.'

Trix unsheathed the knife. It was a steel, meteorite compound. Not even close to being as sharp as her sword — it couldn't cleave armour, for instance — but it'd still be useful. Like all Kit's knives, the grip had a hand-guard that doubled as a knuckle duster. You know, just in case the ones in his gloves didn't activate. Trix attached the knife horizontally along the back of her belt.

'I didn't get you anything,' she said.

'I'm getting your services as a huntress free of charge, so I'd say we're even.'

'Maybe in a galaxy where scales balance incorrectly.'

Kit laughed. Messaged Cole to tell him they'd be at his position soon. Cole's last message had been geo-tagged, enabling the recipient to receive the sender's exact coordinates. The Dread Phantoms had a squadron orbiting around Nuallar while they planned their attack. Trix received a video call from Cole of Orix just after Kit sent him a message. Cole's face filled the windshield. The Fox's HUD readouts minimised to the corner.

'Haha, Kit, you son of a bitch— oh, Trix.'

'Greetings, Cole.'

'G'day, mate, how are ya?' Kit said, swivelling his chair so he was facing the front of the ship.

'I'm ready to go, baby, you know me. Nothing stops the Cole Train. How bout you?'

'Not bad. You've gotta stop using that nickname though, mate. It doesn't work if you give it to yourself.'

'I'm not taking name suggestions from an idiot who got his from a fucking acronym. Now, what've I done to deserve the honour of being in Trix of Zilvia's presence?'

'You don't deserve shit,' Trix said, lips curling to a smile.

'Always got fire, Valkyrie, that's why I like you. I now see that I'm talking to Kit on your ship. Why would that be, huh, Kit? Did you clog your last toilet so bad you couldn't get her off the ground? Even I was starting to worry when you weren't replying to messages. Where'd you go anyway?'

'Mate, if there's one of us here who's full of shit, it's you, no doubt. And as for my ship, I misplaced it.'

'How'd you manage to get it stolen?'

'Would you believe me if I told you I left the keys in the ignition?'

'Not even if ships still used keys, dumbass. Since you're still a ways out, I'll fill you in on what we know about this situation.'

'We?' Trix said.

'The Dread Phantoms are serious about taking down the Ice Exiles. Damn serious. But we've gotta few Red Wolves here, and things are tense. The Dread Phantoms gave them a pretty good deal in the takeover, but you know how it is.'

'Why would they bring Red Wolves on such an important mission if their loyalty's in question? Doesn't make sense,' Kit said.

'Because this mission's gonna end in a lot of bodies hitting the floor, and Gerdac doesn't wanna waste his own men.'

Ren Gerdac was the Dread Phantoms' leader. He'd been born on Earth to a medcanol father and a human mother. His ears pointed slightly at the top, and he enjoyed a marginally better than average constitution as a result. He grew up in England, on Earth. Ran away from home to Dark's Hide. Worked in a smuggler's employ.

Unfortunately for Ren, he was caught during what was supposed to be a routine mission on the Bastion and was imprisoned for a decade. When he got out, his parole was on Thyria. He'd started building the Dread Phantoms there. Years later, he was finally starting to see his efforts pay off.

'That's why he's paying us,' a woman with a startling red pixie cut said as she came into frame. Kyra of Drion. Her fringe was swept to the side. She had a scar which nicked part of her right eyebrow.

'Greetings, Kyra.'

'Hey, Trix. Glad you're here. You can help me keep these two in line,' Kyra said, nudging Cole. Both the onis were wearing heavy armour. Much thicker than Trix's.

'Anyway,' Cole continued, 'one of the scouts found out where the Ice Exiles are going. The ruins of an ancient kalarik city. I'm talking everything made out of stone. Really old. Probably in ruins before Nuallar was attacked. We did an orbital flyby.'

An image came across the screen showing a ravaged desert with ruins in the centre. It might've been a pyramid once, but most of it had crumbled. Sand dunes buried it. Trix zoomed in. There were ships down there alright.

'Beatrix thinks the Exiles could be searching for big game to sell to the highest bidder,' Kit said.

'The monster's called a gramyriapede in Earthen. Essentially, a gargantuan millipede. Before Nuallar was attacked, it was documented as predominately living in arid continent centres. That's why all buildings contained heavily fortified subterranean levels. Gramyriapedes can create tunnels large enough to collapse entire cities.'

'That'd explain the freight ship the Exiles brought. That, or they're packing more heat than we're equipped to deal with. Either way, that image I just showed you was from thirty minutes ago. Cloud cover's masked the surface since then,' said Cole.

'Speaking of heat, mate, I withstood dragon flames for ten seconds. A greater dragon, no less. How'd ya like that?' Kit said.

'I'd like it a lot better if the dragon had burned your eyebrows off,' said Kyra.

'Maybe the beard too,' Cole nodded.

'You're just jealous of my rugged good looks.'

'Fool, you wish you looked as good as me.'

'Should Kyra and I leave you two alone?' Trix said.

Kyra: 'Yeah, come on, Cole. Ren wants to go over everything one last time.'

'See you soon,' Cole said to Trix and Kit. The communication ended.

Kit: 'What'd you think about those ruins, do they support your monster theory?'

'Even pre-space age kalarik ruins go well below ground. Their catacombs are rumoured to be some of the galaxy's most extensive. Many of them were built in disused gramyriapede tunnels because they led to underground water reservoirs.'

'You think the monsters could've reclaimed the ruins?'

'I guess we'll find out. What I don't understand is how the Exiles think they're going to extract a gramyriapede. The amount of tranquilisers you'd need would cost tens of thousands of orits.'

'Are there any other monsters they could be looking for? Something more pocket-sized?'

'Nothing that'd be worth their time. Serpions exist on Nuallar, or used to, but they usually stick to swampland.'

Serpions were snakes that had fangs, pincers, and a stinger on their tails. Variations could be found on several planets, but they were most common on Nuallar.

'Let's hope that the Exiles have decided to go on an archaeological dig for the hell of it,' said Kit.

'Cole and Kyra didn't mention the Vipers.'

'I noticed. There's a chance that they don't even know we're here. The ruins are far away from any known settlements. But the Vipers don't exactly get off planet a lot, which means they know Nuallar's radioactive wasteland better than anyone else.'

'Hmm.'

'Fourteen minutes until we reach the Dread Phantom squadron,' Sif said.

The Fox continued through hyperspace. Ren Gerdac began addressing his pirates. What nobody understood was why Ren had picked a fight with the Exiles in the first place.

Exiled Wasteland

1

The Fox prepared to dock with Ren Gerdac's ship.

Sif lined up the loading ramp with Ren's galleon. He had several corvettes locked in formation around it. Kit said that Gerdac had a frigate he'd liberated from a trade convoy and refitted it to have a destroyer's power. Clearly he was saving that for direr circumstances.

Before meeting Kit in the cargo bay, Trix ejected the data-drive which housed Sif and inserted it into her comms gauntlet. Nuclear weather could cause all sorts of interference. An initial scan showed the dense clouds were mixed with volcanic soot. Sif said that comms probably wouldn't break through.

Although Sif was no longer physically in the ship, she'd still be able to control it if there was a comms signal.

When the Fox docked, Trix met Kit in the cargo bay.

'Cole told me that Ren can be a bit of a dick, so try not to bite his head off, Beatrix. We stand to make decent paycheck if this goes well, and considering I'm without a ship, I could really use one.'

'No promises,' Trix said as the gateway between the ships stabilised.

Ren's galleon's airlock opened. Cole was waiting on the other side. He was wearing head-to-toe Requiem Corp Armour. It was white, black, and rust orange. The thick plating made Cole appear even musclier than he was. An SMG was attached to his outer left leg. A shotgun was on his back.

'Come on, Ren's waiting,' Cole said.

Sif wirelessly disengaged the Fox's docking mechanism once the machinas were inside. It fell into formation with Ren's ships. Trix had permission to stay within his squadron for now.

'If Ren wants war with the Exiles, why don't you bomb them

from orbit and get it over with?' Trix said.

'Don't ask me, and don't ask Ren. Trix, I know when you're hunting you've gotta ask a lot of questions. But we're paid to not ask questions,' Cole said.

'I haven't been paid anything so I can ask whatever I want.'

'That's the Trix I know, haha. But seriously, until you've given Gerdac a reason not to hate you, don't piss him off.'

Cole led Kit and Trix through the galleon's halls. All ships from galleons upwards had war rooms. These typically contained a central holo-table, analysts, and gunners on the bridge before the cockpit. Ren's ship was no exception. His aesthetic was grey and green. A hologram of the ruins was on the central table.

Men and women were all around it. Those on the left were clad in various shades of grey and green armour. The Dread Phantoms' logo was on their pauldrons: a two-tone skull wearing a bandana over its mouth with crossed rifles beneath it.

A group of Red Wolves were on the right. Obviously Ren Gerdac hadn't had time to order new uniforms. Their armour was onyx black, made to look like it'd been dipped in burgundy blood. Their pauldrons had two mirrored, howling red wolf faces.

Ren Gerdac was at the table's head. He had a ginger quiff, and a moustache that curled at the tips. A jagged scar ran from his chin, over his lips, up past his nose. Ten black spots were tattooed down the right side of his face.

He's been in the Hole, Trix thought. Black Hole Maximum Security Prison in the Never Reach system was the galaxy's most secure lock-up. No one had ever broken in. No one had ever broken out. Ren's black spot tattoos were indicative of his time inside: one for each year.

Anyone could have those spots tattooed on their face, but there was an easy way of telling who'd been an inmate. All Black Hole inmates were branded with a code across their chest, forearms, and back. It ensured that even when they left the Hole — if they were so lucky — that their lives would be ruined. No one was hiring anyone who'd been in there.

Black Hole Prison did this because if ex-inmates couldn't get a job, they'd inevitably turn to crime. And if they turned to crime, there was a strong chance they'd be arrested again. Every race's home planet had its fair share of prisons, but most governments preferred to put lawbreakers off-world if they could help it. For this "out of sight, out of mind" tranquillity, governments paid Black Hole Prison handsomely. It also enabled them to skew the stats of imprisoned people, since the Hole didn't make their numbers public.

'Cole, I see these two are the extra muscle you were telling me about.'

'This is Kit, and Trix.'

'Trix? And she has white hair? You're the notorious huntress, aren't you?'

'Hmm.'

'Well, well, a chooser of the slain, here on my ship.'

'I've already briefed them on the situation,' Cole said.

'Good. And I trust you included that they won't be paid unless we're successful.'

'It was assumed,' said Trix.

'I like you already, Valkyrie. Where was I? Ah yes, we don't want to let the Exiles know we're here. They might know, they might not. I'd like to think they're clueless. We'll be dropping in right next to the ruins. From there, Vicaull, your team is going to secure the Exile ships.'

An Arabic man grunted to affirm he'd understood the command. He was one of the Red Wolves. He didn't look happy with his current position.

'Reda, you're going to back them up, then you're going to hack the ships, see if we can't commandeer them, aye? Vicaull, you better watch her six.'

Reda was a Chinese woman who was part of the Dread Phantoms. She nodded. Unlike Vicaull, she seemed to relish the coming slaughter.

'Finally, that leaves Eosar. You and the machinas are with me.'

Eosar was to Ren's right. 'As you wish, commodore.'

'We're going in. Fall out, you mangy dogs.'

The Dread Phantoms and Red Wolves exited the war room. Headed to the troop carriers. A galleon could easily fit smaller craft in its own hangar. This was useful for entering planet's atmospheres faster, and with more manoeuvrability. It also meant that the fleet's flagship could remain in space to provide orbital support if it had the correct weapons.

The machinas were the last to leave, besides Eosar and Ren.

'Hold on, machinas,' Ren said, walking to join them. Eosar had a shotgun ready. Ren was the same height as Trix. The onis towered over both of them.

'Cole told me about your monster theory,' Ren said. He twisted one corner of his moustache. 'It's not bad. Fits with the Exiles' usual business. I have no interest in transporting live cargo, and if those overgrown worms are as big as they're purported to be, then I don't have the space to transport them anyway. A trophy though, that I could sell. I trust that if we do come across one of these monsters, you'll kill it.'

'You're quick to trust someone you haven't paid yet. I could kill you now, or leave you to die once we reach the surface.'

Eosar's raised his shotgun at Trix, just out of arm's reach. He was clever. Too close and it was easy to find yourself disarmed. Then you'd find your body hitting the floor. Ren wasn't fazed. He forced Eosar's shotgun down with his hand.

'You could kill me. Probably even kill all my men. You're a Valkyrie. That's what you were made for. I know for a fact, that these three,' Ren pointed to Kit, Cole, and Kyra, 'work for the money. And I've heard, Trix of Zilvia, that you only lift a finger to kill monsters when you're being paid.

'That brings us back to your point about betrayal. You could, and you'd get the money I already have. But help me finish the job, and we'll have the combined wealth of the Red Wolves, Dread Phantoms, and the Exiles. I know that might not be much of an argument to someone who lives like a nomad. So let me make this proposition.

'You kill me now and you'll have to contend with my men. You kill me when we're on the ground and my squadron bombs the ruins until you're turned to dust. I give an order, and you're dead. I have more firepower than your ship ten times over.'

Trix and Ren stared each other down. The Oni Three were ready for a fight, though they wished Trix had kept her mouth shut.

'Good,' Trix finally said.

'A strange context for such a phrase to be uttered.'

'I like knowing the people I work for aren't stupid.'

'I was in the Hole for ten years. I begged for death more than a starving man on a deserted planet. Once you want death, truly wish it upon yourself, you don't fear it anymore. I see you don't either. You machinas will ride in my ship on the way down. Move.'

Ren extended his hand to prompt the machinas forward. Trix and the Oni Three walked down the hallway. Cole and Kyra led the way. They knew the hangar's location.

There was a general living area with crappy furniture just past the airlock Trix and Kit had entered before. An elevator was in the centre wall. The machinas hopped in. Cole pressed the button for the hangar.

'That was some ballsy shit, Trix.'

'I wanted to make sure he wasn't a fool.'

'And, you convinced?'

'No. Attacking the Exiles makes no sense. He'd have more luck expanding the Red Wolves' influence on Thyria. There'd be less bloodshed. And a better use of resources.'

'I've never really met a smart criminal. Just ones less stupid than others,' Kit said.

'Ren's made good choices so far. Hiring me, for starters,' Cole said. 'He pays on time and treats his crew better than any other pirates I've worked for. I haven't even seen him kill one of his own to make an impression.'

'But he has tattoos to show he's been in the Hole,' Kyra said.

'Getting tattoos to show you've been in prison,' Trix shook her head. 'That's advertising that you made a mistake. And if it happened once it can happen again.'

The elevator doors opened to the hangar. Both squads were going over their gear one last time. The shuttle pilots carried out pre-flight checks in the cockpits.

Cole walked the machinas to an equipment rack and picked up a metal backpack. He handed it to Kit. Kyra put one on too. It attached to her armour with a locking sound.

'You're gonna want this unless you plan on hitting the ground at terminal velocity.'

'A thruster-pack?' Kit said. Good thing he'd left his backpack on the Fox.

'Yeah, reusable and everything. So try not to break it.'

Cole grabbed one for Trix.

'I don't need one.'

'I forgot, Valkyrie powers.'

Ren and Eosar exited the elevator. The pilots signalled that everything was ready. The Red Wolves filed into their shuttle. The Dread Phantoms did the same.

Troop carrier shuttles could hold 20 people in heavy armour. The machinas took their seats, closest to the loading ramp. Ren stepped inside with Eosar. Smacked the hull. The ramp closed. Engines powered up.

Sif piggybacked on Ren's comms so she could monitor orders. Trix set her comms to only transmit to the Oni Three. Activated her helmet.

Normally, Trix's helmet still showed the top of her head. However, for space walks, and toxic environments, she could set it to be all encompassing. It locked with the rest of her armour. Created a pressurised environment. Her HUD kicked in. She looked around. The Dread Phantoms were activating their own helmets.

Some went old school. Helmets that were totally separate

from chest pieces. They could take more of a beating, but were inconvenient to carry around.

Porthole windows showed the carriers dropping into space. Thrusters propelled them towards Nuallar. The surface was almost invisible from space. Nuclear Winter tended to have that effect.

'Ren, we're reading temperatures of negative ten degrees. Weather's fine, fine as you're gonna get on a shithole like this, anyway. No incoming storms. You're clear to drop once we get below the clouds,' the pilot said over the speakers.

'Take us in. Keep formation with Reda and Vicaull,' Ren said. His accent was British. Halfway between enunciated and rough.

From what Trix could see as she entered the atmosphere, the clouds were thick and black. Mostly soot. Nuallar had a hyper active volcanic belt around the equator which meant lots of sulphur dioxide. This could cause severe acid rain. It was a wonder anything survived on Nuallar at all.

No one spoke as the carrier approached the drop zone. Kit was whistling. Trix could hear it over comms. That damn Ultima lullaby again. It was the only music which had been allowed on Mair Ultima.

Kyra was sitting opposite Trix. Unlike the boys, her helmet was mostly one big visor that could switch between reflective or transparent. Her armour was beige coloured, like Trix's scarf, with black and white accents. Neon red oni logos were plastered on her pauldrons. There was an oni face with III inside the horns embossed above her right breast. It was the Oni Three's logo. Her medallion chain was attached to her armour so that the pendant sat below her neck. Kyra gave Trix an "O" with her fingers. Smiled. Her visor switched to reflective mode. It was pure red. The colour of frozen blood.

Cole was next to Kyra. Trix opened a channel to the machinas. She heard that Cole was listening to music. Rap blasted through his earpieces. His helmet had no visor, only brutal metal angles. It was stored in the back of his armour and unfurled when he entered a command on his comms gauntlet.

Due to having no visors, Cole's vision was completely simulated. Trix couldn't see his face. She was willing to bet his eyes were closed and he was mouthing the words. Rap got Cole fired up. In his downtime he liked rock n roll, and rhythm n blues.

Turbulence hit the shuttle. It was like being inside a tumble drier balanced atop a jack-hammer falling down stairs.

It didn't last long. When it ended, the carrier's porthole windows were caked in soot.

'Sorry, commodore,' the pilot said.

'Are we still on course?'

'Yeah we are. Obe just checked in. They're right beside us. As we approach, they're gonna peel off to the ruins' south side, where the Exiles parked their ships. I'm gonna be dropping you further north in case— oh shit. We've got a bogey coming in hot. Missile. Ground to air. Everyone strap in.'

'Fuck,' Ren said. He slammed the hull with his hand. Sat in the last available seat just as the shuttle banked hard right then dove. 'Damn it, Isaad, you better shake them.'

'Trying, commodore,' the pilot said.

'Xray, this is Zulu,' said Obe. His voice was now coming over the speakers. Trix figured he must've been the other pilot. 'We've got two bogeys on our tail, and one of our thrusters is failing. Fucking soot must've gotten in.'

'Obe, this is Ren. You better get Reda to the drop-zone. We need the Exile ships immobilised.'

'No chance, commodore. They're gaining. Fuck me. Thruster one just failed. *Sonofabtich.* Have to drop early.'

'How far out are they?' Ren said to Eosar.

'Two clicks.'

'Alright. Obe, eject now. Get everyone out of there.'

'Got it.'

'Isaad, you're gonna lose this bogey, then we're gonna circle around and pick up Reda. It'll be tight, but we can fit everyone on.'

The carrier lurched before Isaad could respond. It lurched a second time. Dropped in violent, short bursts.

'Our thrusters are going as well. I'm not gonna be able to keep her in the—'

An explosion rent apart the shuttle's cockpit. The Exile's missile had found its target. The shuttle started going down. Fast.

The Dread Phantoms didn't need an order to jump. They'd be joining Isaad's burnt carcass if they didn't. A Geiger counter appeared on Trix's HUD. It was hovering around 100mSv. All combat armour made was built to be used as a spacesuit, as well as passable radiation, and submersible suits. As long as everyone's armour remained intact, they'd be alright.

The troop carrier spun wildly through the air. The machinas waited until the ship's nose was pointing down, then they dropped like laundry through a chute. Ren and Eosar followed close behind.

Outside, Trix got her first proper look at Nuallar. Wasteland was too generous a noun. You couldn't even call it a piece of shit. At least shit had bacteria. Nuallar's surface was a grey void. Life was the last thing Trix expected to see, monstrous or otherwise. The sand wasn't gold, but an ashy brown instead. Trix saw the ruins. They were pathetic. The way the rocks had weathered made them look whipped. Flayed by time.

To help her suit purify the air — and to stop it getting in the way — Trix brought her scarf up around her helmet's lower portion and fastened it tight. Kit was just below her. To the left. Cole and Kyra were on her right. The Dread Phantoms were further down. So far there'd been no more attacks from the ground.

As everyone approached Nuallar's surface, they activated their thruster-packs. Trix wove in and out of the Dread Phantoms. Moments before she hit the ground, Trix created a low gravity bubble which slowed her descent to a gentle glide. She backflipped. Landed on her feet.

The ground was bone dry. Trix sunk into it a little. Radiation rose to 115mSv.

Kit landed beside her with a crash. Kyra and Cole came next.

'Right, let's get this over with. I thought I'd seen some dumps in my time, but, dick me, this place takes first prize.'

'I've seen the inside of your ship,' Cole said. He'd taken his shotgun out. 'I'd say you could give this place some stiff competition for biggest dump.'

'On the bright side, the radiation's not bad enough to kill us,' Kyra said. Most people would've said that sarcastically. Kyra was serious.

Ren and his pirates landed in the general area. Trix switched her comms to receive Dread Phantom chatter. However, she would still only transmit to the Oni Three.

'Zulu, come in,' Ren said.

Silence on the other end.

'Obe, you reading me?'

'Yeah, commodore, I'm here. We made it out. Zero casualties.'

'Isaad's dead.'

'Shit. Nothing we can do now. We're on our way to the ruins.'

'Get those ships on our side. They might be our only way off this planet thanks to the damn clouds.'

'Understood. Keep you posted.'

Trix saw Ren look around. His hands were balled into tight fists.

'What're you all standing around for, you insolent pups? Move.'

The Dread Phantoms got into gear. Made their way to the ruins at a light jog. Ren and Eosar sprinted to reach the front of the pack. The machinas kept up easily. The ruins could be seen over a couple dunes.

Light was dim. Cloud cover ensured Nuallar was in a near constant state of dusk, or dawn, depending on how you looked at it. At the top of the second dune, Ren called for everyone to get low. They did. The ruins became fully visible as they crawled to the dune's ridge.

'Trix,' Sif said. 'I can barely get a signal to the ship from here. There's too much interference from the soot. If this goes south, I won't be able to perform an extraction. And there's a good chance that bringing the Fox through the clouds will completely fry the thrusters.'

The onis heard Sif's words too.

'That's not what you want,' Kit said as he surveyed the ruins.

Trix: 'Thanks, Sif.'

If Sif couldn't break through the clouds, then there was no way Ren could. His squadron communications would be weak at best.

'Anytime.'

Ren crawled beside Trix.

'What do you see, huntress?'

'Ruins.'

'Anything else?'

'Dirt.'

'Anything *useful*?'

'I can see Exile ships at 10 o'clock. I can also see footprints leading into the structure form the south. No second set. Anyone who's gone down there hasn't come out.'

'No sentries?'

'If I was the Exiles, I would've left crew with the ships. They might be patrolling the dunes. I can't see anyone on the ruins. The entrance might be rigged with tripwire, or motion sensitive explosives.'

'Cole, anything to add?'

'The Valkyrie read my mind.'

'I'll skirt around the perimeter. If there are any bombs, I'll diffuse them. If they can't be diffused, I'll set them off. That's likely to alert the Exiles to our position though,' Kyra said.

'They're down in the ruins. They have nowhere to go. But I'd rather take the dogs by surprise if we can help it.'

Kyra nodded. Rolled forward. Slid down the dune then ran for the ruins' eastern wall.

Reda: 'Ren, we're coming up to the Exile ships.'

'Aye.'

'Fan out,' Reda said over comms. 'Vicaull, on my six. Approaching Exile ships. No signs of any corrachs. Three corvettes. No large transport. Ship number one has its loading ramp down. All units on alert. Investigating.'

Five seconds of radio silence.

'All clear in the cargo bay. Vicaull, open the airlock. Zulu, split up and search the remaining ships.'

Vicaull clearly wasn't big on speaking. He gave no verbal confirmation that he understood Reda's order. Other Zulu members responded as they went to check on the last two ships.

'Nothing beyond the airlock. All clear.'

'Moving up to join Vicaull. Headed for the cockpit. From there I can hack the contr— contact.'

Gunfire.

'Reda, report,' said Ren.

'Exile pilot down. Headshot. Rest of the cockpit clear. Vicaull watching six. Zulu squad, report.'

'Beginning to open the doors on ship two,' a Dread Phantom said.

'Working on ship three,' said another.

'Ren, you're good to enter the ruins. I'll begin my— what the—'

'Reda, respond.'

'The Exile pilot, he was already dead. Message written on his chest. It's... kalarikian. Zulu squad, red alert, the ships have been compromised. Possible Viper presence. Watch yourselves.'

'What does the message say?'

'Running translation algorithm now. It says... *got you*. What?'

'Contact ship two.'

'Contact ship three.'

'Fuck these guys are everywhere.'

And sure enough, they were. The Vipers had reached the Exile ships after the initial force entered the ruins. The remaining corrachs were caught off guard. The Vipers hadn't even known the Dread Phantoms were coming until alerts sounded inside the ships.

The Vipers had decided to wait.

And they were glad they did. Nuallar was their territory. Outsiders weren't welcome.

Trix could see flashes of gunfire from her position. Plasma shooting into the air. She could hear screams and frantic cries through her earpiece.

'I've reached the ruins' entrance,' Kyra said over comms. 'No traps.'

'Proceed as planned,' said Ren. He cut the comms line to Zulu squad. The screaming stopped. Trix could still hear faint yawps from over the dunes. Everyone could hear the gunfire.

Eosar grabbed Ren's shoulder. 'We need to avenge Reda.'

'Aye, losing Reda is unfortunate, but most of the casualties were Red Wolves. I can handle losing those bastards. The longer we spend fighting the Vipers, the deeper the Exiles go into the ruins.'

'You don't want to avenge them, fine. But we need those ships.'

'There'll be another way. Xray, to the ruins.'

The Dread Phantoms went to where Kyra was waiting. A steady gradient led into catacombs. Footprints disappeared into darkness. The Exiles hadn't covered their tracks. This made Trix wary. At least the ruins' entrance was blocked by the dunes. If any Vipers had seen them, they weren't doing anything about it.

Night vision activated. The Dread Phantoms descended into the catacombs.

Deep beneath the surface, Trix swore the ground moved.

The catacombs were ravaged.

Cave-ins abounded near every corner, and support beams looked ready to collapse at any moment. Despite the darkness, the catacombs weren't as bleak as outside. The deeper Ren's squad went, the lower the radiation levels became.

It'd been 28 minutes with no sign of Exiles. The machinas listened to the underworld's sounds. They could hear the Dread Phantoms breathing. Their hearts beating. Footsteps over stones. Shifting armour.

What they were really tuning their ears for was the soft whirring of corrach mech-suits. The Exiles would be packing the heaviest armour available if Trix was correct about the gramyriapede.

Stone walls depicted faded pictures. Art of rituals, sacrifices, and ceremonies. They were walking on hallowed ground. Trix felt a sense of déjà vu.

Balthioul's church entered her mind. She could see his face. The spider he became. Isha, flayed. Her smooth, pink skin. Sharp white teeth. Oh yes, these catacombs had a holy significance to them. But what for?

For a monster, Trix thought. Kept walking.

The machinas were on either side of Ren and Eosar who were taking point. For all his flaws, at least Ren was involved. Not many leaders saw the front lines.

Xray squad rounded a corner. Their night vision outlined a small room. Sand had piled on most surfaces. Dense paintings covered these walls. They were in better shape than the others. The western wall had a section carved out of it. It wasn't a ragged hole. It'd been done with precision. And recently. An altar at the room's northern end was cracked down the middle.

'A church?' Kit said, walking forwards. Looking at the markings on the walls.

'The altar gave it away, huh?' said Kyra.

Cole was inspecting the hole in the wall. The ground on the other side was dirt. Footprints led into gloom. This was strange. The Exiles weren't stupid. They had to know the

Dread Phantoms were tailing them. Why not cover their tracks?

'Ren, we got tracks down here, leading further in,' Cole said.

'Good. We better be close.'

Kit was off to the side with Kyra.

Trix took a closer look at the altar.

Something's broken this right down the middle. There are no remains of seats anywhere else in this room. Church seems unlikely. Though kalarik religious practices usually entail sitting on the floor, so it can't be ruled out. There used to be something on here. The altar's stone is lighter in the centre. In the shape of a circle. Must've been moved recently. But what was it? Trix thought. She went behind the altar. Wiped the dust off the wall. The picture beneath was revealed in greater clarity.

A gramyriapede was eating itself in a circle. Images like that had been on Earth for thousands of years in various cultures. It was supposed to symbolise life's cyclic nature. There were faded symbols in the centre.

Trix looked back at the altar. The circular object that'd been removed. The paintings on the wall. People always wondered how ancient kalarik cities had been built. Without modern technology, the underground tunnels would've taken centuries to dig. Gramyriapedes dug them for free, but they went wherever they damn well pleased. Not much good for planning a city.

'Come on, Beatrix, we're moving,' Kit said.

The pieces were all in the Valkyrie's mind. They refused to form a coherent picture. She acknowledged Kit but didn't move yet. The church's relative safety gave Trix time to think.

She went through kalarik legends. All the ones she knew of, anyway. There was nothing in any of their documented religions about revering gramyriapedes as gods. So why the altar? The only animal sacred to kalariks was the serpion, for they believed they evolved from it. There'd been no serpion images in the catacombs above. That rumbling sound Trix had heard at the catacombs' entrance reached her again. She exchanged a look with the Oni Three. They'd felt it too.

Trix's mind drifted through countless myths. She eventually found herself thinking of Cuthbert's Theroux's *Otherworldly Fables.* It was a huge volume full of stories, anecdotes, footnotes, and illustrations. One that stood out in Trix's mind was a tale called *Song of the Monster.*

The tale told of a kalarik named Jevrak who purported that he could whisper to gramyriapedes, and make them obey his every command. However, he would not do so for free, and demanded payment for his actions. The people paid. Jevrak would disappear into the catacombs. His guttural singing was said to shake stones in their foundations. Sure enough, when he was done, a new tunnel had been dug.

This continued for some time. Jevrak became incredibly wealthy. Wealthy enough for the King to take notice. The King told Jevrak he wished to use a gramyriapede to attack a neighbouring kingdom, for they hadn't offered a gift for the birth of his son. But the King had one condition: he was to be present when Jevrak summoned the beast. As a reward, Jevrak would be allowed to marry the King's eldest daughter.

Jevrak agreed. Travelled to the neighbouring kingdom with the King. Jevrak carried a box with him at all times. It was the only possession he brought on the journey. When they reached the next kingdom, the King and Jevrak went into the catacombs. Jevrak still had his box with him. The King had heard how Jevrak summoned the beasts through songs and was surprised at his silence.

Once they were in position, Jevrak opened his box. Took a large, metal cone out of it. It was how he was "whispering" to the gramyriapedes. Upon seeing how Jevrak operated it, the King killed him to use the machine for himself. Unfortunately, he failed to understand its complexity and died once the beast reached him. Crushed by its enormous girth.

The entire kingdom was razed. It collapsed into the gramyriapede's newly dug tunnels.

No city as described in the story had ever been found, nor had any contraption to control the monsters. Trix had the uneasy feeling that the Exiles had discovered it. The rumbling didn't ease her mind. Hadn't the story told of singing so loud it shook stones in their foundations?

The rumbling grew louder, but Trix began hearing something else. Footsteps. Coming from outside the church door. She scanned the room. Ren's squad members were accounted for. That meant there were no stragglers. And since Zulu squad had died, that left only two other options.

Neither were friendly.

'We've got hostiles in the doorway,' Trix said, broadcasting her observation to Xray squad.

'Move to cover,' Ren said, signalling his team to spread out as much as possible. Trix moved up front with the onis. The footsteps were drawing closer.

Kyra unhooked a grenade from her belt. Rolled it in her palm before putting it back. She'd rather not bring the whole place down.

Trix and Kyra were behind a fallen pillar fifteen metres from the doorway. Kit was to their right behind a mound of rubble. Cole was on the left, right beside the door.

There were a few support columns still standing. It wouldn't take much to knock them down.

'Avoid striking the beams at all costs,' said Ren.

The machinas heard the footsteps stop.

'Vipers on the other side,' Cole said.

Ren: 'How can you know?'

'Man, I can hear a corrach mech-suit a mile away, and these aren't those.'

'Nobody fires until my say so. They might have one of ours.'

'You condemned them to die before, now you want to save them?' said Eosar, trying to hide his anger. Being Ren's righthand wouldn't exempt him from punishment if he stepped too far out of line.

'There's a difference between leaving someone for the good

of the mission and gunning them down in cold blood. I suggest you remember your place—'

Two shapes came from around the corner. They were naked. Bruises covered their skin. Blood was congealing around open wounds. One was a man. The other was a woman. Vicaull and Reda. Their skin was turning yellow and green. Being exposed like this in such an irradiated environment meant death. Even with immediate medical attention, they'd likely never recover to full health.

'Hold your fire,' Ren said.

Reda tried standing. She collapsed to her knees. Her breathing sounded like she was gulping flames. Vicaull moaned. He sounded like a banshee only 10 octaves lower.

'They say... to leave... this place... outsiders. We don't... belong... here,' Reda said. 'This... their land—'

'This is your fault,' said Vicaull. He chucked a weak right hook at Reda's face with bloody knuckles. Trix saw bones sticking out of them. Vicaull's fist made contact with Reda's face.

Ren dropped him with a bullet to the head. Then he finished off Reda.

'What the fuck was that?' Eosar said.

'Vicaull was a motherfucking scoundrel, aye. A coward too.'

'You killed Reda.'

'I ended her suffering. I've seen enough to know when someone is broken.'

Kalariks emerged from the door, guns blazing, drowning the last of Ren's words.

Cole pumped his shotgun twice. Eviscerated the first kalarik.

'That's what you get, baby, that's what you get.'

'Fire at will,' Ren said. His voice was grizzly, like he'd gargled cement.

Another two kalariks entered, rolling this time. They made it as far as Kyra and Trix. Kyra's dual shotguns blew one of the kalarik's heads off. Trix came from behind cover. She grabbed the other kalarik by the throat. Flipped him over herself with a gravity assist. Sliced through his body when he was airborne. Two halves hit the floor.

The doorway blew apart. The altar room shook. Kit and Cole had just enough time to activate their oni barriers. The kalariks had liberated some corrach breaching explosives from the Exile ships. No way they possessed anything that good on Nuallar.

Kalarik Vipers barged through the doorway. Concentrated Dread Phantom fire riddled them with bullets. The Vipers might've had vicious guerrilla tactics, but their equipment wasn't up to a proper firefight.

Trix and Kyra emptied their chambers.

Cole head-butted one kalarik. Caved in his helmet, then used the absorbed energy from his barrier to send out a shockwave. Three Vipers were knocked airborne. Kit kicked one into the others. They smashed against the stone wall. He unloaded his remaining shotgun ammunition into them.

The columns were holding. Dust fell from the ceiling. It looked like everything was going to be alright until a kalarik wearing retrofitted corrach armour ran into the altar room holding four live grenades. Trix reloaded in less than a second. Her finger danced on the trigger. Bullets rent the kalarik's head apart. The grenades flew through the air.

Before Trix could reverse gravity, they struck two central support columns. The Dread Phantoms taking cover behind them were pushed back. Their shields took the brunt of the detonation. Trix could see shrapnel in their armour. They'd live. The roof started coming down.

'Fall back to the tunnel,' Ren said.

Everyone ran for the hole in the wall. The machinas reached it first. No Dread Phantom could match their speed.

The mercenaries who'd been knocked down by the grenades struggled to their feet. Ren went to save them. Eosar pulled him back as the ceiling collapsed. Buried the pirates under rubble.

Silence once again filled the catacombs.

In addition to losing the entirety of Zulu squad, Ren had now lost three other members. Xray squad was down to seven, not including himself, the machinas, and Eosar.

No one moved. Ren stood. Looked at the crumbled wall in front of him. His night vision painted it a depressing green shade.

'We avenged Zulu squad. Happy, Eosar? Everyone move out. We're going further in.'

Ren shoved his way past Eosar so he could take point. Eosar lagged behind him for a moment. The Dread Phantoms fell into line without mourning. Such was a pirate's life.

'This isn't good,' Cole said, transmitting only to the machinas who stayed at the rear. 'Vicaull was the Red Wolves' leader. If the other Red Wolves find out that Ren killed him... shit. There's enough of them on the galleon to potentially overthrow the Dread Phantoms. And if that happens, there goes our extraction.'

'I can't imagine Ren will let the Red Wolves know he shot their commander,' Trix said.

'Who knows how they might find out. We haven't exactly been lucky this far.'

'We've still got Trix's ship if this all turns to shit,' Kit said. 'We'll just need to find a way to boost a signal through the clouds.'

Kyra: 'For now we've gotta leave these catacombs.'

The machinas agreed silently. Kept walking.

3

Ren Gerdac marched further into the tunnel.

His Dread Phantoms followed. It grew so wide only the machinas could see its walls. And even their vision was falling short. The ceiling rose higher.

'Ren,' Trix said.

'Huntress.'

'I think this is an Exile trap.'

'You insult me by assuming I haven't thought the same.'

'Then you're easily insulted.'

'You have another insight? Something pertaining to your monster theory?'

'I think the Exiles have found a way to control gramyriapedes.'

'Assuming there are any left on this world. How the Vipers survive here is beyond me. Nothing can grow. I almost believed you on the ship, but now that I've seen Nuallar for myself, your theory seems flawed.'

'You can hear the rumbling. That's drawing the monster here.'

'Then we shut it off,' Ren said. He increased his pace.

Trix hung back with the machinas. She didn't want her friends dying because Ren was an idiot.

'We heard every word,' Kit said. 'You really think that's what's going on?'

'Nah ah, Trix, nah ah. There is no way I'ma be going up against something that size,' Cole said.

'Thought there was nothing the Cole Train couldn't plough through?' said Kyra.

'Yeah, well, the way Trix talked about those things before, not sure if anything's ploughing through em.'

'If I'm right, then there's not a lot we can do. There's next to no chance of killing one below ground. On the surface is your only option.'

'See, that shit right there, that is not what I want to hear.'

'You can still turn back if you excavate the altar room.'

'Turn back? Haha, no chance. Next time Valentine talks about how awesome you are, I want a slice of that action.'

'You guys seeing that?' Kit said. He pointed to a section of darkness ahead. The machinas saw an object in the cavern's centre once they engaged their helmets' digital zoom. A tiny light was coming from the object's underside.

'That looks like what Jevrak had in the fable,' Trix said. She loosely remembered the illustrations. Only there'd been no light in the book. This version also appeared more like a brass bell than a cone. 'We need to turn it off.'

'I'm on it, baby,' Cole said. He broke into a sprint. His long, muscular legs made him fly over the soft dirt.

Trix ran up beside Ren.

'That's what I was telling you about,' she said, pointing towards Cole's destination.

Cole's voice was transmitted to everyone's earpieces before Ren could respond. 'I'm seeing footprints, leading across the cavern. Fuck, there's another exit up that way. The Exiles led us here on purpose.'

'Everyone, move to that exit, double time. Go go go,' Ren said. He was beginning to realise the situation's direness. Dread Phantoms ran for the cavern's opposite end. The machinas joined Cole while they did that. He was kneeling at the object's base. It was old, hundreds, if not thousands of years old. But the light was new. His medallion vibrated. Magic.

Cole heaved the bell onto its side. It was heavier than he expected. For an oni, that was really saying something.

A device had been fitted to the bottom of the bell. According to Cole's comms gauntlet, it was transmitting a heavily encrypted signal. Kyra knelt beside him.

'No explosives. This isn't a bomb,' she said. 'The bell's markings are unknown, but the transmitter's corrachian.'

Trix: 'It's worse than a bomb. We have to move.'

'Not before I disarm it,' Kyra said. She drew two shotguns and blasted the transmitter. It was blown to pieces. The bell remained unharmed, but the rumbling ceased for a second.

'Now we can—'

The rumbling started again. It was coming from below the machinas' feet. Ren and his team were nearing the cavern's exit. An ambush was probably waiting for them on the other side. If they made it to the other side.

The machinas bolted for the exit. Approximately 200 metres away. They felt the ground sinking beneath them. The previously flat surface became an increasing gradient.

'Jump and activate your thruster-packs on my mark,' Trix

said. They had maybe 10 seconds before gramyriapede's maw entered the cavern.

'Ready,' the onis replied in unison.

'Mark.'

The Oni Three leaped into the air. Their thrusters propelled them forward. Trix altered gravity so they were effectively skydiving towards the exit. She jumped after the onis. Grabbed hold of Kyra's leg, taking care to avoid the thruster propellant. Supporting the weight of three onis in heavy armour was making Trix lightheaded.

Cole: 'Oh hell no, that shit is not alright.'

Kit: 'That's it, boys, I'm cooked.'

A gaping hole formed beneath the machinas. Dirt fell into the abyss. White, pink flesh with hardened brown scabs poked out of the ground. Its mouth was a hundred metres in diameter. It didn't envelope the whole cavern as Trix had expected, but it came close.

The machinas hit the ground hard with a gap of less than five metres. Ren was already ahead. There was no gunfire yet. They would've heard over comms.

The onis ran to join the Dread Phantoms. Trix waited in the entrance. She wanted to see what the monster was going to do. Like any creature that lived almost exclusively underground, gramyriapedes had next to no vision. The monster kept ascending. Its blubbery flesh was covered in toxic growths and pustules, some of which burst against the ground as it passed.

'Beatrix, are you coming?' Kit said.

Trix didn't reply. She noticed that this gramyriapede had lost its legs. Huge scar tissue patches were in their place. Some of them were craterous. Enclaves within the monster's rotting flesh.

That gave Trix an idea. Albeit, a crazy one.

'We can ride back to the surface in this monster.'

'Why would we do that when there's a perfectly good exit up ahead?'

'Because this will get us there faster.'

'Cole, report your position,' Ren said over comms.

'We're in the exit. There's a gramyriapede down here, and it's headed for the surface.'

'Is it hostile?'

'Apart from almost swallowing us whole, no, not yet.'

'Get back now. This mission's failed. We've lost enough already. I'm calling for immediate extraction.'

Trix took one last look at the gramyriapede. Went back to the others. Called Ren.

'We need to reach the surface. The Exiles activated a machine to draw the monster out. That's a lot of trouble just to kill us. If they wanted to do that, they could've collapsed the cavern with us inside. They want the monster for something. I'm sure of it.'

'You'd better be right. We'll standby for you to join us.'

'Go, we can catch up.'

'If this monster ruins our extraction chances, huntress, you better hope you can kill it.'

Considering Trix could run 100m in under nine seconds it didn't take long to re-join Ren. Unlike the tunnel leading from the altar room, this part of the catacombs was built in a steep, zig-zagging pathway. This meant rapid ascension.

It'd taken them just over half an hour of brisk marching to reach the cavern. They'd reach the surface much faster at their current speed.

Trix ran through possibilities in her head now that she knew the gramyriapede was here. The evidence pointed to the Exiles luring it above ground. You could probably fit it on a freight ship if you could convince it to coil and sit still for several hours. Otherwise, you were shit out of luck, Holmes.

Then there was the question of disease containment. There was no telling what vile pathogens and harmful bacteria the gramyriapede was fostering.

The surface drew closer with every step. Trix discarded theory after theory. She was trying to remember anything useful about gramyriapede anatomy. Their insides were a lot like a snake's. Not useful.

They actually ate the dirt they dug through. It was then digested. Soil nutrients were absorbed. That was how gramyriapedes survived. Judging by Nuallar's state, ingesting any soil would be hazardous. That explained the pustules on its skin.

Damn it, what else was there?

Trix accepted that the Exiles may have been on Nuallar for a totally different reason, but she didn't fully believe it. Her deliberating continued until she approached the surface. Triangulation software informed her that she, and the others, were north west of the ruins.

The gramyriapede was still below ground for the moment. There was no sign of the Exiles. Clouds were moving across the sky.

There was a strong breeze.

4

Comms briefly came back online, though they were patchy.

'Moro, we need immediate evac by the ruins. Haven't sighted the Exiles. Mirayna, Otek, and Rath are dead. Zulu squad is dead,' Ren said.

Ren paused, thinking of how to elaborate. His squad's deaths weighed on his mind. Especially Reda. She'd been with him since the Dread Phantoms' beginning. Ren had needed a reliable hacker. He'd found Reda in a dive bar. She'd been evicted from her apartment.

Vicaull's death was much of a muchness. But it had to be handled delicately. Ren's supremacy over the Red Wolves was fragile.

So far, Moro — the galleon's quartermaster — hadn't responded.

'Reda and Vicaull were tortured by Vipers. I killed them out of mercy. Vicaull and Reda had radiation poisoning, severely wounded.'

More radio silence.

'Moro, come in. We need immediate extraction.'

'We've lost comms. They should've received your message,' said Eosar.

'Curse it. Alright, listen up. To the best of our knowledge, the Vipers' didn't wreck the Exiles' ships. And we killed their attacking force in the catacombs. We circle back, take the ships, and get out of here. The fucking Exiles will have to wait another day to die since there's no way the galleon can bomb the ruins accurately with this cloud cover.'

The ground started rumbling again. Part of that was actually caused by the gramyriapede's heartbeat.

'She's coming up,' Cole said. Despite his earlier comments about not wanting to fight the monster, his voice had a keen edge. Cole of Orix was a lot like Yvach Aodun in that he'd never back down from a fight.

'That's it,' Trix said.

'What's it?'

'The gramyriapede's not a she. They're capable of parthenogenesis, asexual reproduction.'

'I wasn't exactly planning on showing that thing a good time.'

Kyra: 'Not my idea of a party either.'

Kit: 'Not even after a million beers and a bottle of rum.'

'If there's even a chance that the gramyriapede—'

'Yo, Trix, that word's a mouthful. Can we just call it, I don't know, Larry.'

'That's probably the worst monster name in the galaxy,' Kit said.

'Fine, we'll go with Larry,' Trix said. 'If there's a chance that Larry's incubating eggs, the Exiles might be after them. Whether or not they're going to be viable after all the radiation is another matter.'

'Then the only question is, where are the Exiles?'

The Dread Phantoms moved for Exile ships. Ren was following a hunch that the Vipers didn't destroy them. If they had, Moro heard their transmission and would be working on a plan to extract them anyway.

Sif spoke to the machinas as they ran.

'I have bad news.'

'What?' Trix said.

'I was piggybacking on Ren's comms, the ones Eosar said should reach the galleon. Only I was able to discern what parts of the message made it through.'

'Playback.'

Ren's recorded voice came through the machinas' earpieces.

'Moro... immediate evac... sighted the Exiles... Zulu squad dead... Vicaull tortured... I killed... Vicaull.'

'God damn. That's not bad news, that's a fucking noose that's been lit on fire and covered in iron spikes,' Cole said.

Trix: 'He only sent it to Moro. What're the chances that the Red Wolves heard and misinterpreted?'

'High. Rosamund Galbrand was Vicaull's second in command. Guess she's first now. From what I could make of their body language, they were involved. So not only will she think Ren killed her boss, but her lover too' Kyra said.

'That doesn't explain how she would've heard the message.'

Cole sighed. 'She was assigned to the bridge. Her job is communications. I've been dealing with her and Vicaull for a few days now. That's enough for me to know that Galbrand isn't someone who keeps her temper in check. She punched a Dread Phantom in the face because he didn't address her as his superior. Our only chance at extraction just got wrecked.'

'Hell hath no fury like a woman scorned,' Kyra said, making her visor transparent. 'And I'd know, I've been there,' she winked. Her visor turned reflective red.

'We can't tell Ren what's happened,' Trix said. 'It'll only make him angry. He's lost too much today already.'

'And he didn't kill any Exiles,' Kit said.

'His reasons better be good.'

'He won't tell you his reasons. He wouldn't even tell me, and nobody says no to this face,' Cole said. The effect was lost since his helmet totally concealed his visage.

'And, mate, that sure isn't because you're pretty.'

'Shut up, fool. I'm the prettiest there is.'

'Would you like a skirt to go with that comeback?'

'Only if you're finished wearing it.'

'You're alright, mate.'

'Yeah, man. I know.'

The Dread Phantoms were running across a sand dune ridge. The ruins were on their left. The Exile ships weren't far. Trix reckoned she could've smelled the gore from where she was standing if it hadn't been for her helmet filters. The wind died. Clouds stopped their lazy sojourn across the sky. Nuallar looked like someone had dunked it in bleach then wrung it out.

The rumbling intensified. Trix thought for sure that Larry would've tunnelled faster than they could run. Then she remembered the stone layers just below the surface. They'd be tough to break through. But Larry could do it. Gramyriapedes were literal garbage guts that could digest just about anything.

They were also sponges, able to take massive damage. Near impossible to stagger. And they were quick above ground. Able to dive in and out of sand like a dolphin in the sea. But there were more places to run above ground. And there was air support.

The Dread Phantoms were almost at the ships when Sif spoke.

'If you can plug me into the ships' long-range comms, I can boost a signal to the Fox.'

'That doesn't solve our re-entry problem. The soot will fry the thrusters.'

'I'll scan Nuallar's cloud cover to find an opening once I re-establish communication.'

'That might take too long.'

'I suppose you have a better idea?'

Trix knew the Fox's features like people knew how to breathe. There had to be something.

'Hmm.'

'Is it crazy?'

'Any normal person would say so.'

'Fortunately for us both, we're not normal.'

'None of it matters if comms can't reach the Fox.'

'There's an 89% chance they will.'

'Alright.'

There was no sign of the Exiles yet. Trix didn't like this. Neither did the onis. They should've been able to hear mech-suits. There was a possibility that the corrachs weren't wearing them, but it was slim. You didn't go monster hunting when you were only five foot three if the game you were chasing could swallow a city block. Trix kept an eye on the ruins. There was enough stonework above ground for the Exiles to be hiding in crevices. If that was the case, why weren't they attacking?

Larry reared his head as Ren reached the Exiles' ships. Stones collapsed downwards like they were being sucked into a whirlpool. There was no reason Larry should attack the ships. But the monster's presence didn't do a lot for preserving tranquillity.

'Let's get these things airborne and get out of here,' Ren said.

'Going through the clouds will disable the thrusters. We won't reach the galleon,' Eosar said.

'We only need to make it into orbit. Moro can extract us from there.'

Dead bodies were stuck in the sand like they were drowning. Spilled blood added much needed colour to the torrid dunes. Whatever the kalariks had done, they hadn't stopped at killing the mercenaries. They'd hacked at the remains.

Trix ascertained that they'd forced their way into the Exile ships then waited inside the cargo bays. Some Dread Phantoms were crushed underneath the loading ramps. Popped like zits.

Larry was still rising into the air. Trix knew that he would extend himself almost all the way above ground before arching into the dunes and beginning his descent.

Monsters & Other Beasts stipulated that while gramyriapedes were slow to burrow, they were agile above ground. Trix figured that going so long with no real, uncontaminated nutrients had made Larry deathly ill.

She walked into the ship Reda and Vicaull had entered. Dread Phantoms were working on the others. The onis stayed with Ren and Eosar who were watching Larry's ascent. Kit looked at Cole. Kyra looked at them both. They'd heard something. Sounded like mech-suits powering up. It was hard to know over the collapsing ruins.

There was a dune between them and any other line of sight. The machinas moved to the ridge. Crouched low. They wanted the first shot when the Exiles showed themselves.

Inside the first Exile ship, Sif ran a preliminary scan. The Vipers had disabled the thrusters. They could be fixed, but repairs would take an hour. That meant Sif's plan to use the comms was their only hope. Reports from the other two ships showed that the same sabotage had befallen their thrusters too.

Trix plugged her gauntlet into the ship's controls. Sif began working.

'They've got a failsafe which means if I try hacking any of the critical systems, the ship detonates. So let me see... no, they don't count comms as critical. Good. I'm in. This is only a hotfix. I won't have wireless control. What's your plan?'

'Contact ruins,' Trix heard Kyra say over the comms.

'All units to my position,' Ren said. 'We've got Exiles on the ruins. Light them up.'

Trix: 'Kit, what're the corrachs doing?'

'Looks like some of em are setting up an explosive ring around Larry's tunnel. The rest are shooting us. What're you doing?'

Looked like it was time for Trix's plan.

'Calling in air support,' she said. 'Sif, contact with the Fox.'

'I have a connection. It's weak, but I can access the controls.'

'First use the camera to see if anything's happened to the

galleon.'

'It's still there.'

'Break formation and come for our position. Don't bother scanning for clear skies.'

A scrolling list of commands on Trix's gauntlet indicated Sif was executing her orders. 'When the ship approaches the clouds activate the Inclement Weather Protocol.'

'You know that's only for when the ship is grounded, right?'

'Do it, Sif.'

The Fox's Inclement Weather Protocol was for truly terrible situations. Volcanic ash clouds, sand storms, blizzards, you name it. It involved blast barriers sliding over the windshield, re-alignment thrusters, rear thrusters, and external life support systems, preventing the hardware from being damaged. This meant the Fox had to power down its engines which meant it'd be falling through the sky.

'Activating IWP now,' Sif said.

The Fox began falling through the clouds somewhere above Trix. If it started tumbling, regaining control would be difficult. Trix knew the ship could come back online before it hit the ground, though it'd be close.

'Mortars incoming,' Cole said over comms. 'Shit, they ain't coming for us. Trix, watch out.'

A mortar hit the ship Trix was in. The cockpit was torn apart. Trix's shields depleted. Worse, she was disconnected from the console which was now wrecked beyond repair, and the Fox was hurtling through the atmosphere with no way of getting the engines back online.

'Sif, tell me something good.'

'I can't get a lock on the Fox with just your comms gauntlet. It's falling too erratically.'

'I said tell me something good.'

'This ship's comms are still operable, but you need to log in to another console. There should be one on the upper level.'

Trix bounded through the cockpit. The ship was like a larger version of the Fox. She climbed up a ladder and entered a hallway with two doors. Both were locked. Sif didn't have time to hack them. Trix placed one hand on the door. Altered its density until it was brittle. Then she made her other hand denser. Punched through the door. Got lucky. The other side was full of terminals, like a scaled down version of the bridge on Ren's galleon.

Trix put her gauntlet into the first console she saw. Sif ran the algorithm again. The Fox was at one and a half thousand feet. The Valkyrie watched as Sif went through the motions. First, IWP was turned off. Now for engines on.

The Fox came to life at 594 feet. Stabilisers reengaged. Thrusters blared.

'We now have full comms,' Sif said.

Trix disconnected from the terminal and returned to the first floor. She exited through the broken cockpit as another mortar hit the ship. If the Exiles were willing to destroy their own transport, it meant they had a backup. But where was it?

Trix re-joined the Dread Phantoms on the dune. The onis had switched their shotguns to secondary firing mode, which enabled them to be used like rifles. This meant their range went from short to medium. Three of the remaining seven Dread Phantoms were trying to flank the Exiles. An RPG put an end to their plan.

'Fuck it all. I'll kill every last one of them,' Ren said.

Larry was now beginning his lumbering descent back into the dunes. That was until stray fire slammed into his pustules. They burst. Gunk fell into the abyss. Larry took notice. Roared.

Then everyone saw how fast he moved. Larry swung his body around, knocking down the ruins' remains. The Exiles jumped from their hiding spots and rolled onto the dunes, firing wildly at the Dread Phantoms, forcing them to take cover. Two remaining Phantoms decided it'd be a good idea to try bringing down Larry with machine guns.

'What're you doing, fool?' Cole said, smacking their rifles away. 'You're gonna draw it over here.'

And Cole was right. Larry began swinging towards the dune.

Ren was shooting every Ice Exile within range. They were still fiddling with the explosives. If they'd wanted to kill the gramyriapede, they would've detonated them near its head.

Eosar pulled Ren back as the Dread Phantoms hurried down the dune. Larry smacked into it, causing the ashy sand to shift like a wave. Then he brought himself around and inhaled. The final four Dread Phantoms who'd been closest to the dune's ridge were sucked in. Their thruster-packs activated but they didn't have enough power.

The machinas, Eosar, and Ren slid towards Larry.

'Sif, bring the ship around and concentrate fire on Larry's head.'

Trix fired her utility cannon at the ship that'd been struck by mortar fire. It achieved a perfect tractor beam. She grabbed Kit's hand. Everyone formed a chain. Ren and Eosar were on the end. Cole had Ren's arm in an oni grip, the only thing stronger than a vice, baby. Trix altered gravity to reduce the strain on her utility cannon. It wasn't rated to handle so much weight and would fail before much longer, even with the Valkyrie's magic.

The Fox roared overhead and pumped plasma into Larry's face. Rotted flesh chunks fell away. Larry kept inhaling.

Sif: 'Trix, I'm reading inbound bogeys approaching our position fast. I think they're corrachian.'

'Hit him again.'

The Fox did a one-eighty. Fired again. Larry abetted. Trix reeled everyone back to the original Exile landing site. Irradiated gore spewed from Larry. The corrach ships were already visible. They must've been risking hypersonic speed. All non-essential systems had to have been rerouted to shields and thrusters.

'Coming in for landing,' said Sif.

'We're getting out of here,' Trix said to everyone.

'You don't give the orders here, huntress,' Ren said.

'That's funny. I have a ship. And you have no air support, and no men. I'm in charge now. If you don't like that then I respect your right to die here.'

The corrachian ships swung into position above the ruins. They were modified interceptors with almost no stock parts left on them. Tractor beams hauled up the remaining Ice Exiles. Mounted cannons took aim at Larry's body. It looked like they'd forgone whatever they planned on doing with the explosives.

Harpoons with reinforced adamant joints slammed into Larry in a triangular pattern. The ships engaged full thrusters. Began wrenching him out of the tunnel.

Ren still hadn't responded to Trix.

'I'm leaving, pirate.'

'Fine, huntress, I'll come aboard your ship. But you'd better bring those Exiles down.'

Kit, Kyra, and Cole were already inside the cargo bay. Sif started takeoff as Ren and Eosar stepped inside. The corrachian ships hadn't fired on them yet. Apart from the harpoon guns, it didn't look like they had any weapons at all.

Trix stepped into the airlock. Normally she wouldn't bother with a decontamination shower, but after Nuallar's toxic atmosphere, she thought it'd be for the best.

Once that was done, she ran for the pilot's chair. Larry was fully out of his tunnel. There was a blinking string of lights around the bottom of his body.

The explosives, Trix thought. What the fuck?

The Oni Three entered the cockpit behind her.

'We told Ren and Eosar to stay put,' Kyra said.

'Good.'

'Bring those ships down, huntress,' Ren said. His voice was frantic. Once this was over, Trix was going to find out why Ren wanted the Exiles so badly even if she had to strangle him. To hell with his threats.

Trix fired. The three corrachian ships were performing an aerial manoeuvre, like a loop-de-loop. The amount of power to accomplish such a feat while towing a gramyriapede had to be immense. Not to mention the cable and hull strength.

The Valkyrie focused her guns on the leftmost ship. Their formation would become unbalanced if she blew that up.

'Their shields are holding steady. From my scans I can tell those ships are built purely for defence and speed,' Sif said.

'I have to shoot the cables,' Trix said.

That was easier said than done in a dogfight. What happened next made it even more confusing.

The Ice Exiles had Larry close to horizontal in the air. Harpoons detached. An explosion. The bombs around the monster's rear went off. Severed it clean. Larry fell back to the sand. Torrents of blood and intestines spilled out. They were thick as tree trunks. The harpoons lodged into the severed chunk of Larry's flesh. The corrachian ships booked it in three separate directions.

What remained of Larry's backside was ripped in three. The harpoons on all three ships reeled the pieces into their cargo bays.

Trix parked the Fox. Engaged her weapons. The Exiles' shields were still holding. Corrachian ships were some of the strongest in the galaxy. Though if a ship was nigh on impenetrable, the chances were its offensive capabilities were slim.

'Fuck these things are tough,' she said. The corrachian ships were space bound in the opposite direction of Ren's galleon. Trix pursued. They were going well over supersonic speeds. Ashen desert blew past beneath them.

Ren had muscled his way into the cockpit with Eosar. It was far too crowded for Trix's liking. Kit and Kyra were sitting in the only other two command chairs. Four passenger seats were along the back wall.

'You better not lose those ships,' Ren said.

'If you're going to be in this cockpit, you better sit the hell down and shut the fuck up,' said Trix.

Ren held his tongue and strapped himself into one of the backseats. They were tight. Eosar sat beside him. Cole remained standing. The chase was taking them to the other side of Nuallar. Speeds were approaching hypersonic.

Cole: 'Trix, get close. I'll jump off and bring em down.'

Kyra: 'They'll only shake you off. Jumping out's not gonna do any good at these speeds. Maybe if you had a tracking device, that'd be useful. But getting you back on the ship would be a pain in the ass.'

Kit: 'Kyra's right, mate.'

'Worth a shot,' Cole said.

Sif: 'Trix, the corrachian ships are increasing their climb.'

'We can't go through the clouds or we'll burn out the thrusters,' said Trix, thinking she'd need to engage the IWP again. 'Cole, you might want to sit for this.'

Cole knew Trix well enough to know she was the Queen of Unorthodox Ideas. Whatever she was planning, it was going to be somewhere between madness and brilliance.

The corrachian ships disappeared into the cloud cover.

They must be betting that they can make it back to space before their thrusters cut out, Trix guessed. That was what she wanted. Once they crossed the clouds, the corrachs would be hindered, whereas the Fox would be nimble as ever.

'Sif, we need an exact 30 degree angle.'

'Alright.'

'Time to punch it.'

Trix shifted past hypersonic. This was becoming a bad habit. The clouds rushed to greet her. The Valkyrie's fingers danced on the control panel.

Everything had shut off last time she engaged IWP. Trix needed to keep systems like inertial dampeners, and life support on in case events didn't go according to plan. She also needed to keep the vertical stabilisers engaged. With any luck, the Fox would soar straight through the clouds.

Trix engaged IWP at the last possible moment. The windshield darkened. Visuals weren't replaced with simulated imagery. Shit, how was Trix going to know when she was out of the clouds? IWP protected all external lenses, which meant the cameras and the windshield.

The Fox was still moving through the sky. No one had experienced a falling sensation yet.

'Sif, I need the nose lens back now.'

The HUD became a textured black with faint light spots. Damn soot. Trix maximised the HUD's speedometer. Watched its numbers race towards zero. The Fox would start falling soon. To ensure Trix didn't reengage the thrusters in the soot clouds — because that would fry them almost immediately — Trix waited until the speed was dangerously low.

'All systems up. We're jumping straight to top gear.'

The outside world became visible again. Clouds were behind the ship. Just.

'The corrachs are at the atmosphere's edge,' Sif said.

Trix couldn't catch them. Tried anyway. The Fox went hypersonic again. The shields drained. Reached critical just as Trix entered space. The Exile ships she'd been chasing had conked out as she'd suspected. Right in the middle of the Ice Exiles' fleet.

They fired.

Trix evaded with every manoeuvre in the book, and a slew of ones she'd made up. She was good, but not good enough to take on a fleet by herself. Now that she was in space, hypersonic speeds were possible without damaging the ship. So were ultrasonic (30,000kph) speeds. She accelerated towards Ren's squadron. She wasn't pursued. The Ice Exiles clearly weren't as reckless as the Dread Phantoms. For all they knew, Trix was a distraction, meant to lure them into a trap.

Once Trix was satisfied she was safe, she let Sif control the ship. She left her seat, retracted her helmet, and pulled down her scarf. Stared Ren in the eyes.

'This is how the rest of this mission is going to go. You tell me why you want to destroy the Ice Exiles. If you don't, I'll kill you. You can choose how. Sword, pistol, bare hands, or being jettisoned from the airlock.'

Ren had taken off his helmet. He was matching Trix's stare. She had to give him that one, Ren wasn't easily scared. If he was, he was good at hiding it.

The rest of the machinas had disengaged their helmets. Cole was visibly pissed at Ren. This mission had not been what he expected. Not knowing Ren's motives hadn't bothered him before, but he wanted an explanation now. Kyra looked content. They'd escaped alive. And any day that happened was a great one in her books.

Kit was watching Trix berate Ren with a smirk. He couldn't wait for the pirate to crack.

Trix let the power of her last words hang in silence. No one broke it. Silence usually made people talk. That was why she kept speaking to a minimum when handling monster contracts. People in those situations were always reluctant to talk.

When the silence became uncomfortable, Trix let it simmer a moment longer before resuming.

'Now, if you tell me your reasons, then we can begin renegotiating terms, but you're in my house now, dickhead. And that means I have the last say.'

Trix had finished her piece. She leaned back on her chair, fixing her white pupils into Ren's black ones. Trix activated her x-ray vision, causing her pupils to become slits, for added intimidation. A crooked smile twitched her lips. It made her look hungry.

The Oni Three exited the cockpit. Kit grabbed Eosar out of his seat and forced him into Trix's living room. He knew intimidation tactics tended to work better one on one. Made the victim feel more alone. And if Ren thought that they were torturing Eosar, all the better for Trix.

In the silence following an ultimatum, the first person to speak was always the loser.

PHANTOMS & WOLVES

1

Ren Gerdac spoke.

'You were right about the monster.'

Trix remained silent.

'Knowing my reason changes nothing for you.'

The Valkyrie didn't budge. Didn't blink. Didn't breathe. If it weren't for the savagery in her eyes, you would've thought she was frozen in time.

Ren saw he was making no progress. He wasn't used to being on the receiving end of such treatment. For that reason alone, he knew he'd already lost. No point in delaying the inevitable. He rested his head against the back wall and spoke to the ceiling. Trix maintained her gaze. A strand of white hair hung across her face.

'The Ghirsioc Raithexils are scum. I know this because I worked for the man who would become their leader many years ago, when I was a smuggler. His name is Dheizir Crohl. And he's the bastard who betrayed me. He's the reason I spent ten years in the Hole.' Ren wasn't frantic. Trix didn't think he was afraid. She thought he was relieved. Just strolling down Memory Lane with Trix in tow.

'You know when they sentence you for jail time in the Hole, they don't tell you how long? Nobody does. Everyone goes in thinking they're never going to come out. Something to do with them being privately owned. Legally, they don't have to tell you. Crohl's betrayal is the reason I want him dead. Him and all his men.'

'How did he betray you?'

'If any Bastion officials ask you, this conversation never happened. I pleaded innocent on my mother's grave.' Ren looked at Trix again. She softened her gaze a touch. Didn't want to overdo it. Ren needed to remember with whom he was dealing.

'I was making a run into the Bastion, that and the other capital planets are the riskiest places to make a drop, so the reward is massive. We were transporting drugs. Dheizir hadn't gotten into rare animals and monsters full time yet. He'd only just started dabbling. Drugs were still where the money was, and Dheizir always followed the money. He was a bloody dog, the way he could sniff it out, dig it up. By the size of his fleet, probably still is. We had some synthetic psygotaic hallucinogens on board. It was the kind of shit that'd make you believe you were on a beach when in reality you were in the middle of a blizzard, stark naked. In small doses, it's actually used as a treatment for stress disorders, memory loss, all kinds of mental diseases. We were selling it for people to get fucked up.'

'Today, Gerdac.'

Trix's tone was fierce, but Ren was in no hurry. Despite prior, contrary evidence, he wasn't an idiot. He was telling the Valkyrie what she wanted to hear. She wouldn't kill him now. Though the Valkyrie could cause him tremendous pain.

'Dheizir wasn't with me. This was one of the few times I'd been out on my own. Crohl wasn't big on trusting people, but I was getting pretty good. I was handsome, back then, believe it or not. Had a way with women.' He gave Trix a look.

Trix unsheathed Kit's bowie knife and pressed the tip lightly into her index finger. Spun it several times. 'Will you speak faster if I loosen your tongue with this?'

'I'm walking to the security check-in. The drugs are inside my ship. In powder form. Like aquamarine sugar. I'd hidden them inside computer terminal cases. I had my fake ID that'd been inserted into the Bastion database on another op. I was feeling great, surveying the guards, seeing which one looked like the easiest to schmooze. Saw a young woman. She was flustered. First day on the job, maybe. I figure she's my way in. That's when I see Dheizir himself. Dressed like a fucking dandy, strolling up to the same woman I had my eye on.'

Ren sat up straight in his seat. Trix still had her knife out. Ren continued.

'I slink back into the crowded docks and watch them. He has a conversation with the woman. I see her relax, laugh a bit. They even shake hands. As you know, that's against protocol. Security staff aren't supposed to be chummy with the people they're letting through. I keep to my plan, and I go towards the girl. I let her know that I have cargo to bring in. Give her my fake ID, the cargo recipient's name, which was actually a doctor's office. That was part of Dheizir's brilliance.'

Ren folded his arms. Smiled.

'Dheizir's business was legit He sold a whole heap of things and used them as drug containers. That way he had a totally legal order to show security and they'd let him through with minimal hassle. Since Dheizir didn't care about the legal goods, he sold them at enough to break even. We were never without a way in because of the cheap prices. People always wanted to buy something. The drugs were where he made the killer profit anyway. We'd unload them from the legal goods, then transfer them to their required locations. Easy.'

Trix kept playing with her knife. Despite her projected impatience, she was in no rush to be anywhere. But Ren was verging on blathering territory. And Trix hated that place.

'She was smiling the whole time,' Ren said, partially lost in a daydream. 'When I finished my spiel, she demanded that I take the contents of my ship for inspection. I tried telling her that wouldn't be necessary. This woman ended up being bolder than I'd her pegged for. She told me she'd received a tip off about my business, and that if I didn't comply with her orders, I would be arrested. I knew that if I submitted my ship for a full search I'd be found out, so I tried to get out of it again. That was when she arrested me.'

'Just because you saw Dheizir doesn't mean he was the one who tipped off security,' Trix said.

'He was my phone call. I explained everything that'd happened. Told him he needed to have some of his contacts pull some strings. He was silent the whole time. When I finished, all he said was: *if you want something done right, do it yourself.* Then he hung up. I was put on trial, and I went in the Hole. The doctor on the Bastion had been caught up in it as well. Somehow the judges thought that he was buying the drugs. He kept saying he'd been set-up. He got to sweat out his sentence in Bastion prison cells. I got the Hole since I was the smuggler. That was 26 years ago.'

'If it was 26 years ago, it shouldn't matter. Thirty-four of your men died because you were too busy holding a grudge. Why bother attacking Dheizir's men at all? Why not find him and put a bullet through his head, or hire an assassin to kill him?'

'Revenge is the only deck of cards that the player must deal, not the House,' Ren said. 'I don't want to kill him. I want him to be imprisoned until his skin falls off his bones and he'd rather bathe in boiling oil for eternity than live another second. I want to break the empire he's built so that he has nothing. And if you want something done right, you have to do it yourself.'

'I don't know if your reason is good enough to justify letting you go. My friends and I could've died.'

'There are more shameful ways to die than by a Valkyrie's hand. I already told you, I don't fear death. I know that doesn't rule out torture, but all pain is fleeting.'

'Ironic, coming from someone who's holding onto the pain of a 26 year old betrayal.'

'I'm holding onto a debt of betrayal, and its payment is long overdue. Even though you've effectively imprisoned me on your ship, huntress, I'm no fool. I know you and your friends are valuable assets. These circumstances don't change the fact that I will pay you to help me bring Dheizir down.'

'Why didn't you say this to begin with?'

'A man can have his secrets. It wouldn't serve for the Dread Phantoms to know that this mission could end with all of us dead, though I suspect they know that now. I promised them orits, and ships. The Ghirsioc Raithexils have astounding custom rigs, as you saw on Nuallar. I wouldn't mind having some for myself, but Dheizir is the end game. He's no longer just a business man, he's an extremist. Soon his endeavours will go from exotic animals to full time terrorism.'

'What's stopping me from going to Dheizir and telling him of your plan? Killing you and bringing him your head would net me more money than you can currently afford.'

'The onis will stay with me. They have their own three-person gang for hire. It would hardly do them well for ongoing business if they were known to ditch their employers whenever the mood struck them.'

'Huh,' Trix said. 'So, the Ice Exiles on one side,' she gestured with her knife, 'your Phantoms and Wolves on the other,' she brought the knife to her sternum, just below her medallion. 'And me, right in the middle.'

'Which way will you choose?' Ren said. He got up. Stood across from Trix, no more than an arm's length away. 'You know that although I'm a pirate, I'm a good man, fighting for a just cause. I only steal ships from those who are bad themselves.'

'Badness is a perception that differs depending on the beholder. I suppose you're going to tell me that you give the ships you steal to the poor, too?'

'No, I keep them for myself. I've been keeping them, selling them, buying new ones, all so I can bring Dheizir to justice.'

Trix let the silence hang. It was a corpse hanging from a gnarled branch on a desolate battlefield. Crows pecked its eyes. Maggots writhed beneath its flesh. It was a silence that lingered long after everything else was dead.

'We're not friends, so I'll expect payment for my help. You'll give me 5,000 orits as soon as we're back on your ship. The rest of my reward will be flexible until the deed is done. But I can guarantee it'll be expensive. I don't like you, Gerdac, but you promised to pay my friends, and I want to stick with them. If Dheizir plans on becoming a full time terrorist, then he deserves to die, if only a little more than you.'

'We're all guilty of something.'

Trix had heard those exact words before. During an infiltration mission on Thyria with the princess of Xardiassant. A corrachian mercenary under Daquarius Farosi's command had spoken them. Trix was sure he hadn't been the first person to ever utter those words. But it was how he'd said them. In the face of certain death.

'And ain't that the truth?' Trix said. She was posing the question to herself as much as Ren. She still didn't trust him. He was a pirate. They weren't renowned for honesty. Still, in the midst of all the fuck-ups, Trix began to see a plan on the horizon. Two gangs. One trying to take on the other.

And me, right in the middle, Trix thought.

Until she knew who was the lesser of two evils, she was her own gang. Just her and Sif. Ride or die.

Trix and Ren didn't shake on their deal. Each offered the other a small nod. 'Alright, Sif, let's return to the galleon.'

'About that. I tried contacting Moro so we could dock without hassle. He's not responding. I'm getting nothing from the galleon at all.'

'Your comms must've been damaged in the soot,' Ren said. His voice betrayed no concern. Failed comms wouldn't unsettle his nerves after having a machina threaten him.

'All comms are fully functional. I'm an AI,' Sif said, her hologram appearing on the Fox's console. Her golden, coded face death-stared Ren. 'I think I would know.'

Ren's brow furrowed. He tapped commands on his comms gauntlet.

'Phantom Squadron, this is Ren Gerdac. Confirm.'

'Reading you loud and clear, commodore.'

'Leroy, give me a status update on the galleon.'

'I can see it to port, commodore. No signs of damage. Still in formation. We haven't seen anyone, though we got some heavy activity readouts coming from across the planet. We're guessing Ice Exiles. Ready to engage if you are, boss.'

'Do not engage. They've got a whole damn fleet. We barely

made it out alive. Everyone besides me, Eosar, and the machinas, are dead.'

'Shit,' Leroy said. 'Well... I, I'm sorry for your loss, commodore. I know Reda was a good friend of yours.'

'She was,' Ren said.

Trix could see his mind ticking. There was sadness, but it had a cunning edge. Ren saw a way to use this to his advantage.

'Boss, not to question your judgement, but why'd we come here anyway? Nuallar's a wasteland. There's nothing here but radiation crazed kalariks.'

'I had reason to believe that the Ice Exiles were using Nuallar to stockpile weapons, and other valuable goods. Aye, I thought we could liberate them.'

Trix noticed that Ren lied as easy as he breathed. She'd have to assume he had told her the truth for now. Though she wasn't going to trust him.

'Were they?'

'No, we think they were after a monster. They captured parts of one and flew into space. We followed close behind, but we couldn't take on their fleet alone. Now we're going after them for revenge, pure and simple.'

'Damn right. We'll show those dwarves they shouldn't fuck with the Dread Phantoms.'

'That's what I like to hear, Leroy,' Ren was smiling. It was a devious look. 'Can you contact Moro?'

'Galleon's comms are fine, but he's not replying. No one is.'

'Keep trying to make contact. I'm coming back now, on the huntress' ship.'

'Got it, commodore.'

Trix decided to tell Ren what he'd actually said to Moro. What Rosamund Galbrand would've overheard.

'Your transmission was fragmented when you contacted the galleon.'

'Eosar told me comms were online.'

'Play the recording, Sif.'

Sif played the recording. Trix watched as Ren's face became

aghast.

'No, no, no, no.' Ren punched his open palm with every word. 'Take us back.'

'Sif, punch it.'

The Fox took off towards Ren's squadron. Trix ushered Ren into the living room. Kit and Kyra were sitting on Trix's sofa. Eosar was sitting on the armchair. They weren't talking. Kit was whistling. Cole exited the armoury. He was holding his shotgun. Must've been cleaning it.

Kit: 'So, either you're satisfied with what Ren said, or you're going to kill him out here for all of us to see.'

Ren: 'The huntress has agreed to help, for a fee.'

'Speaking of which, mate, I would like mine sooner rather than later. If the next mission goes anything like the last. You might not be around to pay me.'

'You'll all be getting advancements,' Ren said. The words were forced out of his teeth like they were being pulled in a tug of war. 'Provided we can take back the galleon.'

'What do you mean, take it back?' Eosar said.

'The huntress informed me that the transmission you assured me could reach the ship was fragmented. By what made it through, Galbrand has every reason to believe I killed Vicaull in cold blood. Next time you give me a guarantee, you'd better be ready to stake your life on it, Eosar, because that's what I'll take if you're wrong.'

Eosar nodded.

Kyra: 'If the galleon is under Red Wolf control, and we have to assume it is since there's no response, we're not gonna be able to dock.'

Trix: 'We'll fall back into formation, then we'll exit from the cargo bay and go for the portside entrance we used before. Can you three breach it?'

'Not without explosives,' Kyra said.

'Zero gravity makes it pretty hard to swing a punch, and busting open your suit in space isn't recommended,' said Kit.

Trix had some breaching explosives in her armoury. The

only alternative was having one of Ren's corvettes blow a hole in the airlock. The problem with that was the blast could go straight through. If there was anyone inside, they wouldn't be inside for long.

'I have explosives,' Trix said. She walked into the armoury. Cole followed since he was at the door already.

Trix pulled out a drawer. Riven Drill Mines were inside. She only had one lot of them. Drill Mines were diamond tipped and burrowed into just about any desired surface before detonating on the inside. The blast wasn't huge, but it didn't have to be. They'd work as long as the explosives were placed over locking mechanisms.

Due to the finesse their placement required, you had to have a vast knowledge of door mechanisms, or access to a database with schematics. Ships tended to have some schematics online. Custom jobs rarely did. That was when training came into play. Thankfully, Trix was friends with three onis.

And onis, in addition to being close quarters combat specialists, were breaching experts.

'Oh, Trix, oh baby,' Cole said, picking up the drill mines. 'This is top notch right here.'

'Can you break into the airlock with these?'

'Haha, the Oni Three could get you through just about any door with these.'

'But you have to leave the door intact.'

'Yeah, can't have the rest of the ship flying out the airlock. Shouldn't be a problem. Sif can probably hack the emergency door from inside. We close that one, depressurise the airlock, then we're golden, baby.'

'We could be facing a hostage situation on the other side.'

'Galbrand wouldn't take prisoners, well, I doubt she would. If she hasn't been put down already, she's gotten her Wolves to kill every last Phantom on that ship.'

'How many were there?'

'I was hired to bust skulls, not take roll call. If I had to guess, I'd reckon about 80 Phantoms, now that our two squads ate it.

Probably 50 Wolves. Ren wanted to keep the numbers in our favour in case they tried something.'

'The only thing greater than numbers is surprise.'

'Then let's try not to make too much noise,' Cole said as he grabbed a handful of drill mines. He stood in the doorway and tossed them to Kyra and Kit.

'We need to go over this,' Ren said. 'The ship's integrity is paramount we'll need it to attack Crohl's fleet.'

'Do you have a dreadnought?'

'I have a destroyer. It's running on a skeleton crew.'

'Going up against the Ice Exiles would be suicide.'

'That's why it's my last resort.'

'Why risk all of that?' Eosar said. His response was genuine. Trix heard his heart spike. 'None of us asked you why you wanted to come here, but we did it anyway. Now Reda's dead, and Obe, and everyone else and you're talking about taking on a fleet of corrachian ships for no reason.'

'I'd received intel that the corrachs were stockpiling weapons on Nuallar. Powerful ones. Top of the line Riven gear that only the best mercenaries and Special Forces units can get their hands on.'

Ren spoke with such conviction that Trix almost believed him. She checked her gauntlet. The Fox was closing on the squadron. Instead of listening to Ren's repeated bullshit spiel, Trix wondered what the outside of her ship looked like. What happened when you mixed Noccril Rust with Nuallar Soot?

Kit motioned with his eyes towards Ren. Raised his eyebrow a touch. If anyone else had seen it, they might've thought it was a facial twitch. Trix knew he was questioning Ren's story. She ran her right hand through her hair. Sign for, *you're right*. Kit rolled his shoulders back. *Okay.*

'This is about avenging the people we just lost. The crew will understand,' Ren said.

'Only because they didn't see the way you left Reda to die. We were right there. We could've killed the Vipers. We might've been able to save some—'

Ren clocked Eosar across the face. It wasn't hard enough to break bone, but it'd bruise. Nice and dark.

'You want valour, honour, and all that shit? Join the fucking army. This isn't a fairy tale. And there're no shining knights. Only the glint of money and blood against the stars. You know the pirate code as well as I, for I was the one who taught it to you. There's no shame in saving your squad if you've got what you came for, if you think you can get away clean. If not, then they know for what they signed up.'

'If you really believed that you wouldn't have tried to save Beck in the altar room.'

'Eosar, you question me again and I'll make you beg for what the Vipers did to Reda.'

Eosar said nothing more. He knew he was right. Ren's anger attested to that.

'Galleon's in sight. The squadron's moving to accommodate the Fox,' said Sif.

Trix: 'Ren, give your pilots orders to stand down. I don't want them attacking us when they see we're fitting explosives to the side of the galleon.'

'Leroy, this is Ren. We've got reason to believe that the galleon's been compromised. We have to break in using explosives on the portside airlock. This is meant to happen. Stand down.'

Leroy wanted to ask why the ship had been compromised, and more importantly, how? But he wasn't paid for that. He was paid to agree.

'Yes, commodore.'

'Everyone suit up,' Trix said. She looked at Eosar and Ren. 'You two will be going in front of me.'

Ren: 'Still don't trust me?'

Trix lowered her hand to her pistol in case the pirates needed extra motivation to enter the cargo bay. They didn't. The Oni Three were already there. Each of them had two Drill Mines on their belts. In the event that Sif couldn't hack the internal door, they'd have to bust it open as well.

Trix stepped into the cargo bay. Artificial gravity was disabled. Zero gravity reigned. The loading ramp was open. The Fox arrived at the galleon's portside airlock. The Oni Three were at the cargo bay's edge, holding onto the ceiling handles. They still had their thruster-packs on.

'Okay, boys, looks like a stock standard airlock door. Four point locking mechanism opening outwards from a hinge on the left,' Kyra said. 'Kit, Cole and I will take the first door. Hold your two mines until the interior.'

'You know it, Kyra.'

'Alright, let's go.'

The Oni Three pushed off the loading ramp. Shot for the airlock in perfect formation. Activated their reverse thrusters before slamming into the hull. While there was no sound in space, three heavily armoured machinas knocking about outside would be heard from within.

Cole and Kyra placed their mines at the four points Kyra had specified. Armed them. Small explosions synchronised around the door. The result was immediate.

The airlock door opened. Air rushed into the void.

Kyra: 'Trix, we're ready.'

The Valkyrie gestured for Ren and Eosar to go first. They did. Trix followed. Arrived in the airlock. The onis swung themselves off the hull. Entered. Cole closed the door, though it could no longer contain pressure. Four holes tended to have that effect.

Trix plugged Sif into the command console. It was flashing red. Airlock breach. Trix activated the emergency exterior door without needing to hack anything. Now to take back the ship. The console requested confirmation.

'Gerdac, how about you save us some time and see if your codes still work?'

Ren made a series of taps on the screen. It flashed green twice. The interior door unlocked.

'Shoot to kill. If Galbrand's taken hostages, try and save them.' He paused. Trix swore she could hear him thinking. 'We

OF EXILES & PIRATES

need to disable this ship's long-range comms. If Galbrand's managed to message the rest of the Red Wolves, they'll revolt, and we'll be finished.'

'Where are the rest of your men stationed?' Trix said.

'My fleet is in the Red Reef asteroid field, though I have men in Thyrian Strongholds keeping an eye on the Wolves protection racket. We're also anticipating retaliation from the Hidden.'

Gerdac's empire was falling as quickly as it had risen.

Trix: 'We'll split up. Kit, Ren, you're with me. We'll go for the long-range comms. Kyra, Cole, and Eosar, you search for survivors and help where you can.'

'On it, Trix. Come on, fool,' Cole said to Eosar. 'Let's go.'

Cole and Kyra exited the airlock. The hallway showed no signs of life. Only corpses. Red Wolf and Dread Phantom alike. Eosar followed Cole. Headed to the bridge.

'The comms are on the top level, Valkyrie.'

'Lead the way.'

Ren nodded.

There were potentially 50 Red Wolves on the galleon.

And they travelled in packs.

2

Oni Tag Team

Cole and Kyra moved to the bridge.

Eosar watched their sixes. He looked like an untrained novice who'd never been in a firefight compared to the onis. Nevertheless, the trio reached the war room at the bridge. Kyra held up her fist. Stop. There were ten Red Wolves tossing something back and forth between them. It was a Dread Phantom helmet. The head was still inside.

The onis slunk back. Spoke in machina whispers.

Kyra: 'I'll circle around. Take them from the right.'

Cole: 'Not a lot of cover in there.'

'We're not gonna give them a chance to shoot.'

'That's what I like to hear, baby.'

Kyra went back the way she'd come. Didn't encounter any resistance.

'Ready,' she said over comms.

'Wait. I'm gonna make a *di*version, then you spray the hell outta them.'

'They're gonna *die* in this *version*,' Kyra said.

'Oh yeah,' Cole turned to Eosar. 'Stay here, fool.'

Cole strode out. Shotgun in hand. He switched it to rifle mode. Hip fired. The head the Red Wolves were using as a ball blew up in their faces.

'Oh hell, man. I'm sorry. Was that not for target practice?'

The Red Wolves drew their guns. Cole had to give it to them, they were quick. Seasoned. Cole activated his oni barrier as Kyra entered. Fired her two shotguns. No shells came out. They had an alternate firing mode made for crowd control. Buckets were required for the aftermath.

Two discs flew into the war room's centre, one above the other. They were capable of spreading two shotgun blasts 360-degrees.

They fired.

Shields burst across the war room. The Red Wolves ducked for cover. Kyra couldn't fire her weapons until the discs were retracted.

Cole was up.

Three Wolves furthest from Kyra's blast unleashed their machine gun chambers into Cole's oni barrier. He was going to fire a shockwave before remembering he was inside a space ship. Not the best move.

Cole dropped his barrier and let off a three-round burst once they ran out of ammo. His assailants were knocked to the ground. A sniper rifle round hit Cole in the chest. His shields cut out. Another wolf fired his pistol. Cole unleashed the energy he'd been storing in a controlled blast.

The wind was knocked out of the pistol wielding Wolf. Kyra's shotguns reassembled themselves. Jammed halfway through. She holstered them.

'Fuck it,' she said. Kyra sprinted towards the Wolf reloading his sniper rifle. Jumped. She wound her legs around the wolf's neck and spun. Circled him three times before body slamming him. Broke his neck with two kicks to his head.

Cole used his shotgun to kill the first three guys while Kyra finished reloading the sniper rifle that'd fallen to the floor. Fired it one-handed. Its bullets entered the ear of a Wolf trying to find cover. He died before it came out the other side.

Five Wolves were left, and they were backing up towards the cockpit. Cole still had some gas in the tank from his oni barrier. Not enough for anything major. It was about the amount of energy you'd need to pull a trigger.

Cole threw his shotgun with a spin. Made for the leftmost Wolf. The spinning shotgun always drew attention. Kyra ran for the right-hand wolf. Her oni barrier activated. Bullets peppered it. Kyra put the energy into an armour breaking kick. The wolf hit the back wall. Dented it.

Kyra saw Cole's shotgun coming. Ducked while sweeping a wolf's legs from underneath him. As he fell, Kyra kicked him back into the air, level with Cole's shotgun. Cole mirrored her manoeuvre, albeit, more crudely. Pulled the shotgun's trigger remotely using his oni magic. Two Wolves' heads were wrought from their bodies. Two more left. They were too scared to shoot. They'd never seen anything like the massacre they'd just witnessed.

For their last trick, Cole and Kyra sprung off the floor in synchronised mule kicks, hitting both remaining Wolves in their crotches. They became airborne before being crushed into the ship's floor. Their pelvises shattered. Cole caught his shotgun before it fell. Used its last shell to blow apart the Wolf's head.

Kyra, well, she wanted to go the extra mile. Jumping off the Wolf's pelvis, she grabbed his head and leaned back in mid-air. Put her feet on his shoulders. Crouched. Then pulled. His head tore off. The skin ripped in jagged lines. Kyra landed on her feet, holding the Wolf's head. She tossed it to Cole.

'Ah hell, what're you doing that for? That shit was overkill, baby.'

'I wanted to see what the appeal was.'

'And? You see it?' Cole tossed the head backwards and holstered his shotgun.

'No,' Kyra shrugged. Wiped the side of her face. Blood smeared on her cheek. 'Not really.'

'You're crazy.'

'You love it.'

'Mmmhmm.'

Eosar emerged from the hallway.

'Now, you see what we just did,' Cole said, gesturing to the dead Red Wolves like he'd redecorated a living room, 'that's top dollar, baby, and once we get this ship back, I want orits or I'm walking.'

Kyra: 'Same goes for me.'

Eosar: 'You'll get your money. For now we have to check the comms log.'

'You do that, we'll keep an eye out,' Kyra said, jerking her thumb towards the cockpit.

Eosar nodded. Walked in. It was all clear. Moro was dead. Shot. Point-blanc range. Pistol. Small calibre. Nothing like Trix's .44 Magnum Opus. That would've taken his head off.

Eosar began checking the comms logs when a crash came from behind him. He drew his weapon and spun.

'Fodio,' the man said. He was a medcanol. His double pointed ears gave it away. There was a touch of human in his face. Electric blue hair stuck up in a shaggy mop. A cap had fallen off his head. The logo on the front was a hawk with a lightning bolt between its claws. It was the symbol of the South African Goshawks, the state's premier smashball team.

Kyra and Cole entered the cockpit, shotguns raised. The medcanol was wearing Dread Phantom gear. He'd come from one of the ceiling's life support vents. It would've been a tight fit.

'Don't shoot him. This is Griff, one of our mechanics,' Eosar said.

'That's Griffauron Fulum Raivad to you, Eosar,' Griff coughed. 'Hysi, you're right, that is a mouthful. Call me Griff.' He dusted his cap off and put it on. 'Now would anyone care to tell me what the fodio is happening here?'

Fodio was zirean slang for fuck.

Kyra: 'The Red Wolves think Gerdac killed Vicaull. Now they're out for blood.'

'Hysi, that'll do it, won't it? That explains why Rosa's in the hangar taking prisoners and thinking of ways to kill the others. I didn't stick around.'

Cole looked at Eosar and raised an eyebrow.

'This guy seems a little jumpy to be working on equipment.'

'Hah, that's what the C.A.F. said too. Apparently my modifications were, how'd they put it? Unsanctioned, untested, and unsafe. I told them they were using outdated mechanics, but they just wouldn't listen. So, one ship blew up, hysi, I accept that. In my defence, my math was off. Forgot to account for hull warping under stress from different angles. Now I've got it right. But I was discharged, so what're you gonna do?'

'You're telling me the Consortium Air Force hired you? Fool, you've gotta be kidding me.'

'No, sir, I was a Captain before the ship blew up. Pilot got out okay, in case you were wondering.'

'Why'd you run to the cockpit?' Eosar said.

'I couldn't stay in the hangar or I would've died. If Moro hadn't cut out the comms, everyone else would probably be dead too.'

'Moro stopped the comms?'

'Hysi.'

'How'd you know?'

'Messaged me,' Griff looked at Moro's body. 'Must've been right before he died. Bright stars and clear skies, mufy rami,' *my friend.*

Eosar: 'Why would he message you? You're just the mechanic.'

'Just the mechanic?' Griff's eyes went wide. '*Just* the mechanic. Then I guess I'll *just* stop maintaining the warpdrive, engine, thrusters, fusion cells, life support, that's right, without me, you'd be in a heap of trouble. Besides, Moro agreed I'd be the pilot if anything happened to him.'

'You fly too?' Kyra said, smiling.

'You fly?' said Cole, not smiling.

'Better than anyone you've ever seen, sir. If it's got an engine and it's made to be airborne, I can fly it.'

'Nah ah, Eosar. You see that look in his eyes. This guy shouldn't be operating a simulator, let alone a ship.'

'At the moment, we don't have much choice, unless either of you are familiar with flying a ship this size?'

'I'll make myself familiar if that's what it takes.'

'You're coming with me to scout the rest of the ship,' Eosar said. 'Griff, what were you planning to do once you got here?'

'Override the hangar controls and send Rosa into space.'

'Our men would die as well.'

'Be better than whatever Rosa's planning for them.'

'Hold off doing that. For now, keep the cockpit secure.'

'We'll go search the rest of the ship,' Kyra said.

'Any of you have a gun I can borrow? Couldn't fit my rifle through the vents and I lost my pistol in a game of Faet with Obe last night.'

Cole walked into the war room's carnage. Grabbed a pistol and a rifle off the floor. Handed them both to Griff.

'You know how to use a gun?'

'I can rebuild a ship engine with my eyes closed. I can use a gun.'

Griff holstered his weapons, making faces as he saw the blood still dripping off them.

'Why's a zirean wearing a South African Goshawk hat?' Kyra said. Despite having just killed a room full of people, you might've thought she'd strolled into a low-key soiree.

'I go for Xardiassant in the galactic tournament. But my mother was a half-breed from South Africa. I spent a lot of time living there. Went to a lot of games. Nice place. You three better get going. Don't think Rosa's gonna be waiting long before she decides to kill everyone. I'll try and keep her off the comms if I can.'

'Thanks, Griff,' Eosar said.

'Better than anyone I've ever seen,' Cole shook his head, thinking about Griff's boasting. 'I'll believe that when I see it.'

He left with Kyra and Eosar. Griff locked the door behind them. Sat in the pilot's chair.

'Eloa, harbon. Dapi y'trefcas.'

Hello, beautiful. Daddy's home.

3
Cutting Communications

Ren took point.

He led Kit and Trix to the living quarters. A few more corpses were around, slumped on tables in plates full of food. Murdered while they'd been eating. The ratio of Phantom to Wolf corpses was high.

'If Galbrand's on the top level, she'll have someone watching the central elevator. We'll take a service ladder,' Ren said. He kept moving around the corner to a door. Punched in a few numbers on the screen. It slid open. A ladder was on the other side.

'Gonna be a tight fit for me, mate,' Kit said, looking up the LED strip illuminated ladder.

Trix slapped him on the stomach. 'Suck it in.' She went first. Thought about sending Ren. But that would've made it too easy for him to kick her in the face. Trix didn't want to tempt him. She wanted to be paid. Really though, Trix wanted to finish this. Being in the middle of a galactic gang war was more involved than she liked being. Then again, when compared to kidnapping a princess, she supposed it was relatively insignificant.

Ren followed Trix. Kit followed him. Trix came to a grate on the top level. Listened. Two people were on the other side.

Hard to tell if they were Wolves or Phantoms.

Trix opened the grate. Emerged and stayed low to the floor. Whoever was in the room didn't hear her. They were talking loudly. Bitching about the comms being offline. Cursing Moro. And that their tech experts had been sent to Nuallar to assist with Reda's hijacking. They were Wolves.

'Can't believe Ren killed Vicaull,' one of them said.

'If I ever see that bastard I'll cut his balls off and make him eat them,' said the other.

'They're too big for a bitch like you to swallow,' Ren said, stepping onto the floor. 'But here's something you can chew on.'

The Wolves had left their guns on the terminal they were working on. Didn't reach them fast enough. Ren fired two bullets. Each of them went into the Wolves' mouths. Their teeth shattered. The wolves didn't die right away. Ren's bullets must've missed their spines.

Ren watched them claw for their pistols before he put them out of their misery with headshots.

'We need to destroy these comms systems. No point having them back online. Any of the other ships can contact the fleet,' Ren said.

'Part of the comms system will be outside the ship. They could patch into it remotely,' said Trix.

'Can you disable it?'

Trix plugged her comms gauntlet into the terminal. 'No, but Sif can.'

'That's right, I'm still here,' the AI said. 'This'll go faster if you give me your command codes, Ren.'

Ren obliged Sif's request. Sif was done within a minute.

'All long-range comms have been severed. There's no way for them to wirelessly connect with the rest of the squadron without pilot permission.'

'My pilots wouldn't give the Wolves access to their comms without my say so.'

Trix: 'Now we go find Galbrand.'

Kit: 'Any cameras we can use?'

'Cameras? On a pirate ship? No such thing. If this were to fall into police hands, I don't want them seeing what goes on. Even the logs are wiped at the end of every day.'

'Good way to go about it,' Kit said.

'I've been doing this a while, oni. There's a chance Galbrand could be waiting for me in my quarters. They're through here.'

Ren opened the comms hub door. A hallway with an elevator was on the other side. Ren walked right until he reached the last door. Unlike the others, this required triple threat security — handprint, retinal scan, and voice recognition — to enter.

Instead of opening the door, Ren performed a log check. The last time it'd opened had been before Ren left for Nuallar. That meant no one had entered since him. The door showed no signs of forced entry. It was adamant plated. Anyone trying to get in would be noticed. You couldn't just pop the lock cover with a crowbar then jimmy it with a hairpin.

'She won't be in there. No one will. We sweep this floor then we go to the hangar.'

Trix, Kit, and Ren checked the rest of the top floor. Massive crew's quarters had been thrashed. Trix could tell most of the occupants had been killed in their sleep. There was a human woman with purple skin — half corrach — who was sitting in a ratty armchair. She'd been shot in the gut. It'd been the ruptured femoral artery that'd killed her though. The chair was soaked with blood. Like a sponge left in a serial killer's sink. A dead Red Wolf was at her feet. He'd been shot in the back. Trix rolled him over. The front as well. She heard a rasping breath. Turned around. There was a man dressed in casual clothes in the room's nearest corner. Trix went to him.

'What happened to the others?'

'Others?' the man said. One of his shoulders had been crushed. His pelvic bone was partially collapsed.

Trix glanced at the marks on the floor. People had been dragged out of the upstairs crew's quarters. She was sure of it.

Kit had gone to the next room over. Ren was with him.

'The ones who weren't killed.'

'Rosa... wanted... example... hangar.'

The man died before uttering another word.

'Find anything?' Kit said, sticking his head into Trix's room.

'Evidence of people being dragged. You can see the marks on the floor, and streaks through the blood. They must've been carried the rest of the way.'

Kit nodded. 'There's no evidence of a struggle in the halls, you know, besides the corpses.'

'Apparently they're in the hangar.'

'How'd you know that?'

'This guy's last words.'

'I've counted six Red Wolf corpses up here, that's including the two guys Ren killed.'

'So have I. Cole guessed there were 80 phantoms and 50 wolves.'

'From this level and the living room below, I make that 49 phantoms and 44 wolves.'

'Depending on how many Cole and Kyra have found,' Trix nodded.

Ren stepped behind Kit. His face was dour.

'Some of these people were like my family.'

Trix: 'Anyone who's still alive is in the hangar.'

'Then that's where we're going. First, I need to make an announcement.'

Commodore Ren Gerdac tapped his gauntlet. The ship's PA system came to life. 'Rosamund Galbrand, this is Ren Gerdac. I know where you are, and I'm coming for you. I only killed Vicaull out of mercy, for the same reason I killed Reda, one of my oldest friends. They'd been tortured by the Vipers and irradiated beyond hope of recovery. I had no other choice. I am willing to forgive your betrayal if you stand down, and release the Phantoms in your custody.'

Ren paused. He had to be careful what he said next.

'If you do not, you will give me no choice but to dump you on

Nuallar with no armour so you can feel the pain Vicaull did before I saved him.'

No reply. There was an intercom system in the hangar that didn't require permission to use. Rosa was ignoring him on purpose. Ren held his nerve.

Finally, Rosa replied.

'Come to me unarmed, then we'll renegotiate terms. I need to see in your eyes that you're telling the truth. I'll kill another one of your Phantoms for every minute you make me wait.'

Rosa cut the transmission.

Cole's voice came over private comms.

'Yo, Trix, we've swept the ground floor. Nothing but corpses.'

Kyra: 'There were ten Wolves, but we tore them apart.'

Eosar: 'Ren, I don't know if you were bluffing on your announcement, but Galbrand's in the hangar.'

'How did you know that?'

'Griff told us. He escaped through the vents. He's locked himself in the cockpit. Said he can remotely access the hangar doors from there. Something to keep in mind.'

'We might be able to use that to our advantage. Wait, who's Griff?'

'One of your mechanics. Medcanol. Blue hair.'

'Him? Isn't he certifiably insane?'

Cole: 'Ayo, he looks it. Seriously, man, his eyes look like they've got minds of their own.'

Kyra: 'He's the new pilot.'

'As long as he's not blind I don't care. Where are you?'

'Headed to the central elevator.'

'We'll meet you there.'

In less than a minute, Rosamund Galbrand would begin murdering phantoms.

Ren Gerdac needed a plan.

Thankfully for him, Trix of Zilvia had one.

Ren Gerdac's rag-tag team of hired guns rendezvoused in front of the central elevator.

The galleon had taken on a ghostly feel. The deaths were turning it into a phantom. Everything looked the same as it had before going to Nuallar except for the blood. Except for the corpses.

'How many dead Wolves were on this level?' Trix said.

'We killed ten. There were three corpses in the halls,' said Kyra.

'Roughly thirty of them left then. Probably less than fifty Phantoms. Ren, how many ways can we reach the hangar?'

'There's this elevator. And there's a freight elevator at the ship's stern. There're also service ladders on the port and starboard sides.'

Cole: 'What's the plan, baby?'

All animals had instincts. Even humans. In fact, all the Milky Way's humanoid races had relatively similar natures. Machinas had their own instincts. And one of them was to defer leadership of any given squad to a Valkyrie. An oni, dragon, or a spectre could take charge if they had a better idea. But there was something that told them to look to Valkyries in times of need.

Trix's mind raced. There were six of them. There was also the new pilot, Griff, in the cockpit. He said he could flush the hangar. But formulating a plan was difficult without knowing the battlefield's layout. That was it. Trix needed eyes in the hangar.

'Ren, you're going to take this elevator. Rosa didn't stipulate you should come alone in her transmission. That means she thinks you're alone already. You're going to link your helmet to my AI, Sif, now. Then you'll transmit what you see to our HUDs. You just have to keep Rosa talking. And you have to keep your helmet on. We'll join you once we can see what we're dealing with, provided you can't make her stand down.'

Ren looked into Trix's eyes. Reckoned she was telling the truth.

'Alright.'

A voice on the intercom. It was Rosa.

'A minute's passed, Ren. You mustn't care about your crew that much. What's your name?'

Another voice on the intercom. Shaky, but not terrified. 'Remmal,' the man said.

'Know that Ren Gerdac's tardiness condemned you.'

A gunshot.

'Damn it, Galbrand. I'm coming. Central elevator.' Ren entered the elevator. Put on his helmet. Sif made a connection. Everyone else activated their own. Their HUDs' top left corners showed Ren's POV.

Ren Gerdac stared at the elevator doors until they opened. Rosamund Galbrand was standing on the opposite side of the airlock doors, where the troop carriers had been. There was still one remaining. Its left thruster was missing. Otherwise, its hull was capable of being pressurised. Ren's crew were kneeling on the doors that opened the floor to space.

Trix could see where the freight elevator would exit. She could also see where the service ladders were. She counted 31 Red Wolves and 44 Dread Phantoms. Though a lot of them weren't even wearing armour. Their arms showed severe bruising. Many had broken noses, black eyes, and missing teeth.

Ren stepped through the airlock. Held up his hands. Two Wolves confiscated his weapons.

'How do I know that's you under there, Gerdac?' Rosa said. She looked young. Freckles dotted her cheeks. Her hair was in a tight bun. Pulling back her forehead's skin.

'Eosar is the only other person with me.'

'Interesting that you should say so,' Rosa said. She had one foot on the back of Remmal, the menisel she'd just shot. 'Because I can't contact the team I sent to guard the cockpit. I would've known you were coming sooner, but Moro messed with the comms. I also can't contact the men I sent to the comms hub. So, I say it's interesting that only you and Eosar are here.'

'You don't believe we could kill all your men? Aye, the only reason you have so many of my crew here is that you caught them off guard. We trusted you as our allies.'

'Off guard? Hah, a pirate insinuating that he would've emerged victorious under the rules of a fair fight is as hilarious as it is ridiculous. And you didn't trust us as your allies, you tried absorbing us into your Dread Phantoms. This time next week our red and black would've been covered by your green and grey. You're just a punk who doesn't know what he's doing. As for you and Eosar killing my men, I might've believed it, except I'm no fool. Twelve of them died in two separate locations. You would stand no chance by yourselves. The machinas you hired. They're still with you.'

Ren kept silent. On the floor above, Trix waited before she voiced her plan. There was a chance for Ren to resolve this without bloodshed, but it was slim.

Rosa cocked her head at Ren.

'Take that helmet off, Gerdac. You're insulting me. If you came here to make me stand down then you're doing a poor job. First, you came here with weapons. If you hadn't raised your hands immediately you'd be holier than the Bible. Second, you wear a helmet. And since I'm the one with the guns, I decide what insults me and what doesn't. Take it off or another one of your Phantoms dies.'

Not good, Trix thought.

Ren hesitated a moment. Knew his helmet would still transmit even if the view wasn't ideal. He took it off.

'Hand it over,' Rosa said.

Ren passed it to her. She threw it across the hangar. It landed by the broken-down shuttle. Kyra was reminded of the wolves who'd been tossing the severed head back and forth.

'What do you want from me?' Ren said. He could've been a waiter asking if Rosa was ready to order, though his audio could barely be heard since his helmet had been removed. Trix's visuals now consisted of a low angle from the hangar's rear. The camera was focused on the starboard service ladder. There was a Red Wolf right in front of it.

'I want you to confess to killing Vicaull. I want you to send a message to all the Red Wolves now under my command, telling them you killed their commander.'

'I told you, I did it out of mercy. He was in pain.'

Trix heard a slap. Guessed Rosa had backhanded Ren.

'You lie about being alone when I know you're not. Now you lie about this. Worst of all, you lie about why you came here. I did some digging into your past, Ren Gerdac. And you've got so many skeletons in your closet it could be mistaken for a mass grave. You came here with the Red Wolves in your ranks because you believed that you could finally rival the Ice Exiles. You claimed their leader set you up for smuggling illicit hallucinogens into the Bastion. I was just going to kill you, but I think your idea's better. You told me you were going to leave me on Nuallar to suffer how Vicaull suffered? Now you'll get to experience his fate. Move, into the shuttle. All of you Phantoms. Wolves, keep an eye on the doors. I know the machinas are here.'

The guard in front of the starboard service ladder moved away as he ushered imprisoned Phantoms into the shuttle. There were over forty of them in a space built for twenty. It was going to be a tight fit.

Kit: 'Beatrix, if we're gonna do something, we'll have to do it now.'

Trix: 'No, this is good.'

'This isn't good,' Eosar nearly screamed. 'You're out of your mind. If by some miracle they survive the crash landing, they'll die from radiation poisoning. And if the ship stays intact, they won't be able to leave and they'll starve to death unless we reach them.'

'That's why we're not going to let the ship crash. Once everyone's inside, we'll have Griff trigger the airlock.'

'Hysi: Standing by,' Griff said. 'Ready to see if Red Wolves can swim in the star ocean.'

Kit: 'We won't know when everyone's inside. We've lost visual on everything that's happening.'

As Trix was about to make a move, Ren spoke.

'There's no need for this. We can come to an arrangement.'

'Speak fast or die faster.'

'I still have enough men to destroy your entire operation. Accounting for my full force, I outnumber you two to one. Even as we speak, my Dread Phantoms are making the rounds on Thyria. Your protection money is being transferred to me from now on. Kill me, and you'll have an uphill battle to reclaim your clientele. And, unlike you, Rosamund, I have a fleet. So help me I'll bomb you off the face of Thyria. I'll be labelled a terrorist, aye, but they already sent me to the Hole. All my ships have unlocked fusion cores. I could hide on the galaxy's edge and never be found.

'Face it, Galbrand, you're outgunned. Just because you've got the numbers here, don't fool yourself into thinking you're close to winning. My pilot is primed to depressurise this entire hangar. We'll all die, but Eosar is still alive. He'll salvage the Dread Phantoms from this defeat while there will be no one to take on the Red Wolves.'

There was a pause.

'Cole, Kyra, go to the freight elevator. Wait for my signal. Kit and I will take the service ladders. Eosar, you activate the central elevator on my command, then return to the cockpit. If this goes to shit, we need insurance that the Dread Phantoms won't blow us out of the sky.'

'Why would I activate the elevator if I'm not inside it?'

'Misdirection, mate,' Kit slapped him on the back.

'Hold on. Ren hasn't bargained yet, but I'm betting he will.'

As if the future was Trix's to control, Ren continued speaking.

'You bring up my motives, Rosamund. The only motive that matters is this. The Ice Exiles have money. Lots of it. Their fleet is a defensive masterpiece. The tactical advantages to procuring those ships are immeasurable. But I understand you not being able to comprehend that. Aye, you're a petty thief. You intimidate people into giving you money. To board ships, raid their cargo, kill those who won't join you, that's proper business. That's piracy.

'Damn it, it's more than piracy. It's freedom. If you submit to me as your leader, properly this time, without the backstabbing you're doing now, we'll merge our gangs. The Phantom Wolves. You will control Thyria to the point where you own the planet. I will control the skies. No ship's cargo will be safe from us. With my fleet your business can expand onto every planet in the galaxy. We'll be rich beyond measure, Rosa. This is what I'm offering you. The only alternative is death.'

'You speak like we'll be equals, yet I know you'll be the true ruler of this empire of which you speak. Get into the fucking shuttle, Gerdac. Even if we did rule equally, you killed Vicaull.'

'I also killed Reda. My oldest friend. I loved her dearly. I couldn't see her suffer. I know you loved Vicaull. I did him a favour. Trust me.'

'Into the fucking shuttle now! Gerdac, you fucking piece of shit. Get in there.'

A gunshot. Someone moved Ren's helmet. It was now facing the floor. The mic was covered, reducing noises to a hush. Trix terminated the feed. It was all but useless.

'Move, machinas,' Trix said. She slid down the port service ladder. Kit went down the starboard one. Cole and Kyra got the service elevator moving. Eosar activated the central elevator then legged it for the cockpit.

Ren's terms might not have appealed to Rosamund Galbrand, but they'd obviously appealed to someone.

And that someone had a gun.

Power does not lay in firing a weapon. Power lays in making others fire theirs. Ultimate power, however, makes all weapons lay still.
Cuthbert Theroux

5

Civil wars were part of history and a future certainty.

Statistically, they were inevitable. You couldn't have so many people living in one place until opposing ideologies clashed in displays of terrible force. Such a war was happening in the Dread Phantoms' galleon's hangar.

Trix saw that anarchy had taken the reigns of Ren Gerdac's negotiation. And it was a poor driver. Kit was across the hangar. Red Wolves were going at each other like savages. In the midst of it all, Dread Phantoms were hustling towards the airlock, and the central elevator.

The three Red Wolves who were keeping an eye on it watched as it descended. It was empty. The distraction ended up having no value to Trix, though it did allow a group of Dread Phantoms to rush them from behind. They disarmed the Red Wolves, shooting them at point-blanc.

Cole and Kyra stopped the freight elevator near the ceiling. Jumped off. There was only one problem. They weren't sure who they were supposed to be fighting.

Ren was duking it out with Rosa. He'd disarmed her. They fought hand-to-hand. Ren Gerdac was half zirean. He was naturally faster than regular humans. Had he been a djurel, the fight would've ended already. Ren punched Rosa so hard in the face her bun loosened. She retaliated with a reverse hammer-strike to Ren's neck. He evaded. Rosa dropped into a shoulder charge. Caught Ren in the chest. Trix couldn't get a clear shot.

Then Red Wolves behind cargo crates opened fire on Trix.

They'd signed their death certificates, but they were still alive. Trix smiled. It was the crooked one born from sudden adrenaline and visualisation of death. The one Yvach called crazy.

Trix altered gravity around one of the Red Wolves. Sent him falling towards her. The Valkyrie's sword was in her right hand. Her pistol was in her left. She emerged from behind cover in a pirouette that cut the falling Wolf from shoulder to hip. His corpse split around Trix as her shields stopped Red Wolf plasma.

From the corner of her eye, she saw Ren kick Rosa off him. He went for a jab. It was a feint. Looked like drunken boxing. A knife shot into Ren's waiting palm from his left gauntlet. He grabbed it in reverse grip. Rosa dodged right. Blood streamed from her broken nose.

Cole and Kyra were coming up from Trix's left, working in perfect tandem. They coordinated their barriers so they were never without protection. This wouldn't have been possible in a larger fight. But in a skirmish like this one, easy.

From what Trix could see through the cargo shelves, Kit was helping Dread Phantoms through the airlock. Telling them to return to the bridge while covering their escape. Trix's shields burst. She used the movement from her pirouette to half turn behind another shelf. It wasn't going to last long under fire from eight Red Wolves. And making them all fall towards her would drain a lot of energy.

But magic wouldn't be necessary. It was just a matter of gravity.

'Griff, this is Trix of Zilvia.'

'I'm reading you clearer than Xardiassant's skies. You want me to flush the hangar?'

'No. Roll the ship 75 degrees portside. Now.'

'Hysi, ma'am.'

Griff's voice came over the intercom. His mishmash zirean/South African accent bubbling with mirth was jarring against the anarchic fray.

'Attention all passengers, this is Former Captain Griff of the C.A.F. and pilot extraordinaire speaking but you can call me Daddy Blue. Hold on because we're going for a ride that inertial dampeners won't soften. As always, Go, Go, Goshawks.'

'What the hell is that fool doing?' Cole said. He shoulder charged a Wolf. Sent him airborne. Kyra grabbed the wolf's legs. Used him as a club.

'He's rolling the ship portside,' Trix said over comms. 'Get ready.'

Griff began his manoeuvre with its realignment thrusters.

He could've done it without looking. His unsanctioned modifications to Consortium Air Force vehicles had largely involved thruster enhancements. A ship that Griff had modified — with him at the helm — could dance across space in ways most people never thought possible.

The Red Wolves attacking Trix started sliding. They'd stopped to reload their weapons. Now they were trying to grab hold of shelves so they weren't sent crashing into the portside hull. It was a decent fall. It'd probably break their legs if they didn't roll out of it right.

Trix sheathed her sword. Gripped the shelf. Like everything else in the hangar, it was bolted down. No risk of falling.

'Griff, I changed my mind. Give us 90 degree roll.'

'Lady, I like you.'

Griff kept rolling. The nearly impossible slope became a vertical drop. All the Dread Phantoms were piling into the elevator. Only Red Wolves and machinas were left in the hangar. Trix saw Ren and Rosa slam into a cargo shelf to her three o'clock. Ren was on top. Still wielding his knife. Rosa was struggling to stop it from carving her face.

'Kit, make sure Ren survives,' Trix said. 'I have to take care of something.'

Trix emerged from behind cover. Fired at the shelving unit the Red Wolves were holding. It broke. The eight Wolves fell towards the hangar's new floor. Trix propelled herself across the gap to meet them. Drew her sword mid-air.

'Griff, pitch down 60 degrees.'

Griff performed the manoeuvre instead of replying. Now Trix was falling into the Red Wolves. Her new direction and increased momentum enabled her to slice through the Wolves as she fell. They stood no chance. Trix was soaked in blood once they were all dead.

'Alright, Griff. Straighten up.'

The hangar shifted again. Trix flipped. Landed on her feet. Bodies that'd been cleaved in two hit the floor with squelching noises like boots in mud. Cole and Kyra joined her.

'I've gotta get me one of those,' Cole said, looking at Trix's sword. It ran with blood. Trix gave it a few twirls. The blood came off. The blade sang. The hangar was silent except for Rosa. Trix, Cole, and Kyra walked around the shelves to see Kit holding Rosa by the throat. Up against the airlock.

She had a gash running across her nose. Her hair was plastered to her face with sweat. Ren was hunched over on Kit's right. His cheek had been split open. One of his eyes was pure red. Rosa must've tried gouging it. Ren still held his dagger.

There were three Red Wolves looking chuffed with themselves to Kit's left. One woman. Two men. All three human. Trix sheathed her sword. Went to see what was happening.

Ren straightened up. A spasm made him groan low and long. Blood ran from his eye socket when he blinked.

'You should've taken my offer, Rosa.'

'You killed Vicaull, you killed him. You killed my Vicaull! And you,' Rosa craned her neck as much as she could to face the Red Wolves who'd betrayed her. 'You really think that Gerdac will keep his word. He'll kill you like he killed Vicaull.'

One of the men shrugged. 'Of course, the other possibility is that he won't, and now I'll be incredibly rich. He said he killed Vicaull out of mercy. I believe him. I won't let you condemn the rest of us to die for your ire. Danser sur un volcan est le seule moyen de vivre.'

The man was from Earth. France. Trix wasn't familiar with French, but Sif translated his last sentence. He'd said: *To dance on a volcano is the only way to live.*

'They won't follow you, Reno. They never will.'

'Never is God's favourite joke.'

'What'd you want me to do with her, mate?' Kit said, still holding Rosa. To her credit, she didn't stop trying to escape the oni's grasp.

Ren looked at the havoc behind him. He identified seven more Dread Phantoms that'd been caught in the crossfire. 'Too many of my crew have died to let your death be an easy one, Rosa,' Ren grabbed Rosa's comms gauntlet. Removed it. 'Kit, take her to the shuttle. Box her in.'

Kit hesitated. What Ren was about to do was cruel. Perhaps it was justified by Rosa's actions. He didn't know. Either way, Kit was being paid, so he did as instructed. He'd killed countless people of every race and he still slept fine.

Some nights, after meaningless sexual conquests, Kit wondered if he should feel bad. Thinking about it made him numb. He couldn't imagine having a "normal" job. This was normal to him. Although, the current situation was certainly an outlier.

The oni put Rosamund Galbrand into the shuttle's pilot's seat and strapped her in so she couldn't move. He closed the door on his way out. Her screams could be heard through the glass, but only by the machinas.

'I owe you my thanks,' Ren said to Reno. He put his dagger back in its concealed compartment. Handed Rosa's comms gauntlet to the woman. Shook Reno's hand. 'My crew and I would be dead without you.'

'I did it for the money,' Reno said. 'But I also believe you were telling the truth. You may not be a better leader than Vicaull, though I think you shall be better than Rosamund. Neither of them, however, had any vision. You strike me as a man with vision, Ren Gerdac. As for your motives, I don't care. A person's private matters are theirs and theirs alone. Forgive me, this is Trinity Marquise,' he said, gesturing to the woman beside him. She looked Spanish, maybe South American. 'And this is Kanoa Ulani.'

Kanoa was tall, though still shorter than the oni machinas. He was an islander. Hawaiian, probably.

'And I'm Luc Reno, commodore.'

'Luc, you're now in command of all Phantom Wolves' Thyrian operations. Once we get comms online, we'll inform the rest of the fleet, and those on Thyria, together. Will they follow you?'

'With us vouching for him,' Trinity said.

'Besides, we're the only ones to see what happened here. We can spin them any story we want,' said Kanoa.

'Aye, how true,' Ren said, leaning against the airlock door. He needed medical attention. He turned to speak with the machinas.

Trix noticed his eyes widen at the sight of her. She smirked.

Ren: 'I owe you all money, and more than I originally said. That was excellent work. Get me to the med-bay. Then I'll transfer the funds.' Ren cast another look at Rosamund. She was no longer screaming. Just staring straight ahead. It didn't even look like her chest was rising.

The machinas and Phantom Wolves passed through the airlock. Ren unlocked the shuttle from its docking mechanism once they were on the other side. He wiped his bloody palm on the console. The hangar was ready to be opened.

'Griff, send word to the squadron. We're entering low orbit.'

'Re-entering the atmosphere, commodore?'

'No. Just dropping something off.'

'Hysi, sir. Attention, Dread Phantom squadron, this is Daddy Blue speaking, the galleon's newest pilot. The Commodore has requested a low orbit flyby. Everyone in position.'

Trix: 'Sif, you getting this?'

Sif: 'I'll keep the Fox in formation.'

Griff got the galleon moving. It entered a gradual dive towards Nuallar. Ren kept his hand over the hangar's OPEN button.

'In position.'

Ren didn't wait. Purged the hangar. The shuttle fell into space. It'd be carried by the planet's orbit before crashing into Nuallar's surface. The corpses — Dread Phantom and Red Wolf alike — were sucked into space's vacuum. Ren closed the hangar. He was glad to be rid of Rosamund Galbrand. Not once in all his years of piracy had he experienced losing control of his own ship. It was not an event he wanted to repeat.

Rasping for breath, Ren Gerdac entered the central elevator.

The others followed. Now the mutiny had been handled, he needed his next move. It was elusive, slipping through his fingers like smoke in a gale. A storm brewed in the distance.

Ren Gerdac could not have picked a more interesting time to exact revenge on Dheizir Crohl.

UPGRADES

1

Ren's squadron flew to the edge of Shifting Sanctum space.

Every surviving Dread Phantom needed varying degrees of medical attention. Ren insisted that his crew were tended to before him. His best medics had died during the mutiny, but others made do. Nothing was so bad as to need surgery. Eosar and Griff set to work re-establishing long-range comms for Luc and Ren's transmission.

Hours rolled past one after the other. Trix took a decontamination shower to wash the blood off her armour. Then the machinas raided one of the crew rooms for food and drink. They swapped stories. Talked about old times, and those immediately ahead. The onis wanted to know what'd really happened on Xardiassant with Iglessia Vialle. Trix told them bits and pieces. She wasn't big on embellishing when it came to telling stories. That was Valentine's job. Literally.

Yvach Aodun, on the other hand, he embellished free of charge.

A clean-up of epic proportions was happening around the machinas as they spoke. Corpses were being moved to airlocks. Blood was scrubbed off metal. Trix walked to the cockpit, leaving the onis to reminisce by themselves. She wanted to meet the pilot who'd helped her.

Griffauron Raivad was sitting in the pilot's chair, feet up on the console in front of him. A Phantom Wolf was dragging Moro's body towards the airlock.

'Greetings, Griff.'

'Don't tell me,' Griff covered his eyes. Didn't turn around. 'I know that voice... Trix of Zilvia.'

'Hmm.'

'Hysi, I knew it,' Griff left his seat and gave Trix a flamboyant zirean bow, followed by a zirean salute. One hand behind the lower back. The other, three fingers extended, at an angle against the forehead. 'I was just admiring your ship,' Griff said. Pointed out the cockpit. The Fox still had soot clinging to its hull. It desperately needed a wash. Probably a service as well to check none of the thrusters or weapons had been damaged.

'Fox Transport, isn't it?'

'That's right.'

'Good brand. Reliable. Not as advanced straight out of the box as zirean manufacturers, but you're pretty much guaranteed not to break down. How old's that model now? I'm willing to bet fifty years, maybe more.'

'About that.'

'Panelling looks a little damaged on one of the wings. My guess is friction. Knowing what you do, I'd say going hypersonic within atmosphere. You ever thought about upgrading? Hysi, your weapons are more dated than an escort.'

'They get the job done.'

'So does cryo-stasis and light speed. So does anti-matter fuel. But the point is, those things are old now. Not obsolete, mind you. We could go back to them if Transfers stopped working or cold fusion failed. Considering your line of work, I'd have those weapons upgraded. That's all I'm saying.'

'I'm a huntress, not a mercenary. And I'm not licensed to have a ship with heavier weapons. Acquiring some would be more trouble than extra firepower's worth.'

'If you're gonna help Ren attack the Ice Exiles, then you'll need more firepower. And a reinforced hull. No doubt he'll want you with him after what you've done so far.'

'Upgrades cost a lot of money.'

'Fortunately that's why I talked Ren into giving you more orits than you know what to do with.'

'Really?' Trix raised an eyebrow.

'Yes and no. This is for you,' Ren handed Trix a preloaded orit card with 10,000 orits, double what she'd asked Ren for. 'The rest is for me. Gerdac's a good man. Well, good pirate. Jury's still out on if he's a good man. But that's how it is for all of us, I guess. As much as I'd like to be among the stars with Vitliaeth when I bite the dust, I don't think there's anything after death, though I reckon you do get a reward.'

'What's that?' Trix folded her arms. Whereas Cole saw raving madness in the zirean's eyes, Trix saw incessant thought, like an AI constantly evaluating variables.

'Before you go wherever it is you go, you get to know if you're a good person.'

'Is that important?'

'Maybe not, but it's interesting.'

'You spend a lot of time thinking about it?'

'No. It'll be answered for me one day if Vitliaeth wills it. Right now, all I have to wonder is if I'm the galaxy's best pilot.'

'And where's the jury at on that one?'

'A resounding yes. Hysi, maybe in every galaxy.'

'Big claim.'

'Life's too short for small ones.'

'Did Ren tell you anything else?'

'He's got a plan forming. The fighting sobered him up. Seeing corpses in your own ship is different to seeing ships explode in the star ocean. I've only been with the Phantoms for a couple of years, but I know this is the most men he's ever lost.'

'How'd he keep the body count so low before?'

'As you know, boarding a ship at pretty much any speed in space is impossible, even when you're the galaxy's best pilot. That's why Ren's boarding parties do their work when the ship they want is docked. They place a device in the ship that tricks the systems to thinking that the inertial dampeners might breakdown. This drops the ship out of hyperspace and eases the thrusters to slowly begin a full diagnostic. And Ren's right there, waiting for them when they stop. Most of the time they never fought. Especially if Ren had more firepower than the other guy.'

'What's Ren's plan?'

'Still subject to change, I fron.'

'What does he mean to do?'

'First, we've gotta find the Exiles. We know they're somewhere in the Sea of Bones, but that's like saying you lost your keys in the ocean. Only the ocean's space. Then when that's all done, he hinted at sending in a small crew to infiltrate Crohl's dreadnought, then boom, bang, thank you, ma'am, all sewn up. And we'll land ourselves a dreadnought.'

'You don't care that this is a personal vendetta?' Trix said. She had a feeling that the small crew would comprise of machinas.

Griff shrugged. 'Maybe when I was just the mechanic. But now I have a chance to fly, hysi, I say bring on the conflict. The more ships the better. I want to dance through the stars, thrusters at maximum, swinging in and out of armadas while weapons pump as fast as they can.'

Griff adjusted his cap. Some of his blue hair flopped onto his face. He swept it back up. Zireans naturally had strange coloured hair. Interspecies breeding seemed to make it more likely. In certain light, zirean hair almost looked like velvet.

'Then there's curiosity. I want to know what Crohl wants with that gramyriapede carcass.'

'His name was Larry.'

'You're full of surprises.'

'Hmm. I'll be seeing you, I expect.'

'Well, hysi, who do you think's gonna be upgrading your ship?'

Ren's plan clicked in Trix's mind. 'He wants to use the Fox against Crohl?'

'I thought that was obvious.'

'Trix,' Ren said over comms. 'I want you and the onis on the top level by the central elevator. Now.'

'I have to go.'

Griff: 'No doubt Ren wants to fill you in on his plan.'

'Who'll pilot the galleon if you're repairing my ship?'

'There're others on board who can fly it. And as long as Ren doesn't plan on entering combat, auto-pilot will get it to the Red Reef.'

'Farewell,' Trix said.

Griff saluted again. Vaulted over his seat. Pulled up a screen detailing smashball. There were hundreds of teams. Griff checked in on the South African Goshawks. The season was beginning soon. He wanted to know the starting line-up and how analysts thought they were tracking.

Trix was sceptical about Griff's prowess behind the yokes. But he seemed to know the theory.

'You're not going to let him fly the Fox, are you?' Sif said.

'He can't be any worse than Yvach.'

'Yvach's not that bad. Don't tell him I said that.'

Trix laughed. It was harshly juxtaposed against the corpse clean-up.

2

Ren Gerdac was waiting in a converted storage space at the galleon's stern.

It served as a secondary war room. Kanoa was standing outside. He smiled at the machinas. Opened the door for them. Ren, Eosar, Luc, and Trinity were talking around a galactic holo-map showing the Sea of Bones. Trix recognised Raursioc instantly.

Ren: 'Here they are, the best guns I've ever hired.'

'You pay good, Gerdac, real good,' Cole said. He'd gotten 10,000 orits as well. They all had.

Luc: 'I talked the Red Wolves around. We were able to access all Red Wolf funds with Rosa's gauntlet. She and Vicaull had been hoarding.'

Kyra: 'How much?'

Luc shook his head. Chuckled. Took the cigarette he was smoking out of his mouth. 'Ma cherie, one must not discuss three things in detail: how much money one has, and how much information one has.'

'Clever.'

Trinity: 'It's a large sum, though not large enough to procure a dreadnought to rival Crohl's. We wouldn't even have enough crew to staff it.'

'I trust you've all come to an agreement,' Trix said. Although she was pleased with her payment, she didn't want any more internal trouble.

Ren gestured to Luc.

'We will work on expanding the protection scheme Vicaull started. He'd been too content for years, sitting in the southern-hemisphere. Not wanting to budge. It made my arse twitch. All the waiting. And being on Thyria didn't help. Doesn't do much for the esprit de corps, mais c'est la vie, non?'

Luc exhaled, creating a thick smoke cloud. Trix noticed that his right hand had bionic fingers. Maybe he used to be a thief? Some gangs punished thieves by breaking fingers. Other just lopped them off and called it a day.

'So, we will be expanding, gathering income, resources, all that. We keep 49% to reinvest in expansion. Ren will get 51% to better the fleet.'

'When're the new uniforms coming in, mate?' Kit said.

It was Ren who spoke this time. 'We'll be the Phantom Wolves privately, but we'll publicly remain two separate gangs. What better way to drive up protection prices than to threaten someone with orbital bombing?'

Eosar: 'We figured it would expedite new Red Wolf clientele as well.'

'And I agreed,' Luc said, extinguishing his cigarette against his armour. 'Once the fleet grows and we've saturated Thyria's market, we'll expand to other planets.'

'Provided you give us men for the attack on Crohl's fleet,' Eosar reminded him.

'Bien sûr.'

Trix: 'Griff said you planned on sending in a fireteam to infiltrate Crohl's dreadnought. And he said you wanted to use my ship.'

Ren curled the tips of his moustache. He was sitting on a stool. Looked like he hadn't slept in three weeks and drunk nothing but whiskey. Rosa had put up an unexpected fight.

'I was merely familiarising myself with the purported best pilot in the galaxy when he remarked upon the robust qualities of Fox Transport ships. He said that they were the easiest to customise. Especially the older models. I asked him if a ship like yours would serve for an infiltration mission. He said Zirean Stealth interceptors would be better for infiltration. But if they're discovered, they're easily destroyed.'

Trix gave Ren a look that told him to hurry up. Paying for Trix's help didn't mean you'd bought her. She still did whatever she damn well pleased.

'As it stands, my fleet can't match Crohl's. That's why we'll serve as a distraction while the Fox boards his dreadnought. If we play it defensive, we should be able to hold out with minimum casualties.'

'And do you plan on investigating what he was doing on Nuallar?' Trix said.

'I came here because I thought they'd be vulnerable. Aye, I admit, I was wrong. And those fucking Vipers didn't help the situation. I don't care what he does with his newest haul. After being pursued, I doubt Dheizir will come out into the open. He hasn't been sighted in years.'

'How do you know he's not already dead?'

'News of death travels. I would've heard. His fleet is the only chance we've got.'

'Griff was telling me how you board ships. Seems like it'd be better to wait for one of his to make port, then hijack it and use its signature to dock with his dreadnought.'

'You don't think we've tried that? We always miss them.'

Kit: 'They'll have to dock sometime if they plan on selling Larry's arse.'

Cole: 'They'd have to dock for supplies anyway, fool. But now that they know heat's on em, they might do all their transactions in space.'

Kyra: 'This doesn't change the fact that we don't know where they're moored. If Crohl's half as smart as you think he is, he's probably moving around the Sea of Bones every day.'

The Valkyrie had an idea. It nearly bowled her over. She held her tongue. Didn't want anyone else to know what she did. Maybe she'd tell Kit, but not right now.

Trix: 'I have a few contacts who might be able to help.'

Ren: 'Who are these contacts?'

'Mine, not yours.'

'I see. Well, you speak to them and let me know if you find anything. I have spies of my own.'

Luc: 'And I just inherited quite a few. I'll put them on the trail. All Vicaull ever used them for was checking that his clients weren't trying to skip town. A waste of resources. Le feu.'

'Aye, then it seems like we've discussed all that needs discussing. The Ice Exiles are growing stronger all the time. The sooner we can attack them, the better. Huntress, Griff will take your ship and bring it up to his standards of unsanctioned excellence, as I believe he told me. I made sure he has more than enough capital to do so.'

'This Griff,' Kit said. 'He doesn't happen to have blue hair, an unhealthy smashball obsession, and a twinkle in his eye that looks like explosions glinting off a knife's edge, does he?'

'Well, he has blue hair,' Cole said.

'Oh mate, I thought his voice sounded familiar but I was too distracted smacking down Red Wolves to notice for sure.'

Trix: 'I'll be going with Griff to a mechanic of my choosing. And since the Ice Exile fleet saw the Fox, Kit will come with me should they decide to go hunting.'

Ren: 'Have it your way. But the moment Griff has finished his upgrades, I want you back with the fleet. I've already done you a great favour by choosing your ship to infiltrate the dreadnought.'

'It wasn't a favour. You knew that I wouldn't be leading any mission unless it was in my ship.'

Ren ignored her insubordination. He was too tired to argue. 'Cole, Kyra, you'll stay with me. I'm not anticipating an attack, but I want you by my side as bodyguards. Rosa didn't leave me in a condition to do much.'

Cole: 'You keep paying me like you been paying me, Gerdac, and I'll stick around.'

Kyra: 'Me too.'

'Huntress, Kit, you two can leave. We'll be going to Thyria when you're gone so Luc and Trinity can begin rebuilding Vicaull's former empire.'

'Farewell,' Trix said to the mercenaries. Turned to Cole and Kyra. 'See you soon.'

Cole offered his hand. Trix shook it. 'Been good catching up, Trix.'

Trix went to shake Kyra's hand, but she knew Kyra wouldn't have a bar of it. Kyra moved in for a hug.

'I feel sorry for you. Having to spend so much time with Kit,' Kyra said.

'I'm right here. Come on now,' Kit laughed. He and Cole engaged in a bro-hug, slapping each other hard on the back. 'See you later, mate. Might want to start hitting the gym again. You're looking a bit small.'

'Whatever helps you sleep at night, fool.'

'You get used to him,' Trix said to Kyra.

With their goodbyes said, Trix and Kit left the secondary war room. Kanoa farewelled them as they walked back to the central elevator.

'So, you have a mechanic in mind?' Kit said.

'The one you talked about earlier seems like a good choice. And there's less chance of us being tracked to Earth. Can they do illegal weapon modifications?'

'It offends me, Beatrix, that you think I'd even suggest a mechanic if they didn't. All the best ones do. Griff worked there for a while.' Kit counted backwards in his mind. 'About five years ago. He had an operation going on Xardiassant before that, but the authorities cracked onto him. Then he moved to South Africa. Came close to being busted again. Finally settled in Australia.'

'Did you ever see him fly?'

'Nope. I do remember how he tried getting me to replace my ship's alignment thrusters with his custom designs. I also remember thinking he was more bananas than a plantation. But there's no denying it, that man's seen a few mango seasons.'

'I think I might've lied to Kyra.'

'How's that?'

'I don't think anyone ever gets used to you.'

'A bona fide, Beatrix Westwood Truth Bullet, ladies and gentlemen. Bypasses shields, barriers, and decency. Straight for the heart.'

'You're a walking melodrama.'

'As opposed to all those sitting melodramas.'

'Keep this up and I'll make sure you can only sit in your fondest memories.'

'Now who's being melodramatic?'

Trix and Kit entered the central elevator. Griff was standing in front of them when they came out. He had a backpack that was bulging with goods. The zip was struggling to hold it all in. The Red Wolf machine gun Cole had given him was slung across his chest. The pistol was on a Kevlar mag-panel.

'Eloa, Kit. Good to see you again. Though last time I recall you didn't have very nice things to say about my thruster designs.'

'That doesn't sound like me.'

'Well you were right. They weren't ready back then. They are now. Where're we going?'

'Where else? Desert Star Engines.'

Griff's enthusiastic face faltered for a second. 'Hysi, let's go.'

'Do these guys have junkers lying around?' Trix said. She'd noticed Griff's slight change in mood. Something told her he would've preferred to go elsewhere. But since he'd worked at Desert Star Engines before, Trix thought there was a better chance of him being able to do his own work. She didn't want any more complications.

'Sure. Why?' said Kit.

'Just wondering,' Trix said. That was a lie. Part of her plan involved leaving Earth the day after she arrived. She wanted an audience with Dheizir Crohl. And she reckoned she knew how to get one.

The Valkyrie went to the starboard airlock. Sif moved the Fox into position. The Dread Phantoms who were disposing of corpses were grateful for the reprieve. It was heavy work in every sense of the word.

When Trix boarded the Fox, she laid down ground rules for Griff.

'You can sleep in there,' she said, pointing to her crew's quarters which comprised of two bunk beds and a small bathroom. 'Top floor is my quarters, bottom is the engine bay. That door's the armoury. You can clean your guns in there. Help yourself to the food in the fridge, but go easy on the beer.'

'I call top,' Griff said, running into the crew's quarters.

'Was he like this before?'

Kit scratched his chin. 'Maybe a bit less.'

'Great. I'm taking a shower. We've got a long way to Earth.'

Uldarian Transfers were typically thirty light minutes from the nearest habitable planet. About 400 million kilometres. However, the Solar System's Transfer was just past Neptune, roughly 4.3 billion kilometres from Earth. That was four hours and nineteen minutes of lightspeed travel time.

It'd actually been worse. Once the Transfer had previously been locked into Eris' orbit. Eris was an uninhabited dwarf planet which only fully orbited the sun every 569 Earth years. This made the time to Earth a staggering 21 hours at its longest point.

This became problematic for travelling to and from Earth, especially in space travel's early days when anti-matter fuel had been used. When cold fusion became available, so too did near infinite power. However, although the core didn't run hot, the thrusters most certainly did. And burning them at light speed for 21 hours straight was not advisable. In fact, any time over five hours was deemed risky. Every five hours, thrusters had to be given time to cool, and had to be checked for repairs.

As the Transfer's orbit overlapped with Neptune's, Earth's top astrophysicists devised a plan to push the Transfer into Neptune's orbit around the Sun. Thrusters were retrofitted to the Transfer and remotely activated. It seemed like the Transfer'd had a way of counteracting the thrust, though it'd eventually budged.

Still, four hours to Earth was the longest time to reach any of the galaxy's capital planets. With that in mind, Trix had Sif start moving the Fox towards the Shifting Sanctum's Transfer.

Kit made a move to follow Trix to her quarters. She turned around.

'What're you doing?'

'Having a shower.'

'Your shower's in the crew's quarters.'

'Along with my bed. Got it.'

While Griff was setting himself up on the top bunk, Kit went to the armoury. He put his chest piece into Trix's auto-repair locker. A diagnostic scan said the damage was minimal. Estimated time of completion, 20 minutes. Kit took his shotgun apart. Cleaned it. Oiled his knives.

Upstairs, Trix stripped to her underwear. She was about to get in the shower when she saw Sif had printed a bound copy of Garth Roche's ramblings. It was thick. Sif's hologram appeared on her terminal.

'I analysed what I could and added all relevant annotations as well as trying to separate overly crowded pages. The originals all appear in an appendix at the back of the book.'

'Thanks, Sif.'

'There's also a digital copy on your comms gauntlet. And in the ship.'

'Alright. I need you to contact some people for me. You can't let Griff or Kit know.'

'Who first?'

'Noctius Saberil.'

Sif sighed. 'I don't even want to know what you're planning.'

'Tell Noctius that the whale coos at noon whereas the wolf howls at midnight.'

'Okay, that's ready to send. What else?'

'Tell Andy Tozier that I want him and Aetta trawling the Bastion's database for the galaxy's most wanted criminals and their last known whereabouts.'

'Anything else?'

'No. I'll call Yvach myself once I get out of the shower.'

Trix washed and dried herself in five minutes. Dressed in the casual sweats she'd worn after leaving Mair Ultima. Once she performed her usual equipment maintenance, she retired to her quarters, but she didn't sleep.

Kit and Griff played Faet, the zirean strategy card game in the living room. Players took control of two opposing factions — namely real armies — each with different abilities to amass a greater force than their opponent over three rounds. Griff had a sizable card collection at his disposal. You could buy digital versions, but true Faet enthusiasts always preferred real cards.

Originally, Faet had been the buying and selling of military commanders' portraits on Xardiassant. Prices were attributed to the success of the painting's subject, and the art's quality. These portraits gradually inspired playing card sized versions. Over centuries — and galactic influence — Faet (which effectively meant *battle* in Earthen) developed into what zireans believed was the ultimate strategy game.

They felt chess was lacking because there was no luck element. Armies never started on equal terms in real life. Hence the use of cards with different abilities.

Kit and Griff shuffled their decks.

In her quarters, Trix called Yvach Aodun.

3

Yvach's purple face and bushy moustache filled most of the screen.

From what Trix could see of the room behind him, he was

on Raursioc. Specifically, in his Crescent Crown Mountains' abode.

'Greetings, Yvach.'

'Machina, I feel like it hasn't been that long.'

'That's because it hasn't. A few days, I think. How's being back on Raursioc?'

'Better than I thought it would be. But I suppose that's because it's home. I'm familiarising myself with everything again before I start trying to climb the ladder of command. I expect you're calling me because you've got yourself a situation.'

'We both thought it would be the other way around.'

'Jata. I thought I'd find myself in the shitter almost as soon as I stepped onto the planet. Maybe some of your luck rubbed off on me, huh, machina?'

'You'll need more than a few days without incident to prove that theory.'

'Jata, jata. How can I help?'

'I'm surprised you're home.'

'I have a, ah, lady friend coming over.'

'That explains it.'

'What?'

'Why you don't look filthy.'

'That comes later, machina,' Yvach winked.

'I need to pick your brain before all the blood goes from your head.'

'Those are slim pickings.'

'Quality, not quantity, old friend.'

'Jata.'

'What can you tell me about the Ghirsioc Raithexils?'

Yvach's face contorted. His moustache wriggled as if it were alive. The scarification on Yvach's forehead — meant to be symbolic of a crown — sunk as his brow furrowed. 'What're you playing at now, Trix? Monsters not paying the bills?'

As it turns out, the last one paid me nothing but cost me half my right ear and my temporary sanity, Trix thought. Yvach didn't need to know that. It would only worry him the way all close friends worried.

'A favour for Kit.'

Yvach's face became a giant grin. His chompers were wide like marble bricks. 'You two again, huh?'

'Not like that.'

'I know better than to get into your personal affairs. Don't worry.'

Yvach leaned back in his chair. His fur-lined shirt was open enough to see his muscular chest. Scarification continued down his torso.

'Look, the Ice Exiles are becoming an increasingly bigger thorn in our government's side. They've got followers, you see. They lobby to try and make our government exorcise corrachs from the Consortium. They call for higher taxes on galactic goods that aren't corrachian made. Of course, these people are just followers. They're not part of the gang. In fact, actual gang members never show themselves, what with being exiled. And a lot of the lobbyists find themselves exiled before too long. Usually they try and get the Ice Exiles to recruit them. If not,' Yvach shrugged and scratched his neck, 'they lead pretty shit lives.'

Trix nodded. She'd met an exiled corrach on Desraxe. He was a miserable sack.

'Bunch of tarclabers. It disgusts me that Crohl was a Mountain King, but I suppose all clans have their fair share of disgraces,' Yvach shook his head. 'Thing is, not all clans think the Ice Exiles are totally in the wrong. They're starting to support them. Not publicly, mind you. But, there's a divide growing on Raursioc, Trix. I can feel it. There are those who want war with everyone, to terrorise the galaxy until corrachs reign supreme. I'd be lying if I said I wasn't concerned. Hate spreads like fire on a dry day. For now they can't do anything but wave their dicks around. But I reckon there'll come a time when the government is run by them.'

'Looks like you've picked a perfect time to enter politics.'

'Don't remind me.'

'What can you tell me about their location?'

'That we don't know about it. All we do know is that they're somewhere in the Sea of Bones. Searching space is a little harder than looking for spare ammunition behind the couch.'

'Agreed. Would Vidal Laigalt know their whereabouts?'

'I could try and patch you through, but you know as well as I do that Consortium Reps, no matter how friendly you are with them, don't come running whenever you want. Maybe if we could contact them directly. When you have to go through secretaries, forget it. I also don't know if us contacting him would be a good idea. Been less than a week since we were acquitted from a thousand criminal charges. And he's on the record saying he would've acquitted us. I dunno, it would seem off if I was looking at it from the outside.'

'Let me know if you hear anything.'

'You'll be the first. I'll try and contact Vidal some other way. Don't hold your breath. If he knew anything about the Ice Exiles' location, our military would've been informed. I've still got friends in the armed forces. I'll try going through them.'

Yvach looked at Trix. Stared deep into her machina eyes. Her golden irises crackled like a lightning storm. Even from billions upon billions of kilometres away, Yvach could sense what Trix was up to.

'You already know something about the Ice Exiles, don't you?'

'You're becoming more observant in your old age.'

'Old age. Don't you be talking to me about old age, machina. You might prove to live older than all of us yet.'

'I know what the Ice Exiles are peddling.'

Realisation dawned over the scarred landscape that was Yvach Aodun's face.

'Sweet, sweet Raursioc. Careful, machina.'

'That word means nothing coming from someone as reckless as you.'

'Oh, I know. But as your friend I feel obliged to say so. Not even Nadira Vega deals in live goods.'

'That's because she has a rule. Never work with children or animals.'

'And isn't the ambiguity of Nadira working with either cause for nightmares?'

'My nightmares are at capacity.'

'The sign of a life hard lived.'

'I better let you prepare for your *friend.*'

'Machina, you know I'd tell anyone to hold the fuck up if you needed help. Anything else you want to ask?'

'The Ice Exiles' whereabouts should be enough.'

'I'll keep your name out of it. It'll be better that way. Do you need me to suit up, come and join you? I'll be there in a Raursioc minute if you want. Can't let you and that oni bastard get all the glory.'

A Raursioc minute was the same length of time as any other minute, but because Raursioc's years were shorter than Earth's, it was something Yvach liked to joke about.

'Thanks for the offer, my friend. I'll let you know. Farewell.'

Yvach picked up a whiskey bottle from out of frame. Took a swig. 'Always, machina. For glorious honour.'

Yvach smiled then signed off.

His new information about the Ice Exiles was food for thought. They were trying to radicalise Raursioc's population. Yvach said there were no actual gang members on the planet, but how could he know? Corrachs who hadn't yet been exiled could be actively working for the Ghirsioc Raithexils' agenda.

Strange information fragments came to Trix's mind. The attack during a Formula X race. The gramyriapede. Radical corrachs. Trix couldn't make sense of it. Checked her terminal.

The Fox was in the Solar System now, hurtling towards Earth at 300,000 metres a second.

4

The Fox reached Earth four hours, nineteen minutes, and eighteen seconds after entering the Solar System.

The United Nations Space Station sat in Earth's orbit. Constant experiments were conducted on its many decks. Orbital defence cannons waited for trouble, like cannons on the walls of forts back when pirates sailed the seas.

Trix took off her casual clothes. Put her armour back on. She activated all the security possible in her quarters as well as the armoury. She wouldn't be hanging around once the Fox was in Desert Star Engines. She was going to find a ship and head for Hariyfir, where Noctius Saberil would be waiting. She'd received his transmission an hour before arriving at Earth.

Tell me, little fish, what is your plight?

But would Noctius be able to help?

Trix had flipped through Garth Roche's compiled notes before falling asleep on the journey to Earth. Ragnarök, the Ancient Norse doomsday, was mentioned above all else. Notes of wolves eating suns, a serpent filling the skies, and a giant with a flaming sword abounded. It was Odin's Valkyries who would gather worthy warriors to Valhalla, then they'd fight for all existence. Trix's short sleep was rich with dreams about gods, monsters, and, at some points, a lonesome fisherman.

Griff was making himself coffee when Trix awoke and entered the main living quarters. Kit was on the sofa. Looked like he was listening to music. He sensed Trix looking at him. Opened his eyes.

'What do you think's gonna happen down there?' Kit said.

'You never know.'

Kit rolled his massive shoulders, trying to get comfortable in his armour. 'Shame Desert Star Engines doesn't sell clothes. I could go for some jeans and a t-shirt.'

Griff, whose armour was considerably lighter, more segmented, finished making his coffee. 'Well, we do have a ship. We can go somewhere that does sell clothes.'

'I'd rather not mess with the schedule. Sounds like you have a lot of work to do in a week.'

'Hysi, this baby is gonna be unrecognisable when I'm done with her. Don't worry, I'll leave the interior as it is. But I could probably spruce it up if I have some time.'

Sif: 'It's early morning in Queensland, Australia. March 3rd, 2799.'

Kit moved to the cockpit. 'You beauty,' he said, looking at his adopted homeland. 'The shop'll be closed. But Cid lives next door and he'll open it for us.'

Trix saw Griff nearly choke on his coffee at the mention of Cid's name.

'There a problem, Griff?'

'Hotter than I thought. Hysi, I'm fine, captain.'

Trix nodded. 'Take us down, Sif.'

The Fox descended in a pre-ordained flight pattern. Earth had so many ships coming and going that there had to be a system or the skies would be chaos. Powerful scanners checked incoming ships for their registration. This was to flag any fugitives and people on Earth's Governing Council's watchlist. If there was a match, the ship would be hailed to dock at the UNSS and be subjected to searches.

These scanners could be fooled if you were a competent hacker. What the UNSS didn't like telling people was that their systems were fooled more often than they liked. And it was virtually impossible to scan every incoming ship.

It was important to note that the UNSS was the headquarters for United Nations Space Command. They handled military and science endeavours for Earth's Governing Council (EGC) who were responsible for interplanetary relations.

The vertical stabilisers engaged as the Fox entered Earth's atmosphere. Sif punched it beyond supersonic. They arrived at Desert Star Engines within minutes.

Most of Australia's deserts were full of manufacturing. People didn't like to live in them since it was so damn hot. However, hectares of land were lush thanks to terraforming experiments near the ICBA (International Centre for Botany and Agriculture). There were also factories as far as the eye could see. Thanks to cold fusion, they didn't produce smog associated with fossil fuels.

Sif landed the Fox outside Desert Star Engines' hangar in far west Queensland. Its logo was the sun directly over the Glass House Mountains. Off to the side of the main hangar — which was five smashball fields in length and half a field high — was a simple home. Corrugated iron roof. Crème, wooden panelling that'd been turned red by dust. There was a manmade pond out the back. Grass grew within the fence perimeter. The house itself was three stories. Trix guessed more than one person lived inside.

Kit walked towards Cid's house. It was coming off summer in Australia, though it was a bit cooler in the morning. Griff walked behind Trix. The zirean was on edge. She could smell it.

Kit rapped on the door three times fast.

'Hey, Cid, you lazy arse, get out here.'

No response, but the machinas heard someone moving inside. Trix turned her pupils to slits, activating her x-ray vision. The walls were too thick. She wasn't getting through.

'Come on, Cid, I know you're up there playing with yourself, mate.'

The door swung open. A bald man with a handlebar moustache so tough it could've flexed stood in the doorway. A shotgun was in his hand. He was wearing a sweat stained singlet and boxer shorts. They were the colours of the Australian smashball team, the Smasheroos. Green and gold.

Griff stood behind Trix.

'G'day, mate,' Kit said.

'Kit, fuck you for waking me up, you bloody dingo,' said the man.

'Nice to see you too, Cid.'

'Yeah, yeah. What is it this time? You need the thrusters replaced on your ship? A hot tub in your quarters? A fucking sense of decency?'

'Mate, I don't need any of those things. My ship got stolen.'

'I'm not a dealership, son.'

Trix was hit by the oddest feeling of déjà vu. Seeing Cid go off was like seeing Cortland Caine lose his temper. They even had the same, tan leather skin.

'I know, Cid. Jesus, you'd swear I just stopped you from scoring with a supermodel.'

'How'd you know what I was dreaming about?'

'This is my friend, Trix,' Kit said. 'Her ship's the one that needs fixing. And cleaning. And some serious upgrading.' Despite being in the middle of the Outback, Kit dropped his voice to a whisper. 'And not strictly speaking the legal kind, aye?'

This made Cid's moustache smile.

'Oh, I'm picking up what you're putting down, alright, son. Thing is, me and the lads are swamped at the moment. Got tons of work. The hangar's fuller than a fat girl's undies.'

'Thankfully, I brought my own mechanic,' Kit gestured to where he thought Griff was standing. He wasn't there. Trix stepped aside. Griff was acting like he had no idea what was happening. Looking out over the desert.

'Griff,' Trix nudged him on the back.

'You,' Cid tossed his shotgun down and ran at Griff like bulls ran at matadors. Griff vaulted the porch fence with surprising agility. Cid leaped over it. Hit the zirean in the back. They crashed into the dirt with an insubstantial poof.

Cid flipped Griff over. Grabbed him around the neck.

'You son of a bitch. You and your goddamned modifications. You blew up my ship.'

Kit walked to Cid. Pulled him off Griff with one arm.

'Easy, fellas. Sure there's a way to resolve this.'

'You're right. And it's by the door. Don't go anywhere, Bluey. Wouldn't want you to get out of range,' said Cid.

'Time to go?' Griff said. He turned to run back to the Fox.

Trix thought about giving him a warning shot. She altered gravity around Griff and sent him falling back to the porch instead. He landed on the wooden beams with a thud. Cid picked up his shotgun. Trix disarmed him with gravity magic. Then she dismantled it as easy as a child breaking apart building blocks.

'Great, so first he blows up my ship, now you've taken apart my shotgun. Pick better friends, Kit.'

'We can sort this out, mate.'

'Griff, you told me you only blew up one ship in the C.A.F.,' Trix said.

'Hysi. When I blew up Cid's I wasn't in the C.A.F. I'd already been discharged.'

'But you said you've worked out the kinks.'

'I have now.'

'Alright. Cid, let us in the hangar.'

'I've only just met you. You think I'm gonna let you into *my* shop and let that nutcase use *my* equipment?'

Kit: 'We'll pay you well for your trouble, of course. Come on, Cid. For old time's sake, aye? Besides, you know we won't be using any of your hangar space. We'll need to work in the Bunker.'

'For illegal weapon upgrades, I know you would. That is, if I had any illegal weapon upgrades, which I don't. But, if I had such things, I'd tell you they're damn expensive, and that you never got them from me. Understand?'

'Bloody oath.'

Cid gave Griff another look. Then back to Kit.

'You'll keep an eye on him? Make sure he doesn't do anything stupid?'

Kit being responsible, Trix thought. This guy's a regular comedian.

Kit: 'You know it. No flies on me.'

Cid was silent for close to a minute. The sun was rising. He looked at each of the trio. Trix. Griff. Kit.

'Alright, fine. But one more condition.'

'Anything,' Kit nodded.

Cid was a skinny-fat sort of bloke. Bit of a beer belly. But he moved fast. Cid unleashed a right jab into Griff's nose. Caused the zirean to stumble backwards. His nose hadn't been broken. Only dislocated. He popped it back in place. Zireans had marginally denser bone structure than humans.

Cid: 'We're still not square, but I feel better.'

Kit: 'So you'll take us in?'

'Fuck no. I'm going back to bed. I'll get Jo'ara. Wait here.'

'Cheers, Cid.'

'Yeah, whatever. Thank me by not blowing anything up.'

Cid didn't bother closing the door as he walked down the hallway to a staircase. A djurel-human half-breed descended five minutes later.

Djurels and Humans had a harder time crossbreeding than other species. But it was possible. Jo'ara had mostly human features. However, instead of human ears, she had feline ears protruding from the top of her head. Her nails were closer to claws. Her face possessed stripe patterns on the cheeks, though they weren't furry. The other telling sign — besides cat eyes — was a feline tail which poked through a hole in her cargo pants.

Djurels and kalariks were the only humanoid species born with tails. Although they could move them, they couldn't use them acrobatically like monkeys. That being said, when a djurel crossbred successfully with a human, the human's simian ancestry kicked in, allowing them full use of their tail to climb and pick things up.

'G'day, Jo,' Kit said.

Jo slapped him in the face. Kit moved with the blow so she didn't break her hand.

'That's from Cid, for waking him up.'

'Well—'

Jo slapped him again.

'That was from me.'

Kit rubbed his cheek.

'Yeah, alright. That seems fair enough then.'

Jo smiled. Extended a hand to Trix. 'Jo'ara Zahaan, but everyone calls me Jo.'

'Trix of Zilvia.'

Jo nodded. Then she saw Griff.

'Hello, Griff.'

'Eloa, Jo.'

'Didn't blow up enough last time, huh?'

'I've got the balance right, I swear it.'

'I'll believe it when I see it. Though according to our official logs, you were never here.'

Jo tapped her sleek, civilian comms gauntlet. The hangar doors rolled opened with nary a sound.

'Let's get you set up,' Jo said.

5

Sif flew the Fox remotely as the trio and Jo entered the hangar.

Ships from civilian, to transport, to military were docked along the hangar walls. Some were just shuttles, like the troop carriers Ren had used on Nuallar. The biggest they got were galleons. Any larger ship was typically fixed in space.

Jo took the trio to an empty dock. Sif landed the Fox. Jo approached the dock's console. Entered a string of commands. Placed her palm on the screen.

The Fox's platform started descending into the ground. Jo motioned for everyone to hop on. They did.

Once everyone was on board, Jo tapped her comms gauntlet to make the lift move faster. Headed to the Bunker.

Griff was giving Jo a list of everything he needed for the upgrades while this happened. Everything from panelling to thrusters was listed. It never seemed to end. Finally, he came to the weapons.

Griff: 'You got the Riven Co. Strife Railgun?'

Jo: 'Yes. Are we supposed to have it? No.'

'If you wanted illegal parts, how would you get them without raising suspicion?' Trix said.

'We'd have them dismantled off-world, have the pieces shipped to us at different times, then reassemble them here.'

Trix smirked. The Strife Railgun that Griff had asked about was one of Riven's older designs. Though by all accounts, it still carved a ship's hull like Trix's sword severed limbs.

The lift reached the Bunker. It was pitch black. Jo — whose feline eyes allowed her to see in the dark almost as well as Trix — strode off to the side. Trix heard her pull a lever. The ceiling became an illuminated white mass.

'This is more like it,' Kit said.

There was space for ten corvettes. Five on either side of a central hallway that terminated in a vault at each end. Every work station had a cramped living quarters with bunk beds and a basic kitchen behind it.

'Kit, you know how this works. You have to contact me or Cid before exiting the Bunker. You can only do that after we're closed for the day. And everything you take from the vaults is catalogued. You'll be billed accordingly. No labour fees since you're doing it yourself. If you need help, then you'll pay the standard rate. Lastly, if there's so much as one explosion, I don't care how small, you're out, and you're not coming back,' said Jo.

'Sounds like terms we can agree on,' Kit said, shaking Jo's hand.

'Since you two know where everything is, I'll be going. Weapons vault is on the left. Armour vault to the right,' Jo typed a command on the dock console. A door in the floor slid open, revealing a large ramp that led further underground. 'General stores are down here, things like paint, spare tools, the rest.'

'It feels good to be back,' Griff said, looking at the Fox. Though he wasn't really looking at it. He was looking into the future. By the time Griff was done, it was going to be the galaxy's best corvette.

Jo had already used her comms gauntlet to rearrange the vaults so that the pieces Griff requested would be right on the other side of the doors.

When Kit looked at the Fox, all he could see was its future paint job. Sleek black with pearlescent gold trim, subtle, not gaudy. Right near the cockpit he wanted to paint a white, humanoid fox, smoking a cigar. Kind of a vintage pin-up girl cartoon.

As the men relished the work ahead, Trix took Jo aside. Spoke to her privately.

'Is there a ship I can borrow to reach Hariyfir?'

'We've got a few junkers out back, but I wouldn't trust them in space. They're derelict. We've got two company ships. You can take one out on loan for a fee. They're strictly pedestrian though. No weapons.'

'I'll give you a thousand orits for a week.'

'So you're not sticking around?'

'No.'

Jo opened a comms channel to Trix's gauntlet and transferred temporary registration of a civilian cruiser to her. Trix transferred a thousand orits.

'You'll have to wait until tonight to leave. We're going to open soon, and you'll want to leave when there's less chance of Cid seeing you since he won't approve. He's out on a limb letting you use the Bunker as it is, especially with Griff here.'

'Griff says he's the best pilot in the galaxy.'

'He's the most delusional.'

'How come you're letting me rent a company ship if Cid wouldn't allow it?'

'You pay well. And I don't blame you, leaving for a week. Griff's best in small doses. He and Kit always seemed to get along though.'

'Thanks, Jo.'

'You can thank me by bringing the ship back without a scratch. Contact me at 10:30 tonight. I'll take you to it.'

Jo'ara walked into the living quarters behind the Fox's dock. A secret door opened. She entered. Trix figured it was an elevator that went to the hangar's ground floor.

'Hysi, you two,' Griff clapped his hands together. Turned his cap backwards. 'We've got a lot of work to do. First, I'm gonna need...'

Talk about a busy day at work.

The first port of call was washing the Fox's hull. Thankfully that was all automatic. This was to make sure none of the soot layer fell into underlying circuitry when Griff started removing panels. Despite Kit's eagerness, accessories and paintjobs had to be done last.

As the automatic cleaner scrubbed the Fox spotless, Kit and Trix helped Griff gather what he needed. The hull needed to be overhauled before Griff could fit any weapons. The realignment thrusters, and the vertical takeoff thrusters also had to be scrapped. Trix insisted they were fine. Griff laughed.

'They might be fine for realigning the ship and helping it takeoff, but that's not good enough.'

'That's their primary function.'

'Not when I'm done.'

Halfway through helping Griff repanel the Fox, Trix had received a call from Andy Tozier. He and Aetta had done some digging into the Ice Exiles. As much as they could without being discovered anyway.

'Marked Exile ships have been sighted on research planets, specifically targeting bases that deal in biological and genetic enhancements as well as biochemistry. We can't arrest them because everything they're looking into is legal, and we don't have hard evidence about any of their other activities,' Andy had said.

Trix enquired as to the Exile Fleet's whereabouts. Unfortunately, not even Aetta, who was one of the Bastion's top data analysts, had been able to find that. Trix doubted the Exiles were suddenly going to venture into scientific research, though it was plausible. Maybe they were trying to figure out how their existing exotic animals could be enhanced to fetch higher prices.

Trix suspected that this was related to gramyriapedes. After all, the part of Larry's carcass that they'd stolen was where his eggs would've been. Trix decided not to think about it until she rendezvoused with Noctius. He could help her get answers, if not an audience, with the Exiles.

As the day drew to a close, the Fox looked like a skeleton. Bits and pieces were strewn everywhere. Griff had already replaced about half the existing realignment thrusters. He'd also added countless more. Trix and Kit enjoyed beers while they watched Griff tinker. The time was coming up on 10:30pm.

Kit: 'I've been thinking about the Uldarian prism.'

Trix: 'Happen to see anything else?'

'No, just the vision repeating itself. It kept coming to me in dreams on our way here. It has to have something to do with machinas.'

'Yvach thought the same thing. He's all for it. Wants to fight in the war to end all wars.'

'I can't see us joining the military. Don't know if they'd have us. We could do it as independent mercenaries though. The most elite group the galaxy has ever seen.'

'You watch too much television.'

'Think about it. We could have you, obviously, me, Cole, Kyra, Yvach, that spectre you were talking about, Dai. Griff, if he's as good as he says. Who knows, maybe if everything goes well, Ren and Luc can join up too.'

'If there's a war coming, it's a long way off.'

'Exactly. Think about how many more people could be part of the team when it arrives.'

'You've already thought of a name, haven't you?'

'And logos. Want to hear about them?'

'No.'

'Well, the main unit, the best of the best, will be called Strife Squad. Then everyone else will be part of the larger one: Ultima Company. *Then* there're the mottos. For Strife Squad: Semper Victores. Always Victorious. For Ultima Company: Omnia Vincit Ultima. Ultima Conquers All.'

Trix was never big on team names. She wasn't even big on teams. But all Valkyries were trained to be leaders whether they liked it or not. It wasn't in their blood, but leadership had been engraved with a firebrand during training, figuratively speaking.

'Latin mottos?'

'Just like the machina academies.'

The Valkyrie sipped her beer. She had to give Kit credit where credit was due. The names were far more creative than the Oni Three. Thankfully, these ones didn't rhyme.

Trix didn't bother quelling Kit's enthusiasm by reminding him that they probably wouldn't live to see the return of whatever killed the Uldarians. But the Oni Academy motto wasn't Ad Finem — To The End — for nothing. She decided to humour him.

'And the logos?'

'A Valkyrie skull with a sword going through its centre. All in black and gold on a white shield for Strife Squad. Ultima Company's would be similar, only instead of a sword there'd be two crossed pistols beneath the skull.'

'Why a Valkyrie skull?'

'Because you'd be our leader, Beatrix. Don't act so surprised. If I had to follow anyone to certain death, I'd want it to be you. Yvach would feel the same.'

'Any scenario where you're my subordinate is a win in my eyes.'

'Don't flatter yourself now. It's hardwired into every machina that Valkyries are supposed to lead us into battle, and to victory. I've got no choice. Damn military brainwashing,' Kit laughed. Some beer ran down his chin. He wiped it off with the back of his hand.

'You're not brainwashed. You just know I'm smarter than you. There's no shame in that.'

'I have no shame about anything.'

'One of your many flaws,' Trix finished her beer. The time was 10:20pm. 'I have to go.'

'To sleep?'

'Out. I should be back within a week.'

'I'll come with you. Griff's got this. He could stand to do

some heavy lifting anyway.'

'I need to go alone. Besides, Cid won't let Griff stay here unsupervised.'

'Alright,' Kit said. He put his beer down. Stood. 'I'd say if you have any trouble to call us, but depending on where we're at with the ship, it may not be flyable.'

'I'll be fine,' Trix said. She messaged Jo'ara to come escort her. 'Like I said, should be back in a week.'

'Mind telling me what you're doing?'

'Shopping,' Trix smirked. She wasn't even joking.

'Point taken. I'll stay out of it.'

Kit and Trix hugged. Jo'ara buzzed Trix's comms gauntlet. She was ready.

'Griff,' Trix said.

'Hysi, captain.'

'Don't wreck my ship.'

'Never, well, not on purpose.'

'Hmm.'

Trix walked to her dock's crew's quarters. A number six was painted on the door. Jo'ara was waiting in the private elevator. Trix stepped inside. They went to the hangar.

'Won't Cid know that one of his ships is gone?'

'He will, but asking Cid for forgiveness is a lot easier than asking for permission.'

'Didn't seem that way when Griff showed up this morning.'

'Blowing up a ship and borrowing one are two different matters. Just don't blow it up. You saw what he did to Griff,' Jo'ara paused. Looked at Trix. 'Actually, I don't think you've got anything to worry about. You're a Valkyrie. Cid has as much chance of laying a finger on you as getting a hand on the fucking sun.'

The hangar was in almost total darkness. Jo'ara led Trix to the front. Two small ships, not much bigger than shuttles, were beside the hangar door. They were sleek, like tiny fighter jets. Looked like ex-military gear, just stripped of weapons.

'Yours is the one on the left,' Jo'ara said.

'Thanks.'

'You'll be able to open the hangar door once you're inside.'

Jo left out a small door built into the hangar's main ones. She was certainly as silent as a cat. There was a reason djurels made for great thieves and assassins. However, unlike kalariks who emitted next to no scent, djurels had a distinct musk.

Trix went to her ship's stern. Opened the cargo bay. It was tiny. Four cramped seats preceded an airlock. She went on inside.

A hallway only just big enough for two average sized people to stand side-by-side led to the cockpit. Four sleeping pods were built into the walls. The shower lay behind a sliding door. So did the toilet. There was a pantry and a mini fridge. Both were empty.

The Valkyrie entered the cockpit. There was an equipment rack. She put her sword on it. Sat in the pilot's chair. Booted up the ship.

Trix had been flying the Fox for 50 years. She'd never been without it during that time. Sadness crept over her. This ship wasn't the same. The seat didn't feel right. The yokes didn't meld to her palms. Trix realised she was more maudlin than she first thought.

The ship's thrusters activated.

Desert Star Engines' hangar doors slid open wide enough to accommodate the ship. Trix flew out slowly. Coasted away from Cid's house for a while before gunning the engine fast as it would go.

Back towards the stars.

<h2 style="text-align:center">7</h2>

Hariyfir lay in the Azure Zone system.

Trix entered hyperspace once she was out of Earth's atmosphere. Satisfied that the ship's software could take her to the Uldarian Transfer, Trix reclined the pilot's chair. Activated her helmet so it only covered the top half of her face. Brought up the digital version of Garth Roche's notes on her HUD.

Started sifting through them.

Ragnarök was repeatedly mentioned. Roche had an obsession with it. Sif's annotations explained that Ragnarök was supposed to be a battle in which many prominent gods from Norse Mythology would die. It was seen as the end of the world. Fenrir, the great wolf, would eat the suns. Jörmungandr, the Midgard serpent, would slither through the star ocean, his tremendous size enough to wrench planets from orbit. Then Surtr, the giant, would level everything that remained with his flaming sword.

Sounds like a lot of work, Trix thought as she kept reading. Even though Sif had cleaned up Roche's scrawl considerably, his ramblings were dense. Trix persevered. Unfortunately, it didn't look as though Roche's experiments had been documented in his journal. Trix guessed he would've kept them on a computer.

She found herself thinking of the photo she'd found. Garth Roche and Alpha Omega, smiling. The more she thought about it, the more she was convinced that Alpha had stolen Kit's ship. He was going home to daddy. Maybe to kill him, if he was bitter about being left on Mair Ultima by himself.

While Roche's notes were interesting, they verged on conspiracy theory territory. Trix was about to stop reading when she came upon verses of an ancient poem, the *Poetic Edda*. They referred specifically to Ragnarök.

It sates itself on the life-blood
of fated men,
paints red the powers' homes
with crimson gore.
Black become the suns' beams
in the summers that follow,
weathers all treacherous.
Do you still seek to know? And What?

Roche had commented on the poem. In the original, it had referred to *suns'* as *sun's*. Not a big difference if you didn't have a handle on grammar, but an important one. In the time of Norse Mythology, it would've been thought that there was only one sun. Roche had amended the apostrophe. After it, he had scrawled:

SUNS OR TRANSFERS???

SUPERMASSIVE BLACK HOLE 20

Trix couldn't see any connection. Nor did Sif's annotations ever point to Transfers being called suns. Another verse from later in the same poem followed.

Brothers will fight and kill each other;
sisters' children will defile kinship.
It is harsh in the world,
whoredom rife
—an axe age, a sword age
—shields are riven—
a wind age, a wolf age—
before the world goes headlong.
No man will have mercy on another.

Roche had named machinas. He'd also named the academies. It might've only been a coincidence that he named the Valkyrie Academy what he did.

Maybe he already knew, Trix thought, re-reading the poem. Maybe Roche saw something in us beyond white hair. Beyond unique powers.

Trix made other connections, but they were far-fetched. For instance, the line about sisters' children. Hadn't the Valkyries called each other sisters? They thought their white hair was a familial trait, even though they knew they weren't related. Then there was the issue of machinas being infertile.

Another line that struck Trix as funny was the one about shields being riven. Riven Co. specialised in weapons, though they did make shields too. Funny how the world worked. How the worlds worked.

You are the fish, the hare, the bird, the bear...

Mireleth's Poem came to Trix again. She didn't think she

would ever forget it. She typed it into her comms gauntlet and saved it as a footnote in Roche's notes to be sure. Mireleth's Poem pointed to death. The end of all things.

All the worlds hear their echoes.

Scientists of all races had been pointing to alternate dimensions and multi-verses for close to a thousand years. All connected by some shared consciousness. Something that tied them altogether.

Mages thought that the only way to access these worlds was through magical teleportation. That was rich. Spectre machinas were the best at teleporting, and they couldn't go more than a few metres. Many couldn't even teleport others with them. It appeared alternate universes would be forever out of reach since mage portals required too much energy for long-distance travel.

Alternate universes were to what the last line of Mireleth's Poem was referring. Every variation of life, each reality, all of them were going to die.

'The Gravedigger's been here from the start,' Trix whispered.

Ragnarök and Mireleth's Poem were connected somehow. Trix retracted her helmet. She told herself that this was nothing but a madman's delirium. Someone who'd tortured children to feel like a god.

Deep down, Trix knew there was more to it.

Trix let her mind drift until it was free from Mair Ultima's mysteries. Eventually, it returned to her present situation. Knowing that she could only plan her interaction so many times, Trix entered one of the sleep pods. Machinas needed far less sleep than humans to function in peak condition. However, being sleepy and tired were two different things.

Noctius Saberil was one of the criminal underworld's shadiest figures.

And Trix planned on having a drink with him.

ACCORD GONE AWRY

1

Sif roused Trix.

The shuttle was five minutes from the Transfer. Trix put her armour on and climbed into the pilot's seat. Set her course for the Azure Zone. It was roughly 28 minutes to Hariyfir.

'I hope you know what you're doing,' Sif said.

'Hmm.'

'Noctius Saberil isn't like Nadira Vega. You two aren't exactly friends.'

'We're not enemies either.'

'Why can't you just work for Ren Gerdac without seeing what the Ice Exiles have on offer?'

'Because Gerdac's a pirate. And I think he's cleverer than he acts.'

'But he doesn't act the fool.'

'No. If you act the fool, it's only fools you'll deceive. I think he's using Luc Reno's philosophy. He's not showing all his cards. I want to hear the Ice Exiles' side of the story.'

'And what makes you think they'll tell you?'

'It's all a matter of leverage.'

'I know. You don't have any.'

'I have Ren's plan.'

'Ren hasn't given you any direct orders that we have on file. They could think you're bluffing.'

'Perhaps. The Dread Phantoms and the Ice Exiles are no saints. Ren said he was leaving piracy once he took out the Exiles, but his plans with Luc are long term.'

'Are you feeling alright?'

'Why wouldn't I be?'

'You're getting far more involved than usual. This time you don't have to. I know you want to do right by the Oni Three, but that doesn't mean you have to see Noctius.'

Trix said nothing. Sif was right. She hated involvement. But she had a hunch. Had to see it through.

The ship arrived at Hariyfir around 3:00am Australian time. Griff would still be working on the Fox unless he'd fallen asleep.

Hariyfir looked like a stained-glass marble. Its oceans were diverse shades of blue. Its continents were small. Mostly archipelagos. They were lush with tropical greenery, save for the poles. Ice caps like Earth's kept the poles cool year-round.

Yujius was Hariyfir's capital city. It was a submerged metropolis that partially stretched above water. This was so ships could dock on its tower. Then their occupants could take an elevator directly into the city's heart.

Psygotas had evolved from sea dwelling mammals. Eventually they became something that resembled mermaids in Earthen stories, only their entire bodies were mixtures of fish-like scales, and skin comparable to Earthen dolphins. Slowly, their tails turned into split fins, then into legs. From there they journeyed onto land. Psygotas quickly discovered that they couldn't survive outside water for more than thirty minutes, but they couldn't expand their civilisation too much underwater. Building beneath the ocean was difficult with primitive technology.

Trix descended into the atmosphere. Compared to the Fox, her shuttle handled like the Riven Star Cannon she'd driven on Noccril with Yvach and Dai.

She came in on the colossal tower that was close to kissing the stars. Smaller vehicles were only permitted to dock on the upper levels. Larger ships occupied the lower levels.

Trix found a spot and docked the shuttle. Checked she'd left nothing behind then exited out the cargo bay. She didn't know how long she'd be staying. Bought a two-day pass for 250 orits. She would've been paying close to five times that with a larger ship. The Valkyrie stepped into the elevator that'd take her to the city. 459 storeys below.

When the elevator opened into Yujius' grand square, Trix

was hit by familiar humidity. The city's humidity was constantly kept high as the increased water vapour in the air meant psygotas didn't have to wear neck-braces. As a result, Hariyfir cities always felt like a rainforest on a spring morning when the air was cool and dew settled on every surface.

The grand square was populated by eateries, apartments, and retail shops. It was like the 21st century when you came off a plane and there were gift shops everywhere. Tourists in Yujius tended to stick to the grand square.

Trix made a move for the train station. She was going as far away from tourist attractions as she could. It was late afternoon on Hariyfir. The ocean's Twilight Zone held dim light outside Yujius' domed walls. Yujius' lowest city section descended into the Midnight Zone.

Different sections of psygotaic cities were connected by walkways, elevators, and train lines to accommodate for more distant neighbourhoods. The trains were shaped like capsules and shot through tubes with extreme efficiency. If you took Yujius out of the water, it'd look like a giant chemistry set, or the galaxy's most complicated terrarium.

Trix waved her comms gauntlet over the train gate. Twenty orits were deposited. That gave her unlimited train usage for one hour. After that, she'd pay again. Trains in Yujius came every minute. Trix found her appropriate platform. The train arrived. She stepped aboard. Donned her travelling cloak. Her weapons drew too much attention. So did her armour.

The Valkyrie emerged in one of Yujius' middle sections eight minutes later. It was far less busy than the grand square. There were more offices and apartments. Trix was looking for a particular bar with a name that translated to "Siren Call" in Earthen. Sirens were monsters that existed near the coastlines of Hariyfir's continents. They were winged water serpents whose calls could be heard by other sirens up to 300km away. A group of sirens was called a harem after the Earthen stories where sirens were salacious mermaids. Harems would often contest water wyverns as they both made nests on coastal land.

Since Nuallar's destruction, Hariyfir's islands had become popular holiday destinations if you weren't rich enough to afford Drion. Trix had blown up a few siren nests in her time as a huntress. Their screeches weren't as bad as banshees'. Their teeth were worse though, due to their barbed nature.

Siren Call was one of Yujius' busiest bars. A tourist attraction off the beaten path. Since there were no cars in psygotaic cities, walkways occupied the space between buildings. Trix walked across the street adjacent to the train station. There was a park in the centre.

Parks in psygotaic cities were different to parks in human ones. They were entrances to oceanic bubbles: heated, saline swimming pools populated with aquatic flora and fauna. Trix saw two children swimming happily inside. It looked like they were playing tag.

Through the distorted world beyond the warped glass, Trix saw Siren Call's neon sign. She walked straight for it. The children in the park came up to the glass and stuck their tongues out at Trix. She turned to them. They swam away, laughing bubbles out of their gills. Seeing this, they laughed more.

Trix kept walking. Pushed through Siren's Call's batwing doors. Took a seat at the bar.

The whale coos at noon whereas the wolf howls at midnight. Tell me, little fish, what is your plight?

2

Something comes soon. Something not right.

Siren's Call was filling with patrons. After all, it was late afternoon. Clocking off early from work was a galactic trait. There was a psygotaic woman singing in the corner. Psygotas had an amazing ability to make their voices echo. Their music involved no lyrics. Only choir-like chants. This one was soothing with upbeat undertones. Warming everyone up for a fun night. There'd be dancing later. Now, there was drinking, talking, and more drinking.

Trix lowered her hood. Placed her hands on the translucent bar. The barkeep came to her. A female psygota with emerald skin and scales. She spoke Earthen. Along with zireans, psygotas were the galaxy's most voracious language learners. Humans and corrachs tied for third.

The woman was smiling until she noticed Trix's eyes. Her smile faltered. Trix detected an increase in the woman's heartrate.

'What would you like?'

'Something not right,' Trix said. She spoke her order with the nonchalance of ordering a standard beer.

A male psygota sat three chairs down from Trix. His skin was viridian. His scales were teal.

'Oh, little fish, don't you know? Demons can bite.' He muttered this so quietly only the machina could hear.

'I'm sorry, I'm not sure what you mean. Is it an Earthen drink?' the barkeep said. Trix noted she was wringing her hands. Was going to have a conniption.

'Just a joke. I'll have the house beer,' Trix said.

'Jiyo,' the barkeep said. She put a glass onto a nozzle. The alcohol came in through the bottom. The end result was artful enough to be in a gallery. And Siren's Call was far from the fanciest bar in Yujius.

Trix thanked the barkeep. Took a sip. Psygotaic ale. It was strong. All their alcohol was. Their livers were powerhouses.

Trix sat where she was for a moment, making like she was enjoying the music. She was. But it wasn't what she came for. Trix went to one of the booths. The man who'd spoken three seats down from her followed. Sat opposite her. His tentacle appendages that were the psygotaic equivalent of hair were naturally slicked back.

Trix took another sip of beer. The psygota leaned back. His black eyes had a barely distinguishable pupil in the centre.

'Greetings, Noctius.'

'Trix of Zilvia. Why has the tide brought you to me?'

Both of them spoke low. The noise from the rest of the bar was enough to drown them out in case anyone was eavesdropping.

Trix smiled. Drank more beer. Activated her x-ray vision for a moment. She made out no less than four psygotas who were packing impressive concealed weapons. They were talking with friends and colleagues, but Trix knew better. They were Noctius' guards. Unlike Daquarius Farosi, Noctius wasn't so audacious as to give them matching uniforms.

'Now that you've established I've brought company, you better answer my question,' Noctius said. He was calm. Measured. Wore clothes you wouldn't look back at. Nice, expensive, but non-descript.

'I'm in the market for exotic animals.'

'Thinking of buying a pet? Quaint, Trix, very quaint. I know approximately how much your huntress salary is. You can't afford exotic animals, unless you're looking for a colour swapped vludde, or striped bojax.'

'I want a gramyriapede.'

'I thought you were a huntress? You know that those monsters were native to Nuallar, a planet which has been buried in a nuclear winter for nigh on a century.'

'And I thought you were well informed?'

'I enjoy teasing you, little fish.'

Trix took a long drink. Her eyes were locked on Noctius'.

'I am well informed. That's how I know the Ghirsioc Raithexils have harvested a crop of gramyriapede eggs. Heavily irradiated, though scans show the young will survive,' Trix said, fabricating the last part.

Noctius Saberil was the Middle Man of all Middle Men. He brokered illegal deals across the galaxy. He helped buyers find sellers, then took a commission. In all his business years, he'd never been caught, nor had he ratted anyone to the authorities. Most people didn't even know he existed. But if you were hunting for black market goods, chances were, Noctius would find you.

'You can't afford them, machina.'

'Try me.'

'You misunderstand. The eggs are not for sale.'

Trix shrugged. Finished the rest of her beer in one go. 'Then it's a good thing I have something to trade.'

'You continue to be one of my most interesting clients. What is this trade?'

'I'll only tell the Ice Exiles.'

'Ah, jiyo. If you'll only tell them, then I can presume your trade is one of information. Little fish, the problem with trades is that they make it difficult for me to take a precise cut. Too many arguments are involved, and arguments can lead to mess. I despise mess, little fish. It dirties the water.'

'This trade will see that I'm paid for my trouble. You'll get your cut.'

'Had we never done business before, I'd excuse myself without another word. You have intrigued me.'

'Will you arrange a meeting?'

Noctius rubbed his hands, seemingly lost in thought.

'It should be possible.'

'I only want an audience with Dheizir Crohl.'

Noctius' eyes went wide. He wasn't just surprised, he was surprised at his surprise. He thought that emotion had been lost around the same time as his empathy, not long after his moral compass broke. His mind was all databases. His heart nothing but an organ that pumped blood. Noctius was business to his core.

'That, however, will not be possible.'

'It's improbable, Noctius, but you can do it.'

'No one has seen him in years, much less communicated with him. I'm telling you, this meeting will not happen. Mahdre? If you have nothing else to discuss, I say it's time you left. I don't indulge in social calls unless they involve nudity.'

Trix said nothing. Noctius rose. Trix spoke before he could leave the booth.

'Tell Dheizir Crohl that his fleet will be annihilated if he doesn't speak to me.'

'Farewell, little fish.'

Noctius left. His guards didn't. That would be too obvious. He'd have more in the street anyway.

'Fuck,' Trix said under her breath. She signalled the barkeep for another beer.

This hadn't been part of the plan.

3

Trix drank two more beers.

Her machina metabolism could take a beating though she was verging on tipsy as she exited Siren's Call. Psygotaic ale was similar in strength to clear Earthen spirits, after all.

Trix had rented Desert Star's shuttle for an entire week. She could stay. Although, Noctius agreeing to a second meeting was unlikely. He wouldn't see any point to further discussing an impossible audience.

Deciding not to waste her time, Trix visited some of Yujius' weapon shops. Stocked up on .44 ammo for her pistol. The Desert Star shuttle's storage unit could accommodate at least that much.

Instead of booking a room in the city, Trix headed back to her ship. Docks were cleverly designed. They had life-sign sensors. If you stayed in your ship as opposed to a hotel room, you had to pay extra for parking.

Trix stored her extra bullets then sat half out of her sleep pod. Yvach hadn't contacted her with more news. Neither had Andy. She was holding out for Ren Gerdac to come good on finding Crohl's fleet.

Hariyfir's day turned to night. No messages came.

The sun rose over the horizon. Still nothing.

The Valkyrie received a message from Kit and Griff. The ship was coming along, albeit slowly. Griff was being meticulous, testing each new thruster before adding others. A short video accompanied the message.

'Eloa, this is Daddy Blue reporting in, testing the starboard bridge realignment thrusters. Standing by for ignition.'

'This isn't going to go well,' Sif said.

The feed cut to Kit's POV. He was standing by the nose.

'Fire her up, mate.'

A blast so strong it nearly took the Fox off its docking station made Kit jump out of the way.

The video cut back to Griff. He readjusted his hat. Gave a thumbs up.

'Hysi, going good, captain.'

Trix wasn't so sure. She also wasn't sure why she was still on Hariyfir. She didn't want to admit it, but she hoped Noctius would get back to her with good news.

Around noon on her second day, Trix was buzzed by Cole.

'Yo, Trix, what's happening? The upgrades going well?'

Sif had rerouted Trix's communications through the Fox before leaving Earth. That way anyone who contacted Trix would think she was still there.

'Griff hasn't blown the ship up yet.'

'Haha. Sounds like everything's going as well as can be expected.'

'Hmm.'

Nothing was going as well as could be expected. But that was because Trix had expected too much.

'How's the fleet?' she said.

'Oh baby, you won't believe what we got. Luc Reno sent the Red Wolves on a fucking blitz and brought in a tonne of orits.'

'Plan on paying the Exiles to kill themselves?'

'No, but Ren found a dreadnought. It's old. Earthen make. Would've been better if it was zirean, but we'll take what we can get. Thing is, it's busted.'

'How'd he "find" a dreadnought?'

'It's a defunct husk used for military training exercises. Ren bought it with the orits the Red Wolves are raking in.'

'So you have the husk of a dreadnought.'

'That's all we need.'

Trix went through the options in her head. Ren wanted to

strike as quickly as possible. That meant rebuilding it was out of the question.

'You're going to use it as a hellburner.'

'Haha, you know it.'

A hellburner was a fireship variant. In the days when battles were carried out on oceans in wooden vessels, fireships were disused ships sent into an enemy fleet with the purpose of setting it afire. Hellburners were similar, only instead of being lit on fire they were filled with explosives, aiming to cause maximum, unavoidable damage.

'We're hollowing it out right now. Everything besides the engines.'

'Blowing up a dreadnought's cold fusion core isn't a good idea. If the Dread Phantom fleet is too close, we could be collateral damage.'

'That's why we've set the core to eject before the explosion. By then it'll have enough momentum to reach the heart of Crohl's fleet. Ren doesn't want to blow them all up in one go anyway. He just wants to thin the herd.'

'And what'd you plan on using for explosives?'

'Anti-matter bombs. Nice and simple. Nasty as an anghenfil with warts, but anti-matter fuel is so damn cheap to buy.'

Anti-matter fuel was created by taking matter and anti-matter, then colliding them in controlled bursts for massive amounts of power. It was originally created to facilitate interstellar travel. However, like all scientific discoveries, it didn't take long before someone weaponised it. Now, weapons were pretty much the only way it was still used.

'Try not to blow yourselves up.'

'That's why we left Griff with you. Later, Trix.'

'Farewell, Cole.'

The transmission ended.

'Using a hellburner,' Sif said. 'Risky move. And with an AMB at that. The explosion will be uncontrollable. Not to mention the chain reactions other ships might set off.'

'And Ren wants us right in the middle,' said Trix.

'Ren will be going with you since he wants to kill Crohl himself, or at least bring him to justice.'

'Gerdac's justice won't involve a trial.'

'You think he's going to send you into the middle of the fleet and hope you blow up as well?'

'Upgrading the Fox could be his way of making it seem like he wants us to succeed. Then there's the fact that Ren ordered Griff to make the upgrades. Upgrades that seem to end in explosions.'

'You think Ren's trying to doublecross us?'

'He's a pirate.'

'Are we heading back to Earth?'

'We'll give it one more day.'

There was no message the next day. Trix insisted on one more. That was when she received the message for which she'd been hoping.

The fish swims in the ocean but the fox runs in the woods.

Noctius had something for Trix. But would it be what she wanted?

4

Tell me, big fish, where are my goods?

It was night on Hariyfir. This time, Noctius wanted to meet in the grand square. At a café instead of a bar. Trix couldn't see him as she approached. That didn't bother her. Noctius wasn't seen unless he wanted to be. For this, Trix was grateful he wasn't an assassin. Trix had never heard of Noctius Saberil fighting. But she knew he could handle himself by the way he moved.

The Valkyrie sat at a free table. Psygotas hadn't invented coffee before galactic trade came around. However, they loved it now they had access to it. Unfortunately, they loved it bitter enough to send an optimist into a depressive spiral. Trix ordered one anyway.

An order came to her immediately. It wasn't coffee but an entrée of fish with a seaweed sauce. The sauce was poured in flowing cursive. It spelled out a message.

Oh, little fish, don't you know? The best thieves don't wear hoods.

The words were angled to a table in the corner. It was empty. Trix knew Noctius would show himself once she sat down.

The waiter who'd given Trix the fish returned and apologised for bringing her the wrong order. Trix told him not to worry and went to the corner table. As if appearing out of thin air, Noctius sat in front of her. He wasn't as collected as normal.

'You have an audience with Dheizir Crohl.'

'I told you it was only improbable.'

'Two of his men are waiting across the square. They're at your two o'clock.'

Trix saw the corrachs. They didn't blend as well as Noctius' employees.

'Crohl has laid out his terms. Leave for your ship when this is over. They'll follow you.'

'You spoke with him directly.'

'No, the man is a ghost, and I cannot speak to the dead.'

'You think this is a trick?'

'I think this is an odd business move.'

'Then why did he make it. I don't want to enter this blind.'

'Little fish, you're going to the ocean's depths, and down there in the darkness, there are monsters that can see far better than you.'

'What did you say to the Ice Exiles?'

'I passed on your message as you, the client, requested. It was foolish. They only replied to me last night, Hariyfir time. Now, they have a message for you. Apparently it comes from Crohl himself. He said that he wants to meet the Valkyrie in league with Ren Gerdac, the man who would destroy him.'

Trix's heart sunk. How did Crohl know that?

'You cannot back out now, little fish. I need my commission. And the Exiles were insistent you meet with them.'

'You told them nothing other than what I said?'

'Only your name and your message, passed on in person, as always.'

Crohl knows about Ren's dreadnought. Maybe he doesn't know it's a junker. Maybe he believes my bluff. Either way, how'd he know I was working for Ren? 'I'd love to keep speaking, Noctius, but it appears I have a date.'

'Caution, little fish. You're facing a shark with blood in the water.'

Trix stood before Noctius could move. Her coffee hadn't even come yet. That was a small win. Trix made her way to the elevators. Noticed that the corrachs followed her. They were wearing mech-suits made for speed, not combat. Trix could still kill them easily. She could draw her sword before they could blink. The last thing they'd hear on Hariyfir would be the singing of her blade as it sliced through the air.

If Dheizir Crohl was as smart as Trix thought he was, then killing his lackeys would be pointless. They'd have nothing on them that could lead her to the fleet. Trix entered the elevator. The corrachs joined her before the doors closed. She requested floor number 459. The elevator ascended.

The corrachs didn't speak Earthen. The Ice Exiles, despite being banished from Raursioc, loved it fiercely. They did everything to "better" corrachian standing in the galaxy. Sif translated their words.

'Dheizir Crohl wishes to speak with you.'

'Why?'

'We do not question him.'

'Are you afraid?'

'Corrachs do not feel fear.'

'Then why don't you question him?'

'For he will lead us back to Raursioc. Under his command, Corrachs will conquer the galaxy.'

'You're formidable warriors, but no singular race can control the galaxy. The anghenfil had a chance, once. And that was only because no one would unite to fight them.'

'You're a nikker. You don't understand.'

'I'm an exile, just like you.'

'Your people may spit on you, but you can go wherever you please. We cannot go home. Our brothers and sisters think we have disgraced them. They're wrong. We'll show them how wrong they are. Then they will beg Dheizir to show them the way to salvation. Our empire will last until Verhaseir comes, maybe even longer.'

'You're delusional.'

'Crohl has instructed us not to hurt you, but we know nikkers heal quickly. We could hurt you. He would never find out.'

'Why would you go against the orders of a man you revere?'

'Crohl believes all those who look down on corrachs should be punished, the same goes for those who insult our kind. Make no mistake, nikker, you are the ultimate insult. You're a barbaric, unnatural creation, and we know you have been sworn in by the Mountain Kings as an honorary daughter. The Mountain Kings will see the error of their ways, just as others will.'

'If Crohl feels so strongly about those who insult corrachs, isn't he a traitor for not wanting me punished?'

'Crohl will punish you himself.'

Trix gave up. There was no arguing with fanatics. They twisted everything to either be against their cause or for it, depending on what suited them.

The elevator reached the 459th floor. Trix exited. Walked towards her ship. She went to sit in the pilot's seat once she and the corrachs were inside. One of the corrachs — whose skin was eggplant purple — brought his arm out to stop Trix.

'We will fly.'

'Give us your left arm,' the other said. He was purple like a bruised plum with grey extremities.

'I'm rather attached to it.'

'We can fix that, if you desire.'

Trix fought the urge to retort, *"just try it, dickhead."*

The eggplant corrach brought out a bracelet which went over Trix's comms gauntlet. Sif could still speak to her in offline mode, though all other communications were severed. The greyish corrach scanned the ship. Found what he was looking for: the long-range communications. Opened up the panel. Wrenched the necessary components from their slots. Trix saw him leave and throw them off the docking tower.

Jo'ara had told Trix not to blow up the ship. She hadn't said anything about disabling its comms. Short-range was still available. Trix guessed it was so the corrachs could hail the Exile fleet.

'Sit down,' the eggplant corrach said. Trix did. A gun was levelled at her face. The greyish one came back inside. Sat in the pilot's seat. Took off for the Azure Zone Transfer, then to the Sea of Bones. There'd be no way for Trix to know where they were once reaching the fleet. Fuck, if Kit had been here he could've tailed her.

The ship left the atmosphere.

The shark hadn't spotted Trix yet. When he did, she hoped she had a plan.

5

The Azure Zone became the Sea of Bones.

Trix had no way of telling which direction she'd gone. All that remained was to count the hours. That would let her know how far away the fleet was from the Sea of Bones Transfer. But the more time passed, the wider the search area became.

Two hours and 18 minutes later, the shuttle emerged from hyperspace. Now there were more than stars outside. There were ships. Trix's eyes darted, trying to count them all. She'd seen them after escaping Nuallar. At the time she'd been too busy avoiding being shot to take a headcount. There were three squadrons of interceptors. That made 45 ships already. Then there was a frigate, two galleons, and of course, the dreadnought. Crohl must've had thousands of corrachs under his command. Even with a hellburner, Trix doubted Ren's ability to emerge victorious.

The corrachs began speaking into the shuttle's comms. The eggplant corrach who'd been holding his gun to Trix's head had sat at some point during their journey through the Sea of Bones. He hadn't stopped looking at her, though.

Confirmation came from the dreadnought. The shuttle pilot eased it forward, weaving his way between ships. A docking bay opened. The ship's interior was dim. There were no fancy trimmings. Everything was bare bones. Grates, exposed pipes, haphazard control panels, the works.

It may look like shit, but I bet all the guns are still operable, Trix thought.

The shuttle landed. The corrachs didn't bother cuffing her. Trix thought that was a bold move. She was in their base now. She could go on a killing spree and take over the ship. Clearly, the corrachs weren't concerned.

The only other ship nearby was partially covered. Ice Exiles worked on it as though their master's whip flayed them. Trix caught a glimpse of the exterior. It looked like a Raursioc Military ship. They were probably repurposing it, ready for use in the Ice Exiles' fleet.

All the Ice Exile ships were cobalt. Faint arctic trim was visible on the interceptors' wings. That was all. There were no insignias. Just enough of a colour scheme to avoid friendly fire.

Trix's corrach escorts guided her through drab hallways. They didn't walk far before they arrived at an adamant door. Judging by the rest of the ship, she half expected the doors to be made of wood. Then it clicked. The door wasn't adamant because it kept people out of Dheizir Crohl's room. It was adamant because it kept people in.

This room would be her prison.

There was an instant before the door opened. Trix went through all the possibilities in her head.

Could she kill her captors? Absolutely.

Could she kill everyone else on the ship? Improbably.

Could she escape the fleet?

Jo'ara's words came to Trix.

More chance of getting a hand on the fucking sun.

Alright, it looked like she was going to be a jailbird. If the rest of the cell was pure adamant, then escape would be nigh on impossible. Even if only the door was, she didn't like her chances. There was only so much you could do with a pistol and a sword. She'd burn out her gun before breaking through adamant with plasma. The heatsink would be cooked.

'You'll wait in here. Dheizir Crohl is not ready for you yet.'

The room wasn't a torture chamber. It was a bare, hollow cube. No furniture. No amenities. Trix would be its sole occupant and only feature. She walked inside. The corrachs didn't take her weapons. They shut the door.

Trix had been able to hear the ship's sounds in the hallway. Now she heard nothing but her own breathing. Her own steady heart.

Although her gauntlet had no communications functionality anymore, Sif still worked. And that meant the galactic clock still worked. Trix figured she could pry the bracelet off her gauntlet, but her room was likely a faraday cage. No transmissions in or out. At least that meant any conversation Trix had with Sif couldn't be monitored.

'Sif, if you could get a signal, could you hack open the door?'

'Unlikely. The Exiles would roadblock me at every turn.'

'What about piggybacking their long-range comms and sending a message to Kit?'

'Look, I could try, but you know that won't work. And we don't know what they'll do to you if you attempt escape.'

'Alright, we'll call that our last resort,' Trix said. She sat against the back wall, facing the door. 'We might be here when Ren attacks.'

'In that case I would recommend putting your helmet on and preparing to exit via any rupture caused by the hellburner.'

'That was my first idea.'

'Would they go through with the plan without you?'

'Ren still has three oni machinas at his disposal. That's more than enough for a breaching mission if they can reach the dreadnought. Though I guess that's what the hellburner's for. A diversion. Maybe that's what this dreadnought is for.'

'Trix, you saw from the dock that the corrachs don't plan on tanking this ship.'

'No, not for a hellburner. Maybe it's here as a diversion. Crohl could be on any of the ships. He may not even be in the fleet.'

'That'd be risky. A dreadnought's still safer than an interceptor.'

'Hmm.'

'Still think trying to best two galactic gangs was a good idea?'

'It's not my worst idea.'

'Yet. Let's say that the Exiles know about Ren's dreadnought. There goes your leverage.'

'I've considered that.'

'And? Have you given any thought to what you'll do if that happens?'

Trix air fired her pistol at the door.

'Nice to see your tactical training on Mair Ultima didn't go to waste.'

'I'll use my sword too.'

'Now I feel much better.'

'I'm glad.'

Trix tried to make herself comfortable against the metal wall. There were vents so she wouldn't die of asphyxiation but they were only two hand widths wide. She couldn't crawl through them.

The Valkyrie had Sif play some music through her earpieces.

Then she waited, alternating her focus between the door and the clock.

6

Including the time she'd spent on Hariyfir, Trix had been away from Kit and Griff for six Earth days.

Another 24 hours and Ren Gerdac would be expecting her back with his fleet. Trix had spent almost two days locked up on the Ice Exiles' dreadnought. It would take her far longer than a normal human to die of thirst or starvation. Though that didn't mean she wasn't feeling a little on the parched side.

She was holding her pistol over her communications gauntlet. Debated whether or not she should remove the comms blocking shackle. She hadn't heard a soul on the other side of the adamant door for 48 hours. Trix's ears pricked up. There was movement. Like a normal person's eyes became accustomed to darkness, so too did a machina's hearing attune to silence.

Trix holstered her pistol. Watched the door. It swung open. The two corrachs who'd escorted her from Hariyfir were on the other side. Even though her communications were severed, Sif could still translate their words. Trix knew a little Corrachian as well. Most people learned just enough of a language to get laid and find directions.

The Valkyrie learned just enough to threaten people.

'Dheizir Crohl is ready for you now.'

'Was he doing his hair?'

'Such remarks will get you killed in Crohl's presence,' Eggplant said.

'Death would be more exciting than spending another second in this room.'

'And here I thought I was good company,' Sif said so only Trix could hear.

Trix walked into the hallway. Her two Exile friends had brought guards. Eight corrachs dressed in heavy battle-armour with tank-shell-stopping mech-suits had their guns trained on her. Rifles. Burst Fire. Big slugs.

'Walk,' Greyish said.

Trix continued up the hall. There were surprisingly few crew members for a dreadnought. Trix began wondering about the Ice Exiles' strength. Ren could have a chance.

The hallway came to freight elevators. Trix stepped inside.

So did the corrachs. Eggplant pressed a button. The elevator arrived at another drab hallway. Trix tried her x-ray vision. The walls were too thick.

The Valkyrie committed the route she was taking to memory. Planned her escape. There would undoubtedly be a multitude of other docks. Dreadnoughts weren't huge because they were overcompensating. But, the adage of "stick with what you know" held true for a lot of things. Escape routes most of all.

Finally, Trix's banal walk terminated at another adamant door. She was patient. Huntresses had to be. Some notoriously tough monsters were close to invulnerable until the opportune moment. Though that didn't mean Trix was looking forward to another stint in Dheizir Crohl's Luxury Motels.

Greyish opened the door. Trix walked inside. This time her corrach friends came with her. There was a desk. Behind it there was a corrach. He had grey hair, like an aging wizard. His eyes were young. Blizzards whipped behind the arctic blue irises. Dark purple tinged the edges. Trix's first guess: Dheizir Crohl.

She sat on the chair. Eggplant — who was mercifully not wearing a mech-suit — punched her across the face. Trix's dense bones meant nothing was broken. But her cheek would swell.

'You do not sit until Admiral Crohl says you can sit, nikker.'

Crohl held up his hand. It was calloused like the soles of a pilgrim's feet. He clenched it into a fist. Eggplant stepped back.

'Leave us.'

'Admiral—'

'Leave.'

The corrachs filed out the door. Eggplant and Greyish cast hateful stares over their shoulders as they left. The door closed. The room was dimly illuminated by small overhead lights.

Trix waited for Crohl to speak. Didn't want anything she said to influence what he might say. This silence lasted for three minutes. The Valkyrie and the Exiled Admiral. They regarded each other as if they were playing a high stakes game of Faet. In a way, they were.

Crohl spoke. To Trix's surprise, he spoke in Earthen.

'Noctius Saberil gave me your message.'

'Hmm.'

'You wanted to purchase gramyriapede eggs.'

'And if I told you I only wanted an audience with the great Dheizir Crohl, would you be flattered?'

'I would not be surprised. You know about the eggs. You were on Nuallar. That alone would not be enough for you to know. But you are a huntress. And I know that you know the eggs are not for sale.'

'You sell exotic animals and dangerous monsters for a living. Why would you keep such a valuable prize for yourself? I can tell you that gramyriapedes cannot be domesticated, no matter what the tales say.'

'Then how was it that we lured the gramyriapede to the surface? The bell from the story was different than described, but it existed, as almost every fabled item does, in one way or another.'

'Why do you want the eggs?'

'Because I want to play a game with them, nikker.' Crohl's tone was almost sarcastic. His expression pure cunning. Trix didn't know what to make of it.

'Why did you agree to speak with me if you knew I had chased you on Nuallar?'

'It was precisely for that reason that I agreed to speak with you. You being on Nuallar had to mean that you are in league with Ren Gerdac.'

'You sent him to the Hole.'

'Ah, so he told you that story, did he? I heard he didn't like talking about it, tried cultivating an air of mystery.'

'I didn't give him much choice.'

Crohl's eyes walked up Trix's body, from pistol to sword pommel. 'I expect you didn't. Gerdac was a good employee. He learned fast. Could talk his way in to anywhere without a problem. I expect the Hole robbed him of his charm. Everyone who comes out of that place is only an echo of who they once were. I did betray him, nikker. If that's what you came here to find out, then you have your answer. He was becoming too good. I didn't trust him. Didn't think he was ready for the next step in my business. If you want something done right, do it yourself.'

'Would've been more effective to kill him.'

'Of course a nikker would think that, but you're right. Death is the only absolute. I couldn't kill him. He'd done his job well. One of the best. I expect it's why he went into piracy. It has parallels with smuggling. Now, apparently he's coming for me, with a dreadnought no less.'

'He wanted me to infiltrate this ship so he could kill you.'

'Well, here you are, and without so much as a drop of blood spilt.'

'If he finds you, Crohl, you will die.'

'He'll find the fleet. I cannot say whether he'll find me.'

This floored Trix. How the fuck was Ren Gerdac going to find the fleet when it could've been anywhere two light hours away from the Sea of Bones Transfer?

'If his spies are of any value at all, he'll have this location by now.'

'You don't seem concerned.'

'Why would I? I want him to find my fleet. I'm old. I can still crack a man's skull if I have to, but I'd prefer not to travel too far. Ren was a dear friend once. It would be nice to see him again.'

'How can he have been a dear friend if he's not a corrach?'

'Humans say that dogs are man's best friend.'

Trix frowned. Dheizir was too calm. Why did he want Ren Gerdac to find his fleet? The puzzle pieces in Trix's mind jumbled. Shaken by a child who was trying to figure out why the pieces didn't look like the picture on the box. Ren Gerdac's hellburner. Crohl's bare bones dreadnought. The dock with

only two ships. Griff talking about smashball. Upgrading the
Fox. Biochemical engineering. Radical corrach beliefs.
Teaching the Mountain Kings a lesson. Formula X attack.

Fucking hell it was infuriating. The answer was right in front
of Trix. She tried seeing the picture on the box. It'd changed.
Griff was giving two thumbs up. Winking. A comical speech
bubble saying "GO, GO, GOSHAWKS!" was coming from his
mouth.

Trix had no information to give Crohl. Nothing to bluff with.

'I can kill Ren Gerdac for you, for a price. You don't have to
lose your fleet.'

In truth, Trix was preparing to accept a payment from Crohl,
kill him, then commandeer the dreadnought. Technically it
wouldn't be stealing. Commandeer was a nautical term.

'I don't want you to kill Ren Gerdac. In fact, nikker, once this
conversation has run its course, all I want you to do is return
to Earth. My spies know that's where you were before
Hariyfir.'

Trix thought the Dread Phantoms had been compromised. If
they had, it was too late. It looked like Ren was the good guy
after all. "Good" in this situation being a relative term. This had
gone to pot. Then the pot had been thrown out the window, set
on fire, and shot before exploding into a thousand pieces.

'I trust you've paid Noctius Saberil.'

'I have, for he brought me what I asked for. You.' Crohl
smiled with the perversion of rapists and paedophiles. 'Well,
I'd say this course has now been run. I may see you soon, Trix
of Zilvia, if Ren's plan follows through. I expect it will be an
interesting fight. He's no doubt salivating over his revenge.'

Crohl pressed a button on his comms gauntlet. Trix's escorts
came through the door. She only just noticed the dull pain in
her cheek. The inside of her mouth was bleeding. Trix was
yanked from her chair. Crohl turned his attention to the screen
on his desk. The door closed before Trix could see its contents.

Trix was taken back to the dock she'd entered on her first
day in Crohl's dreadnought. The corrachs pulled her down to

her knees. Eggplant punched her in the face again. Her bones held. She saw stars. They twinkled light years away. A sensory deprivation bag was placed over her head. No x-ray vision. Just before it had covered her eyes, Trix noticed her shuttle was gone. The corrach shuttle was in its place. What was more, in the corner of her eye, she swore she had seen part of Ren's shuttle, the one she'd ridden in to Nuallar's surface.

Trix tried breaking out of her captor's grip. They had her by her arms and legs. She expected to feel shackles. Instead, she was thrown into the shuttle. The airlock door closed. Trix scrambled to stand, but the cockpit filled with gas. It was strong. Trix fought to activate her helmet. Darkness came closer and closer.

Finally, it embraced her.

SPECIAL DELIVERY

1

Schalata Tobas was a synthesised Corrachian gas.

It translated to Sleep of Death in Earthen and induced comas. It was one of the corrachs favourite biological weapons. If you could get even one vial into a ship's life support, its crew would be out in minutes. It could be consumed in liquid form as well, though that slowed its effects.

What made the gas impressive wasn't how quickly it dropped people. Or how effectively it bypassed filters. It was virtually undetectable. Whole towns could be found comatose, as if put under a magic curse. Victims could only be roused with heavy blood transfusions, as the gas lingered in veins for decades. And even with transfusions, victims often developed insomnia, or narcolepsy, or both.

Full recovery was rare.

The dosage that the Ice Exiles had given Trix should've been enough to keep her comatose indefinitely. It probably would've killed any normal humanoid being.

But Trix was a machina, and a Valkyrie at that. Uldarian DNA laughed at the Sleep of Death. And Trix awoke as her shuttle entered Earth's atmosphere. Close to five hours had passed since succumbing to the noxious gas.

Trix was groggy when she ripped the sensory deprivation bag off her head. The swelling on her cheeks had gone down. Bruises lingered, she guessed. Judging by the faint pain.

'Trix,' Sif said. The AI was shouting. Now that she was housed in Trix's comms gauntlet, her hologram could appear on Trix's forearm.

'What?' Trix said. Her voice slurred.

'I think we're in trouble.'

'What'd you mean?'

'I don't know, this damn bracelet won't let me access any

comms, remember?'

Trix looked at her comms gauntlet. Drew the knife Kit had given her and went at it. She was in the cockpit. The ship wasn't over Australia. It was at cruising altitude above Europe. That made Trix more alert. What really woke her up like a slap in the face was the cockpit itself. There was a pilot's chair, but there were no controls. No yokes, no switches, no anything. It was bare.

Trix continued trying to cut the bracelet off. The knife scored its edges but wouldn't cut through.

'Fuck this,' Trix said. She sheathed her knife. Whipped out her sword. Its tungsten carbide edge devoured the bracelet. Sif's comms began rebooting. They last went offline on Hariyfir. It would take several minutes to triangulate and connect to Earthen networks.

Now that was sorted, Trix inspected the rest of the ship. It was full of anti-matter bombs, each rigged to explode on impact. Trix couldn't set them off at a safe altitude due to how the bombs worked. Matter had to mix with anti-matter. Shooting it would do nothing.

Anti-matter bombs were useful since they passed through most scans. And, like Ren Gerdac knew, it was cheap. The trouble was keeping the components separate until the desired moment.

The cargo bay was also stocked with bombs. They covered the airlock. Trix saw that the door was welded shut. No way out. Trix activated her helmet so Sif could provide information through her HUD.

'Sif, we have a problem.'

'Tampering with any of this will set it off, and judging by how the Exiles have packed it, I don't think you could. Actually, I'm positive you couldn't.'

Trix went to the cockpit. They were over Europe alright. It was early morning. Lights sparkled in dying darkness. It'd be around noon in Australia. Trix looked for any port to plug Sif into, but she couldn't find one. There wasn't even an edge to what should've been the command console. Trix was reluctant to cut it open in case there were more bombs underneath, or more of that comatose gas. The shuttle accelerated. It looked like it was aiming for France. Maybe England. It was too hard to tell. Though Trix didn't need to hack into the ship's systems to know what was happening.

This was a terrorist attack. Part of the puzzle in Trix's mind slotted together. Two ships. One was Earthen ex-military. The other was Corrachian ex-military. Trix was kept locked up for two days. When she came back, the Earthen ship was gone. Crohl wanted to make it look like Earth had attacked Raursioc. But who was he framing?

The scraps of Ren's shuttle. The Exiles had recovered the broken pieces. Put the guts into Trix's rented ship. Ren Gerdac would be framed by Dheizir Crohl again. And the ship's ex-military nature would call the E.G.C.'s involvement into question. There'd be an investigation. Fuck, forget that. There'd be an outrage. One Consortium Race attacking another. Tensions would be high enough to see your house from.

The corrachs would've gone to war immediately in the past. Centuries of trade and cooperation had dulled their fangs of yore, though their veins still ran with fire. If his countrymen wouldn't retaliate, Crohl would have to do it for them. Instead of wasting one of his Exiled brothers, he chose to use Trix. Not only did she bring him an Earthen ship, but it was documented that she was a daughter of the Mountain Kings.

Dheizir Crohl wasn't so different to Ren Gerdac. Only Crohl believed that his revenge against his former clan was helping them. Setting them on the right path.

'Sif, you don't need to bother connecting to the ship. We're heading to UNSC HQ, Paris, France.'

'The amount of explosives in this ship will level the entire building, and all city blocks in a 3km radius.'

Trix looked out the windshield. She and Sif didn't have long before the ship crashed. Earth would be on high alert, waiting for Corrachian retaliation. As soon as Trix drew too close, the air force would greet her. Trix would have no way to respond. She'd be blown out of the sky. That didn't matter. An explosion of that size would smash the anti-matter and matter together. The result would still destroy a good portion of Paris.

'We don't have much time to figure this out.'

'We don't have any way of disarming the bombs. Unless you can alter the gravity around this ship, we're going down. Your only option is to break the windshield. If you can crack it with a few shots from your pistol, the force from the wind outside should cave it in.'

'Those people down there will die if we don't do something.'

'Trix, there's no way to save them. If we're not destroyed by the air force, we will be when we hit the ground. We can't even radio ahead. Trying to reboot comms from scratch while moving this fast isn't easy.'

Trix didn't like getting involved. Now she'd done so of her own volition. She'd underestimated the Ice Exiles. But this time her mistake would cost thousands of people their lives.

Time to try something stupid.

Trix fired her pistol at the windshield. Magnum Opus' roar was stentorian. Its .44 slugs burst forth, hungry to destroy. They were tungsten, armour piercing rounds. It took a full clip of 18 bullets before the windshield began cracking. Trix had half expected that the gunfire would set the explosives off. But that was irrational. The bombs were housed in canisters stronger than the windshield.

Cracks spread over the windshield. Trix closed the cockpit door to stop any debris from hitting the explosives. She didn't want her rescue attempt to end in her death. Better to be cautious.

The Ice Exiles had expected her to be comatose. Their mistake.

The more Trix thought about her plan, the more alive she felt. Her nerves bristled. Adrenaline raced through her body as if it were being delivered by the galaxy's best Formula X racers.

More cracks appeared on the windshield.

'Come on, you son of a bitch.'

The cracks kept splitting the glass. Trix made sure her gear was in check. Fired another bullet. Holstered her pistol. The glass irrupted. Wind rushed the cockpit. Trix had already pressed herself flush against the wall so she wouldn't be knocked back.

'Now what are you planning to do?'

'I'm going to fly the ship.'

'And what if you crash?'

There's no situation so bad you can't make it worse.

'I won't.'

Trix climbed out of the broken windshield. The wind buffeted her. Tried shaking her off. It was as if nature itself was working for Dheizir Crohl.

Thankfully, handles covered the shuttle's hull. This was in case a spacewalk was necessary to repair damage. Trix used them as she climbed on the wings, though she made a mental note to get goddamn mag-boots.

In space, thrusters controlled a ship's direction. Flaps were useless when there was no wind resistance. Though they were still easier in atmosphere. Trix reckoned the ship was at 30,000 feet. Descending in a wide arc. It could dive at any time. She had to be ready.

First, she needed a plan. Trix thought about using her sword to upturn the wings. Force the ship into a climb. But now she was holding onto the exterior, she saw that wouldn't be possible. The corrach ship was too sturdy. Her sword might've been able to cut through the thinner metal around the wings. But she'd still have to furl them upwards.

Maybe she would've had a chance if she was an oni and on solid ground. Though she could alter the wing density. The danger was that she could only make objects dense or brittle. The wind resistance could shatter the wing. Then she'd be up Shit Creek in a leaky canoe without a paddle.

It was still the best idea she'd had so far. Worth a shot. Below Trix, Paris' lights twinkled blissfully unaware of the big bad wolf coming to blow them out.

Trix climbed onto the right wing. Her progress was slow to avoid being blown off. Once she reached the wing, she fired her utility cannon at the hull. Attached it back on its mag-panel to secure herself.

Next, she created heavier gravity around her so she could stand on the wing. It'd be a miracle if she didn't pass out. Trix bent down and began altering the wing's density at its thinnest point. Pulled back.

The wing started bending. Trix felt lightheaded. Her plan was working. With any luck, the UNSC would realise something was wrong and destroy the ship at a safe altitude. The wing bent further.

Then the ship dove.

Trix was slammed onto the hull.

'Shit.'

She could see the Eiffel Tower below. The UNSC HQ flanked it on all sides. A picturesque garden courtyard lay between it and the tower. The dive had done two things. The first was knocking Trix onto the hull. The second was that it exacerbated the wing's damage. It tore clean off, making the ship catastrophically unbalanced.

It kept hurtling towards the city.

'The ship's readjusting with thrusters. By my calculations we'll crash into the Seine, but the explosion will still affect the HQ.'

'Next time,' Trix said, hauling herself back on top, 'your calculations should take me into account.'

'Scanners are detecting bogeys. I don't think they're going for peaceful resolution.'

No amount of swearing was going to make Trix feel better. The ship was nearly vertical. She was holding onto the external handles, watching the ground approach. The ship was correcting its flight path with thrusters.

Thrusters, meet Trix of Zilvia. She's pissed as hell. You better watch out, son.

Then the missiles hit.

The explosion enveloped the ship, but didn't destroy it.

Corrachian shields, Trix thought. They formed a bubble around the ship. A bubble she was inside. She remembered how Crohl's ships on Nuallar had taken a beating from the Fox. Dheizir Crohl would've made sure this ship would reach its destination too.

But he'd also omitted Trix from his calculations.

12,000 feet until impact. Trix could see the City of Lights clearer now. If Crohl's payload hit, that name would no longer be appropriate.

Trix clambered to the thrusters. Reattached herself to the ship with her utility cannon.

She couldn't touch the thrusters without burning her hands off. Or could she? Mireleth had blessed her and Kit. She didn't know what the blessings entailed. She thought it would be greater heat resistance. She was willing to roll that dice.

Trix retracted her gloves. Doubted Mireleth's blessings extended to her equipment. Placed her hands up near the thrusters. Her HUD blared red, warning of dangerous temperatures. Trix ignored them. Her hands touched the top of the thruster cones. The rest of her body was lying against the ship's roof. She pushed.

The heat didn't even sear her skin. She felt a warm tingling sensation like sitting by an open fire. It might've just been because she was lightheaded from her magic use, but she could've sworn she saw frost forming on the thruster cone.

Bad news.

The thruster wasn't moving.

8,000 feet.

Trix looked for a way to loosen it. She could've fired her pistol at the joints if she'd been at a different angle. But she wasn't.

More missiles were coming.

6,000 feet.

Last idea.

Trix detached her utility cannon. Slid towards the ship's nose. Entered the cockpit. Started pushing up the ceiling, altering its density to create a flap which would hopefully make the ship pull up. The ceiling was made from sturdier material than the wings, but that also meant it took more energy to bend. Trix had to stop or she'd pass out.

5,000 feet.

'Trix, you have to leave. I don't know if the shields can take two more hits.'

'We're too close to the ground.'

'You have to. You've got ten seconds, nine...'

Sif started her countdown. Trix was weak at the knees. She'd failed. Dheizir had to pay. Ren Gerdac was no longer the only one who wanted revenge. With any luck, the detonation wouldn't kill too many people.

Trix jumped out of the cockpit. Pushed herself away from the ship. Bullet dived towards the ground. Turning in mid-air, Trix saw the missiles hit the empty kamikaze ship. The first struck the shields. The second made contact.

The shockwave was immense. Fire followed. It was like the sky itself had been set ablaze. The ship had exploded 3,000 feet above the Eiffel Tower's tip.

Trix was falling just out of the flames' grasp.

She saw buildings get hit. The top of the tower was rocked by the shockwave. Swallowed by fire. Destruction reigned and rained. People's screams reached Trix's ears. She was approaching the Seine. She slowed her descent just enough to dive safely.

The world was subdued underwater.

Trix had failed. Never mind that breaking one of the wings had stopped the ship from exploding over a denser area. People had still died. That meant failure. Images of the possessed townsfolk she'd killed in Fenwick rushed towards her from the river's depths.

There'd be time to lament this tragedy. Now, Trix had to escape. Her comms would come back online in a minute. She needed to reach Kit and Griff. She'd be a galactic fugitive for the second time in two months.

Trix swam deeper into the river. Being detected would mean being brought in for questioning. The only way to stop Dheizir Crohl was by taking him out, and that started with his fleet.

He wanted Ren to find him, a sinister voice whispered in Trix's head. Trix ignored it. Crohl needed to be brought to justice.

And after what he'd done to Trix, justice was a .44 bullet right between the eyes.

Blink and you'll miss it, dickhead.

2

Night covered Europe like the Reaper's cloak.

The destruction wrought by Dheizir Crohl's kamikaze ship had been extensive, despite the altitude at which it detonated. People on the streets had been flung by the shockwave. Hundreds were injured. Tourists on the Eiffel Tower were cooked. Its tip had been blown clean off, landing in the gardens below. Apartments on the other side of the Seine had been eviscerated. Experts were still trying to recover the data from the ship's log. When they did, they'd discover that the ship had been registered to Trix of Zilvia, Daughter of the Mountain Kings.

They'd also discover a message from an unexpected source.

This was only the beginning. For attacking Raursioc, you will see the games we can play. And then you will scream. You will die.

Trix of Zilvia didn't know this just yet. She'd left her comms gauntlet turned to private. She received nothing. Transmitted nothing.

After landing in the Seine, Trix knew she needed extraction. There was no way she could risk anywhere in France. To be safe, Trix ventured 700km to St. Agnes' island, south of Penzance, England. She'd swum out of Paris in the Seine, then went to Rouen. From there she caught a train to Lannion. She'd stopped every few towns to switch lines, sometimes walking to the next stop in case she was being followed. She wanted to leave as little a trail as possible.

When she'd arrived at Lannion, she'd bartered passage to St. Agnes from a local and made it as the sun was setting.

The isle was abandoned. Only then had she checked the ENN to see what'd befallen Paris. She'd seen worse destruction. After all, she'd witnessed the Machina Academies' Last Day. But this was different. Machinas were made to kill, and they'd all accepted that they would be soldiers. Would die. These had been innocent people killed on a racist madman's whim.

Trix had been right about Raursioc as well. There'd been an attack. Crohl would've known the clan chiefs' council chambers were too strong. Not enough people would die. Instead, he'd sent the ship to the Frost Gardens, the largest public park in Raursioc's capital city of Ceanstadach. Close to a thousand corrachs had died.

Trix checked the backlog of messages she'd received while being Crohl's prisoner. There was one from Yvach. He was safe.

Trix could've used a cigar. She was out.

Deciding that she was safe for extraction on St. Agnes, she contacted Kit and Griff.

'Beatrix, where've you been?' Kit said. He was laidback pretty much all the time. Hearing him slightly panicked was strange.

'Is the ship ready?'

'Yeah.'

'I'm sending you my coordinates.'

'Bugger me, what're you doing in Europe? Did you have something to do with the terrorist attack?'

'Get here and I'll tell you.'

'Alright, just gotta have Jo let us out. She's not seeing the ship she loaned you again, is she?'

'She can see it as many times as she wants if she watches the footage of Raursioc's Frost Gardens being attacked.'

'Jesus, Mary, and Joseph. Hold tight. We're coming.'

Trix ended the communication. Went back to staring at the Celtic Sea. Numbness soaked into her bones. She didn't feel cold. Didn't feel anything.

Back in Australia, Kit and Griff suited up. They'd finished the Fox yesterday. Kit'd even had time to give it a fresh lick of paint and a few decals. Jo reluctantly let them out of the Bunker even though Desert Star Engines was close to opening. Kit dodged the questions Jo asked about the ship she'd loaned Trix. But that didn't stop Cid from figuring out what'd happened. Kit had to talk him down from bursting a blood vessel.

Griff gunned it for space once the new and improved Fox left the hangar. Punched it to ultrasonic when he hit low orbit. The Valkyrie didn't move as she waited.

'They're close,' Sif said, appearing on Trix's comms gauntlet. 'Wow.'

'What?'

'I can read what they've done to the ship. I hate to say it but they've done an incredible job.'

The Fox's engines filled Trix's ears before she could reply. What'd once been a grey hull with midnight navy blue trim was now black as a starless night. The windshield was tinted gold, like her visor. Realignment thrusters were everywhere. A railgun had replaced her ship's primary plasma cannon. It was thin and pressed against the hull so it didn't disrupt the Fox's aerodynamics.

The Fox turned around. There was a white fox painted by the windshield. She was smoking a cigar. "Fox Vanquish" was written beside her in cursive script.

The loading ramp faced Trix. Opened. Kit was standing in the cargo bay. Trix ascended the ramp and held him. He held her. Their embrace was short. They both walked to the cockpit when it ended. Griff was beaming ear to ear.

'Captain, the ship's singing like a vludde in the springtime.'

'Now can you tell us what happened?' said Kit.

'Once we're out of here,' Trix said. She'd simmered down plenty during the day. But she still wanted to blow Crohl's head off. Maybe she'd decapitate him instead. There were so many options. Trix had spent the better portion of her journey to St. Agnes mulling over them. She still didn't know what to do about attacking Crohl's fleet. Trix figured that destroying his ships couldn't possibly hurt. 'Griff, show me what my ship can do. And step on it. If I'm right, I'm about to become wanted for terrorism.'

'Hysi, captain.' Griff put his hat backwards. Cracked his knuckles.

Trix was taking in the new control panel. There were new knobs, yokes, and levers. There was no way everything could possibly have a useful function. Trix was about to put Sif back into the ship when she decided against it. Better to leave Sif with her.

Griff went to push the thrusters. 'You need to sit down and strap in. Inertial dampeners aren't gonna help us with what I'm about to do.'

Trix sat in the navigator's seat. Kit sat in the gunner's. Griff punched it. Started explaining the new features.

'Hysi, so, let's say you're flying along and you've got someone on your tail. They start shooting at you. Good luck to them. Barrel-rolling used to be a hassle, just like banking. Now, with the added realignment thrusters and extra power, they're as simple as...' Griff's fingers danced on the yoke buttons. He'd added extra paddles too.

The starboard realignment thrusters activated, sending the Fox into an instant spiral faster than any conventional barrel-roll. 'Now for the banking, but not the boring financial kind.'

Griff stopped the barrel-rolls. Righted the ship. Activated the vertical takeoff gear under the wings. The ship strafed violently to port, then starboard. Zig-zagged through the sky.

Griff: 'You beautiful thing. It works!'

Trix: 'What do you mean, *it works*?'

'Well, uh, we hadn't exactly tested the systems at this speed, or outside the Bunker. We'd tested all the thrusters in isolation, so we knew it'd be fine in theory,' Griff said.

Trix was impressed. The Fox would've never been able to do anything like that before.

'I can't show you the weapons now. Earth's probably a bit jumpy considering what happened earlier this morning. But those were the basic handling manoeuvres. You can combine the Fox's thrusters to make it dance better than any ship in the galaxy. Well, I'll be able to make her dance, you might need some practice.'

'There'll be time to use the weapons when we attack Crohl's fleet.'

'How'd you know Ren found the Ice Exiles' fleet?'

'Dheizir Crohl told me Ren would find out.'

Kit: 'You spoke to Dheizir Crohl? How?'

'Take us to the Red Reef, Griff. We need to see Ren.'

'Hysi, captain. I'd say we do.'

Griff showed off some more aerial acrobatics before sending the Fox into a near vertical climb. 'By the way, see this?' Griff pointed to a switch near the yokes.

'Hmm.'

'This bad-boy controls shield modes. This setting, where it is now, is your default. What the ship came with standard. Stops plasma, ballistic projectiles, and most debris you might hit while travelling at high speeds. Top setting reduces the shields' effectiveness from massive impact. Shells, missiles, rocket propelled grenades, bombs—'

'I get it.'

'Hysi. So while it reduces effectiveness against concentrated impact, it increases effectiveness for prolonged stress. This might be constant bombardment of smaller projectiles. But most notably,' Griff grinned like a maniac as he pushed the thrusters beyond supersonic, then to hypersonic, 'it allows sustained flight at hypersonic speeds for longer than before. No one's gonna outrun this baby now.'

'I had my doubts, Griff. But this is great. Thank you,' Trix said.

'How about that fox on the outside though?' said Kit.

'Not bad.'

'I'll take what I can get.'

The Fox left Earth's atmosphere. Griff jumped to hyperspace. Leaned back in the pilot's chair. Brought up the Galactic Smashball Association on the windshield's HUD. Trix felt puzzle pieces being put together in her head. She had a hunch. Smashball was part of this somehow.

You had a hunch about Crohl. Look how that turned out, her sinister internal voice said. Trix realised with harrowing fascination that the voice — while internal — had taken the shape of the twins in Fenwick. The ones who'd been playing with the ball in the street. Trix pushed them away. Their faces were stuck in limbo. Half spider, half human. Trix heard Balthioul howl with laughter in her mind's recesses. The children spoke again, repeating Balthioul's words back to her.

You're a murderer and a monster. You fill the star ocean with blood to keep yourself afloat. You, Valkyrie, are death, and you have chosen it for everyone but yourself. One day you shall drown in the blood you've spilt. You will be alone in a galactic graveyard, the ultimate monster.

'Alright, now that we're away from Earth, can you tell us where you went? I asked Jo and she said you mentioned Hariyfir. Needed to take a vacation? Kill some sirens?'

Kit's words dragged Trix away from memories of Fenwick. Her skin crawled with gooseflesh. Her face betrayed nothing. The numbness that'd made a home in her bones wasn't thawing. It was comfortable. But Trix was aware of its presence. Unsure of her feelings. Surely this meant she wasn't a monster like Balthioul claimed.

Not yet, maybe. But there is time, Valkyrie. No machina has ever died in their own bed.

Trix told Kit and Griff about her trip to Hariyfir, meetings with Noctius Saberil, her imprisonment upon Dheizir Crohl's dreadnought, and her subsequent time aboard the terrorist ship. Griff had stopped looking at the smashball page. He could hardly believe what he was hearing. Even Kit didn't interrupt once.

The Fox was silent when Trix finished.

'There was nothing you could do,' Kit said.

'I might've been able to tamper with the bomb and blow up the ship while it'd still been well above the city.'

'Then you would've been dead.'

Trix said nothing. Kit was right. Retelling her story drudged up self-loathing feelings. There were no more useless feelings in the world, except angry ones. Anger possessed incredible power, though all too often it was blind.

'What've you heard from Ren?'

'You know the part about him finding the Exile fleet's location. Luc's boys tailed a suspected exile ship that turned out to be legit. Trinity thought it was too easy. Too convenient considering the haste of Ren's plans. Luc felt the same way. Ren refused to believe it was a trap. He put it down to the skill of Luc's spies.' Kit shrugged as if to say "what're you gonna do?"

'We're going straight for Crohl once we get back to the Dread Phantom fleet. The hellburner's ready. Luc Reno, Trinity Marquise, and Kanoa Ulani are taking care of the Red Wolves and won't be joining us. The plan, unless Gerdac changes it once he finds out that this is what Crohl wanted all along, was to send the hellburner in first. Thin out the fleet. Then, with Griff piloting the Fox—'

'Daddy Blue,' the zirean fake coughed.

'Mate, for the last time, I'm not calling you that. Anyway, with Griff piloting the Fox, we, that's all of us plus Cole, Kyra, and Ren, weave through the debris and enter Crohl's dreadnought. Ren didn't mention what to do when we apprehend Crohl.'

'Gerdac said he wanted Crohl to be imprisoned until the skin fell off his bones.'

'Looks like we won't be killing him then.'

'Ren may not be, but if I see him, I'm killing him.'

'You'd cross Ren like that?'

'Thousands have died because of Crohl's agenda. So far he's fooled us at every turn. I wouldn't be surprised if he could worm his way out of jail. People are easier to outsmart when they're dead.'

'Do what you have to do, Beatrix. Just be ready for Ren to be pissed.'

'Uh, Trix, you might want to put ENN on the HUD,' Sif said.

'Do it.'

Griff's smashball page minimised. Two anchors from the Earth News Network, Veronica Auburn and Kumar Mohajit, took its place. They broadcasted from a studio aboard the UNSS.

'New leads have surfaced in the recent terrorist attack on the UNSC HQ in Paris, France, as data recovery specialists have determined the ship's owner,' Veronica said. 'According to the ship's computer, the ex-corrach military vessel began its journey on Raursioc, specifically the region home to the Mountain King clan. The log mentioned that the ship's pilot was Trix of Zilvia, an individual known in popular culture as Jinx of Zyr, the heroine of Aleks Valentine's most successful novels. Witnesses say they saw a person jump from the ship moments before it was halted by UNSC HQ missiles.'

'Aleks Valentine has been reached for comment. This is what he had to say. Be advised, the following video contains strong language.'

The feed cut to a mid-shot of a tan man with a mostly shaved head. An off-screen reporter asked a question.

'Mr Valentine, what do you think of Trix of Zilvia's involvement in the terrorist attack on Paris?'

'What do I think? What the fuck are you wasting my time with a question like that for, you fookin idiot?'

'She is your known friend and confirmed muse. You've written over twenty stories detailing her adventures.'

'Trix committing a terrorist attack is as likely as putting a bullet through your skull and living.'

'She was recently linked with charges regarding massive destruction of property on Thyria as well as carrying illegal weapons into the Bastion. Is that not terrorist behaviour?'

'Son, if you did your homework, you'd know Trix was acquitted four to one by the Consortium fucking Council and the President of Xardiassant. Any time she's done anything dangerous, it's been to save more lives than you could ever hope to even if you weren't a little bitch.'

'Are you suggesting her vigilante behaviour is not only to be condoned, but admired, even welcomed?'

'Only pussies suggest anything. I state my opinions as blunt as a poker up the arse. I've seen the footage. It looked like she was trying to stop that ship from hitting the ground.'

'If that was the case, why didn't she contact the UNSC and explain her situation?'

Valentine's face went red with rage. Trix thought she could smell the alcohol on his breath. His shirt was unbuttoned, revealing a love heart tattoo with a keyhole in the middle.

'Probably because she was set up. Anyone thinking these attacks are the work of the Raursioc or the Earthen Government needs to get their heads out of the sand. Why would the military send a terrorist ship to Raursioc under the command of a bloke who was imprisoned on smuggling charges 26 years ago? You know what, get this camera out of my face before I—'

The video cut back to the ENN studio. Trix was smiling. Valentine was a loyal friend. He'd happily pick a fight with anyone who badmouthed his mates, or him, or his mum. This was partially because he was perpetually in a semi-drunken stupor and exhaled cigar smoke like most people exhaled CO_2, but that didn't make him any less reliable. Writers had to drink like surgeons had to cut patients open. It was all part of the job.

'Trix of Zilvia was last seen in Lannion, France. Anyone with information as to her whereabouts is urged to contact the relevant authorities,' Veronica said.

'The Consortium Council has been called to oversee an emergency hearing between Earth and Raursioc governments. Ronald T. Duckworth has said that he hopes these matters will be resolved peacefully, without any further bloodshed,' said Kumar.

'Representative Duckworth was unable to divulge his personal opinions on the matter. He and the corrach representative, Vidal Laigalt, were seen conversing calmly as they entered their chambers in the Bastion's Main Square.' As Veronica finished speaking, she looked to her side. She was receiving new information.

'I have just been informed that a message has been found in the ship's log. We are airing it in a galaxy first, here on ENN.'

'This was only the beginning. For attacking Raursioc, you will see the games we can play. And then you will scream. You will die.'

The voice was deep, flavoured with Corrachian dialect. It sounded oddly familiar to Trix. Not Crohl's voice. He wouldn't be so stupid.

'UNSC Special Investigators have matched the voice to...' Kumar hesitated. Even Veronica's jaw slackened. Whatever they were reading on their contact lens autocues was the opposite of good news.

'I apologise for my shock, ladies and gentlemen. Special investigators have matched the message's voice to Vidal Laigalt with an 89% similarity rate.'

'For more on this story as it develops, stay tuned to ENN.'

Kumar and Veronica switched to the next topic, though they were still visibly rattled by the Exile story. How could Vidal Laigalt have said such things? He was a Consortium Representative, and supposed to hold all races in equal esteem.

Trix: 'Crohl must've found a way to alter existing soundbites from Vidal's speeches and suture them in a message.'

Sif: 'It would be possible. With the right software, at least. I could probably do it. The problems would come from trying to match the cadence. Chances are Vidal has never uttered many of those words in a row. The timing would be all off. You could transpose it onto another piece of dialogue. That could be a reason why it only matched at 89%. A percentage of at least 99.1% is needed to unlock anything secured with voice recognition software.'

'Eighty-nine per cent is still enough for people to be outraged. The corrachs on Raursioc who are sympathetic to Crohl's point of view will see this as an opportunity to hang the Consortium rules and start a war,' Trix said.

'Forget that. What about Earth? We were already stupid enough to exorcise ourselves from the Consortium once before. If people think that other Council members have it out for us, they'll be calling for Earth's resignation. Then the Consortium would collapse on itself with only two races,' Kit said.

'Wonder who'd get the Bastion if that happened,' said Griff. He didn't seem worried at all. Truth of it was that as long as Griff was behind a ship's yokes, almost nothing rocked his confidence.

'Not all of Raursioc would want a war with Earth. They'd fight among themselves before that happened. If the wrong people won that civil war, then they'd come after Earth. But if the situation deteriorates that badly, Earth would strike while were killing themselves. Raursioc could be the next Nuallar,' Trix said. She knew that the only way to stop this would be having Crohl confess. That was going to be a problem. Crohl would kill himself to further his cause.

Kit: 'We don't have any more leads about what Crohl is planning. Our last hope is that wanting Ren to find him was a double bluff.'

'Then we shouldn't hold out much hope. He knows Ren has a dreadnought. But he didn't indicate he knew about it being a hellburner. I think it's safe to assume that he knows what we do with how he's played us so far. He has 49 ships under his command. The hellburner should destroy most of the interceptors. Might damage the frigate and the galleons. Since we're going to need Crohl alive, we'll have to detonate the hellburner away from his dreadnought.'

'What about the freight ship? The one that was sighted above Nuallar. And those three that we chased on the surface,' said Kit.

'I didn't see any of those ships in the fleet.'

'Then that begs the question, doesn't it? Where's the freight ship?'

Griff: 'Hysi, and what's it carrying?'

You will see the games we can play.

Gramyriapedes.

Not for sale. Why?

Because I want to play a game with them, nikker.

Genetic, biochemical enhancements.

Trix was so close to figuring out the connection, but her recent failures bred self-doubt.

'I think it might be carrying gramyriapedes.'

'You saw as well as I did that they blew Larry into chunks, Beatrix. And Crohl may not have the eggs. That could be why they're not for sale. But that's beside the point. If he does have them, and we'll say for the sake of this argument that he does, then they're only eggs. Sure, I'd wager they're big eggs. Not enough to warrant a freight ship though. You could fit them in a galleon's hangar.'

Trix knew that Kit was right about the eggs.

'Crohl might've found a way to expedite the growth process with biological enhancements. He's had a full week since Nuallar. Who knows what he's done?'

'When we take his ship and you've got him cuffed to a chair, you can ask him.' Kit activated his knuckle dusters. 'Or I can ask him a few times. Or we can take turns. Bad Cop, Worse Cop.'

Trix nodded. Discussing the subject further would just be throwing useless "*what ifs*" around. The undesirable fact of the matter was that they had nothing else to go on. Unease brewed in Trix's stomach. It broiled and bubbled and churned like someone had put it on a stove, cranked up the heat, then buggered off. Never mind that they might burn down the house.

For the rest of the flight to the Red Reef, Trix felt something on the tip of her tongue. The answer to her predicament. She knew she should leave it alone. That the idea wouldn't come if she kept looking at it. But she couldn't focus on anything else. Not reading, not music, not idle conversation. Nothing.

Her trigger finger itched. She wanted to shoot something. And if it couldn't be Dheizir Crohl, then his crew would have to do.

3

Ren Gerdac was aboard his frigate, settled in the Red Reef asteroid belt for which the system was named.

Griff docked the Fox to one of its many airlocks. Trix and Kit went aboard. Griff stayed put. Didn't figure there was any sense in leaving when they'd be coming right back. It was 40 minutes from the Red Reef Transfer to Ren's position. That meant it'd be a two hour and fifty-eight minute journey to Crohl's fleet. Griff was restless.

As much as he wanted to put the Fox through its paces in a big ship battle, he was wary about Crohl's plans. The bastard wanted them to come. Fine. But Griff was going to fly so damn well that Crohl would regret inviting him.

Aboard the frigate, Trix and Kit were escorted by two of Ren's Dread Phantoms to the central war room. It was three times bigger than the galleon's largest one. Trix saw Cole and Kyra. They were beside Ren.

'Huntress, where the fuck have you been?' Ren said. He was angry. Fevered with anticipation of his grand plan's culmination. His eyes were bloodshot. Trix reckoned he hadn't been sleeping much. He smelled of rum but his words weren't slurred.

Trix could've called ahead to explain her situation. But her seeing Dheizir Crohl could sound, to Ren Gerdac, a lot like betrayal. Such delicate matters were always best handled in person. And it had been a potential betrayal. Trix had wanted to see if Gerdac's story checked out. She'd also wanted to see what Dheizir was like. She'd learned everything for which she'd hoped, but at great cost. Ren Gerdac might've been a pirate though he was the lesser evil compared to Crohl.

Given the choice between two evils, Trix would rather choose neither. Evil was evil. That was somewhat of a double standard on her part. She'd done plenty of questionable things in her 80 years. She'd justified them to herself by saying they were necessary to prevent worse things happening. Valentine called it making tough choices. The ENN called it vigilante behaviour. Really, it was just a lie. An excuse so she could sleep at night. And wasn't there a part of her that relished combat's thrill, the challenge of impossible odds, and the way blood spilled?

In some way, evil was necessary, like how some poisons in small doses could be medicinal.

Comparing evils made Trix think of Cortland Caine, and how he'd evaluate the Valkyries' strategies during training. Their first attempts usually weren't good enough.

'You're giving me two shit options,' he would say. 'Give me a third that's not shit.'

I could use a third option right now, Sir, Trix thought. She looked at Ren Gerdac. This was where the Exile debacle began to end. For better or worse, they were going in.

'I was trying to kill Dheizir Crohl,' she said. A partial lie. She'd never been trying to kill him, though she had considered it at the time. 'I gained access to his dreadnought where he kept me as a prisoner before allowing me to speak with him. He knows you know where he is. He told me that he's an old man, and he wants you, his old friend, to visit.'

Murmurs ran through the war room. Cole and Kyra remained the calmest. Machinas were made to adapt in endlessly changing situations. And there was no situation as ever changing as battle, no matter how big or small.

'And how did you reach this dreadnought, I wonder?' said Ren. His voice had soothed. He was no longer a bear enraged by a hunter's bullet, but a snake slithering through the grass, looking for a weakness. An exposed ankle, perhaps?

'I had hired a ship from Desert Star Engines. Two of Crohl's men piloted it. Despite saying he wanted you to come, he didn't let me see his fleet's coordinates. He knew I could've told you where it was.'

Trix's last two sentences were unintentionally verbalised thoughts. She hadn't considered them before. Crohl could've just let the coordinates slip to Trix. That gave some credence to Griff's double bluff theory.

'Damn it, it was the ship that you took there then. That must've been it. The one with which they framed me. Because of you, huntress, I've been branded a terrorist.'

'In case you aren't aware, pirate, so have I. I was sent to Earth in a ship full of explosives originally intended to hit the UNSC HQ, but I redirected its course.' The dryness with which Trix spoke could've sucked all the humidity from Yujius.

'Aye, I understand what you were trying to do. I care not for how you did it. And I have no need to seek revenge for the same fate that has befallen me has now befallen you. We're in this together now, Trix of Zilvia. Bound by a common enemy. No doubt you share my bloodlust to take everything that bastard has and crush it.'

The high-ranking Dread Phantoms around the war room fell silent. No one dared whisper. Interrupting this discourse wouldn't be wise.

'But,' Kit said, 'just remember, mate, if you kill Crohl, then the only bloke who can clear both your names won't exactly be able to do so. Sure,' Kit began walking towards Cole and Kyra, 'you could kill him. I understand that before this whole terrorist fuck up, you wanted to imprison Crohl. Well, if your boiling blood is somewhat beyond that now, then just remember, there's always necromancy. But if he's not willing to confess when he's alive, I doubt he'll throw you a bone when he's carked it.'

Commodore Gerdac looked at Kit as if to say "what are you blathering about?"

Kit: 'I only wanted to point out that despite your rage, and poetically justifiable reasons for murder, killing Crohl would be incredibly stupid.'

Ren: 'I don't plan on killing him until he's confessed, oni. But I do plan on enjoying the process of making him confess. Huntress, you must've been taken to a dock to board Crohl's dreadnought. Could you find it again?'

'Hmm.'

Ren cleared his throat. 'Alright. Ladies, gentlemen. Today, we cleanse the star ocean of the Ice Exiles' filth. When we take out their fleet, we open up more of the galaxy for ourselves. We purge vermin from their holes. You may be wondering why we're attacking Dheizir Crohl's fleet. I'll tell you why.'

Ren Gerdac moved from the head of the war room holo-table. A hologram showing Ren's fleet was projected above it. Trix joined the oni three. Ren continued his speech.

'From his terrorist attacks, you can see that he'll stop at nothing until the galaxy is under his corrachian boot heels. Our trade would become near impossible. War is not useful for pirates. We need times to be prosperous and relaxed so there's more loot for the taking. For the more people have, the more they worry about loss. And that scenario bodes much better for our Red Wolf brothers and sisters than a galaxy where people have been so ravaged by war there's nothing left for us. Heed my words, if Crohl continues as is, the Milky Way will descend into a worse state than when the anghenfil were at the height of their powers.'

Ren's Dread Phantoms gave a cheer. His words ignited their bloodlust better than drink or drugs.

'Crohl wants us to come, aye. This means we could be flying into a trap, but I see no other option. You've all seen what he did to Earth. No one else knows where he is but us. We cannot contact the authorities for their guns are plugged with red tape, their mouths gagged, and their hands bound.'

'That and they'll take us to jail,' Kit whispered to Trix, who was standing beside Kyra.

Ren kept speaking. 'This is not just the chance to ensure our survival, and to ease our future piratical endeavours, but the chance to avenge people who have died on a madman's whim. We have ancestors from Earth, all. And they wouldn't see it hurt when we can do something about it. When we reach Crohl's fleet, the hellburner shall go first. It'll be as much a smokescreen as their demise. It will thin his interceptors as well as weaken the dreadnought's shields. Kilo Squadron, you'll protect the frigate and the galleon as they attack the dreadnought. We're not trying to blow it up. Just deplete its shields. All other squadrons will swarm Crohl's frigate and his galleons, but don't play with them. If you see an opportunity to tear them apart, seize it by the fucking throat. Eosar will be in charge of the fleet while I board the dreadnought with the machinas. Then we will capture Dheizir Crohl. Once we have him, everyone is to rendezvous here.'

The war room fell silent. Ren had commanded everyone's attention masterfully. There was a long pause. The plan was simple. It was usually better that way. The simpler the plan, the more flexible. And in Trix's experience, flexibility was more important than intricate details.

'I understand that if this truly is a trap, many of us may die. That's why we're sending the hellburner first. But as we've seen,' Ren looked at Trix. There was pity in his eyes. There was also gratitude. It was good to have someone who understood what it felt like to be deceived by Dheizir Crohl. 'As we've seen, he's deceitful. His thick corrach skull houses a mind sharper than that of any blade. However, any sword may be shattered if hit in the right way. If anyone here has a better plan, share it now, or take your words to your grave.'

Silence again. It appeared that no one had any better ideas.

'Alright, you dogs, you know what to do. Let's kick this dwarf motherfucker's arse.'

More cheers from the crew. People scurried to their stations. Orders were relayed for confirmation. Ren's speech had been broadcast to the entire fleet which was one frigate, one galleon, thirty-five corvettes, and a dreadnought hellburner packed with enough explosives to shatter a moon. They weren't going to be horrendously outmatched, though Crohl's fully functioning dreadnought would make all the difference. Success largely depended on how lucky they were with the hellburner's explosion.

Ren walked back to the machinas. He still looked tired. His eyes were more alive than before. Victory's possibility flickered behind his pupils.

'It's time we went to your ship. I trust that Griff has made the necessary upgrades?'

Trix: 'I've never seen a ship handle anything like it.'

'And hopefully Crohl's fleet never will again. Are the weapons upgraded too?'

Kit: 'There's a mighty fine railgun on there now. You combine that with the plasma cannons on the wings, and I reckon we've got a good chance of making a hole.'

'Then let's go.'

Ren walked with the machinas. They boarded the Fox together. Griff was bouncing around his chair with excitement. The Oni Three conversed among themselves. Kit did most of the talking. He explained what happened on Earth, and Trix's deal with Noctius Saberil in greater detail. Cole and Kyra were impressed. They'd heard of Noctius. Neither of them had met him.

Griff went through the new controls with Trix as she hadn't been in the mood after leaving Earth. A lot of the switches, buttons, and touchscreens were to alter settings. Trix could change the power of each individual realignment and vertical takeoff thruster from the cockpit. There were also controls for each weapon. For example, each wing on the Fox had six plasma cannons. Previously rapid fire only. Now she could use a different mode on each one: rapid fire, burst fire, or charged impact shot.

Trix had been sceptical of Ren wanting to upgrade her ship. She'd been sceptical of Ren in general. She still wouldn't trust him to keep a secret, or with her life if she had something he wanted. But she knew he'd cooperate to bring Crohl down. If Trix hadn't doubted Ren, then she would've never gone to see Dheizir Crohl, then he mightn't have blown up Paris. That was a fool's hope. Crohl would've found another way. He probably hadn't even considered Trix as a viable option until Noctius delivered her message.

Trix could almost hear Luc Reno saying *"c'est la vie."*

Ren received word that the fleet was ready to ship out. Griff undocked the Fox from the frigate. The hellburner jumped to hyperspace. It was followed by the rest of the fleet.

Close to three hours until battle. Were it only to be a battle, Trix would've been calm. She'd been in so many that nerves didn't inhibit her anymore. However, they were also closing in on a potential trap. That made the waiting worse. Caused minds to work in overdrive, trying to compensate for every possible scenario.

While improvisation was favoured by machinas, madmen, and lucky rogues, it took an awful lot of forethought to be spontaneous.

When the battle finally arrived after considering a thousand scenarios, you ceased to think. The thinking had been done beforehand. Although your conscious mind forgot, the problems — and more importantly, the answers — remained in the subconscious. That was how instinct came about.

Of course, unimaginable scenarios always arose. That was when instinct failed.

Therein lay true improvisation.

The edge between madness and brilliance.

MISDIRECTION

1

The Fox flew through hyperspace.

Griff was catching some shut eye on the pilot's chair. He'd worked tirelessly on the ship's upgrades and wanted to be at his best for the upcoming battle. Well, maybe best was a stretch. He wanted to be at least a little rested.

Trix sat with the Oni Three as they regaled each other with tales, each more outrageous than the last. Trix was quieter than usual. She was still fiddling with the puzzle in her mind. She thought everyone was going in the wrong direction more than once.

Ren sat on the armchair, not really paying attention. Though his expression did change accordingly based on what story was being told. He went to the crew's quarters thirty minutes into the voyage. Trix followed him.

Gerdac was sitting on the lowest bunkbed's edge with his arms on his legs. Head hanging low.

'Ren,' Trix said.

'Sit down, huntress.'

Trix did.

Ren: 'You know, my parents were good people. Well off, too. Very well off.'

'Why are you telling me?'

'Because as I was sitting out there, listening to all those stories, I realised that there isn't a living soul who knows much of mine. Rumours, yes. Fragments, of course. But my life before I went into the Hole is a mystery.'

Trix said nothing. Ren filled the silence.

'It occurs to me that this battle could mark my death.'

'Each battle could mark death,' Trix said. She absently touched her freshest scars. The ones dealt by Isha under Balthioul's influence. The arachnid twins giggled in her mind.

Their gunk filled eyes wept pus.

'Yes, it could, but you don't always feel it, do you? I feel it this time. It doesn't feel like fear. It feels like nothing, but that cannot be so, can it? Nothing by its definition should not feel like anything. Rather I think that this,' Ren gestured vaguely over his body. 'This is the absence of something. What has taken its place, I can't say. The privilege of knowing how one feels and knowing how to express those feelings lies with artists, not pirates or ex-convicts.'

'You seem to be doing a fine job of it so far.'

'Aye, my parents paid for me to attend a fine school. Funny, isn't it? How a word that means superior quality has been reduced to meaning "okay," or "alright."'

'Nothing's exempt from time's ravages, not words, not stories, not imagination. Perhaps it is greedy.'

'Cuthbert Theroux,' Ren nodded. 'There's a man who could explain my current state. I read a fair bit of his works in school. He has many others besides his popular fables.'

'Why did you become a smuggler if your parents were rich?'

'I saw them both, day after day, never getting any happier. Yes, they made money. We could holiday, we could have nice things. I wanted for nothing. But the older I grew, the more perceptive I became. They were hollow inside. They had no tales like you and the others of which to speak. People always associate poverty with surviving, not living,' Ren looked up at Trix. While he still appeared haggard, the fire in his eyes was growing. His words were stoking the flames.

'Conversely, people look to the rich, they see their fancy clothes, their ships, their houses, and they see that as living. I've done both.'

'Is this where you wax lyrical about the humbling benefits of living in poverty?'

'No, living in poverty is shit. I wouldn't wish it on anyone. There is nothing noble in going hungry, or wondering if you'll die from the cold. Far better to suffer misfortune's slings in comfort than in the gutter, aye. But, my point, huntress, is that the rich live in a prison, slaves to the matron that is wealth. They are whipped by money. Compelled by it. Addicted to it. They shovel it into their emptiness, hoping to fill themselves.'

'That's rich. A pirate who condemns making money.'

'I don't condemn it. Money allows me to have ships. To have freedom. That's just it. Money is grand if you know how to use it. Why, it may be one of the grandest things there is besides sailing among the stars. There's a good reason that the phrase "trappings of wealth" exists, huntress. Because that's precisely what they are, traps. The houses and such. They lock you in.'

'Your prison metaphor.'

'Precisely. You buy and buy and buy, unknowingly doubling the guards, adding bars, and throwing away keys. You become conditioned to a luxurious life. Unable to let it go. This makes you worried. What if I lose all that I've acquired? What shall I do then? You can't escape. If you do, you might just kill yourself. Thus, you continue making your money, further imprisoning yourself with each orit.'

'And what's your solution?' Trix was intrigued about what Ren was saying even if it was just the classic *money can't buy happiness* spiel delivered in a magniloquent manner. He said that expression was a privilege reserved for artists, but he seemed to be doing a good job.

'You can make money so long as you separate it from yourself. So long as you don't live for it. I think that's how most people start until they have a taste. Me, I like having lots of money. More ships, more drink, more company. Those are all bonuses. Additions to my happiness. Not my happiness itself. Aye, I'm a simple man. I want to see what the galaxy has to offer on my own ship. It doesn't have to be grandiose, just enough to fly. Everything else,' Ren shrugged, 'bonuses.'

'So you became a smuggler to escape your parents' prison of wealth?'

Ren nodded. There was a devilish smirk on his face. 'I suppose that's another condition to my happiness. The thrill of taking what you can and giving nothing back. The rush of taking another's life. The possibility of death. When you stop fearing the Reaper, death can be seen as an exciting eventuality instead of a pathetic possibility.'

'It's an eventuality no matter what adjective precedes it.'

'People across the galaxy would disagree with you. Most refuse to believe that they will die. More now than ever considering how long medical science can allow us to live. People lie to themselves every day about their impending mortality.' Ren looked at Trix, tilting his head to one side. Similar expressions could be found in art galleries when experts inspected statues, looking for nuance. 'Although, you may never experience that, huntress. You may outlive everything else.'

'No one can live forever.'

'And on that count you would be correct. But living longer than all else would be close enough.'

'You wish for immortality?'

'It would have its drawbacks. I like to think I'll try everything once. Twice if it's good. Thrice if it's great.'

'Is this why you're opening up? You're seeing what it feels like?'

'No. We're entering battle together. This time, unlike Nuallar, I'd prefer we did it on better terms,' Ren smiled a fool's smile. Shook his head lightly. 'Even though you met Dheizir Crohl to see if he could offer you a better price than I. What was it you said? Phantoms on one side, Exiles on the other, and you, right in the middle?'

'Then why haven't you killed me?'

'Because I would've done the exact same. You'd make a good pirate, Trix, if you weren't a huntress.'

'You might make a good man if you weren't a pirate.'

'What makes you say that?'

'You talked about avenging those who died on Earth. Can't help but think you were actually telling the truth.'

'Every word, huntress.'

'Is this a first? Doing something noble?'

'I wouldn't call it noble, huntress. I'm doing it for my own skin.'

'I don't believe you.'

'Dishonesty is the hallmark of every good pirate.'

'And what of the great ones?'

'Not dying.'

'I meant to give you thanks, for the ship. It's better than I expected.'

'Consider it given.'

'It's a generous gift. So generous it made me suspicious.'

'Once again, your ship being upgraded was another benefit to me. Call it a test run before Griff upgrades my ships in a similar manner.'

'Dangerous for you to be aboard for the maiden battle.'

'What better way to see how a ship performs than to be in it?'

'Watching a video would suffice.'

'So it would.'

'After Nuallar you told me that all you wanted was to take revenge on Crohl. You don't plan on stopping your pirate ways once this is over.'

'Like I said, dishonesty. But wouldn't you rather have me live than that psychopath? I haven't seen him in decades. What does he look like now?'

'A stern face with cunning eyes.'

'About the same as when I knew him then.' Ren sat up a bit straighter. 'I was surprised you were silent when I asked for ideas back on the frigate.'

'I think it'd be foolish to try and anticipate Crohl's plan. Griff reckons his words are a double bluff.'

'Crohl was adept at those, but I'm sure you can guess his favourite tactic by how he smuggled goods.'

'Misdirection.'

'Aye, misdirection.'

'I've been feeling that we're going the wrong way.'

'And what would the right way be?'

'I don't know.'

'Crohl might be relying on other factors such as his freight ship and gramyriapedes to rattle you. Impede your judgement. They could easily be a smokescreen to have you think that he's planning something else, when he really has no intention of abandoning his fleet, or even moving it. He believes that he can crush us. Our hellburner will break his legs. He won't be able to squash an ant by the time we're done with him. Honestly, I think he just let himself slip, and instead of taking this opportunity to flee, he's seeing it as a moment to finish what he started when he sent me to the Hole.'

'We'll see soon enough.'

'Aye. Now if you'll excuse me, huntress, I'd like to rest before we arrive.'

'Alright,' Trix said, rising to leave.

'Huntress.'

'Hmm.'

'If Crohl is about to escape and nor you nor your oni friends can capture him, I want you to take the shot. I'll clear my name another way.'

'And what if I want him to clear my name?'

'Pirate, remember?'

'It's an inescapable fact.'

Ren smirked, took his boots off, and lay in bed. His face was still covered in bruises from his fight with Rosamund Galbrand.

Trix re-joined the Oni Three, though Ren's words kept circling her mind.

'Didn't know you fancied half-breeds, Trix,' Cole chuckled, his eyes flitting suggestively to the crew's quarters.

Kyra smacked him on the back of the head.

'Not everything's about sex.'

Kit: 'Sex is the root of all life, mate. There's no escaping it.'

Cole laughed. 'I always knew you were a smart man. A regular scholar.'

'If it weren't for you, Kyra, I'd think that idiocy was Oni

Academy's only admission requirement,' Trix said.

Kyra: 'I do my best to uphold our prestigious name, it's true.'

'Machinas are about as prestigious as easting fast-food straight from the bag while wearing a stained shirt as tomato sauce dribbles through your three month unemployment beard,' Kit said.

'You ever wonder what we'd be doing if Earth didn't submit to the zireans' terms for aid?' Cole said, leaning back on the sofa. His hand was near Kyra's. Their fingers brushed lightly against each other.

The Valkyrie hoped they wouldn't have sex in her bed.

'We'd be in a crack military squad,' said Kit. 'We were trained as soldiers, mate. What else did you think we'd be doing? As an honorary scholar courtesy of your comment not 30 seconds ago, I can safely say you're no closer to being a scholar yourself. You're on the janitorial staff in a community college at best.'

'Alright, smartass. What I meant was, what would we be like?'

Trix: 'Well, Kit would have to follow orders. So he'd probably be crazy. Desert the army in search of the galaxy's best pub and stay there, telling war stories about fighting the anghenfil.'

'I killed a whole platoon with just this hand,' Kit said, holding up his right hand as if it was a powerful weapon. Considering he could cave in a man's skull with a single punch, it kind of was.

Kyra: 'The only thing you kill with that hand is millions of potential children. Come on, you left yourself wide open.'

Trix snickered. Cole let out a whooping laugh that was almost a cheer.

'That would've been hilarious, mate, if it weren't for the small matter of being as barren as a farm during drought.'

'No, it was still funny.'

'Then when this is all over I'll be having a magnificent barbecue, a really big one, and you can all get fucked. Except for Griff, he can come.'

The cockpit door was open. Kit shouted in its direction.

'Oi, Griff, wanna come to a barbecue? I'm buying. We can put on some smashball, have a feed, sink some tins.'

There was silence. Then Griff responded:

'Only if you wash those potential children off your hands first. That's not the kind of sauce I like on my meat.'

'That's it, you're off the list. I'll have a barbecue by myself.'

'Is that what you're calling it now?' Trix said. Her expression was so deadpan it could've wiped the smile off a child at an amusement park.

Cole guffawed. Bent over and grabbed his stomach. Kyra laughed hard, her cheeks turning as red as her hair. Griff came out of the cockpit. He wasn't wearing his hat. His blue hair was dishevelled over his face. He was chuckling.

Even Trix started laughing. Kit joined in soon after.

For all they knew, they were going to their deaths.

Best to get some laughs in while they could.

2

Final preparations were being made.

Weapons were double checked. Armour was triple checked. There was every chance that they'd end up in space's cold void. Losing suit pressure wasn't what you wanted. Griff had made himself strong coffee. Drank it right from the plunger. To Trix's disgust, he scraped the bottom and ate the grounds.

Griffauron Fulum Raivad was no stranger to ship battles. He adjusted the Fox's settings accordingly. Sif insisted she could do it for him, but he wanted to do it himself. That way he knew it'd been done right. Sif, true to her nature — which was becoming more nuanced, and, well, more human, by the day — took this as an insult and told Griff to shove it.

'That's Quartermaster Daddy Blue to you, Sif,' Griff had chortled. He made six of the Fox's 12 plasma cannons have charged fire, and the other six rapid fire. Griff believed in a healthy balance. He left the shields in their default position.

You never knew what you were going to be smacked with in a dogfight. Better to be prepared for anything then adjust as needed.

Sif then apologised to Griff. She hadn't really meant her insult and would still do whatever Trix said. She'd even pilot the Fox as she'd done before if need be. However, Trix began wondering how much longer Sif would obey her every command. She was well past the recommended AI lifespan. Though they were questions for another time.

Like Trix had suspected, Cole and Kyra had sex. Just not in her bed. Trix's quarters were locked tight. They'd done it in the cargo bay. At least that meant they had to take a decontamination shower before returning to the ship's living space.

Ren woke up. Looked worse than before he went to sleep. Joined the machinas in the cockpit. They were nine minutes away from Crohl's fleet. None of them knew what to expect. The hellburner was scheduled to explode one minute before they arrived. It was longer than Ren would've liked. A minute could give Crohl's fleet time to flee. But he didn't want to be caught in the explosion's aftermath.

Thus a minute was both as short and long as he wanted to leave it.

'If the hellburner does what you want it to do, boss,' Griff said, talking to Ren, 'then we're gonna be entering a debris field that makes the Reed Reef look like bump in the road. You're all gonna have to strap in. I'd recommend the cargo bay, because if there's an opening in the dreadnought, chances are I won't be able to dock and let you off, go inside for a piss, that kind of thing. Depending on how bad the situation is, I'd say you'll have to drop as I do a flyby. Hysi, I'll be getting close enough to kiss the dreadnought, but not enough for it to be classed as sexual assault.'

'One question, quartermaster Griff,' Kit said, raising his hand like a school boy.

'If you want to know what sexual assault is, look it up

yourself. I don't have time to explain.'

'I bloody know what it is, mate. What I want to know is that after you do this flyby—'

'Hysi.'

'After you do it, we've busted in, painted the walls red, and caught Crohl, how do you plan on getting us out?'

'All going well, I dock the ship, you scurry aboard, then we take turns beating Crohl like a piñata.'

'And what if it all goes to shit?' Cole raised an eyebrow.

Griff opened his mouth to speak. Closed it again. Made an upturned smile. Something like a sigh escaped his lips.

'I'm not saying that I don't want to go in without an exit strategy, but then again I am saying that I'd prefer to have one,' Kyra said.

'Hysi, I'll think of something.'

Sif: 'The dreadnought will likely have ships on board that you can commandeer. Failing that, and being able to land, you'll have to do another flyby. All of you have thruster-packs, except Trix, and she can alter her own flightpath.'

Kit: 'That won't be difficult at all. There'll only be a dogfight and a sea of debris around us.'

Trix: 'That's just another day in training to a dragon machina.'

'I don't know if my massive physique gives it away, but I'm no dragon machina, Beatrix.'

'I'm aware. The ones I trained with didn't whinge anywhere near as much as you.'

'Maybe being blessed by Mireleth will help me fly.'

'I don't think the blessing is that generous, but we might be impervious to heat.'

'Beatrix, I know I'm hot. Just because you can stand next to me without being burned doesn't mean anything.'

Cole: 'Hold up. Blessed by who?'

Kyra: 'Who's Mireleth?'

Trix gave Kit a look that said "*idiot,*" in every language. Never mind that she supported Kit's claim by mentioning the blessing as well.

'No one really, mate,' Kit said. 'A distant friend of a friend's brother's aunty, twice removed. Plays the bongos. Cooks a mean steak. Nice guy, really. A holy man. His hands work miracles.'

'More shit comes outta your mouth than goes into toilets,' Cole said.

'Alright, I confess that might not have been entirely true. But now's not exactly the right time to explain.'

'Folklore superstition says that keeping a secret from friends, accidently revealing that secret, and then lying to cover it up is frightful bad luck,' Kyra said.

Cole played along. 'Ayo, and I've heard that the only way to counter it is for the man who did the lying to buy the people he lied to a drink while they listen to the truth from the man who did the lying.'

'I think you've both been spending too much time together. Jesus Christos and the Virgin Mary, you're mad. Where the hell are you pulling shit like that from? But that being said, you know I'll never turn down the chance to drink with friends.'

'You turn us down whenever we suggest you buy,' Kyra said.

'If a man doesn't stand firm on his principles then he doesn't stand at all, mate.'

'Shut up, fool. Which real scholar did you steal that from?'

'Made it up myself just then,' Kit winked. 'Good, aye?'

Griff: 'Not to break this up, but we're approaching the fleet. Everyone in the cargo bay. Hysi, and please, for the love of vluddes singing in the springtime, strap yourselves in. I'll not have this fine vessel's maiden battle be marred by one of you dying before you've made it off the ship. Fodio mufy, I haven't even christened her yet.'

'Don't worry, Daddy Blue,' Cole put one of his massive hands on Griff's shoulder. 'Kyra and I christened her just before. Twice.'

Kyra fist-bumped Cole.

'Then it's a good thing you're wearing gloves,' Griff said. He wasn't all that mad. Cole had agreed to call him Daddy Blue. The catch was that he had to call Cole "Cole Train." 'I've lived with humans for a long time. You're all still strange to me.'

Cole: 'Aren't you a quarter human?'

'Thankfully I don't look it,' Griff smiled. 'Your faces are so, soft. I have cheekbones like daggers.'

'Let's move,' Ren said. He'd remained silent for most of what was supposed to be Griff's brief. Turned for the cargo bay.

'Griff, for the second time, don't wreck my ship,' said Trix.

'Hysi, captain. You needn't worry. I built her back from being a skeleton. She's as much mine as she is yours, and I look after my girls.'

'Glad to hear it, even if *it* was strange.'

Griff saluted. Put his cap on backwards. Game time.

Trix left the cockpit. Joined everyone in the cargo bay. Cole and Kyra were sitting opposite each other. Ren was beside Kit who'd already activated his helmet. Ren put his on. Cole's foreboding metal visage slid into place. Kyra's visor flashed to blood red. Trix sat next to her. Set her comms to have two battle-net configurations. Her default would transmit to Ren, Cole, Kyra, Kit, and Griff. However, she would also receive all squadron leader transmissions. If something went pear-shaped she wanted to know about it immediately. Her second pre-set would allow communication with Ren's fleet, namely Eosar, who would be commanding the frigate, and therefore, the most firepower.

'Alright, everyone, this is Daddy Blue reporting. The hellburner is going to hit in five, four, three, two, one. Awaiting blast confirmation.'

The minute between the hellburner's explosion and entering the fight began. Trix felt unusual. She was typically the pilot during dogfights. Now someone she'd only met a week ago, who might've lost his marbles so badly that he'd forgotten he'd any in the first place, was in control. And when Trix wasn't flying, Sif was. It was comforting having the AI in her gauntlet. Had Sif not been with her aboard Crohl's dreadnought, she might've grown restless enough to try escaping.

Something told her that Crohl wouldn't have taken kindly to that.

'Griff, has the explosion been confirmed?' Ren said.

'Hysi. We're exiting hyperspace in ten seconds. Everyone brace for evasive manoeuvres.'

When Cole of Orix had asked Griff how good a pilot he was, Griff had said that he was better than anyone Cole had ever seen.

Griff's claim was about to be put to the test.

3

Hyperspace disengaged.

The cargo bay depressurised so it could open without sucking everyone out. Everyone's helmets showed what was happening from Griff's point of view via their HUDs.

Space had become a swirling debris maze. True to his word, Griff began evasive manoeuvres. Sif was working the Fox's HUD remotely to help Griff identify threats. She saw that twenty of Crohl's interceptors had been wasted. So had one of his galleons. The other was barely functional. However, his frigate was in fine form. So was his dreadnought.

'Scans are showing that the dreadnought's shields have taken a hit. No hull damage.'

'Focus all galleon fire on the dreadnought. All hands to the guns. Give them everything we've got,' Eosar said. 'We have to get Ren inside, and if we don't disable its weapons, we'll all be dead.'

'Kilo Squadron moving to defend the flagship,' Kilo Leader said over the comms. 'We've got incoming interceptors. No quarter. Let's take these bastards out.'

'The dreadnought's firing. Divert power to thrusters. We're gonna need to avoid its blast.'

'Fuck me these ships take a beating,' another squadron leader said. 'Their shields are nearly impenetrable.'

Corrachian shielding, Trix thought, just like on Nuallar. Except, unlike Nuallar, these ships had weapons, and their pilots knew how to use them.

As if he'd heard Trix's thoughts, Griff contacted the fleet.

'Corrachian shields are strong against rapid fire. You'll never bring them down spraying and praying. Hysi, wait for the opportune moment, gents, then hit them with your cannons. Once the shields are down, aim for the thrusters.'

'Roger that. Changing tactics. We can out manoeuvre them but— fuck, they took down Tavia!'

'Break formation, their cannons will rip right through us. Pick a target and stay on em.'

'Alright, we can hold this position for now.'

'Firing all weapons at the dreadnought,' Eosar said.

Corrachian dreadnoughts were leviathans. The central hull consisted of one rectangular prism while extras formed the massive rear thrusters. Guns covered every available surface allowing omnidirectional fire. The only safe approach angle — which wasn't that safe, because you could still be hit by missiles — was along the central prism's edge. It was the only place where there were no guns.

Even the thrusters had weapons between them. This was so enemy ships couldn't approach from behind if the shields were drained. Powerful railguns struck with precision, bringing down anyone who dared flying too close.

While the rest of Ren's fleet did battle with Crohl's interceptors, Griff flew through the debris field. His enhanced realignment thrusters allowed the Fox to turn tighter than ever before. It also allowed for it to spin on every axis, even flip over itself. Griff was approaching the dreadnought.

Sif: 'The shields are still at 75%. They'll take a while to recharge but we still have to keep hitting them.'

Eosar's frigate fired all on the dreadnought.

'Shields at 69%. We barely made a dent,' Sif said.

More Ice Exile interceptors started streaming from the dreadnought's keel. 'Hysi, let's boogie. Apologies in advance,

I've gotta feeling that there's gonna be murder on the dancefloor.'

Then the dreadnought fired. Eosar's frigate evaded behind a mass of debris but the plasma cut straight through.

'Frigate shields at 60%, and that wasn't even a direct hit. We can't afford more of that.'

'Eosar, sir, the Exiles' frigate is coming about. Readying their broadside cannons,' one of Eosar's gunners said.

'Leroy, focus all galleon fire on that frigate. Lima Squadron, give him a hand.'

'Copy that. Heading to the galleon. We'll get it done.'

As that happened, the dreadnought recharged its weapons. The interceptors that'd come from its docks were headed for the Fox. Griff switched off all non-essential systems. The lighting dimmed. Emergency only. Artificial gravity stopped. It didn't matter since everyone aboard the Fox was strapped in.

'Griff, thirty interceptors are coming for us. Marking them for you now,' Sif said.

'You're not half bad,' Griff smiled. He strafed the Fox downwards, underneath a metal sheet that'd once been part of the hellburner. 'Attention all squadron leaders, this is Daddy Blue. I've got thirty bogeys on my tail. Do not attempt to help. I repeat, do not attempt to help. Worry about yourselves. I hear the debris field's nice this time of year. Hysi, I'm gonna give em the grand tour. Come on, baby,' Griff said to the Fox. 'Let's show them what you can do.'

Griff's hands worked magic on the controls. Watching him at a ship's yokes was like watching Beatrix Westwood in a combat trance: awe inspiring in its majesty, graceful in its flow, and downright ruthless in its efficiency.

Daddy Blue gunned the Fox for the oncoming interceptors. They were approaching in a wall. He switched the Fox's shields to their impact setting. Corrachs didn't piss around with rapid fire on ships despite their affinity for machine guns in warfare.

Trix watched the ships on her HUD. Griff was on a collision course. What the fuck was he doing?

The interceptors fired. Griff engaged the realignment thrusters on the Fox's nose, bringing it vertical in nearly an instant. Another boon of the impact shields was that they could be redistributed. This meant that the shields' full strength could cover the impacted area only, making it nigh on impenetrable within reason. It wasn't going to stop a dreadnought cannon or heavy railgun, but it could more than handle stray hit from an interceptor barrage.

Once the ship was vertical, Griff punched it past hypersonic. Evaded most of the shots. The few he didn't were blocked by the shields. He laughed with joy. His designs worked. And they didn't just work. They were sensational.

Hot damn, boys. Call the papers, run the presses and get the president on the phone. We've got a winner. By Jove, we've got a winner. A real fucking humdinger. Yessir, a bona fide, genuine zinger.

Now that Griff had the interceptors' attention he began his tour. They followed him into the debris field which circled the Exile dreadnought. Griff eased off the speed. Hypersonic through any sort of dense obstacles wasn't advisable. He was mad, but not that mad. Not yet anyway.

'Yo, Daddy Blue, why aren't you shooting these fools?' Cole said.

'Don't need to waste the power. There isn't a ship built today that can withstand a collision at these speeds. They're gonna blow themselves up.' With that in mind, Griff redirected power from six of the Fox's plasma cannons to the shields. He didn't need any more speed.

'Come and join me on Daddy Blue's Inaugural Debris Field Tour in the Sea of Bones. I'm your host, but you can call me the Best Pilot You've Ever Seen. Hysi, this is gonna get real mean. Join me as I play all the hits. Namely you, crashing into debris.'

Kit: 'You've gotta stop mixing your metaphors, mate. You said you were on a dancefloor before.'

'Please don't insult the pilot while the ship is in motion. Hold all retorts until the victory party,' Griff said.

As Griff was approaching a debris chunk with a hole just big enough for the Fox, Eosar was trying to avoid destruction. When he struck the dreadnought the first time, he saw that they were using a bubble shield. Whereas most ships' shields hugged the hull — personal armour shields worked much the same way — the Exiles' dreadnought created a bubble that encompassed everything. The less complex shape meant that it was easier to maintain, but it made the already big ship bigger, not ideal for handling. Though that wasn't really important for a dreadnought.

Lima squadron swarmed the Exile frigate. They'd only lost three out of their fifteen corvettes. Ren's third squadron — Uniform — was split between helping Lima and Kilo. The Exile ships that weren't attacking the Fox were attacking Eosar's frigate. Since it had a destroyer's power, the Phantom Frigate took out ten interceptors with the squadrons' help. The Exiles only had fifteen interceptors left, not including the ones after Trix.

The problem was that while they were preoccupied with the interceptors, the frigate couldn't whittle away the dreadnought's shields. And its weapons were almost fully recharged.

Griff was still among the debris field. The corrachs on his tail were better than he thought they'd be, but six of them had already fallen victim to collisions. That still left twenty-four. Griff was wondering how to kill the rest of them. The corrachs grew a little smarter with each ship he felled.

Eosar: 'The dreadnought's weapons are almost back online. We're going to be hit. We don't have enough guns to destroy the interceptors and the dreadnought at the same time. And our shields cannot take a direct hit. If we're left exposed, the interceptors will finish us off.'

Griff: 'Almost charged you say?'

'Yes, that's what I said.'

'I'm bringing in extra shielding for you, Eosar. Hold tight.'

Griff activated the Fox's underside rear realignment

thrusters at the same time as ones above the nose. The Fox cartwheeled over a chain of broken interceptor parts. Whether they were bewildered by the move, or they were tiring, three more corrachs fell victim to Griff's prowess.

'When you say you're bringing in some extra shielding—' Kyra began.

'Hysi, it's exactly what you're thinking. Sif, I need you to scan that dreadnought and put the countdown on the HUD.'

'Trust me a bit more now?'

'Like I said, you're not a half bad co-pilot.'

The timer appeared on the HUD. Griff zig-zagged out of the debris. He was above Eosar's frigate. Saw an attacking interceptor below.

'Sif, railgun that bastard.'

The Fox's new railgun charged. Fired. The corrach ship was wasted.

'One less.'

Twenty ships were still pursuing Griff. He was coming between the Exile Dreadnought and the Phantom Frigate. This was going to be mighty close. But if it worked, he saved the frigate, and annihilated his pursuers in one go.

Then he still needed to figure out how to enter the dreadnought. Even with the frigate's firepower, Griff doubted they'd break through. He had a theory about how to bypass the bubble shield, but it was a hunch based on guesswork. It'd be fine if the shield wasn't custom.

If not, Kit's barbecue would be hosted in hell.

Mind the brimstone.

4

Griff played with his attackers a while longer.

His plan involved making sure the dreadnought didn't have time to belay its attack. Its crew likely wouldn't fall for the same trick twice. Without any debris in the way, evading was becoming harder, but the Exile interceptors were slow. Marred by conventional manoeuvring methods. Griff wasn't worried.

Kilo squadron had destroyed another five interceptors. Only three more were attacking their frigate. Seeing that Kilo had the situation under control, Uniform focused its fire on the Exile frigate Lima was attacking. Ren's galleon was also laying down heavy fire.

The Dread Phantoms had lost eight corvettes in total. But it looked like they were going to emerge victorious. The Ice Exiles' frigate's shields depleted. Every hit was now direct to the hull.

'Uniform, target the life support systems. Lima, take the main cannons offline,' Lima squadron leader said. 'We're sinking this frigate.'

Order confirmations were relayed between the remaining pilots. The Dread Phantoms were competent warriors, but their true skill lay behind ships' yokes. They were pirates after all.

The Fox's crew heard this chatter. It was good news.

'Griff, the dreadnought's weapons have reached critical mass. They have to fire.'

Griff: 'Hysi, never thought I'd hear a woman say more beautiful words.'

Cole raised his eyebrows. Understood Griff's plan.

'Haha, baby, cook these fools. I repeat, cook these fools.'

'That's the plan, Cole Train.'

The Fox flew parallel to the dreadnought. Between it and Eosar's frigate. Griff redirected shields to port. This was a risky move. If any interceptors behind him scored a shot before their demise, they could land a direct hit on the Fox. But Griff was feeling lucky.

The dreadnought's starboard cannons came to life in a spectacular lightshow. Fireworks fit for a serial killer. Griff strafed the Fox upwards. Spun it 180 degrees. Avoided two railgun blasts by flying inverted between them. The corrachian ships on his tail couldn't evade fast enough. Griff swung the Fox around.

Thanks to his thruster upgrades, the Fox could move

backwards almost as fast as it could move forwards. Such a manoeuvre would never work within atmosphere, but in space, aerodynamics had as much bearing on flight capability as the price of beer in Timbuctoo.

Griff switched the Fox's shielding to starboard then fired up the railgun to take out the stragglers. A whopping 16 of the pursuing interceptors had been wasted in the dreadnought's attack.

'Sif, if you'd be so kind as to auto-target those ships while I focus on getting us out of here alive, I'd appreciate it.'

Sif lined up the railgun while Griff continued dancing the ship, in reverse, through plasma lasers. It was like that scene from that old heist film where the protagonist puts on some music and slinks through a room of laser beams to reach priceless treasure. Only this was at thousands of kilometres an hour. In space. And hitting these lasers would kill you.

The Riven Strife Railgun was adept at destroying shields, then still having enough spare juice to penetrate the hull. The dreadnought's onslaught ended. It began recharging. Thanks to Griff's flying, the pursuing interceptors had been laid to waste.

Unfortunately, Griff had underestimated the strength of the dreadnought's weapons. The Exiles' weapons had ploughed straight through their interceptors and hit Eosar's frigate which was now at one per cent shields.

Griff went to Eosar's aid when he saw that it was pointless.

'Fodio, they're dive bombing the frigate,' Griff said.

'Squadron leaders, this is Eosar, we're taking heavy damage. Shields are gone, repeat shields are—'

Eosar's transmission cut out. From what Trix could see, the frigate hadn't been completely destroyed, though it wouldn't fly again. The hull damage had likely severed the comms. Crew members were sucked into space. Eosar's voice came back. The signal was weak.

'Heavy damage. Life support's failed. Artificial gravity's out. We need to abandon ship.'

'Eosar, get all survivors to the shuttles, and get the hell out of there. That's an order,' Ren said. If he was upset about losing the frigate, he didn't show it.

'Have to perform a spacewalk to reach the hangar. Can't get the schematics online. It's separated from the bridge. Don't know if the shuttles will still be intact.'

Griff: 'I can see the hangar, Eosar. The damage is minimal. Hysi, the shuttles should still be flyable. But you better move. If you're not outta here by the time their weapons finish charging—'

'I'm aware.'

Eosar ended the transmission.

Ren: 'All ships, focus fire on the dreadnought. We need to buy Eosar some time.'

'Commodore,' one of the squadron leaders said, 'the frigate still has weapons online. They could pick us off if we leave them as they are. Their weapons don't need half the time the dreadnought's do.'

'Belay that. Belay the commodore's orders, you're to keep firing on that frigate until it's a new addition to the debris,' said Griff.

'Quartermaster, you don't have the authority to defy my command. We need to drop the dreadnought's shields.'

'Unless we have a 100 corvettes, those shields are staying exactly as they are. Hysi, I have a plan, just keep your men on the Exile frigate.'

'You better know what you're doing. Squadrons, focus fire on the frigate. Once it's destroyed, then and only then are you to fire on the dreadnought. Alright, Griff. What's your plan?'

'Commodore, we could hit those shields until the universe collapses on itself. We don't stand a chance without our frigate. However, they're using a bubble shield configuration.

'Bubble shields are made to keep large objects out unless they're travelling at super slow speeds. This is so that when a dreadnought's docked, they can keep their shields up, but ships can still enter the hangar. And before you say anything, we can't try that because their close-range weapons will rail us. There is another way though.'

'Flyby?' Kit said.

'Hysi. Your bodies should be small enough to not be registered as missiles. And if I time it right, your speed won't be registered either.'

'Hang on, *should* be small enough?'

'Well I can't be sure of how the shields are calibrated without seeing the specs. And I don't think they're gonna send them over, even if I ask politely.'

Sif: 'There's an 80% chance Griff's assumption is correct.'

Kit: 'That other 20% is as comforting as a bed made from broken glass, mate.'

Kyra: 'Eighty per cent works for me. Let's go.'

Trix tapped some commands on her comms gauntlet. She was telling Griff the location of the docking bay she'd entered. Sif transposed the information into a virtual flight path which showed Griff the best trajectory at which to release the machinas.

'Ayo, we've got one problem. Sure, we land on the ship. No problem. But we've got nothing to break into the docks with, and the dreadnought is crawling with weapons that can pick us off before we land on the fucking hull,' said Cole.

He was right. They'd been relying on the Fox to blow a hole in the dreadnought. Without its firepower, they were done before they began.

'We still have a way,' Kit said. He tapped one of his armour compartments. 'When we were infiltrating the galleon, we never had to use my drill mines because Sif opened the interior door.'

Trix: 'You only have two, and this isn't an external airlock door. This is a hangar door.'

Kyra: 'Sif, can you find an alternate entrance? One that's just an airlock door?'

'Possibly, it's hard to scan something that's not emitting energy with the shield in the way. We'll need to get closer.'

'How close?' Griff said.

'Just above the shield.'

'We're worse than dead if they fire on us from that range. Can't you wirelessly hack into their systems and reverse the shield's direction? That way they'll be blowing themselves up when they fire.'

'You don't think I've tried that already? There's no way I can hack them without being in a terminal.'

'I don't like the idea of being so close to the shields.'

Sif activated a HUD filter that let Griff perceive the bubble shield. It was still pretty tight over the ship, but the machinas would have more than enough space to breach.

Cheers erupted on the wider battle-net. The Exile frigate was no more. And not a moment too soon. The dreadnought would be ready to fire again before long. Commodore Ren Gerdac started commanding. There wasn't much time. Had he been a business man like his father, he might've called his actions delegation, or effective resource management. Ren called it a coordinated attack.

'All squadrons, swarm the dreadnought. Attack if you can, but focus on evasive manoeuvres. We need to give them as many targets as possible while Eosar evacuates the others.'

'Ren, it's no good. The shuttles have come loose of their moorings. They're drifting out in space. Two of them are badly damaged.'

'Kilo squadron, accompany our galleon to the frigate. They're on lifeboat duty. Get everyone off the frigate alive or you'll be praying to the devil to save your souls. Dock on the portside. If the dreadnought looses a shot, hope that its weapons hit the frigate's hull before they hit your shields, or you'll drown in the star ocean like the rest of them.'

'Roger that, commodore. Beginning evacuation. No one else is going down with that ship.'

'Honour among pirates?' Trix said to Ren. 'I was under the impression that anyone who fell behind was left behind.'

'And for the most part this is true, though it is also honourable. If you stop the rest of the crew from succeeding, then that's hardly worth saving you for, is it, aye? But if you don't show your men that you're willing to make a sacrifice from time to time, then mutiny becomes more likely than continuing loyalty, especially after what happened on Nuallar.'

'I think you're only saving them because without enough men, or ships, Luc Reno will hold more power than you, and there goes your leverage. Then you work for the Red Wolves, and the Dread Phantoms are finished.'

'We'll make a pirate out of you yet, huntress,' said Ren.

'Hysi, if you thought that the ride's been bumpy so far, you haven't seen anything yet,' Daddy Blue said.

Griff adjusted his hat with one hand on the yokes. It helped keep the sweat off his face. Zireans sweated less than humans. Altaeifs liked to think it was because they were more refined.

'Squadron leaders, Daddy Blue. I'm transmitting scanning specs to you now. I need you to sweep the dreadnought from front to back, close as your dare then closer again. We're looking for an airlock door. I have some passengers who're hankering to get aboard, and they need a window. So let's give them one.'

'Roger, running the scanning parameters now.'

'Copy that, Blue, we're linking our scanners. We'll find you an airlock.'

'Hysi, appreciate it, boys. Watch yourselves out there.'

Kit: 'There you go again, mate. First you said you were looking for an airlock door, then you're talking about windows. Dreadnoughts don't have windows, and if they do, they're covered in blast shields during combat.'

'Damn it, Kit. What'd I tell you about talking to the pilot while the ship was in motion?'

'Just trying to understand your metaphors, mate.'

Griff let a string of zirean curse words fly. They were savage.

Uniform and Lima squadrons fell into a formation that, at first glance, looked erratic. In truth, it was a formation Ren had customised himself. Custom formations were much like smashball plays. The whole point was to fool your enemy.

Although the formation, which Ren had dubbed the Phantom's Chain, appeared structureless, it allowed ships to easily swap positions and left plenty of space to evade which was perfect for facing a dreadnought.

Griff gunned for the dreadnought's nose. Uniform fell into position along the starboard side. Lima took portside. Then the dreadnought's close-range weapons engaged. They didn't pack the same amount of oomph as the broadside cannons. But they could fire rapidly, giving no reprieve. Griff switched the shields to the Fox's keel and calibrated them to withstand rapid attacks.

Even with his flying, Griff couldn't avoid every blow. The shields were dropping fast.

'Come on, baby. We've got this. We've got this.'

In an attempt to fool the dreadnought's targeting system, Griff punched the Fox faster. This wasn't ideal for scanning, but with the other squadrons helping, he could afford the lack in quality. It was better to have the ship in one piece.

Sif's hologram appeared on the console. She put her hands on her hips. Stared at the HUD.

'The scan's successful so far, but I'm not seeing any airlocks.'

'Are you telling me this thing has no airlock doors at all?'

'Looks like it. Hang on... got two. One to starboard, one to port.'

'Are you sure there're none below? That'd be much easier.'

The squadrons completed their scan. Peeled away from the dreadnought. There'd been no casualties. The Dread Phantoms had come too far to die now. This had been the craziest endeavour they'd ever undertaken, and they planned on talking about it later.

'The scan's complete. There might be another one below, but we'd have to scan the dreadnought's keel. I don't think we'll be lucky enough to survive a second run. The shields dropped to nine per cent.'

'That had nothing to do with luck. That was all skill.'

'Alright. Then I don't think you're skilful enough to do it

again. There are two options. You've got to pick one or the other. There is a third option, but that's running away.'

Cortland Caine's voice echoed in Trix's head as if she'd just told him Sif's idea for taking the dreadnought. *You're giving me two shit options. Give me a third that's not shit.*

Hard as she tried, Trix couldn't. Scanning the dreadnought's keel wasn't any better than going for one of the side airlocks. And even those would require flying dangerously close to the shields again.

Sorry, Sir Cortland, looks like this time I'm shit outta luck.

Ren: 'We'll go portside. That way any stray fire won't hit the frigate.'

Sif: 'Dreadnought's starboard cannons are ready to fire in thirty seconds.'

'Eosar, tell me everyone's on board the galleon.'

'We made it. We're coming to attack the dreadnought.'

'No, get out of here now. That's not up for negotiation. Get back to the reef.'

'But—'

'Now.'

'By your leave, Ren.'

The galleon jumped to hyperspace not a moment too soon. That was one less thing to worry about. Now that the galleon was gone, Kilo squadron could begin swarming the dreadnought.

Griff: 'All squadrons to port. Draw fire. I repeat, draw fire, we have cargo going in hot. Let's see if we can reduce the heat.'

'Kilo squadron in position.'

'Uniform ready.'

'Lima is go.'

'All of you ready to drop?' Daddy Blue said.

Cole: 'You know it, baby.'

Kit: 'Bloody oath.'

Kyra: 'Always.'

Trix: 'Hmm.'

Ren was silent.

'Hysi, opening the loading ramp. Everyone take positions.'

The machinas stood. Space unfolded before them.

'To avoid you splattering on the hull, I'm gonna take her up real close, then yaw 180 degrees. In that brief moment when the ship is stationary, and you're facing the hull, you have to jump.'

'By my count you'll have 300m before you reach the hull,' Sif said.

Cole: 'That's a long way.'

Kit: 'Mate, I think you're getting metres confused with kilometres. We could run that in twenty-four seconds.'

'You know how they say the camera adds ten pounds?'

'Yeah.'

'Well each gun adds ten kilometres,' Kyra said. 'And how many guns do you think are on that dreadnought?'

'Point taken, mate.'

'Beginning approach,' Griff said.

The run on the dreadnought had officially begun. Dheizir Crohl was waiting inside.

At least, Ren Gerdac hoped he was.

5

All squadrons drew fire as the Fox cut through the middle.

Despite his best efforts — which were extraordinary by anyone's standards — Griff couldn't avoid all the dreadnought's shots. None of them hit him dead on, but they skimmed the shields enough to drain them. And the Dread Phantoms lost three more ships in their distraction efforts. Piloting spacecraft in a dogfight was exhausting. People were beginning to make mistakes. Thankfully, Griff was more or less in fine form.

'Hysi, coming up. Get ready.'

Sif highlighted the dreadnought's shield so Griff wouldn't fly into it by accident. Daddy Blue yawed, cutting the thrusters at the shield's edge. He could only stop for a second. Rerouted the Fox's shields to the stern. As soon as the machinas were aboard the dreadnought, Griff was returning to the debris field. There'd be less chance of being hit in there. Avoiding space junk was easy. It wasn't actively trying to kill you.

The machinas and Ren jumped. Trix had debated wearing her flight-suit, but she wanted full mobility once she boarded the dreadnought.

I really need to invest in a newer model, Trix thought, like she was reminding herself to get milk. She grabbed onto Kit's legs as he activated his thruster-pack. They soared towards the dreadnought. Through the shields. Now they just needed to reach the airlock and breach it. A walk in the park.

If that park was full of death traps.

'Oni Three, up front,' Cole said. Kit and Kyra joined him. Cole was in the middle. Ren and Trix were behind them. They were joined together, flying in formation. None of the guns had targeted them so far. The Oni Three were moving erratically. Their HUDs showed the correct route to the airlock door so they could readjust after every evasion.

Another reason the Oni Three were taking point — besides the fact that Kit had the drill mines — was so they could merge their oni barriers into one. A unified oni barrier could absorb a dreadnought shot, maybe two, before the casters' hearts exploded.

Kyra: 'Incoming at two o'clock.'

Cole: 'Bank hard left then roll right.'

The onis did as Cole said. He'd liked dragon training more than the others on Mair Ultima. He was far from being as masterful as a dragon machina, but his talents served well enough.

Trix saw plasma brush past close enough for her HUD to blare with alarms.

Sif: 'Trix, one hit from these blasts and we're dead.'

Trix: 'We?'

'I'm in your gauntlet.'

'You could've stayed on the ship.'

'I could've, but you need me more than Griff.'

'Hmm.'

The onis smashed into the dreadnought's hull a moment before being incinerated by a plasma cannon. Dreadnoughts in the military — whether it was Human, Corrachian, Zirean, or Psygotaic — possessed ballistic weapons as well. Notably, missiles, and shells. However, since gangs of marauders, pirates, and other miscreants didn't have the manpower to staff dreadnoughts that required so much manual reloading — not to mention the cost and trouble of buying illegal ammunition — they relied on plasma cannons. They only needed to recharge.

The machinas pressed against the dreadnought. They couldn't be fired upon so close to the hull.

Kyra was examining the door. She tried x-ray vision. Better to try the obvious in case it yielded results than to forgo it altogether. The door was too thick to show where the locking mechanisms were located. Kyra had an idea of where they would be though. Cole and Kit left the decision up to her. Kyra had always been better than them at breaching since she'd paid more attention in theory classes.

She showed Kit where to place the drill mines. The lack of noise in spacewalks always heightened the tension. Trix's helmet could simulate noise based on visuals to prevent disorientation, but it wasn't the same. No soundtrack was as unsettling as your own heart pounding in your ears.

Kit placed the drill mines. Activated them. Heard Griff throwing shade at the Exiles over comms. None of which they'd be able to hear, but whatever worked for him.

Ren: 'All squadrons to the dreadnought's starboard side.'

The squadrons obeyed Ren's command. The portside cannons stopped firing now they had no more targets. The onis watched the drill mines with bated breath. Kyra hadn't been certain about their placement.

Red lights turned blue, signalling the drilling's completion. Cole moved back. Used his thruster-pack to shoulder charge the door. Nothing happened. He tried again. Same result.

'Fuck, it's still locked.'

'We could try the hangar doors,' Kyra said. She spoke like they'd only suffered a minor setback. Someone might've scraped a knee instead of being stranded outside a hostile ship.

'They'll be even harder to breach. We may as well try moving a fucking mountain.'

That gave Kit of Aros an idea. It was unquestionably the stupidest idea he — and possibly anyone else — had ever had. That said a lot considering that Kit had requested a dragon to douse him in flames only last week. A greater dragon, no less.

Kit: 'I know a way to get the door open, mate.'

Trix put Cole's last sentence together with Kit's sudden plan. 'You're mad.'

'Am not, Beatrix. I've just had a bloody good idea. Cole, I'm gonna need your help.'

'You tell me what we're doing first.'

'We're gonna get hit by a dreadnought plasma cannon.'

'On purpose?'

'Yeah, mate. On purpose. We can use the energy we get from the blast to blow open the door. It'll be like a shot from the Fox's weapons, only bypassing the shields.'

Sif: 'Ah, Trix I'm picking up a problem. A really bad one. The dreadnought's shields are contracting. The drill mines alerted them to your attempted breach. If they get the shields to form fit the ship, you'll never break through.'

'Come on, Cole Train. Let's get you up to speed,' said Kit.

'Fool, you're one crazy motherfucker.'

'Glad you're seeing it my way.'

Kit and Cole got beside each other. Pressed their feet against the airlock door.

Trix: 'The energy you absorb could be enough to burst your heart.'

'Exactly why there's two of us going.'

'I'll come with you,' Kyra said, getting into formation.

'Trix will need a breaching expert if we explode,' said Cole.

'We've only got one shot, so I'm coming with you.'

Kyra was in position. Her resolve would be harder to move than Cole's aforementioned mountain.

'Alright. Oni Three, move out.'

They pushed off together. Their thruster-packs activated. Sif created a filter on their HUDs so they could see the approaching shield. It was definitely moving closer.

The Oni Three hovered a safe distance from the cannons. Only nothing was firing.

Kyra drew her guns. Started shooting. She wanted to draw their attention. The dreadnought was likely occupied by the starboard squadrons. A cannon started charging. Kyra holstered her guns with blistering speed. The onis summoned a barrier. They could feel their immense strength waning. Then the blast hit. The Exiles must've figured it was unnecessary to fully charge the cannon. After all, they were only aiming at three people.

The Oni Three activated their thrusters to counteract the force. That stopped them from hurtling into space but it pushed them beyond the rapidly shrinking shield. If it formed to the airlock before it irrupted, they wouldn't be up Shit Creek in a leaky canoe, they'd capsize completely.

The energy coursing through the onis' bodies was unlike anything they'd ever felt. Even dragon fire hadn't compared to this. Gold shattered the blacks of their eyes. Their white pupils enlarged to the size of small moons. Their skin bristled underneath their armour. Heads pounded. Storms thrashed inside them. Fissures split their brains. Tidal waves churned their guts. Their hearts were beating three hundred times a minute and climbing. An oni machina could operate at 400 beats per minute before catastrophic heart failure, in the form of an aortic explosion, became reality.

If only Kit and Cole had taken the hit, they would've been so dead a post would've seemed lively in comparison.

Stunned by the blast, the Oni Three watched the shield shrinking, dimly aware they had to move. The dreadnought would fire again. With any luck, the gunner would be just as stunned as the trio who'd survived the blast. They wouldn't be making that mistake again. Next time they'd hit those demons with the dreadnought's full force. There wouldn't even be a mess to clean afterwards.

Kit: 'We've got to move.'

Cole: 'Kit, fuck you.'

The Oni Three formed up once again. Pushed their thrusters as fast as they could go.

At the airlock, Trix and Ren moved out of the way. Took care not to place themselves over any cannons. Trix didn't know how big the onis' resulting blast would be, but she guessed it'd do more than blow the door off.

Even with their thrusters, the Oni Three couldn't catch up to the shield. It was accelerating every second.

Kyra: 'We need to release some of this energy to get more speed.'

Heartrate was at 360.

Each of the onis released an infinitesimal amount compared to the vast energy oceans that ran deep within them. Their acceleration was like seeing the Fox go from supersonic to hypersonic.

The Oni Three passed the shield. Shoulder charged the airlock. What happened next was a sight none of them would live to see again. Well, probably not. Anything was possible. And it was a well-known fact that, despite the age-old proverb, lightning could strike the same place twice.

The dreadnought's side caved. The Oni Three's shoulder charge preceded by a magic shockwave didn't just blow through the outer airlock door, it tore off the inner one as well. Surprised corrachs had just enough time to see what they thought was a human cannonball before being sucked into space. The onis clung to the hull's remains.

Despite their massive energy expenditure, they still had more in the tank. They let a shockwave tear up the dreadnought's hallway, pushing the hull outwards. Corrachs who'd put their helmets on were fumbling for weapons before being steamrolled.

The Oni Three returned to normal. Their heartrates dropped back below sixty. The feeling they had was like finally pissing after holding it in for so long your bladder started aching, only one hundred-fold.

Trix and Ren entered the hallway which was now filled with floating corrach corpses.

Ren: 'You were only supposed to blow the bloody door off.'

Cole: 'We were supposed to get us inside. And look at that, we're here.'

At the hallway's terminus, Trix saw an internal airlock door closing to preserve the rest of the ship's pressure. She, the Oni Three, and Ren, booked it to the door. Made it just in time. The section of the ship they were now in pressurised. The interior looked as Trix remembered it. Cold, exposed metal. Everyone kept their helmets on. They didn't know what the corrachs had planned.

Unfortunately, the room they'd entered was full of mech-suit clad Ice Exiles. All of whom were drawing their weapons.

The dreadnought was massive. Trix had no idea where Dheizir Crohl was hiding. They'd have to sweep it from top to bottom. She'd run out of bullets before she killed her fair share of Ice Exiles.

Now wasn't the time to worry about that.

Now, she had to fight.

6

Kit had made more improvements to the Fox than just the decal by the windshield.

What Trix hadn't seen yet were the decals on each wing. They were the logos for Strife Squad and Ultima Company respectively. A 6V had been painted in white on the ship's centre as well. Kit thought Trix would like it even if she hadn't shown a great deal of enthusiasm when discussing ideas.

With that in mind, Kit was already thinking of their current team — Ren included — as the very beginning of Strife Squad.

Strife Squad were in a square room towards the ship's rear. Sif highlighted the enemies. There were twenty-five corrachs in total. Each of them was preparing to fire. Surprisingly, the room looked like a lab. That was about the last thing Trix had expected to see in an Ice Exile dreadnought.

Andy Tozier's words about Crohl researching biochemical engineering came to her mind. She might've had to search the rest of the ship to find Dheizir, but what he'd been doing with the gramyriapedes could be in the lab. If there was anything left of it after the fight, she intended to find out.

The corrachs raising their weapons at Strife Squad were certainly no scientists. Scientists — even corrachian ones — wouldn't be wearing battle-armour and mech-suits in a lab. They were too bulky. Not appropriate for delicate work.

They're here to destroy it, Trix thought. To erase the evidence.

The Oni Three ducked for cover. Ren dove with Kit. Cole and Kyra were together behind a bench. Everything was bolted down due to being part of a spaceship. Wouldn't want floating furniture if the artificial gravity failed or the hull was breached. Especially not if harmful experiments were in progress.

Trix contemplated using spells to disarm some of the corrachs. Decided against it. They'd have a vice grip on their rifles. It'd be too taxing to make it worthwhile.

The Valkyrie drew her weapons. Vaulted the first bench. Aimed to plunge her sword into the helmet of the corrach standing behind it. He evaded left with thrusters. Trix anticipated the move. Changed her sword to reverse grip. Impaled his head. She'd learned from previous encounters to avoid striking mech-suits directly with her blade, as they sometimes had adamant layers which her sword couldn't cut through.

Trix hit the bench in front of her, with the corrach's corpse beneath her feet. She looted him for grenades. Found five. You could always count on corrachs to carry explosives. Trix was reluctant to use them in case she damaged the equipment. But she'd prefer to live and find another way to discover what Crohl was doing.

Twenty-four corrachs remained. They were near the back wall, moving crates towards airlock doors. They must've been going to dump them in outer space. Maybe incinerating them first.

Ren rose from behind cover equipped with a burst-fire zirean rifle. He was on the room's left side. Trix was to the right, one bench up. Kit was directly beside Ren. One of the corrachs used his mech-suit thrusters to skirt around the lab benches to flank Ren.

Commodore Ren Gerdac ducked behind cover to avoid being shot by the other corrachs who were shooting his position. The flanking corrach came around the bench. Ren rolled away, firing into the corrach's head. The corrach's shield held steady. A blast from Kit's shotgun depleted it. Ren used his thrusters to propel him forwards. A plasma bayonet extended from his rifle.

He skidded along the floor. Jammed the bayonet into the back of the corrach's helmet. Fired point-blanc. The corrach fell to his knees. Ren extracted his bayonet. Searched the Exile's body. Grenades. Perfect. Only 23 mercenaries left.

Cole and Kyra were pinned on the room's right side. Seeing two Exiles die was clearly enough to make the others switch their tactics. Two grenades flew for Cole and Kyra. Cole switched his shotgun to rifle mode. No-scoped the grenade coming for him. It exploded in the lab's dead zone. The shrapnel hit Trix's shields but didn't bring them down.

Kyra opted for a different approach.

'Cover,' she said to Cole.

'Go.'

Kyra jumped over the bench. Wielded her shotgun by the barrel. Batted away the incoming grenade. It sailed back to the corrach who'd thrown it. Kyra hit the floor. Used her thrusters to skid.

The grenade exploded. She absorbed the blast with an oni

barrier. The grenadier was still standing. As was the corrach to his left. Trix rolled from her bench to Cole's position. Emerged from cover. A couple plasma shots to the head dropped the grenadier's shields. Two pumps from Cole's shotgun caused him to stumble. The grenadier's friend unloaded heavy machine gun fire into Kyra's shields. They burst. She was in trouble.

Kyra dropped the grenadier with a shotgun headshot. It rent open his helmet. Revealed a bloody face. Cole charged the HMG wielding corrach. Caused the gunner to panic.

On the room's left side, Kit and Ren were trying to advance towards the rear airlocks. Ren had liberated a dead corrach's helmet from his corpse. It was going to come in handy.

The men had developed a system without speaking. Kit would emerge from cover. Use his shotgun to deplete shields. Ren would then take his place, using his rifle's accuracy to score headshots. In the event he missed, or the corrachs' helmets stopped his bullets, Kit would unleash more shotgun shells. They'd killed two corrachs each using this method and passed just over the lab's halfway point.

'Ren, watch out,' Kit said.

Ren turned. Saw a corrach on his left. Kit raised his shotgun to fire but Ren was in the way. Ren tried using his thrusters to strafe backwards. Now he was out of cover. The corrachs on the far side of the lab shot his thruster-pack. His shields weren't covering it. His thrusters malfunctioned. Sent Ren into his assailant who shot him in the chest. Ren's shields held.

Kit forced the other corrachs back into cover with rapid fire shotgun bursts. Ren tried evading the Exile attacking him but was coat-hangered on his mech-suit. The corrach grabbed his arm at the elbow. Squeezed. Ren's armour wasn't heavy like the onis'. It caved from the elbow down. Ren's right forearm came off in a ragged tear. Shattered bone and torn skin protruded from inside his armour.

Kit pulled Ren to the floor. Shoulder charged the attacking corrach. Followed up with a kick. The Exile threw a servo powered punch at Kit's head. The oni was too fast. He bobbed. Went to fire his shotgun. Out of ammo. Kit holstered it. Tackled the corrach as a bullet fusillade hit his shields. They burst.

On the other side of the room, Kyra's armour was peppered with bullets. None had penetrated her skin, but her armour was becoming weaker. And the constant damage meant her shields couldn't recharge. She'd dispatched the grenadier with a mule kick to the face. It'd bowed his skull. He could live if he received immediate medical attention. But Strife Squad only gave out death certificates.

Trix had killed Kyra's assailant with Cole's help. He'd dropped the corrach's shields. Trix's .44 armour piercing rounds did the rest. Kyra was three benches up from Trix and Cole. And there were only three more benches before the back wall where the corrachs were situated. All eighteen of them.

Kyra crouched behind her bench. Reloaded her weapons. The corrachs were laying down suppressive fire on Trix and Cole. The lab benches were sturdy, but they weren't bulletproof. The machinas had to move. Trix saw that two corrachs were attempting to flank Kyra. Others were moving towards Kit. More were combing the aisles for Ren.

Trix focused her attention on the corrachs trying to flank Kyra.

'Cole, you need to kill those corrachs at the back.' Trix handed him two grenades.

'Yeah, baby. I can make these work.'

Trix broke cover. Ran across the right aisle and back to the centre benches.

'Kyra, make another barrier. Now.'

'Okay.'

Trix threw a grenade to where Kyra was sitting. The explosion weakened the flanking corrachs' shields significantly. Kyra used a shockwave to disarm the Exiles with the energy she'd absorbed from the explosion. Trix jumped from her position. Altered gravity so she fell towards the stunned corrachs.

Cole threw the grenades Trix had given him. The corrachs laying down cover abetted enough to give Trix a chance.

The Valkyrie fired three bullets into the first corrach's head. He made one final grab for Kyra then went limp. The second one wound back for a punch. Trix twisted her body away. Rent his helmet with her sword. Skidded along another bench before dropping back into cover. Saw that Cole was opposite her. He reloaded his shotgun in a blink. Sprung towards the back wall.

Cole's grenades went off. Now the corrachs' shields would be down. He was going to rip them apart.

Kit was trying to do the same thing. He'd subdued the corrach he was boxing. Kit grabbed the sides of the Exile's helmet. Twisted his neck until it was facing the other way, like a demon from some nightmarish plane.

The oni looked back at Ren. He'd used armour resin to seal his stump arm. It would've hurt like a motherfucker but that shit could fix spacesuits and armour. It could easily stop bleeding. Taking it off though, that would redefine pain. That was if Ren stayed conscious. Kit saw Ren putting the grenades he'd taken off the first corrach into the looted helmet. Three Exiles were moving towards Ren. The others were still at the back of the room.

'What's wrong, fellas? You scared? Don't worry, I won't bite,' Kit said.

He had to save Ren. If the pirate died, Kit could forget his paycheck. Considering he needed a new ship, he needed as many of those as he could get his hands on. Besides, Ren was an alright bloke. One of the better guys Kit had worked for in any case. Kit reloaded his shotgun. Jumped onto the nearest bench. Bounded over the others towards Ren's would-be attackers. They saw Kit immediately. It wasn't hard since he was seven feet tall. He summoned an oni barrier to absorb the bullets. Leaped with the energy coursing through him.

The oni body-slammed one of the three corrachs who was almost at Ren's position. The other two were knocked back, but quickly regained their balance. Fired, trying to pin Kit down with their mech-suit boots. Kit was grateful for his thick bone density and thicker armour. Though it wouldn't hold much longer. Kit's HUD showed his shields draining faster than air from a depressurising vessel.

Kyra rushed behind the Exile on Kit's right. Dropped his shields with four shotgun blasts. She shot him in the head. There weren't many other weak points on mech-suits. She holstered her shotgun. Snatched the machine gun from her most recent kill. Kyra emptied its chamber in the other Exile attacking Kit. Kit pulled the corrach to the floor. Ripped off the Exile's helmet. Head-butted him. The corrach's thick skull cracked under his skin. Kit finished him with a knuckleduster punch to the cheek. Skin pierced. Blood spurted. Teeth chipped. Bones broke.

The Exile's left eye was squished so hard in its socket that it burst like a grape beneath a winemaker's feet.

'See, told you I wouldn't bite.' He scrambled to cover. 'Thanks, Kyra.'

'If anyone's gonna kick you while you're down, I want it to be me.'

'Wouldn't have it any other way.'

Behind them, Ren was still fumbling with the grenades. He'd been right handed. And his right hand was currently four metres away. Its index finger still twitched slightly. Trying to pull the trigger on a spectral gun. Ren finally put all the grenades into the helmet. It'd slide along the metal floor nicely.

Trix: 'Sif, how many Exiles left?'

'Thirteen.'

Ren grunted. Pain was causing him to see stars. Darkness pressed against his eyeballs. He felt faint. Any sense of urgency was fleeting. He wanted to lie down. Before he'd put the resin on his stump arm, he'd cauterised the wound with his plasma bayonet. That had hurt almost more than having his arm torn off. The resin was to pressurise the suit. Strife Squad weren't even close to being out of trouble, and if they needed to escape by leaving through an airlock, he'd prefer not to die from exposure.

Commodore Gerdac shuffled to the edge of the bench. Primed one of the grenades.

He hoped he didn't miss.

7

Cole of Orix was fighting five Exiles at once.

The Cole Train didn't believe in biting off more than you could chew. He held the staunch opinion that you just had to chew harder. Unlike Kit, he would bite.

Cole was moving fast. Light on his feet. Quick with his hands. He'd been Oni Academy's boxing champion. When he fought in the ring above the pit, he'd only been thrown off once. Scars running his torso's length served as haunting mementos. The rocks had torn his left pectoral's nipple clean off in a jagged chunk. He remembered falling. How a rock had almost gouged his neck.

No one was going to knock Cole out of the ring again. Nothing stopped the Cole Train, baby.

He tried keeping one Exile between him and the others. Harder for them to shoot that way. He hated mech-suits with a passion. It was more difficult to throw your enemies around when they weighed several hundred kilos. This time he had something else in mind. Like Kit's knuckledusters, Cole's armour had its own special function. Flexing his palms just so made his gloves course with voltage powerful enough to knock out most electronic devices. Including mech-suits.

'Haha, that's it baby,' Cole said. He disarmed the corrach in front of him by grazing his wrist with light voltage. Then he broke said Exile's weapon over his knee. Rocked backwards to avoid a punch. Lunged forward. Cole reached up with his open palm. Placed one hand on the Exile's crotch. Cranked the voltage to maximum. 'Church is in session. Bow down, motherfucker.'

When a corrach's mech-suit was hit by an EMP, the corrach

inside was ejected as a safety precaution. Cole released his grip on the mech-suit. Uppercut the Exile so hard his helmet cracked. The oni ripped it open. Delivered another electric shock to the corrach's head. His skin was crisped.

The other corrachs came closer. Dropped Cole's shields with their shotguns. Shells hit him between his armour plating. They broke through flesh and muscle. Struck bone. Fuck it stung. Cole summoned a barrier as Trix of Zilvia came to his aid.

She'd been engaged in close quarters combat with the last corrach out of the five attacking Cole. Valkyrie Academy had focused closer on mixed martial arts than boxing. In that respect, they were more similar to Spectre and Dragon Academies.

Trix sliced the Exile's gun in half. Didn't bother trying to hit him. Evaded his every move while pumping his shields full of plasma. She was waiting for the opportune moment. It came when the Exile thought a servo-punch would be a good idea. Trix reversed gravity. Fell towards the ceiling. Brought herself down on his fist. Increased her density. The corrach tipped forwards. Trix thrusted her sword into his helmet.

The Valkyrie didn't stop moving. She ran up the Exile's arm and jumped off his head, simultaneously wrenching her sword up through his skull. Brain juices slicked the titanium blade. Its tungsten carbide edge glimmered. Trix increased gravity around herself, and her density to boot. She landed on the next corrach's head so hard that she flattened his helmet. Forced his head inside his body like a turtle.

She saw the last two Exiles filling Cole's armour with bullets.

'On your left,' Trix said, springing from the crumpled Exile's head and delivering a kick to the back of the corrach on her right. This made him stumble forward.

Cole spun out of the falling Exile's way. Dropped low. This was to avoid more bullets from the corrach on his right. It was also useful for achieving proper leverage. He smacked into the stumbling Exile's legs like a professional smashball player.

Cole lifted the Exile up. Put him over his shoulder. The Exile outstretched his arms to stop his neck from being broken on the floor.

Too late.

Cole dropped the Exile on his head at angle. There were few things Cole of Orix relished as much as the sound of a neck snapping in the midst of battle. Especially when he was doing the snapping.

The other corrach attacking Cole had refocused his attention on Trix. Her shields gave far easier than the oni's. Her armour wasn't large enough to accommodate a massive generator. Trix sidestepped as a shotgun shell barrage just missed her. Some hit her helmet. Her gold visor cracked. It wasn't enough to stop her HUD working. But it was a reminder that she should finish this quickly.

The Exile feinted right with a kick. Trix realised just in time to avoid the incoming left hook which was followed by a jab. The Exile knew the machina would kill him if he reloaded. Trix was out of bullets as well. She sheathed her sword. Tried reloading her pistol when the corrach knocked her backwards. She crashed into the wall. Her pistol sailed through the air, somewhere beyond her peripheral vision.

And it was caught by Cole.

He fired it at the Exile's head. The bullets were absorbed by his shields. Cole's arms wracked his body with pain. The fucking shotgun shells were grating his nerves like rusted barbed wire against bare skin. He ignored the pain. Holstered Trix's pistol. Warmed up his volt-gloves. Dove for the corrach. The suit short circuited. He was ejected. Cole went to put him in a chokehold when he heard a single note cut through the air. Trix had split his skull with her sword.

'I had him, you know,' Cole said, pulling Trix back into cover. There were still eight Exiles left.

'Hmm.'

'Showing off?'

'Showing you up.'

'That still counted as an assist.'

Trix nodded. Cole gave her pistol back.

A thunderous explosion happened behind them. It sounded like a thousand grenades going off at once. In actuality, it was five.

Ren Gerdac's helmet-bomb had detonated at the back of the lab. Left a crater in its wake. All the lights burst. Even the hull looked like it was in danger of breaking. Strife Squad wouldn't have to worry about combing the entire dreadnought to find Dheizir Crohl. There wouldn't be any ship left by the time they were done.

Two of the eight remaining Exiles died from the blast. The other six had taken cover. Their shields had burst. Trix picked one off with her pistol. Cole cleared three benches in a single leap. Landed on one of the corrach's backs. The impact sent him into the floor. Cole eviscerated the Exile's head with his shotgun. Another corrach raised his gun to Cole's head.

Kyra disarmed him with a shot then broke his visor with a punch. Stunned him. Activated one of the grenades on his bandolier. Heaved him away. The blast tore apart his mech-suit. And his chest cavity.

Three left. They'd regained their composure. Kit focused fire with his rifle but the Exile evaded. Trix hit him as he strafed. Another went for Cole. The oni coat-hangered his assailant. Shot his mech-suit's rear thrusters, causing him to lose control. The Exile flew head first into a bench. His neck bent at an unnatural angle.

One Exile left. He belonged to Kyra. She attacked with her dual shotguns. The first blast disarmed him. The second broke open his visor. The third rent his face open. The fourth and fifth — which were fired within his shattered visor — turned him into slop. Those last shots weren't necessary. The Exile was already dead. Kyra was just pissed.

The liquid-faced Exile fell. His mech-suit made a loud bang as it hit the floor. Strife Squad looked around them. Bullet holes, plasma burns, and explosive residue marked nearly every available surface. Corpses decorated the floor like exotic animal rugs. Blood trimmed the rest with a macabre colour palette. All the boxes in the room's back-left corner were non-existent.

Ren Gerdac stood behind his bench. Only Kit had seen what'd befallen him.

'We need to find Crohl,' Ren said. He sounded like he was delirious with fever during a bad hangover. He'd taken his helmet off. All the colour had gone from his face. It made the black tattoos on his profile appear even darker. Like they led into an abyssal realm where darkness was the sole occupant.

Kit: 'You look bloody awful.'

Cole: 'Yeah, Gerdac. It's not Halloween for months, man. Put the mask away.'

'We need to find Crohl,' he repeated.

Trix: 'You're in no position to find anything except an early grave.'

Ren put his helmet back on. His visor lit up, indicating that his HUD had come to life. 'As long as that grave is big enough for me and Crohl, I don't care.'

Kyra: 'Trix, there'll be reinforcements coming. We need to move.'

'Not before I look around. They were doing important experiments here. And the fact that they were clearing this lab tells us something else. Crohl still wants this dreadnought. Otherwise he would've destroyed it when we turned up.'

'So why did he want me to come here?' Ren said. His voice could only be heard through comms. He was speaking softly. Leaning against the bench. He wanted to retrieve his arm. It was possible for it to be sewn back on, but that was becoming less likely with every passing second. He'd have to go bionic. What with being a galactic fugitive wanted for terrorism, he doubted that any hospital would help him, no matter how much money he paid. Sure, there were people in Dark's Hide's bowels who could give him a hand — and a forearm come to that — but their methods were shoddier, and likelier to fail.

Trix remembered Ren telling her that Crohl was adept at double bluffs. But he favoured misdirection. He wanted them to miss something. Like an illusionist — not someone capable of actual magic, just sleight of hand — making you watch one hand, while the other did the work.

The Valkyrie crossed the lab and started shifting through the boxes. Empty vials with viscous liquid residue were packed in tight racks. Trix picked one up. Smeared its remains on her comms gauntlet. Sif started analysing it.

The Oni Three moved to cover the airlock doors. Crouched beside them. Reloaded. Too many more Ice Exiles though and they'd completely run out of ammo. Kyra scavenged some shells from the fallen corrachs. Split them between Kit, Cole, and herself.

Ren walked to a more secure position. Remembered that he had painkillers on him. Painkillers of old made people drowsy. Especially the strong ones. And since Ren's arm had been torn off, the strong ones were what he needed. Now they came preloaded with stimulants. That way soldiers wounded in battle could remain alert even after suffering horrendous injuries.

Ren took his helmet off again. Slumped to the floor. Drew a syringe of neon green liquid. Slammed it into his neck. His veins thickened. Rose from his skin like aquatic leviathans. His pupils dilated. Ren tossed the syringe. Started feeling better. Putting his helmet back on, he reloaded his rifle and retracted the plasma bayonet.

If he was going to die, he was going to take as many Exiles with him as possible.

8

Sif finished her analysis.

The compound in the vial was a powerful growth hormone. It looked like it'd been specifically engineered to assist in the rapid growth of arthropods. Trix searched the rest of the boxes. All the vials contained varying degrees of the same hormones. Gramyriapedes were close to arthropods. Though their classification differed slightly. They weren't technically monsters seeing as they were only found on Nuallar. However, their size made people overlook that technicality more often than not.

'This is why the eggs weren't for sale,' Trix said to Sif. 'He didn't have any.'

'You think he turned them into fully grown gramyriapedes within a week?'

'Could it be possible with what was in these vials?'

'Of course it *could* be. But such growth over a short time period would cause untold stress on the body of whatever creature to which this compound was administered.'

'It's amazing how much stress a body can endure,' Trix said. She looked at the Oni Three, thinking of how they must've felt being struck by the dreadnought's plasma cannon. Her earliest memories surfaced. Flashes. Glass walls. Pain. The first thing she'd ever known before she even knew she was alive. The grinding of nerves. Seemingly suffocating for days on end yet not dying. The tearing of flesh. Stretching of muscle.

'Andy did say that Crohl was looking into bio-chemical enhancements. It's possible that the gramyriapedes were altered in a way that made them more susceptible to change.'

'But why? He can't have wanted to sell them.'

I want to play a game with them, nikker.

The puzzle was back in Trix's mind. Infuriatingly, the picture on the box was still Griff with a stupid smile, shouting about the Goshawks. The games Crohl played weren't ordinary ones. He took no pleasure in dropping obvious hints. He didn't want to be stopped. He wasn't a comic book villain. Telling the "heroes" — if genetic freaks and a pirate could be called heroes — his plan would be foolish.

He tried to kill me, but he fucked up, Trix thought.

Dheizir Crohl had made a mistake. He'd underestimated Trix of Zilvia. That would prove to be his downfall.

If Trix could figure out his plan.

But if Crohl had made a mistake once, he could make one again. Trix spied a terminal across the room. The screen was blown to hell thanks to Ren Gerdac's helmet bomb. The input, however, was still intact. Trix plugged Sif in.

'Can you find anything about what they were doing in here?'

'The data on these drives has been erased or corrupted. Reinforcements could fill this room a thousand times over before I found anything readable.'

'Yvach's vernacular's been rubbing off on you.'

'Humans have been using 1,000 as a standard measure of hyperbole for centuries.'

Trix unplugged Sif. The longer Strife Squad stayed in the lab, the more they risked being discovered. But Trix didn't know what to do. It was a helpless feeling. Even worse than being shot. At least when you were shot you could yank the bullet out.

Ren spoke. He could now stand without swaying.

'Have you searched enough, huntress?'

You will see the games we can play.

'We can leave.'

'We can't leave. We need to find Crohl.'

'Crohl's not here.'

'He has to be.'

'This was a ruse. I'm not sure how. But no one besides me has seen Crohl in years. He's only seen when he wants to be. This isn't one of those times.'

'He was hoping we'd die before we even reached inside the dreadnought,' Kyra said. 'If we go further in, we mightn't be able to find our way out.'

Kit: 'Well, we have already made a hole. No point in making another one.'

Just as Kit finished speaking, the airlock door they'd entered through exploded open. Strife Squad was pulled towards it. Kyra dove for Ren to stop him from being dragged into space. Trix held a bench's edge. More Exiles were coming. It looked like Strife Squad wouldn't be going back the way they'd come anytime soon.

Cole was by the airlock across from the open one. He blasted it with his shotgun then shoulder charged it. His whole arm howled as the hallway beyond began depressurising. Upon opening, it depressurised another hallway. There were no corrachs in this one. That was as good a reason as any to enter.

The Exiles who'd come through the broken airlock were lighting up the lab with heavy machine gun fire. Benches perforated like they were made from rice paper. Strife Squad made for the airlock Cole had opened. An emergency blast door began closing at the hallway's terminus. They had to move.

Kyra's thrusters were still operational. She flew towards the open door while holding Ren. Cole waved her through. Kit went next. Trix was furthest away. She took a slug to her shoulder. It went straight through. Her suit depressurised. Fuck. She could still survive with her helmet on. All machinas could survive exposed in space for a time. Though when the heat died down, if it did, Trix would have to repair the hole with resin.

Trix reached Cole. He grabbed her arms. Flung her forward. He followed. Strife Squad flew down the hallway. The corrachs were catching up. Trix flipped on her back. Fired to try and make the Exiles retreat. That wasn't going to happen. They knew her pistol would overheat — or run out of bullets — before their shields gave.

The blast door was closing. Trix and Cole weren't going to make it. Trix altered gravity, pushing them lower to the ground and increasing their speed. Cole made it through, just after Trix, a moment before his foot would've been shorn off.

Strife Squad found themselves at a crossroads. A bridge from their position ran to a central square platform. There were sheer drops on either side of its railings. The drops looked like they ran the dreadnought's entire depth. Maybe down to a hangar.

There were more Exiles at the crossroads. Kit, Kyra, and Ren were already engaged in combat. Ren was having a hard time. Reloading with only one arm wasn't difficult. It was a near impossible task. He had to set his rifle down before he could grab a magazine. The doorway Strife Squad held was a poor defensive position. And the Exile reinforcements who'd chased them from the lab would break down the blast door any second.

'I'm calling it,' Trix said. 'We're getting out of here.'

Ren was fumbling with his rifle. 'Fine.'

'Captain,' Griff said over comms. 'We're taking a beating out here. They just won't stop firing. Are you almost done?'

'We're going to find a way out. We'll let you know when we're almost there.'

'How're you gonna know when you're almost there if you don't know where you're going?' said Griff. He didn't sound particularly alarmed. More like a teenager playing a difficult video game knowing that if he died, he'd just respawn at a checkpoint. It probably hadn't crossed Griff's mind that he could die. Trix thought he'd be more upset about the ship blowing up. Or scratching the paint.

The only option was down. Ren no longer had functioning thrusters. The Oni Three did. That would have to be good enough.

'Because we're almost there now.'

'That was quick.'

'Sif, broadcast our position to the Fox.'

'It's going to be weak because of shield interference. But it should be enough.'

'Griff, you seeing us?'

'Hysi, captain. I've got you.'

'We'll be descending to the dreadnought's bottom level.'

'What should I be looking for?'

'Probably a fucking big hole,' Kit said. He'd ducked behind cover again. He could barely fire three shots before his shields gave out. Corrachs were everywhere. What was worse, he heard the ones from the lab on the other side of the blast door.

Strife Squad was about to be surrounded.

'Hysi, I'll keep that in mind. Good thing, too. The first galactic friendly of the Earthen smashball season is starting soon. I hate missing the pre-game show. It helps get me in the mood.'

Time stopped for Trix of Zilvia. Froze in an instant. Sounds were muted. Urgency fled. Thoughts were swept aside like cards from a game of Faet.

I want to play a game with them, nikker.

The Ice Exiles botched a terrorist attack during a Formula X race years ago. Could they be targeting smashball now? With gramyriapedes? That would be more terrifying than any bomb. It was ludicrous. Something akin to a comic book villain's grand plan. Yet, it made perfect sense to Trix. The pieces were all slotting together. Crohl and his talk of games. Rapid gramyriapede growth. Wanting Strife Squad to attack his fleet. He hoped they would die here. If they didn't, and somehow they figured out what he was planning, they would be six hours away from Earth. And they would be too late.

The gramyriapedes would do more than kill people. They'd serve as a symbol. The wish of a man twisted by demented ideologies. Gramyriapedes were remnants of a planet that'd been plunged into a deathly winter. Glassed by plasma, shattered by bombs, and suffocated by ash. That was what Crohl desired for every planet other than Raursioc. The more Trix thought about it, the madder it became. Though all the pieces fit. She looked at the picture on the box again.

Griff's face was no longer there. Instead, a stadium, every seat packed, was being destroyed by enhanced gramyriapedes. Their hides thick carapaces that deflected bullets and dissipated plasma. The stadium's audience would be dead by the time they were put down.

Trix didn't care when this game was. She was going to Earth. She was going to stop it. She'd thought going to Nuallar was ridiculous. If only she could've foreseen what Crohl planned on doing. Hindsight was the cruellest vision of all. It taunted her in the twins from Fenwick's voices. Balthioul's Children. For they had been his. Everyone in Fenwick had been under that monster's control. And she hadn't seen it. Just like she hadn't seen this.

'Everyone, move. We're going down. Oni Three first. Kit, you take Ren.'

'Got it, Beatrix.'

Kit's hulking frame easily shielded Ren's average size. Cole and Kyra jumped the railing. Kit went next. Trix followed last. They began freefalling through the dreadnought. Of course, nothing was ever that easy.

Open platform elevators were moving through the crossroad gaps at different speeds. Strife Squad had to constantly readjust their course to avoid fatal collisions. Bullets howled past them. So did plasma. Now that they were moving, they had to worry less about the Exiles and more about colliding with the dreadnought's interior. Trix contacted Griff as she fell.

'Griff, this smashball game, where's it taking place?'

'Where else? Jets Stadium in New York. The biggest smashball stadium on Earth. It can seat 400,000 people. I've only ever been to one game myself, and that was way in the cheap seats. And let me tell you, captain, when a stadium is that big the—'

'Hold that thought.'

A corrach with a fuck-off-big rocket launcher had his sights set on Trix. He was on one of the bridges. Coming up fast.

Alright, dickhead. You wanna dance? Let's go.

Trix increased gravity. Fell faster. Drew her pistol. Fired four shots into the launcher's barrel. The corrach jimmied his weapon. It was broken. Trix flipped backwards so her legs were facing the Exile. Trix could see in his floundering body language that he knew he'd made a mistake. Hindsight's a real bitch, ain't it?

Trix brought her feet square into the corrach's chest. Sent him over the railing. Trix pushed off him a second time. He hurtled towards an approaching elevator. Made contact. The

Valkyrie kept going. Resumed her conversation with Griff.

'Griff, the game. When's it start?'

'The pre-show starts in about two hours. It usually goes for two, but I think this year they're airing a special anniversary vid that'll add an extra thirty minutes. All in all, the game should start in about four and a half hours. Earthen Gladiators versus the Xardiassian Ceirlos.'

'And how long does the game go for?'

'Four glorious, fifteen minute quarters. But once you include the half-time show, and all the stoppage time between plays, you're looking at about three hours. Each quarter adds new power-ups and pitch augmentations depending on the league too. Seriously, how don't you know this?'

Trix would watch smashball if it was on and she was exceptionally bored. In truth, it was exciting to watch, though she preferred Formula X. More than anything else though, Trix liked reading when she wasn't exploring. Besides, half smashball's fun was keeping up with a certain team, and Trix could never be bothered.

How Dheizir Crohl could've smuggled fully grown gramyriapedes into Jets Stadium was a question for another time. Trix's hunch was so strong it could've enrolled in Oni Academy. She regarded the puzzle in her mind once again. The pieces were as she'd left them.

'Griff, you don't have to worry about missing the game.'

'Because we'll be home toasting to your victory in, say, five minutes?'

'We're going there.'

'To the game?'

'Hmm.'

'Captain, I'm all for being rewarded, but there's no way you could've gotten tickets unless you bought them months ago. And we can't park the ship over the stadium. It's restricted airspace. I only know that because—'

'We're not going to watch. We're going to stop Dheizir Crohl from killing four hundred thousand people.'

'But his dreadnought is here.'

'And the gramyriapedes are not.'

Griff paused. With the way he was holding conversation anyone would've been right to assume he was watching television, idly flicking channels instead of manoeuvring around debris at high speed.

'Fodio mufy.'

Trix was approaching the dreadnought's bottom floor. It rushed to greet her like the Reaper himself. She'd cheated him out of a body so many times he had to be frustrated by now. Trix altered gravity to stop just above the floor. She was in a hangar. More interceptors were being prepped for launch. Ice Exiles were everywhere.

'Yeah,' Trix said. 'Tell me about it.'

Piratical Planning

1

Strife Squad was at the bottom of the crossroads.

Cargo was everywhere. The open platform elevators moving between bridges transported it to upper levels. All packing duties had been waylaid in favour of launching more interceptors. There was no way Strife Squad could escape unseen. The corrachs from above would be on them within the minute.

A huge blast door opened to reveal a shield door at the end of the hangar. It was new generation shield technology which allowed friendly ships to pass through but kept enemies out. This was accomplished by a transmitting signal aboard friendly ships. The shield door's greatest benefit was that you didn't need to worry about airlocks. You just came and went as you pleased.

The Oni Three were evaluating the situation. They thought they could bolt to the shield door, jump out, then have Griff pick them up. That was one of their few flaws. Yes, it would keep enemy ships from entering, but anyone could leave.

Trix was thinking of something else. Her mind churned.

If Crohl planned to unleash gramyriapedes on Earth, then he undoubtedly had a plan to frame someone. Framing Trix was a possibility. She was supposed to have died in the Paris attack, but people saw her jump ship. Then there was Vidal Laigalt who'd been taken in for questioning. It didn't really matter, she supposed, who Crohl framed next. But it would be someone important. Another powder keg added to the stockpile.

Stopping Crohl would be pointless if Trix didn't prove he was behind the attacks. Proving it would also be for naught if Crohl wasn't captured. The Consortium had never caught him. They couldn't even find him. Trix didn't know if foiling Crohl's terrorist attack and bringing him to justice would be possible.

But as she surveyed the hangar, she had an idea.

Elements came together in her mind as if summoned by a sorcerer.

The shield door.

Access transmission.

Ice Exile Fleet coordinates.

Interceptors.

Yes, she had it. Crohl might roam free until he died of natural causes, but if Trix of Zilvia had a say, he'd die powerless, with no influence on the galaxy other than begging for orits on backwater planets.

'We're going to commandeer an interceptor,' Trix said.

'There're five of us, and we're not exactly small,' Kit said, gesturing to himself and the other onis.

'Fine, two interceptors. Kit, you take Ren. Get out of here. Jump to hyperspace and wait for us. Go anywhere. It doesn't matter. Just make it close. Cole, you'll have to fit inside with them. It'll be tight. But a coffin'd be tighter. Kyra, you're coming with me to disable this dreadnought.'

'Since we're carrying deadweight,' Kit said as he ducked behind some crates. They were full of weapons and ammunition. Gangs didn't tend to buy much else. 'Sorry, Ren, you're not dead yet, but you know what I mean. Since we're hauling disabled pirate ass, we'll go first.'

'We'll cover you,' said Kyra.

'I'm liking the look of that interceptor right there,' Cole said, tagging the one he was talking about with his comms gauntlet. The beacon showed up on everyone's HUDs.

'Any particular reason why, mate?'

'It's the closest, dumbass.'

'I'd say you're right.'

Kyra cracked open a weapon crate. Heavy machine guns like the ones the Exiles from the lab had used spilled out. They had massive drum barrel magazines. Originally, they'd actually been turrets on the back of ground vehicles. Mech-suits allowed corrachs to deal with the recoil and weight. Machinas could handle HMGs because of their enhancements. Kyra tossed one to Trix who caught it with her right hand. There was a trolley near the crates similar to the one Kit had used to help Griff haul parts for the Fox.

Ren got on to the middle of the trolley. Cole kneeled at the front like an old ship's figurehead. Kyra and Trix stood on the back. Kit grabbed the trolley handles. Started running. Bullets came from every direction as soon as he left the cargo area.

'Sit the fuck down,' Kyra said, unloading her HMG on the corrachs who'd been helping prep the ships.

Trix did the same on her side. Cole kept his barrier raised at the front. Kit's legs pumped hard. A bullet struck him between his thigh armour plates. It missed shattering his knee cap. He would've been in real trouble if that'd happened.

Strife Squad was approaching the interceptor. The pilots were desperately trying to get it airborne before the machinas reached them. Unlike other, larger ships, interceptors could be entered through the windshield. They lifted up like old fashioned Earthen fighter jets. In the event of ejection, the windshield popped off completely. This was most useful for dogfights within atmospheres, though it could be used in space as well. The seats were fitted with oxygen canisters, adjustment thrusters, and trackers to alert nearby ships to the pilot's position.

Cole knocked the interceptor's pilot off the nose with a shockwave. He went sprawling into the air.

'Everyone ready to jump,' Cole said. It wasn't a question. He took his remaining absorbed energy and hit the front of the trolley with it. It tipped forwards like a catapult. Strife Squad was flung into the air. Kit had pushed upwards on the trolley handles to increase lift. Trix and Kyra got the most height since they'd been standing on the sweet spot. Their weapons were almost dry, and they only had one extra barrel each.

The women swept bullets over the hangar from their airborne positions. Since most of the corrachs were either pilots or engineers, they weren't wearing mech-suits. Some of the mechanics weren't even wearing body armour. The HMGs atomised their bodies. Ren watched this happen. He wasn't half as composed. Losing an arm had thrown him off balance. It was said the same thing happened to djurels who lost their tails.

Cole grabbed Ren in mid-air. Shoved him into the interceptor's gunner's seat. It was already taken by a corrach who raised a pistol to Ren's face. Ren stuck him with his plasma bayonet. Right in the neck. Cole landed in the pilot's seat. Reached over and threw the corrach's corpse outside. Ren squished in the paltry storage compartment behind the gunner's seat. Kit took his place.

Kit: 'Hey mate, no one's flying this but me.'

'I'm already in the pilot's chair,' said Cole, keeping his head low as he finished engaging takeoff protocols. Lucky for him, the Exiles had already entered their activation code. The windshield closed.

'Trix, we're good to go, baby,' Cole said. He powered up the interceptor's vertical thrusters. It lifted into the air.

'Get out of here now.'

'Okay but just before I go, Kit, why don't you play these bastards the song of our people?'

'Fuck oath, mate.'

Kit used the cannons to demolish interceptors on the hangar's opposite side. Cole turned the ship at the crossroads. And the elevators from where reinforcements were spewing. Kit fired again. Rocket launchers started being brought out, and they were taking aim at the ship.

'I think we've sung enough, mate. Throat's a little sore.'

'See you soon, Trix.'

Cole flew the interceptor out the shield door. Back into space around the dreadnought. He'd jump to hyperspace once he was safely away from the dreadnought's cannons.

Trix and Kyra landed underneath the interceptor beside the one Cole had commandeered. It seemed as good an option as any other. As Cole would've said, it was the closest.

Exiles surrounded them. The machinas had reloaded their HMGs before hitting the ground. Interceptors across the hangar decided to hang their pre-flight checks and takeoff. Leaving the hangar to fight Dread Phantom ships seemed safer than staying.

Corrachs who'd survived the elevator blasts took aim at Trix and Kyra. Knowing that the machinas would probably dodge rockets, they aimed at their own interceptor. It hadn't powered up yet. The shields wouldn't be operational. And they would rather have their interceptor in pieces than in filthy nikker hands.

'Incoming,' Kyra said as she held a mechanic by the scruff of his neck. Used him as a meat-shield. She wielded her HMG with her opposite hand. Its bullets were vicious. They didn't just pierce flesh, they split it apart like cannonballs against wood.

Trix saw the rockets. Shot one. It exploded before hitting the interceptor. Kyra's meat-shield had outlived — ha ha ha — its usefulness. She tossed it upwards. Into second rocket's path. Gore rained from the sky. Infused with shrapnel. Roasted in flames. However, the third rocket hit its mark just shy of the interceptor's cockpit.

That was some terrible, terrible damage. Internal components erupted in ribbons of wiring and twisted metal.

'Sif, is it still flyable?'

'Yes, but the inertial dampeners are finished. And without the windshield, well, it has no windshield.'

Trix's original idea changed. She couldn't leave the dreadnought in an interceptor after all. Cole had one. That was all she needed for the larger part of her plan to work. In theory, at least.

The Valkyrie's HMG ran dry. A crying shame. It'd mown down over twenty corrachs in the time she'd used it. She jumped. Pulled herself onto the ship's wings. Into its cockpit. It was covered in metal debris from the blast. But the consoles were still operational. Trix plugged Sif into the gunner's seat's controls. They were safer than the pilot's by a longshot.

'Sif, I need you to get the ships off the ground.'

'How many?'

'All of them.'

'And what should I have them do?'

'Unload all weapons to the dreadnought's rear, then when the shields burst or weapons overheat, make them dive-bomb the hangar.'

Kyra sat in the pilot's seat. Her HMG had run dry as well.

'The only way to be a better target than sitting in a stationary ship would be to strip naked and paint bullseyes on your nipples,' Kyra said as she got the ship airborne. Strafed around the hangar.

Sif: 'I can't make the ships with pilots obey me. In fact, I can't remotely control all of them. That's too many individual actions. They'd easily be overridden. But I can make them copy our ship's actions. They're all linked to the same battle-net. They won't be able to stop us with this one as the host.'

Trix thought about that. She'd hoped Sif could upload a macro. While the Exiles were too busy saving themselves, she and Kyra could slip out the shield door. Sif's new method left them in the danger zone longer than she liked. But that was the way of battle, was it not? If you wanted things to go according to plan, you bought a piece of furniture.

'Keep us in the air,' Trix said to Kyra.

'Long as you do the shooting.'

Trix focused the cannons on the corrachs who'd activated temporary shield barriers. They were reusable generators capable of stopping one tank shell before needing to recharge. Invaluable tools when fighting in an open area. Much like shield doors, weapon fire could come through from the back, but not enter from the front. Each race's military had their own variant.

The ship's cannons made short work of the shield barriers. Rockets flew from the ground. Kyra dodged them. Swung the ship back and forth erratically. Patterns could be read. Could be shot down. Being unpredictable in combat was hammered into all machinas. Onis especially. With their unparalleled ability to take a beating, they could afford to be more brazen than your average soldier.

One by one, interceptors started becoming airborne beside Kyra's. Sif's hack was working. That was because it wasn't really a hack. It was a built-in interceptor function. It allowed pilots of different skill levels to maintain formation easier. Sif was just exploiting it. Activating their formation protocols to the highest setting. Absolute duplication.

Sif had a third of the remaining ships airborne. That made nine of them. The hangar's rear was more torn open than a child's presents on Christmas. Most of the crossroad bridges had collapsed, crushing the underlying levels. Carnage was king, baby.

Then a rocket hit Kyra's wing. It appeared Carnage was interested in making sure all his subjects received equal treatment. The starboard vertical thruster was fried. The interceptor angled downwards. It was completely unbalanced. Consequently, the other ships angled themselves obliquely. Trix killed the bastard who'd shot them. He'd been hiding in the crossroad wreckage.

Kyra: 'We don't have any shields. Good thing it didn't hit the cockpit.'

Sif: 'Trix, there's a rogue ship coming up behind the formation. And it has weapons lock.'

Trix: 'Can you keep the ships under your command if I unplug you?'

'The program's self-sustaining until someone stops it.'

'That's all we need. Kyra, I think this ride's had it.'

'I *know* this ride's had it. Let's get out of here.'

Trix unplugged Sif. Kyra set the thrusters to rev. Once they redlined, the ship would launch at the hangar's rear. It didn't matter if their ship exploded now. Sif's command was repeating itself across nine other interceptors.

Trix jumped onto the ship's hull. Kyra was right behind her. An enemy Exile ship fired all. The machinas leapt off the edge.

Plasma hit exposed thrusters. A shockwave. It pushed the machinas onto the ship in front of them. Their shields were non-existent. Trix hit the wing. Almost slid off. Kyra brought herself onto the windshield. Caused it to crack. She planted her feet against the hull. Tried ripping it off. Sif's interceptors were nearly ready to dive-bomb.

The Ice Exiles on the ground had taken the hint. They were getting the fuck away from the hangar.

Trix came opposite Kyra. Kyra still had a grenade from the corrachs in the lab. She slammed it into the windshield's cracks. Dove with Trix to the back of the ship for cover. The grenade broke the rest of the windshield. Trix killed the pilot with her pistol. Kyra tossed his body out. Blew the gunner's chest asunder with her shotgun. There was no time to actually fly the ship. Trix kicked her foot onto the thruster lever in reverse. The ship started flying backwards as Sif's kamikaze ones flew forwards. Trix and Kyra held onto the broken windshield as they fled the hangar.

Grey walls became lit with white-blue flames. Orange streaked around the edges like neon tubing. The crossroads funnelled the fire upwards. Corrachs on upper levels were incinerated. Even the shield door failed. The hangar depressurised. The objects that hadn't been vaporised were sucked out of the hangar.

Trix and Kyra kept holding on as their ship flew towards the dreadnought's nose.

'Griff, we need extraction.'

'I'm already on my way. I'm tracking you, remember?'

Trix had forgotten in all the excitement. It appeared like she and Kyra were going to make it out with hardly a scratch — if you ignored their multiple bullet wounds. Then an Exile interceptor came to their position.

Trix reached into the cockpit. Jerked the yoke portside. Avoided the interceptor's fire, but the sudden movement caused Trix to slip. Kyra caught her. The bullet hole in Trix's shoulder howled with pain. Though it was being numbed by the star ocean's cold water. Trix never did get a chance to repair her suit.

The attacking ship followed Trix's lazy manoeuvre with ease. Then Ren Gerdac's remaining corvettes dropped its shields.

'Thanks for warming her up for me, boys,' Griff said.

Trix saw the Fox approach on her right. Its railgun charged. Cut through the exposed corrach ship. The Dread Phantoms dispersed. Trix looked back at the hangar. The flames had been extinguished seeing as there was no more oxygen. It wasn't recognisable as anything. It was so abstract that if it'd been an art piece, snooty people with more money than sense would've called it masterful. A steal at only 100,000 orits.

Kyra swung Trix back up to the interceptor's topside. Trix grabbed the Exile gunner's corpse. Held him close. Then she and Kyra pushed off. Trix altered gravity so they fell towards Griff. He'd parked with the cargo bay open. Griff reversed. The machinas were engulfed by the Fox. The loading ramp closed. Gravity was restored. Trix and Kyra hit the floor. The corrach corpse rolled aside.

'HYSI! Daddy Blue makes the catch,' Griff said. 'Kilo, Lima, Uniform, we are outta here. Haul ass to the Reef. These bastards can't catch us. We're flying on Vitliaeth's wings now!'

Vitliae was the zirean word for victory. Vitliaeth was an ancient god representing Fortune who took the form of a gold dragon. It was said that anyone his fire touched wouldn't be burned, but blessed. Griff had a tattoo of Vitliaeth on his right shoulder blade that stretched down his arm.

Trix strapped herself into one of the cargo bay's chairs. Kyra sat next to her. Trix took off her helmet. The visor was split from one corner to the other. It was a miracle that it hadn't shattered. Blood seeped from her shoulder. Another bullet had scraped under her armpit. Her combat vest was riddled with shells. She was going to be covered in bruises.

Kyra had faired a lot better. Her armour was based off tank plating. It allowed for less manoeuvrability and was too heavy for Trix to wear. A shotgun blast had shorn the paint off Kyra's left pauldron. She retracted her helmet.

Trix smiled at her. Both of them were glistening with sweat. The blacks of their eyes were cracked with gold. The machina equivalent of being bloodshot. Kyra grinned. They fist bumped.

'The last time I felt this good in your cargo bay was—'

'I don't need to hear the end of that sentence,' Trix said as she applied nano-gel to her wounds.

'If that unsettles you, you might want to switch seats. Funny that it should considering we're sharing your cargo bay with a corpse.'

'Griff, are we in hyperspace yet?'

'Just have to clear the debris field, captain. And... we've made the jump. This is the greatest ship I've ever flown. No, the finest vessel to have ever flown among the stars. And the most magnificent one that ever will.'

'Would that be because you built it?'

'The folks at Fox Transport deserve a healthy amount of credit. They were the sculptors, but if you wish to see the grand artisan, look no further than the cockpit. Fox Vanquish, you did me proud.'

'Don't kiss my ship.'

'How'd you know? By the way, we're out of hyperspace.'

'Why?'

'Cole Train only made a 10 second jump. More than enough to clear the dreadnought.'

Ten seconds in hyperspace was three million kilometres.

Trix unstrapped herself. Moved for the airlock.

'Get Ren aboard. Tell Cole and Kit to stay with the ship. We're going to need it.'

'Care to let us in on what you're planning? What'd Kyra say about a corpse? And Ren probably needs medical attention. The galleon's med-bay should do the trick.'

'No time to take him to the Reef. I'll let you know what we're doing once we're Earthbound. I need to take my armour in for repairs. Then I need to call Yvach.'

Kyra followed Trix into the airlock. Pain started seeping into her joints. Being a machina afforded a lot of unwanted gifts. But Kyra wouldn't trade the power for anything else. She was proud to be a machina. And she'd fight anyone who said a word against her. All with a grin, too.

Once the women were inside the Fox's living quarters, Griff began the docking procedure with the Ice Exile interceptor. Trix made a beeline for the armoury. Stripped off her armour, down to her 2nd Skin one piece, and fitted it inside the locker. The computer estimated two hours to repair the damage. Most of it was fixable with the materials she possessed. Her helmet would be almost as good as new.

Trix set her weapons down then went to her private terminal. The Fox docked with the interceptor. Ren staggered aboard, barely noticing the corpse on the floor. Passed through the airlock. Crashed onto the sofa. Kyra was checking herself over. Administered nano-gel where needed. She walked to the fridge and grabbed Ren a beer.

Trix: 'Sif, can you control that interceptor remotely?'

'Now that it's separated from the dreadnought, sure. As long as you don't want me flying the Fox, I can do it.'

That was what Trix wanted to hear. She used her terminal to contact Cole and Kit.

'Change of plan, you two can come aboard.'

Cole: 'You mean there was a plan where we had to stay in here? This thing was built for corrachs. Damn it's a tight fit.'

Kit: 'So many jokes off that, mate.'

'The only joke here is you.'

'Um, the phone just rang. It's a lame dude on the other end. He says thank you. Your comeback was so lame that he, by comparison, looks like he can walk.'

'The shit that comes outta your mouth, fool. I will punch you in the face.'

'It's funny because we're mates.'

'Yeah, joke's on me there.'

Trix: 'Just get back on the Fox. But can one of you transport something into the interceptor's pilot's seat?'

'What, Beatrix?'

'A corrachian corpse.'

'I'd say that was a strange request, but I've been asked for weirder,' Kit said, ending the transmission.

Alright, that was done. Trix's plan was coming together. She dialled Yvach. Set the frequency to the highest of urgencies. He answered on the second ring. His face appeared on the screen. It looked like he hadn't slept since speaking to Trix last.

'Trix! It's risky for you to be calling me.'

'It's risky for you to be answering. I expect I'll be labelled a tarclaber for my alleged actions on Earth and exiled from the Mountain Kings.'

'No, we Mountain Kings can smell a rat. We know you wouldn't do such a thing. Well maybe not everyone does, but I do. Raursioc and its 1,000 peaks I'm furious. I haven't slept in a day. Vidal Laigalt's been taken in for questioning. That was hours ago. Still no word on what's happening. Apparently the trial's being conducted in the Bastion's Secret Council Chambers. That they would even think Vidal could've done such a thing.' Yvach spat. 'This was Crohl wasn't it? Those fucking Exiles? As soon as the attack on our gardens happened, I put what you'd told me together with the bombing. Then when I saw what you'd "allegedly" done on Earth, I knew it had to be.'

'It just so happens I know where they are. Well, where their dreadnought is.'

'How'd you find out? We've had a team of our finest spies searching for years.'

'Crohl wanted us to find his fleet. Hoped that our discovery would lead to our obliteration.'

'M'fiak, doesn't he know who he's dealing with?'

Trix could tell from Yvach's face that he was looking for a fight. She intended to give him one.

'We incapacitated his dreadnought. I'm sending you its coordinates.'

'I'm sure the story of how you did this is probably even more thrilling than our last adventure together, hey, machina?'

'Hmm.'

'When you say this dreadnought's incapacitated, how exactly do you mean?'

'We dive-bombed ten interceptors in one of their central hangars after firing the guns until they overheated. From what I saw of the result, I don't think they'll be moving anytime soon. But they'll still have weapons.'

Yvach cracked his knuckles. Smoothed his moustache like someone trying to calm a savage beast. 'So we're still gonna need a considerable force, is what you're saying?'

'I wouldn't risk going in with anything less than a destroyer.'

'A wounded baisiom still has claws. Jata. Thing is, we can't exactly be seen readying a destroyer at the moment. We so much as move a platoon down the road and people are gonna think we're preparing for war. Then Earth prepares. Misconceptions will be the end of us, Trix.'

'You need to find a way. If there's anything that can clear my name, and Vidal's, it's aboard that dreadnought.'

'And where is Crohl?'

'I believe he's going to unleash gramyriapedes during the smashball friendly between Xardiassant and Earth.'

Yvach smacked his forehead. 'I'd completely forgotten about that. Supposed to be a hell of a match. If you're right, I guess it really will be.'

'I don't know if we're going to make it in time.'

'I trust you have a plan? Or as much of a plan as machinas are capable of making?'

'The less you know the better. You're not a great liar.'

'Jata. For lying is just another form of poetry, and as you take every occasion to point out, I'm not a poet either. Trix, boarding this dreadnought sounds more like a stealth job. And we happen to know the galaxy's sneakiest bastard.'

'Can you imagine what would happen if word got out that Xardiassant's Queen's personal bodyguard was sent to commandeer a dreadnought full of fugitives, likely killing them instead of bringing them to trial?'

'That'd be a verhais situation if there ever was one. Still, would've been nice to work with ghost boy again. By the end of it I was really warming up to him. And the shit we pulled on Thyria during that train ride. A glorious victory.'

'Can you board the dreadnought?'

'I've got plenty of swing left, machina. I'm bound to find a crew crazy enough to join me. I mean, I'm friends with everyone I plan on asking. And I've never picked the sanest companions.'

'Where would be the fun in that?'

'Gone, machina, is where it would be.'

'We killed countless of their crew members, but the ship is huge. And they still have a couple interceptors flying around. Be careful, old friend. For your sake, don't attempt to pilot anything.'

'Wouldn't dream of it. What kind of window am I looking at?'

'Within six hours. And it's going to take almost three of travel time from Raursioc.'

'I cannot tell you how thrilled I am to shoot something again.'

'It's only been just over a month.'

'I know. I've developed a nasty itch right here,' Yvach raised his right index finger to the camera.

'There'll be enough exiles on that dreadnought to scratch it raw.'

Yvach's smile broadened wider than a battle-axe. It was just as entrancing to behold. Weapons always held a certain fascination. Regular people when faced with a gun barrel, for instance, would incorrectly assume they were frozen in fear. However, it wasn't the pain of death that rooted them to the spot. It was curiosity. What lay in the life after this one? Only when the will to live subdued curiosity was the person at gunpoint able to move.

In faraway lands, incomparable in their vastness and seemingly stretching longer than time itself, it was said that there were other worlds than these, and death was but a doorway to them. A dark highway. A portal. Corridors between worlds that few had ever seen, and even fewer tramped.

A grove of trees where Colours died, once upon a bye.

Thus came about the tired notion that, mayhap, death was a beginning.

Death being final seemed unlikelier the more people learned about the universe. Infinite wonders existed. Anything was possible. The unsettling caveat to that often misinterpreted quote was that if dreams were real, so were nightmares.

Yvach Aodun, Son of the Mountain Kings, was about to bring a metric fuckload of nightmares upon the Ice Exile dreadnought. Jata, you could count on that.

'Well, machina, as much as I'd like to chat, I apparently have a lot of work to do.'

'Take care, Yvach.'

'Jata, along with some Ice Exiles' lives. For glorious honour.'

Yvach signed off. Trix hoped she hadn't sent one of her dearest friends to an early grave.

Sif: 'Trix, we're headed to Earth. To the Transfer, then to Earth, but you knew that.'

'Then I think it's time I told everyone the plan.'

'How long could that possibly take? All your plans can be surmised in one sentence. Don't die. Don't lose. I could go on.'

'This one might even be two sentences long.'

'Good thing I don't have bones, or your wit would cut me to them.'

Trix shook her head. Walked into the living room. Everyone was there. Griff was engaged in giving a play-by-play of how he flew while Strife Squad had been in the dreadnought.

The Oni Three were beaming. Cole had already patched his shoulder. Ren looked surprisingly at ease for someone who'd lost a limb. He wasn't smiling, but he was far from distraught.

Trix thought that might change once she shared her plan.

2

The Valkyrie sat in her armchair.

Griff was leaning against the wall, trying to maintain an air of cool while recounting his death defying stunts. The Oni Three and Ren were on the couch.

'Ah, captain, you've arrived just in time to hear how I put the Fox through a triple forward flip with a half-turn reversal to fly between two interceptors and a fusillade of dreadnought plasma.'

'Maybe another time, unless you don't want to hear why a commandeered Ice Exile interceptor is currently flying ahead of us with a dead corrach at the helm.'

'Hysi, that I'd like to hear.'

'The reason we couldn't just escape the dreadnought was that once we left, it'd be free to go anywhere, and Crohl wouldn't be stupid enough to tell us its location again.'

Kit: 'So we're going back to the dreadnought after Earth? If we're gonna be making these long trips all the time, you need to buy better mattresses for the crew's quarters.'

'No, Yvach's going to take the dreadnought.'

'Isn't he the corrach who was put on trial with you for your destruction of Thyria?' Ren said.

'He's ex-corrachian military, honourably discharged. One of the best. I trust him with my life. He and his team will take it over. There has to be evidence on that ship somewhere that incriminates Crohl and frees us,' Trix said, looking at Ren.

'And in case that doesn't work, you wanted to frame Crohl for an attack by using a stolen ship?' Cole said.

Trix smiled. 'That's part of the reason. From what Sif found in the lab, I think Crohl's going to release gramyriapedes into Jets Stadium during the smashball game.'

Kit whistled low and loud. 'We can't exactly fly a ship overhead and bomb them. Even if we were allowed, the damage could kill civilians.'

'And our weapons didn't do shit to the one on Nuallar,' said

Cole.

'The stadium's going to be empty,' Kyra said, grinning at Trix. 'You're going to send that interceptor down somewhere close by, and they'll be forced to stop the game.'

Trix nodded. 'Hectares of greenspace surrounds Jets Stadium. Public transport's the only way to reach it unless you feel like walking. Or if you're wealthy, then they'll let you use the private garage. There shouldn't be any casualties. It'll look like the Ice Exiles fucked up, but it'll be enough to postpone the game and have the stadium evacuated. The explosion will also trash the pilot, hiding his shotgun wounds. That should cover our tracks. With any luck, he'll be identified as an Ice Exile.'

'Beatrix, that's all well and good,' Kit paused, like he was saying an inside joke to which only he was privy. 'But let's say Yvach finds no evidence. A single Ice Exile drunk flying into a planet isn't going to absolve you or Ren of your alleged actions.'

'That's why we're going to tip off the UNSC. They'll think we're lying. Telling them the attack will take place in New York when it could happen anywhere else on Earth. When it does happen, they'll be forced to see we were telling the truth.'

Ren: 'Huntress, while you may only be wanted for terrorising a planet, I'm wanted for piracy, and already have a long criminal record. Better you leave my name out of it.'

Trix: 'Have it your way.'

Griff: 'Captain, this is fine if Crohl waits until the game's later stages to attack, but if he chooses to do it in the first quarter, we'll never make it in time.'

'There's nothing we can do about that. Once I inform the UNSC about "our" attack, it'll be up to them whether or not they choose to act.'

Kit: 'You're not telling them about the gramyriapedes, are you? They'll never take you seriously if you say giant worms are going to eat the stadium whole. I barely believe it, and I fought one.'

'That's why I'm not telling them. I can't prove it. The best part about saying a ship is going to kamikaze the stadium is that they can't do a bomb sweep. They'll be wondering whether or not it could happen right up until it does. I'm betting on that angst to make them call off the game.'

'Okay, so let's say everything goes as planned, but the gramyriapedes—'

'Larry's kids,' Cole said.

'Larry's kids show up and the stadium's not fully evacuated. We'll have authorities shooting at us, and gargantuan monsters to deal with. How do we fight them without using a ship?'

'I should've taken some of those damn Exile rocket launchers,' Cole said like he should've remembered to buy bread. Oni grocery lists were more dangerous than average household ones by a longshot.

'Gramyriapedes have thick carapaces that protect blubbery flesh. Nothing we have besides the Fox will penetrate their armour. The reason their carapaces are so dense is that the flesh underneath is extremely sensitive. Think of an exposed intestine. They're covered in nerve endings. A breeze would be enough to render anyone catatonic.'

Kit: 'Failing to see how we'll be disembowelling Larry's kids.'

Cole: 'Damn, Larry didn't have any exo-skeleton on Nuallar. Poor bastard must've wanted to kill himself.'

'Poor bastard? Larry tried eating us, mate.'

'It was the Exiles' fault for drawing him out in the first place,' Kyra said.

'Right, so when they draw his kids out, how are we fighting them?'

'The insides of their mouths are their weakest point. Their legs are useless for anything but movement. They don't attack with them. If you have to watch for anything, it'll be the pincers.'

'Larry didn't have any.'

'That's because Larry was sick. Gramyriapedes have retractable pincers in their mouths to help break down rocks while tunnelling. The flesh inside their mouths is extremely tear resistant. It has to be because of all the foreign matter they ingest.'

Griff: 'It's like shields, isn't it? The flesh inside can take constant friction, but it's weak against impact.'

'Hmm.'

'So we're gonna have to be in front of these things to even have a chance at bringing them down. Last time we did that, Larry damn near inhaled us,' Cole said.

'That's a possibility.'

'You saying we could be inhaled?'

'Yes, though there is a way to counter it. A gramyriapede has jaws but its teeth don't meet. It can't actually crush you. Its teeth spiral inwards to create a funnel that filters whatever it digs through. If you can wedge yourself between the rows, you can survive long enough to escape the next time it exhales.'

'I better not have to do that shit,' Cole said.

'Could be fun. What if we slip and go all the way down?' said Kit.

'Their stomach acids will dissolve you before you can scream.'

Kyra: 'Wonderful.'

'Shooting for their mouths still isn't a great plan. Sure, the target's wide enough that a blind man with no arms could hit it,' Kit looked to Ren. 'Sorry, mate. I forgot.'

Ren: 'You lot helped when I was a liability. No need for sorry.'

'And if we told you that we only saved you for the money you owe us?' Trix said.

'Then I'd believe you. It matters not with what intentions a deed is done. Only the end result. I couldn't care if you only saved me for payment. I'd rather be alive. Pride's killed just as many people as bullets.'

'Pride is normally the reason bullets fly in the first place,' said Kyra.

Ren nodded. Scratched the resin casing over his stump arm.

ALEKS CANARD 423

He hadn't cauterised the flesh beneath it very well. Blood was still leaking. Didn't matter, Ren wouldn't bleed to death any more than he was going to win a beauty pageant.

Griff: 'Captain, I know I told you that I can't fly over the stadium because it's restricted airspace, but what if I did it anyway? The Fox will outmanoeuvre any ships the UNSC send after me. And you're gonna need all the help you can get.'

Trix: 'You know I can't afford to pay you fairly for helping like this, Griff.'

'What can you pay me?'

'Nothing.'

'Sold,' Griff shook Trix's hand. 'Hysi, flying the Fox is payment enough. Though I'll be expecting payment from you, Ren. Trix might be the captain but you're the commodore, and I'm still technically your employee.'

'You'll have your money, Griff.'

'Knew you'd see it my way.'

'Speaking of fleets,' Cole said. 'Now that yours is no more than a handful of corvettes and a galleon, how do you plan on maintaining superiority over the Red Wolves? You've got nothing to offer them without ships. Since they're making the majority of the money, it'd be fair to say that they own you, wouldn't it? Really, man, I don't care either way. Long as those orits find their way to my account, doesn't bother me.'

'The galleon's enough. They don't have any of their own ships. And their men aren't accustomed to pirating. We've honed boarding to a fine art. They wouldn't have as much success expanding without us.'

'For the sake of my bank account, you'd better be right, because that dreadnought stunt ranks pretty high on the list of craziest shit I've ever done.'

'And to think it didn't even involve a toilet,' Kit chuckled.

'Sometimes I think your brains stopped aging as well as your bodies,' Kyra said.

'If anyone has better ideas to handle the gramyriapedes, I'll listen. Now,' Trix stood, 'I'm going to contact the UNSC since they can't trace us in hyperspace.'

Kit: 'Try not to say anything stupid, Beatrix.'

'The Fox's stupid quota's already been filled by you,' she said, returning to her quarters.

Cole had a good laugh at that. Kyra was looking at Ren's arm. She knew Trix had basic medical supplies in the armoury.

'Come on, Gerdac. Let's get that arm of yours fixed properly.'

3

Trix was at her private terminal.

She hadn't expected everyone to like her plan. Then again, machinas were used to the ridiculous. And despite what people thought, they weren't monsters. Even without Ren paying them, the Oni Three would follow Trix to Earth because she asked them to. Four hundred thousand lives and international relations were nothing to disregard. They all lived in the same galaxy. Keeping it functioning somewhat smoothly was always a useful goal.

Sif appeared on the desktop of Trix's terminal. Leaned against an invisible wall, arms folded.

'You sure you want to call the UNSC?'

'So long as you don't patch me through to the ENN by mistake. We don't need what I'm saying sensationalised.'

'They'll be recording your message.'

'I won't say anything incriminating. Put me through, Sif.'

'You're the boss.'

After four dial tones, Trix heard an AI asking her to verbally confirm her preferred language, then a promise that someone would speak with her shortly. All AI help desks were trialled once. They performed exceptionally well, but people thought the experience was impersonal.

'Thank you for calling the United Nations Space Command aboard the UNSS. How may I help you?' a female voice said. Despite people requesting a more personal service, no one operating the UNSC help desk ever gave their name unless asked.

'Greetings. My name is Trix of Zilvia. I'm currently wanted for trying to destroy the UNSC HQ in Paris.'

Trix heard a sharp intake of air on the line's other end. Then there was nothing. Trix thought she might've given the young woman a heart attack.

'Could you stay on the line please, ma'am?'

Trix laughed. As far as responses to terrorists went, the woman handled herself well. 'Of course. In fact, I want to keep speaking with you if that's possible. What's your name?'

'Bronte, ma'am.'

Trix could've sworn the woman's voice had changed.

'Pleasure to be speaking with you, Bronte. I was hoping to talk with someone higher up. Perhaps Roger Hobbes. He and I are on good terms. Well, *were* on good terms after I saved his daughter from a psygotaic arms dealer. I imagine he has his reservations about associating with me after my alleged terrorist attack. I was framed. But for now, that's not what's most important.'

Trix wished she could've just said there was a suicide bomber heading to New York and hung up. Though that was unlikely to be taken seriously. It could've just been some kids who had a dark sense of humour.

'And what is most important, ma'am?'

'I'll call you Bronte, and you call me Trix. Sound good?'

'If you insist, Trix.'

'I was the captive of Dheizir Crohl, leader of a gang known as the Ghirsioc Raithexils. That's Ice Exiles if your Corrachian isn't sharp. During my captivity I learned that he plans to send a suicide bomber into Jets Stadium, New York, during the friendly between Xardiassant and Earth.'

The reason Trix decided it was better speaking with a help desk official as opposed to a superior was that superiors were bound to ask questions. They'd try poking holes in her story. They wouldn't adhere to protocol because they wrote it. And that meant they could break it. Bronte, on the other hand, had to treat Trix like any other person who called regarding suspicious activity and/or potential terrorist threats.

'And did you find out the method of delivery?'

'A ship.'

'What kind of ship?'

Bronte was trying to keep Trix talking. But there was no current software that could track a ship in hyperspace.

'An interceptor. Corrachian build. Navy blue paint. Arctic blue trim. No markings. Probably anti-matter bombs on board, like Paris. It was Dheizir Crohl who attacked Raursioc, and Dheizir Crohl who retaliated against Earth. He aims to start a war so corrachs can become the galaxy's superior race.'

'This information will have to be verified. You understand, don't you, Trix?'

'Perfectly. But, in the event you decide that this won't happen, I'm coming to intercept the bomber myself, though I may not make it in time.'

There was no harm in letting Bronte know she was headed for Earth. The UNSC couldn't stop her without knowing from where she was coming. Besides, catching a ship in hyperspace wasn't possible.

'Trix, our authorities take every precaution for all major events within Earth's atmosphere. If the bomber threat is real, it will be dealt with swiftly. As for your allegations about the "true" nature of recent terrorist attacks, we must ask you into the station for questioning.'

'You know I'm telling the truth. Corrachs would never steep to terrorism. It offends their honour which is their proudest possession. If a corrach has a problem with you, they'll say it to your face. The only ones not capable of such valour are those who've been exiled for cowardice and disgraceful actions. While you may think them brutish, they are noble warriors with strict behaviour codes. With that in mind, I'll decline your offer to join you aboard the UNSS. I've heard stories about how you treat machinas.'

'All races are offered equal treatment when subject to—'

'Don't bullshit me. I know our conversation is being

recorded. I also know that by this time you're surrounded by people giving you orders and feeding you information. Funny how you won't negotiate with terrorists, but you're more than happy to chat with them. Evacuating the stadium could save thousands of lives. If not hundreds of thousands.'

'Ma'am

(they were back to ma'am now)

if you enter Earthen airspace, your ship will be shot down. You were right. We don't negotiate with terrorists. And we will not cancel one of the year's biggest games because of a supposed threat. This would only serve to show those you may be working for that events can be controlled with nothing other than false information. The threat will be neutralised and the show will go on. The only way to stop this is by turning yourself in for questioning. You will be afforded a fair trial under Earthen Jurisdiction, presided over by the Bastion supreme court.'

'Calling someone ma'am loses its professionalism when you threaten them with death. I'm innocent until proven guilty. Killing me without a trial would be murder.'

'Machinas aren't covered by those laws. When it comes to your kind, the laws are more like guidelines.'

If Ren thought Trix could turn pirate, he should've heard Bronte.

'Bet that part won't make it into the recording,' Trix said. They didn't believe what she was saying. If Trix could reach the stadium before the gramyriapedes were unleashed, then there was a chance at evacuation. Either way, she understood that making the UNSC trust her wasn't going to happen. Her new primary objective was to make sure her ship wouldn't be shot down or pursued.

'Shooting down my ship would be fine if it wasn't for two citizens I have on board. The first is Ren Gerdac. Citizen of Earth and Thyria. He served a decade in the Hole for a crime he didn't commit. The second is Griffauron Raivad of Xardiassant and Earth. He was a former captain in the C.A.F. I don't think

Xardiassant would take kindly to one of their people being killed without a trial. Zireans stand on ceremony like corrachs stand on a battlefield. They will demand justice.'

'Ren Gerdac, born Renier von Gerdac, is currently implicated in the attacks on Raursioc. As for Griffauron Raivad, he was dishonourably discharged for poor conduct.'

'Those do not change the facts that they're both Earthen Citizens. Gone are the days when people were content their enemies be slaughtered with impunity. If you don't give these men a trial, people will see you as thugs. Not the best image for a government organisation. But since you were willing to murder me, I'm willing to bet you don't care about image. You can paint whatever image you want with the ENN. However, you should care about breaching Consortium law. Any member of a Consortium Race who is suspected of criminal activity must be given trial with fair representation.'

This gave Bronte pause. With Raursioc's situation and Vidal Laigalt's capture, they couldn't afford to anger the Consortium. Especially not the zireans. Queen Iglessia Vialle was beginning to ease taxes on Earthen goods, but they would take years to be implemented, if they ever were. She, by all accounts, was said to be fair. Her rule hadn't even lasted a zirean month. Her effectiveness remained to be seen. And it didn't matter if she was fair. No King or Queen could pass laws without going through the government first. And their opinions were unlikely to have changed.

The zirean chokehold on humans was another reason the game couldn't be postponed. They had invested hundreds of millions into the friendly match as smashball ratings were among the galaxy's highest. The E.S.A. wasn't fooled by their generous donations. The zireans would make their money back through sponsorships, ratings, and of course, the tariffs which bent Earth over backwards.

Zireans were the galaxy's most powerful race. And now Trix of Zilvia claimed to have two aboard her ship: one zirean, and another with strong lineage.

Besides, broadcasting a terrorist attack live at a location with so much potential for disaster would be a ratings goldmine. Earthen governments were trying to establish new laws which locked down even more airspace and allowed them to build shielding over major landmarks, costing taxpayers exorbitant amounts of money, even though the technology wasn't that expensive. Most of the money would be funnelled into experimental weapons programs. For example, a compactor which could mould any scrap metal into bullets of the user's desired calibre. The next step was making that process happen within the weapon itself.

What it boiled down to was that if any zireans were aboard the machina's ship, she couldn't be legally shot down unless she gave the UNSC cause. It'd be a political nightmare. And they were inescapably tangled webs.

Balthioul spun beautiful webs in the forest before you killed him, Balthioul's Children said in perfect unison. *Shame you didn't walk into one then. But you're in one now. It's even worse than one of daddy's! And you'll never ever escape.*

Bronte: 'How do we know you're not lying?'

Trix opened a channel on the Fox's PA system. 'Griff, Ren, come up here now.'

'Hysi, captain.'

'Bronte, if you accept my video request, you'll be able to see that Griff and Ren are here, as I said. This means you cannot shoot me down, as you said.'

Griff walked into Trix's room followed by Ren. He was out of his armour. Kyra had been in the middle of cleaning his wound.

Ren: 'What's this about, huntress?'

'You're going to show your face so we can't be shot down once we reach Earth.'

'So be it.'

Ren and Griff stood on either side of Trix. Bronte hadn't allowed the video feed to show her face. Sif gave Trix a thumbs-up: the video feed had been established.

'As you can see, both of them are here.'

Griff waved. Ren death stared the camera.

Trix knew Bronte would be running facial recognition through registry bases. For Ren, she'd cross reference her findings with his personal file from the Hole. For Griff, she'd use his military record.

'Gentlemen, if you turn yourselves in to the UNSC you will be treated fairly and allowed to explain your actions. A court will decide your punishment.'

'That's a tempting offer, you faceless woman. I know you can't shoot down this vessel with us on board. You could, but my people wouldn't like it very much. You'd probably find yourself on trial. And, I can't speak for the commodore, I wouldn't want to shove a hand up his ass, but I would be useless on trial. Hysi, I find that I tell lies more often than I should. Small ones. Ones that make people feel better about themselves. Harmless. White lies, I believe humans call them.' Griff took off his cap. Held it in his hands.

'Like now, for example. I said you could shoot us down. With me at the helm, you'd have a better chance of catching a bullet between your teeth. Since I lied just now, I'll tell you a truth as a form of compensation. Trix is right. There's an Ice Exile ship headed to Earth and it's going straight for Jets Stadium. As a lifelong smashball fan, I could say that I don't want to see a stadium full of fans like myself massacred. Really, I'm kinda selfish. I don't want the smashball players to die. Xardiassant's team is the best it's been in years. Be a shame for those lads to be killed because of your foolishness. In short, thank you for your offer. And in the words of Aleks Valentine, shove it up your ass.'

Bronte was silent.

'I, Ren Gerdac, agree with Griffauron. You'd take us in for questioning that would last forever. The problem with innocent until proven guilty is that we're not innocent in your minds, are we? Justice may be blind in theory. In reality, Justice looks only where she is directed by those who see what they want. '

Bronte: 'You won't make it into the atmosphere. You will be apprehended.'

'When you try catching that bullet between your teeth, let me know how it works out for you,' Griff said. 'Speaking might be hard, but I'm sure you can write it down instead. Come on, commodore, let's finish fixing your arm.'

Ren left with Griff. Trix kept her eyes on the camera lens.

'I know you're still thinking of shooting us down. So let me offer one last word of warning. If you so much as try and stop us, I'll release the entire recording of this conversation to every news network in the galaxy. When they see the terrorist threat could've been avoided, they'll blame you.'

'Your vigilante methods have already been called into question in the past month. A drunken novelist's testimony can't help you. It's public knowledge that Luanu Mieshe dissented on your judgement for your actions on Thyria and Xardiassant.'

'Once this is over, I'll come in for trial if I must. On my own terms. So will my team. You have my word. Now that's on the record, people will think differently should you choose to attack me.'

'Your information about the alleged terrorist threat will be analysed for validity. Thank you for your call, ma'am.'

Trix cut the communication.

'You think they'll do anything about it?' Sif said.

'No. There's too much money involved for them to risk anything. I'd release the recording now if that would help. The sheer panic it'd cause wouldn't even require an official evacuation. People would boycott the game for fear of death.'

'But if you do that, Crohl will know that we know. And if those gramyriapedes are released before we reach Earth...' Sif trailed off.

'We need to find where Crohl implanted the gramyriapedes. Most likely somewhere far from the stadium with no security. He'd also have to be in a freighter. There's no other way to transport them. From that point it's just a matter of luring them into the crowds.'

Trix's mind fell through memories. The bell on Nuallar had included a Corrachian transmitter. It hadn't been controlling the bell. It'd been copying the signal to an external location. Saving it for later. For this game.

'We'll split into two teams,' Trix said. She'd unknowingly begun liking using Sif as a sounding board for ideas. Many ideas often seemed great until they were voiced. And Sif never failed to point out flaws. 'Cole and Kit aren't wanted for anything. And it helps that they look like typical smashball fans. They'll infiltrate the stadium and locate the transmitting device. Griff will remain at the helm. Ren, well, he can stay in the gunner's seat. Not much else he can do. Kyra and I will sweep the surrounding areas from the Fox and investigate any anomalies. A freighter anywhere shouldn't be hard to spot.'

'What if Crohl didn't use a freight ship at all? What if he had that in his fleet as a red herring? For all we know, besides when you saw him on the dreadnought, he's been on Earth, overseeing the gramyriapedes' enhancements.'

Trix hadn't considered that. It was obvious now. Damn hindsight again. What a bitch.

'That'll make finding his point of entry harder, but it won't ruin us. You should be able to find any anomalous tunnels with basic scans.'

'New York's subterranean geography criss-crosses more than children doing double-dutch.'

'You're becoming more eloquent with age.'

'When dealing with emotional lifeforms, yes, even machinas are emotional, it's easier to use hyperbole. I could tell you the tunnels' combined lengths, the total building material weight, but numbers are only useful for AI. You need visual aids, even when they're only words.'

'Alright, there're a lot of tunnels. I'm willing to bet not many of them are a hundred metres wide.'

'You'd be right. However,' Sif raised her right hand like a university professor, 'since we don't know how long Crohl has been on Earth, he might've had time to fill them in. You're also making the assumption that the gramyriapedes will be the same size as Larry.'

'True, they could be bigger. Gramyriapedes can incubate up to ten eggs at once. Each is the size of a small car. Considering Larry's radiation, it's difficult to say how many would've been healthy enough to undergo significant enhancements, and if they grew to full size.'

'How many do you think you could handle?'

'There's nothing we can't handle with the Fox.'

'Griff would be overjoyed to hear you say that.'

'I don't make those kinds of statements lightly.'

'I know you don't. So, going to tell everyone your new plan?'

'Once we're closer to Earth.' Trix stood. She was going to clean her weapons. She couldn't recall a time when her blade needed to be sharper, or her pistol better oiled. There'd be resistance, not just from the gramyriapedes, but Ice Exiles and authorities alike. Then there was the question of how Kit and Cole were going to blend into Jets Stadium's crowds. Heavy battle-armour wasn't inconspicuous.

When Trix gave it some more thought — for cleaning her weapons was done in a ritualistic trance — she realised that the onis' armour wouldn't be a problem. Kit and Cole could be taken for dressing up. Smashball armour was similar to theirs. Bulky, beaten, and decorated.

Shotguns, however, weren't typically seen at sporting events. The United States of America was much like the rest of Earth. Guns could be carried anywhere save for certain events. At "gun-free events" — which typically entailed armed security guards — firearms were put into lockboxes at the door and could be claimed afterwards. Every weapon was heavily regulated. Firearm registries ensured that if someone fired a bullet, someone else could trace it as long as they had a device with computing power. Plasma, on the other hand, was more or less untraceable.

Kit and Cole would have to sneak in. Airdropping was out.

The skies would be patrolled. There were too many variables. Trix didn't know the layout save for maps she'd seen. She'd never been to Jets Stadium. Griff had. Maybe he knew something.

That concluded that train of thought. It came to rest at the station. End of the line.

Trix hopped off, not looking at the neon departure boards.

4

The next train she found herself on, as her pistol lay in parts before her, was occupied by none other than Garth Roche.

He was sitting alone in a carriage, head locked forward. Trix was sure she was dreaming. She was vaguely aware of her hands moving corrachian gun oil over Magnum Opus' components.

She was awake in the Fox. And somewhere else. A place not of sleep nor of wakefulness, but somewhere in between.

The train station was stark white. Like her hair. Trix had never met Garth Roche. But like every other person in the galaxy, she knew his face. The Scientist of Death. Trix sat beside him. While the rest of the galaxy was hopeless to see him as anything other than a monster, one Trix could be hired to slay, the Valkyrie couldn't help thinking of him as a father. It was the same way machinas instinctually thought of Valkyries as leaders.

Garth Roche was the man Trix had been meant to serve, only she never had. No machinas had.

'Father?' she said. The word sounded wrong. It slicked her tongue with foul memories. Of that day. The Last Day. Calling Roche "Father" was heresy. Felix Roland Westwood was her father, as Susan Marigold was her mother.

The Valkyrie could see through the train windows. Outside was full of stars. She was in space. Where had the tracks gone? Trix looked down at herself. She was wearing casual clothes. The ones she'd worn to Iglessia Vialle's coronation. Her gambler hat with basilisk band was at a jaunty angle. Her shirt sleeves rolled up. Corrachian gun oil covered her hands.

This place was not natural. But not real? That was harder to say.

The stars became a white tunnel again. No sooner turned into something else. Mair Ultima's Luna Wolf Mountains.

'I made machinas to save not just humanity, but all of us,' said Roche. Still looking ahead.

'From what killed the Uldarians?'

'Yes. The anghenfil were a ruse. I knew that we could stop the anghenfil if we banded together with other races. But humans do so love to bear their problems. We are arrogant to the point where we proudly take responsibility for even the worst atrocities. In the 21st century, when people said that we caused "global warming," for example. They didn't want to see the planet as a being with cycles just as we have cycles. They didn't want to consider that they might've only been accelerating it at first. No. Humans wanted to be the ones who singlehandedly killed Earth. It was all our fault, apparently.'

Roche fell silent. His words weren't like the madness he'd written, but they were approaching insanity. He was an old, combustible engine. Warming up after years of gathering dust in a garage. A relic. A Reliquia.

'This folly you've engaged in, stopping Dheizir Crohl. It pains me to think that it might be necessary. What killed the Uldarians is coming back. And when it does, all the galaxy will need to fight, or you shall perish. Somehow ancient Nordic people knew of this calamity.'

'Ragnarök,' Trix said. She'd always thought that she'd strangle Garth Roche if she met him. Never mind that he gave her life. But had he not ripped Trix from her true mother's womb, she would still be alive. Garth Roche didn't steal Trix's life, he'd exchanged it for one of pain. One of being a machine from the gods. A bastard of the stars.

'Of all the stories foretelling the world's end, Ragnarök fits best with what I have uncovered. The Poetic Edda holds clues. The first signs. But they are not as they seem.'

'You speak like you're no longer part of this world. You said "you shall perish" not *we*.'

'Of course I'm not part of this world,' Roche turned his head so he could see Mair Ultima. His reflection was ghostly in the glass. He looked like a haggard man with terminal illness, flipping through pictures of a bygone era. When he'd been handsome. When the world had been a different place. Before the sickness had taken him over. Happiness was evident in how the corners of his mouth formed a weak smile. But his eyes shimmered with sadness. The knowledge that this too, would end.

But beauty could only be fleeting. It knew no other way.

'I'm in your head, Beatrix. I'm here to remind you not to forget. You must remember that a war is coming. I don't know when. I only know that your enemies will be great. Find me, if you can. For this war shall determine the fate of this world.'

'Of this galaxy?'

'No, of this *world*. This version of reality. Others exist through the corridors. In the portals. Each world has its Final Battle eventually. Light and Darkness will clash. This is how it's always been. How it always will be. No world is exempt, not even balance itself.'

'That doesn't make sense.'

'Inner workings of anything seldom do.'

'This place, balance. What's it called?'

'It is not your concern. It is another Childe's burden. One of another world.'

To Trix, Roche had said child. It made sense. He called machina his children. Childe was an archaic word. It meant one of noble birth. Though in special circumstances it could mean one destined for a great journey. As sure as each world had to face an inevitable battle, each one had a Childe, someone who would champion the Light.

'If you're inside my head, how come you know things I don't?'

'Thoughts enter your mind. They do not come from within.

If they did, people would surely not lie awake at night as their worst mistakes play over and over. These thoughts have come to you because you are receptive to them.'

'Then tell me where you are. Tell me what you know.'

'It doesn't work like that, Beatrix.'

Trix looked out the window. Night had come to Mair Ultima. Mireleth looked straight at her. Right through the window. Then he was gone. The train entered a white tunnel which became fragmented. Walls became trees. Trees became Balthioul's Woods. The train stopped in the clearing. Balthioul's Children were playing there, using Balthioul's carcass as a jungle gym.

'Don't you think you've polished that sword enough?' Roche said.

Trix looked down. She was wearing her 2nd Skin one piece again. Her pistol was back in one piece, resting on her hip. Her sword was in front of her. The blade caught light from the overheads. Shone it in her face. It was radiant. Trix looked around. Roche was gone. So was the train. She had so many questions to ask.

Sif appeared on her weapons bench.

'Your eyes indicated you were sleeping. Your heart rate was barely one beat per minute.'

'I was somewhere else.'

'You were here the whole time.'

Perhaps there were two selves. Physical and mental. While the physical was tied to one place, the mental could roam free. Uninhibited by any laws. Capable of its own magic. Was that not the true meaning of imagination?

'How much longer to Earth?'

'We've entered the Solar System. About four hours. Just as well Griff installed brand new thrusters or we'd have to take a break and let them cool.'

Trix remembered what Griff had said about the pregame show. It would've just started. In fact, he was probably watching it.

As the Gladiators and the Ceirlos would be revising their game plans, so too would Strife Squad.

End-Zone

1

Trix of Zilvia gathered everyone in the living room.

She was dressed in her fully repaired battle-armour. Two bandoliers worth of pistol magazines crossed her chest. This had the potential to be a massive fight. In hindsight, it would've been a good idea to have that much ammo on the dreadnought. No matter. She'd survived.

Everyone stood around Trix's table. It was no fancy war room holo-table like Ren's, but it served well enough.

'Sif probably told you that my call to the UNSC didn't go as we hoped.'

'But it did go as we expected,' Kit said.

'If anything happens before we arrive, the best we can do is kill the gramyriapedes to stop them from being used in future attacks.'

'And if we reach Earth in time?' said Kyra.

'If that happens, Sif will pilot the Exile interceptor for Jets Stadium with a disabled shield. That way Griff can destroy it with a single railgun blast.'

Sif: 'I'll also angle the ship so the debris falls away from the stadium. There shouldn't be any casualties. In fact, it's a highly unlikely scenario.'

'And if anyone's pursuing us, that'll be their life's vocation,' Griff said, fiddling with his hat. Wanting to turn it backwards.

Trix: 'After the "attack" has been stopped, Cole, Kit, you'll enter the stadium and look for the transmitting device.'

Cole: 'Same as the one on the bell from Nuallar. You know it, Trix.'

Kit: 'Hopefully everyone will be too busy worrying about death to notice two giants with shotguns combing the stands.'

'If it's anything like Nuallar, the device will probably be in centre field,' Cole folded his arms.

'That's my guess too, mate. It could be below, where all the turf changes come from. There could even be some around the perimeter.' Kit looked to Trix. 'Don't worry, Beatrix, we'll find them, it, either or.'

'I almost hope it's on the field,' said Cole.

'You want to walk on the smashball field, don't you, mate?'

'Fool, you telling me you never wanted to play smashball once you found out what it was?'

'Why wouldn't I? It's better pay for easier hours.'

'I think I'd miss killing people.'

'Me too, mate.'

'You're belligerent, the both of you,' Kyra said, her vicious gaze turning to a smile. She brushed her firetruck red hair away from her face. 'But I'd miss it to.'

'It's who we are,' Kit said.

Trix thought Kit sounded like he was lamenting his statement as much priding himself on it. 'By the way,' Trix said, regaining control of the conversation, 'Ren, you'll be staying on the ship.'

'That's fair, huntress. I'm not much use until I have another arm. And I'd prefer living to see Crohl brought to his knees.'

Kit: 'You know, I'm having a thought here, Ren. You could get a wooden forearm and a hook. Then you'd be a proper pirate, well, vintage, at least.'

'When I have a bionic arm, I look forward to punching you with it.'

'Long as your left hand is paying me orits, I can handle that.'

'Kyra,' Trix said before Kit could continue his stupid banter. 'Griff's going to fly the Fox over the surrounding area while Sif scans for tunnels that shouldn't exist. We'll see if we can stop whoever Crohl has in charge from releasing the gramyriapedes.'

'Easy.'

'It'll almost certainly not go to plan.'

'I think that if one of our plans did go accordingly, we'd be fucked,' Kit said. 'We're so used to making things up as we go I reckon we'd botch a perfect plan.'

'Only you could botch a perfect plan,' Kyra said.

'You're forgetting that any plan involving Kit is far from perfect,' said Cole.

Griff smiled. 'I still like you.'

'See, there's a real mate. I'm standing over here with Griff.'

Griff smacked his forehead. 'I just thought of something.'

'You actually don't like Kit?' Trix said.

'Who cares about that? If we succeed, we might be given lifetime box tickets to Jets Stadium. Wouldn't that be awesome?'

'You have strange priorities, mate.'

'Don't act like that's not exciting.'

'Yeah, look, you're not wrong.'

Kyra: 'I think we've said all that's needed.'

Trix: 'Agreed. Everyone be combat ready by the time we reach Earth.'

'I'll say. You especially, captain,' Griff said.

'Why?'

'You should've seen Cid's face when he found out you'd probably destroyed his ship.'

'He has more chance of putting a hand on the sun,' Trix said, borrowing Jo'ara's phrasing.

'So he does,' Griff said. 'Now, I'm returning to the cockpit for the pregame show. There might be clues to the attack. Maybe Crohl's infiltrated the highest levels of professional sport? Spooky.'

Trix shook her head with a slight smile. Everyone dispersed. Kit went with Griff to the cockpit. Ren went to the crew's quarters. He was understandably fatigued. Probably going to check in with Eosar. Damage control was sorely needed.

Cole and Kyra sat on the sofa together. Trix returned to her room to study Garth Roche's notes. She received a message from Yvach. It hadn't been easy, but he'd assembled a team of corrachs just as insane as him. They were on route to the Ice Exile dreadnought. Trix wished him glorious honour. Opened

Roche's notes. She ended up staring at the picture of Roche and Omega until her eyelids grew heavy. Sleep took her, if only for a few hours.

Her mind drifted.

The Valkyrie didn't return to the Train Station of Thought. She couldn't. No matter how hard she tried. Instead, she dreamed of wars waged between gods, of children sacrificed.

And of the Uldarians. Theirs deaths tainting the star ocean with penultimate destruction.

2

Griffauron "Daddy Blue" Raivad's rousing voice rang through the Fox.

Trix had fallen asleep at her terminal. She was still holding the picture of Garth Roche and Alpha Omega. She slid it back into the journal Sif had printed for her. Griff spoke as Trix locked it away.

'Attention all passengers, this is quartermaster Daddy Blue speaking. I have good news and I have bad news. I have so much news you could call me Kumar. Only don't do that. It doesn't sound as cool. And my news isn't ceirlo shit.'

'I already know both,' Kit said over comms. 'You want the good news first.'

'Don't spoil it.'

'Just tell them, mate.'

'Hysi, hysi. Good news is that two hours into the game, nothing's happened. The stadium's in one piece. Nobody's died.'

'So what's the bad news?' Trix said.

'The Xardiassian Ceirlos are losing. It's an outrage.'

Cole laughed. 'That's the best bad news I've ever heard.'

'The Gladiators still have plenty of time to lose.'

'How long until we exit hyperspace?'

'Five minutes. If everyone except the Commodore could make their way to the cargo bay, that'd be appreciated. And for those of you already in the cargo bay, put your clothes back on.'

Cole: 'Least I could do is give everyone something beautiful to look at in case we die.'

Trix: 'I don't think we have the time to get you plastic surgery.'

Kit: 'You could throw yourself off the loading ramp and leave Kyra, mate. Then again, you being near her makes her look even better by comparison.'

'Damn, that's cold.'

'Not as cold as space would be without your suit on,' Kit reminded him.

Sif: 'I've dropped the Exile ship out of hyperspace. It's ahead of our position. No one's fired on it so far.'

In New York, it was 2:00am on March 10th. The third quarter was nearing completion.

On Earth, smashball season began on a Wednesday. It was typically a galactic friendly as they pulled the largest crowds and warmed people up before the proper matches on Friday, Saturday, and Sunday nights. In terms of leagues, there was: United States of America Smashball Association, Allied States of South America Smashball Union, European Union Smashball Federation, Austral Asia Smashball League, and United States of Africa Smashball Confederation. There was never a shortage of games, especially if you included college smashball.

These seasons typically lasted three months, culminating at the end of June. From there, the planet's best club teams faced off in all-star matches until the end of July. There was an Earthen Cup every four years. Galactic Cups were held in accordance with other planets' schedules. Usually every two and a half Zirean Years.

After Smashball season came Formula X, and other variants of classic Earthen sports which had been upgraded to be more visually impressive. Paintball Zero, for instance, was another popular sport that involved two fireteams or more playing each other in simulated war games like capture the flag. Many of the players were ex-military. And some of the best players ended up joining the real military.

Strife Squad converged in the cargo bay. Cole and Kyra were grinning at each other.

'Coming out of hyperspace,' Griff said. There was no way to feel changing speed thanks to inertial dampeners. If you could, you'd feel it by hitting the wall hard enough to atomise your blood.

A POV from the Fox's nose appeared on everyone's HUDs. The Exile ship was highlighted in neon pink, on a trajectory with Earth.

'Sif, you better engage one of the false ID logs,' Trix said.

'Sara Fenris?'

'Someone subtler.'

'The UNSS might detect an ID shift this close to Earth. Besides, the time we gain won't be worth it.'

'Never mind then.'

A string of zirean curse words came from the cockpit. 'Fodio mufy. The Gladiators scored again.'

'I think you should just admit defeat, mate.'

'I suppose it doesn't matter. With what we're about to do, the match won't count.'

'It already doesn't count, fool. It's a friendly.'

'A loss is still a loss even if the winners gain nothing by winning.'

'That'd be profound if it weren't so meaningless,' Kyra said.

'Things are about to get hot. Don't make me turn on the "Do Not Talk To The Pilot" sign.'

'This ship doesn't have one of those,' said Trix.

'Oh, doesn't it?'

Thin screens flared red on either side of the airlock. DO NOT TALK TO THE PILOT, they said

'I forgot about them during the dreadnought assault. Somehow I think this'll be less stressful.'

'Good thing none of us believe in jinxes,' Ren said over comms.

'I thought pirates were superstitious?'

'When committing acts of piracy, aye, it's a given certainty. But this is not one of those.'

'Exile ship just entered the atmosphere over the North Atlantic Ocean. I'm punching us to hypersonic. So far so good.'

'Now that really is a jinx, quartermaster.'

'Apologies, commodore.'

The Fox entered Earth's atmosphere. Gave chase to the Exile Ship. Trix didn't feel right. This was going too well. Why hadn't anyone started pursuing them? It was a known fact Earth had so much constant traffic that accurately scanning all incoming ships wasn't possible. But surely the UNSS would've been watching for the Fox. It was heavily modified, but still recognisable as a Fox Transport corvette made on Earth, in Japan.

Trix received a long-range comms call direct to her helmet. It was Yvach.

'This dreadnought's down but it's not out. Raursioc's peaks, machina. It's like you punched a baisiom right in the kisser then slapped it across the face.'

Baisioms stalked Raursioc's mountain ranges. They were like bears, though their immense size made them similar to abominable yetis from Earthen folklore.

'Can you handle it?'

'Jata, we're handling it, but these tarclabers are putting up a fight. We think there's a way in from a hangar in the keel.'

'There should be. I left the door open.'

'Blew the fucker clean off its hinges more like it. I'll call you once we've taken control. These cowards will never best the Mountain Kings.'

Yvach ended his transmission. He sounded confident in his chances. Though he'd never been thrilled about dogfights. He felt like too much was left out of his control. But an honourable corrach never complained about battle.

The Fox came over Lower Bay. The John F. Kennedy Spaceport sprawled over land and sea to starboard. All manner of ships docked there. You could travel to other continents and other planets from the spaceport.

Spaceships weren't like cars. Not everyone owned one. They were expensive to buy, costly to maintain, and difficult to store. Not many people had docks attached to their houses or below their apartments. Machinas had ships either by procuring them as payment for tasks, repairing junkers, or stealing.

Now they were crossing Upper Bay. Manhattan was North-East. Its skyscrapers towered among the clouds. The Exile ship was flying at unsanctioned altitude. Far too low to be considered safe. Griff kept the Fox at the lowest legal height. He didn't want to attract any attention.

Jets Stadium was in Jersey. To combat urban sprawl and keep nature's balance in check, all major cities were forced by the E.G.C. to meet a quota of green space. European Union cities had plenty of space in their countryside. To add more, all roofs were also gardens. New York, New York, had downsized their outer Burroughs, allowing no new high rises to be built. Instead, they gentrified old neighbourhoods and filled them with parklands. Jets Stadium was in the centre.

Elevated walkways were lined with gardens. Trains ran through them. In Formula X season, the train lines were covered so the walkways could be used for the New York Grand Prix. Extra track sections were then added so the course ran through Manhattan's skyscrapers.

Cities built onto water when they wanted to expand. Artificial islands were easy enough to create. Though water displacement had to be carefully considered.

The Exile ship began climbing, ready to kamikaze the smashball field. The third quarter had just ended. The score was 68-46. Gladiators favour. Anything could happen in the last quarter though.

Anything at all.

3

Cheerleaders took the field while both teams readied themselves for the final quarter.

Another 15 minutes lay between them and potential victory. It was almost a shame they'd never know the victor. The Exile ship reached its peak. Sif sent it down in a predictable spiral pattern. This was so the debris would be flung towards the gardens instead of the stands. Griff armed the railgun.

In the stands, zireans and humans drank plentiful alcohol. Fried foods were consumed like the match's outcome depended on it. Light hearted banter was exchanged between groups the way it so often was at sporting events. Had this been for the Galactic Cup, the zireans would've nary said a word to the humans. Though the majority of them were displeased about the match thus far, they accepted that the Earthen Gladiators had been playing exceptionally well.

Griff lined up the shot. No one in the Fox liked that they hadn't been hailed by the authorities. Despite the game's telecast, it was too quiet.

Both teams ran back onto the field. Trix had a deadly premonition that the gramyriapedes would be released as soon as the klaxon sounded. At the start of a smashball quarter, each team started 50m away from the ball which was suspended in a tractor beam in centre field. The first team to reach it started on offense. Then the game continued from there.

The Exile ship broke out of its controlled spiral. Its dark navy paint made it blend into the sky. All the stadium lights were pointed at the field.

Sif: 'Trix, my control of the Exile ship is being manually overridden.'

Cole: 'The pilot's dead. He was missing half his fucking face.'

Kit: 'That'd be a good trick though, mate.'

'How?' Trix said, ignoring the onis.

'Clearance from the highest level. Biometric. I can't stop it.'

Ren: 'It's Crohl. The bastard's here.'

'I can still read the ship's signs. Trix, it's reengaged shields.

Its weapons are powering up.'

'Griff, bring that ship down.'

'Poor choice of words, nikker,' a voice said over comms. It was Dheizir Crohl. Trix would've known it anywhere after only a brief conversation. His tones were the rumblings of storm clouds and the soft patter of dice rolling on felt. His cadence was smooth, almost cursive, like a snake hissing as it slid through the long grass.

'I must admit, I'm surprised you survived my dreadnought. I instructed the crew to give no quarter. Apparently your ship is a demon, able to out manoeuvre any of mine. But, I was more surprised when you survived my attack on Paris. I tell you, that made my icy veins bubble with fires that rage on Raursioc during winter feasts. I killed three of my men in pure outrage. They had assured me that the dosage would keep you under for over a decade. See what your anger has done to me, I'm blabbing, nikker. I haven't blabbed in years. The less you say, the more people are forced to wonder.'

Trix shivered. Daquarius Farosi had pertained to a similar school of thought. He had been one of the vilest creatures with whom she'd ever had the misfortune to cross paths.

The Gladiators and Ceirlos lined up in their opening formations. The announcers continued their useless chatter about the game's outcome when neither of them could be sure. Trix didn't even hear them. Strife Squad was listening to Crohl's every word. Griff wasn't sure what to do, so he kept following the Exile ship which looked like it was flying back to space. He was reluctant to fire now that its shields were on.

Since it was minding its own business, shooting it down would be considered criminal. Thirty seconds until the final quarter commenced. Trix saw Crohl appear in her mind. He was a giant. Picked up her puzzle and threw the pieces into the air.

Fuck your plans, he seemed to say. Puzzles do not change. They do not adapt. You and I have been playing Faet. And my hand trumps yours, nikker.

'When your AI activated the interceptor cloning protocols, I told my men to prepare for an eventuality such as this by opening a backdoor into the UNSS scanners. They detected our ship and yours quite easily. We kept our findings to ourselves of course. We wouldn't want the military spoiling our game.'

Ten seconds.

'Ren might've told you my favourite game is misdirection. It's true. As a boy, I was captivated by magic. I even wanted to be a warlock. That was until I discovered guns were cheaper. And you need not cast spells to fool people. The mere wagging of a tongue can do that.'

The final quarter commenced.

Gladiators and Ceirlos took off in mad sprints for the ball. Ready to tackle each other. There was low rumbling deep below the field. 400,000 people cheering drowned it out.

'Here is the game I want to play with you, machina. At present, I'd love to kill you and be done with it. Even you, Gerdac. I don't care about looking into your eyes as you die. The lot of you seem to be exceptionally lucky. So let's test that. I don't possess the firepower to kill you. But I possess one ship. And as you saw in Paris, one ship can do a lot of damage.'

The rumbling beneath the field grew louder. The Xardiassian Ceirlos grabbed the ball with an impressive deceptive play. It had nothing on Crohl's though. The Gladiators prepared their defence. Zirean fans cheered wildly. This was a good start.

Trix typed a message to Sif.

TRIX: CAN YOU LOCATE CROHL'S POSITION?

SIF: I'M TRYING. I CAN'T DO IT. THERE ARE TOO MANY PROXYS AND MASKED ADDRESSES. HE COULD BE ANYWHERE.

'You have enraged me the most, nikker. And now your corrachian friend is attacking my dreadnought. I thought we had parted on good terms. Here is how this will work. Your ship will leave Jets Stadium. If it so much as lets off one shot at those gramyriapedes you will force me to do something I don't wish. You may have noticed I've ejected the interceptor's dead pilot into the North Atlantic. His body won't be found. And more importantly, won't be traced back to me. Should your ship attempt to destroy my interceptor, I won't stop you.

'However, what you did aboard my dreadnought has given me an excellent idea. If my ship's shields are depleted, it will kamikaze Times Square. I've also set their depletion to arm a nuclear warhead. I have them installed in my best interceptors because it's better to be safe than sorry. I'm sure the people in Times Square will agree. It's full of people watching the smashball game. They couldn't secure tickets. What a pity.'

Crohl sounded like he was talking about a forgotten bag of groceries or a scratch on new paint.

'I am not the monster you think me to be, nikker. I'll bring those people a show they won't soon forget. Not that they'll live long enough to reminisce.'

Strife Squad shifted their attention to the smashball feed. Centre field had started collapsing in on itself. The crowd kept cheering. Sometimes smashball fields altered themselves in the final quarter. They could also be altered by certain power-ups. Only the zireans hadn't made their play yet.

Cheers turned to screams as if two tracks were being played simultaneously, and a spectral DJ crossfaded between them with zero finesse. One writhing mass shot from the field. When the dirt fell, it revealed itself to be not one, but four gramyriapedes entwined like braided steel cables. They were smaller than Larry individually. Each one only had a mouth 50m in diameter.

Together, they created a chasm of teeth 100m across. The players ran to the Gladiators' end-zone, for the Ceirlos' no longer existed. One of the zirean players was still holding the ball. The four Larrys split, each one going for a different portion of the stands.

Their carapaces were dark brown with tan stripes. Entire seating sections were swallowed whole as Larry's children buried into the crowds. Unlike Larry, they could burn through metal and concrete with no problems. Larry'd had a tough time breaking through eroded stone.

Kit: 'Beatrix, we need to get down there now.'

Crohl: 'What will you do, nikker, what will you do?'

From Griff's POV, Strife Squad saw the Ice Exile interceptor start blowing the tops off Manhattan skyscrapers.

'Captain, he's going to block the streets leading away from Times Square. No one will be able to leave. Not that it matters. Not with a nuke,' Griff said.

Trix thought fast. Killing those gramyriapedes would be nigh on impossible without the Fox.

'It looks like you have company, nikker. The UNSC must've received your broadcast. If they deplete my interceptor's shields, you know what will happen. But I think there's a greater chance that they'll be coming after you.'

'What broadcast?'

'The threat you made to the UNSC, obviously. At least, it certainly sounds like you. My, your heart is almost as black as your ship. Farewell, nikker.'

Crohl ended his transmission.

A voice that sounded like Trix's played through the Fox's comms.

'This is Trix of Zilvia. I set the gramyriapedes loose. Now I will nuke Manhattan. You can't stop me. The corrachs have taken me in. We will rule the stars. You are inferior.'

It sounded slightly robotic, but even the onis looked at Trix to check she wasn't speaking. Crohl clearly possessed powerful voice modulation software. He'd probably recorded her during their first meeting, and again now, then extrapolated the sounds he needed to form words she hadn't said. Trix could prove it wasn't her voice under close scrutiny. The current situation didn't really afford time for that, though.

'Captain, we have bogeys coming in. I'm reading six interceptors coming for us from the spaceport. Light shields. Medium firepower. They're approaching damned fast. Three of them are likely to be headed for the Exile ship. The others will be coming for us. Orders?'

The situation raced through Trix's mind. One detail stuck out like a broken nose on the face of her new problem. Crohl had said Trix's heart was as black as her ship. How was that possible? How did he know the Fox's colour? The Exile dreadnought might've relayed that information to Crohl but that seemed unlikely. How would they have known it was her ship? And why would they tell him that?

Crohl can see us, Trix thought. It pierced every other thought she had. She switched her helmet so she was looking at the rapidly falling Manhattan skyline. The interceptor was cutting its way through the buildings around Times Square first.

He's up there somewhere. In a skyscraper. So close. He'd need to be to intercept Sif's control of the Exile interceptor. And Sif said the override came from the highest biometric authority.

That wasn't important right now. She trusted Yvach to procure the evidence she needed from the dreadnought. Her immediate problems were worse.

Gramyriapedes were tearing into the stadium. An unstoppable interceptor was demolishing Manhattan. And if they tried stopping it, it'd vaporise everything in a four-kilometre radius.

Trix had an idea. It wasn't perfect. She didn't have time for perfect. Dheizir Crohl had presented her with two shit options.

And you couldn't polish a turd, but, god damn, you could roll it in glitter.

4

'Griff, take us within slingshot range of the stadium,' Trix said.

'Hysi, captain.'

Griff swung the Fox backwards. Booked it for the stadium. He couldn't go too close or Crohl would know. Somehow.

'Sif, scan for malware. I want to know if Crohl's still listening.'

'He doesn't have a presence aboard this ship. I wouldn't let him.'

'Beatrix, what're you doing?' Kit said.

'You three have to stop the gramyriapedes.'

'What, not coming to back us up?'

'Crohl said we couldn't use the Fox. He never said anything about another ship.'

A basic version of Trix's plan formed in the Oni Three's minds.

'I don't know who's crazier. Us for fighting these overgrown worms, or you,' said Cole.

'Captain, we have interceptors on our tail. Evasive manoeuvres. Make sure everyone's strapped down. I can't go faster or you'll overshoot the stadium when I do the slingshot.'

'Take them out, but don't kill them,' Trix said. 'We can't give them more reasons to believe we're the bad guys.'

'Hysi.'

'Trix, we don't have time to waste with these punks. We can do the slingshot now' Kyra said.

Kyra gripped the cargo bay handles for support. Pulled the loading ramp's manual open lever. Three interceptors were visible in the night sky. Their white and blue paint contrasted against Manhattan's crumbling backdrop. Griff wasn't letting them get a hit in. Cole and Kit stood to join Kyra who was holding onto the rungs outside the cargo bay. Wind whipped hard at their bodies.

'Are you three ready?'

'Clear for lift off, Daddy Blue.'

'Vitliaeth's fire to you, Cole Train.'

Griff whipped the Fox's rear forward and out. The Oni three released. Hurtled through the sky towards Jets Stadium's roof. None of them knew how they were going to handle the gramyriapedes. It seemed like an impossible task without heavy weapons. But those were the only tasks for which machinas were trained.

Sif closed the loading ramp as Griff flew inverted for a few seconds. He was heading back to Manhattan where the Exile interceptor was under fire from three UNSC interceptors.

'Griff, those interceptors are our top priority. Disable their thrusters. Force them to eject.'

'Hysi.'

Griff turned his cap backwards. This was game time. And it sure as hell wasn't a friendly. He dropped one of the interceptor's shields with plasma cannons. The railgun charged simultaneously. It could charge much quicker since it didn't need to be at full power. Griff blew away the thrusters. The pilot scrambled to save the ship. He ejected amidst a sea of neon advertising and falling embers. It looked like the sky was snowing flames.

'One point for Daddy Blue,' Griff said, pumping his fist into the air. Trix didn't know how old he was, but he seemed like a kid.

The other interceptors were swarming the Fox. Griff kept them away by small margins. They were swifter than the corrachian ships.

'Sif, try hailing the interceptors. We need to let them know we're on their side.'

Sif's hologram appeared on Trix's comms gauntlet as if she was dialling an old-fashioned telephone. 'They're not picking up. All I'm getting is a looped message: *We don't negotiate with terrorists.*'

'Of course they don't.'

Griff didn't have to bother depleting the second interceptor's shields. The Exile interceptor did that by itself. Trix was watching it through the POV camera. Its movements seemed planned. It was being flown wirelessly. Probably didn't have the ability to do anything tricky. Griff put the second interceptor's thrusters out of commission. He was making good progress. But this was the easy part. The UNSC wouldn't stop at sending interceptors. Soon they'd send their own corvettes.

And if the situation became catastrophic, they wouldn't hesitate to use a laser guided targeting system to assault Trix from orbit. However, they'd need to be directly over the stadium to use it on the gramyriapedes.

'Sif, I need you to scan Manhattan for the Exile interceptor's command origin.'

'Got it.'

Ren: 'Huntress, if you find Crohl, I'm going after him.'

'You're staying here.'

'I know a way I can best him.'

'How's that?'

'Your flight-suit. The one in the armoury. I saw it when I came aboard. Does it have a neural uplink?'

'It's old.'

'It works, though?'

'Hmm.'

'Then my missing arm will no longer be a problem.'

'Ren, you can't.'

The airlock opened. Ren was in Trix's flight-suit already. He sat in the seat opposite her, struggling not to fall over as Griff moved the Fox as sharply as a slalom skier.

'Too late.'

Trix nodded. It appeared there'd be no stopping him. Besides, if he broke the suit, she'd be forced to buy a new one. That was fine by her.

Sif began scanning. The last interceptor pursuing the Exile ship peeled away to focus on the Fox. Griff was now outflying four pursuers. It would've been futile for a lesser man.

For Griffauron Fulum Raivad, it was just another Wednesday morning.

Only when the UNSS fired up their orbital targeting system (OTS) would he have cause for concern. There wasn't a ship around that could avoid its targeting capabilities.

But mayhap there was a pilot.

5
Take Me Out To The Ball Game

The Oni Three landed on Jets Stadium's roof.

They walked to the edge. It was just over 200 metres above the field. Pandemonium was the game's victor, and no one even knew he'd been playing. What a dickhead.

Larry's kids were piercing the stadium. Primarily situated on the Ceirlos' side of the field. Everyone in the stands was being devoured. People flooded towards the exits in one, shifting mass. The onis could see the smashball players heading to the locker-rooms. Presumably there was a different exit for players.

The holographic rings that granted power-ups were still in play, like the officials expected the game to go ahead. The likelier scenario was that they'd fled when the gramyriapedes arrived.

'Anyone have any ideas?' Kit said, looking at the gramyriapedes. He didn't know how far they stretched underground, but their heads almost reached the roof. Their inhalation sucked people in. The onis could see blood spraying as flesh met teeth.

The onis debated collapsing the roof. Only problem with that was collateral damage. And with no explosives, they weren't collapsing anything. Not unless a dreadnought felt like hitting them with the good stuff.

'These fools have big mouths. I say we shut em up,' said Cole.

Kyra saw hovering platforms that dotted the space above the stadium. They controlled some of the holograms on the field. They also played parts in certain power-ups. There was one useful for charging to the end-zone called the "Lord is My Shepard." On Raursioc it was called "Mountain Winds." On Xardiassant: "Vitliaeth's Fire."

It typically came in to play when the quarterback passed to the wide receiver or tight end. It allowed a teammate to take control of pressurised air cannons above the stadium and shoot the opposing team. The air cannons would be naught but peashooters against the gramyriapedes. But the platforms could be useful.

And it just so happened there was one near the onis, only 50 metres away.

The Oni Three ran towards it. They jumped. Their powerful legs like rockets. They made it to the platform with their thrusters' help. There was a Jets Stadium official cowering under the console. A member of the Earthen Gladiators was watching the mayhem unfold with a jaw slacker than someone whose wife was also their sister.

The Gladiator was a woman of Asian heritage whose black, pink streaked hair was in two buns. She had her hands on the controls. Wasn't moving them.

'Yo, we're big fans,' Cole said. His smooth, resonant voice broke the woman out of her trance. She looked Japanese. Might've played for a Japanese team in Austral Asia Smashball League.

The Gladiator couldn't see the onis' eyes for their helmets. But she did see their medallions. Grinning demons, thrilled at the surrounding destruction.

'Nikkers,' she said, raising her eyebrows.

Kyra: 'Yeah, we get that a lot.'

Kit: 'Why is it that you people can never come up with anything better? Anyway, not important. We're commandeering this platform.'

'Good luck. Unless there's a power-up in play, it can only move around the stadium's edge.'

'Well fuck me. That's not helpful at all.'

'Yo, man,' Cole said, crouching down near the official. 'Can you move this thing?'

In his visorless helmet, Cole looked like an infernal golem.

'N-n-n-no. I can't. It's to prevent cheating. These platforms are hardwired to only move when a power-up is in play.'

'Seriously? Isn't there a contingency plan for emergencies?' said Kyra.

'Lady, you ever seen an emergency like this one?'

'Only on days when I get out of bed.'

Overhead, two interceptors had come to the rescue. Kit watched them approach. Maybe the Oni Three wouldn't need to do anything after all. As they came over the stadium, they swung into park. That would be their last mistake.

They started firing controlled bursts against the gramyriapedes. The onis watched from their platform as ballistic shells bounced off their thick hide. The gramyriapedes stopped their onslaught. Rose up as one. Four heads separated. The pilots tried escaping, but Larry's kids lashed like whips. They brought their carapaces down on the interceptors. Crashed into the hulls.

Cockpits shattered. Pilots were crushed. One of them attempted ejecting. He broke his neck smacking into a gramyriapede's body.

Cole: 'Damn. We gotta get one of these things into its mouth.'

Kyra: 'We're gonna need more than one, boys.'

Kit looked at the end of the stadium that was still intact. 'These platforms can only be activated with a power-up. So let's play ball.'

'I'm QB, baby. You make the catch.'

'You know it.' Kit fist-bumped Cole.

'You two throwing the ball won't do anything. It only registers power-ups when it's touched by our gloves. Otherwise it's just a regular ball.' The Gladiator took her gloves off. She handed one to Cole and one to Kit. They stretched easily over their own armoured gloves. One size did fit all, apparently.

'That platform over there,' Kyra said, pointing to the next one along. Is it Gladiator controlled?'

'Yeah, you'll be good.'

Kyra nodded. 'Get as far away from this place as you can.'

'No way. I'm piloting this straight into that motherfucking worm,' said the Gladiator.

'Come on, fool,' Cole said to Kit, jumping off the platform.

'You two be ready,' Kit said. He was smiling under his helmet. He'd always wanted to play smashball. Albeit, preferably not with gramyriapedes.

The Gladiator turned to Kyra. 'Kimie, by the way, Kimie Tsukakoshi.'

'Kyra of Drion. Don't miss. And make sure you jump out in time.'

'I definitely plan on it. I only just started playing for the Gladiators. Not about to give that up. Who the fuck did this?'

'An exiled corrach called Dheizir Crohl. He wants corrachs to have galactic supremacy.'

'What an asshole,' Kimie said. She wasn't wrong.

Kyra vaulted over the platform's side. Ran for the next one. Her thruster-pack had been used more than it should have. She hoped it held out a little longer.

Cole and Kit launched themselves off the stadium's roof. Fell for the Gladiators' end-zone. It was 100 metres across. Their thrusters propelled them to where they saw the players enter the locker-rooms. Stadium security guards were shooting the gramyriapedes. Their bullets did less than nothing.

The two onis hit the field with synchronised rolls. The ball had been dropped in the end-zone. Must've been force of habit.

Cole picked it up. The holographic rings above glowed brighter at his touch.

'Go long, baby. This is gonna be the mother of all Hail Mary passes right here,' Cole said, jumping up and down on the spot.

'Make it count.'

'The Cole Train don't know any other way of making it.'

Kit took off at sprint. Cole checked out the rings above him. He was well versed in smashball power-ups, though new ones were added all the time. He had his target picked out. A moving holographic ring that would enable the platforms to descend partway into the stadium and fire air cannons. It was an upgraded version of the Lord is My Shepard. The longer a match lasted, the better the power-ups became. This was to make impossible comebacks possible which made for more entertaining viewing.

Cole threw the ball.

The crowd kept screaming.

Kit kept running.

Kyra took position.

Kimie steeled herself.

Today's play of the day, the Oni Three removing a gramyriapede's head from its body.

6
When The Sky Falls, It Crumbles

As Trix and Griff had suspected, the interceptors were only the first in a long line of anti-terrorist measures.

Ten corvettes descended from orbital defence cannon hangars. Only two interceptors remained. Griff could fend off two ships while making a pot of coffee. Sif was still scanning for the signal controlling the Exile ship. In the wake of the crisis, Manhattan was rife with transmissions. Pinpointing Crohl's wasn't going to be easy. Sif kept trying.

'Captain, I've noticed that the Exile ship is following a consistent pattern. We can use it to our advantage.'

'I need to board it.'

'I know you do.'

'You have to keep the shields from dropping.'

'Hysi, captain. That ship's my receiver and I'm left, right, and centre guard. No one's getting past me. I'm bringing you overhead now. The floor's gonna drop you straight into the cockpit.'

Trix stood in the cargo bay's centre.

'Good luck,' she said to Ren.

'And to you, huntress.'

'Coming up in three,' Griff said. He performed a last minute barrel roll to avoid fire from pursuing interceptors. The corvettes would be upon him in a minute. Trix flipped herself so her boots were planted on the cargo bay's ceiling. Held her position by grabbing onto support rungs. Griff opened the cargo bay floor.

Trix pushed off. Out like a missile. Though that wasn't a fair comparison. Trix of Zilvia was far deadlier than a missile.

The Valkyrie saw the Exile ship. Her plan might work after all since she wouldn't have to break into the cockpit. She altered gravity by a fraction. Flipped herself right way up. Landed in the hollow cavity where the pilot's seat had been. The ejection had taken some of the console with it. Back-up controls were in the gunner's seat. She clambered in. The ship stayed on its mysterious course.

'You can't catch the motherfucking Fox. You couldn't catch a lame donkey if I was the one piloting it,' Griff said at his pursuers. Trix saw him guide the Fox, inverted, backwards, between two skybridges connecting opposite skyscrapers. Then Daddy Blue fired up his classic combo: heavy and light plasma fire followed by a thruster disabling railgun blast.

Trix turned her attention to the gunner's console. She couldn't do anything until Sif regained control. She plugged her comms gauntlet in. Sif began working.

'You know I can't give this my all while I'm using the Fox's scanners to search for Crohl.'

'I only need control for a minute.'

'I still don't know what you're planning.'

Crohl spoke through Trix's earpiece before the Valkyrie could respond. He must've had comms access since Sif was plugged into his ship.

'Entering the ship that's doing all the damage, shooting down UNSC interceptors. My, nikker. You certainly are hell bent on making yourself as guilty as possible.'

'You're finished, Crohl.'

Dheizir ended the transmission. Sif continued hacking.

'Trix, it's no good. I can't take control of the ship. Crohl's overriding my every move with biometric security. He has to be nearby. Biometrics only works wirelessly over extremely short-range. Any longer and it'd defeat the security benefits.

Trix unplugged Sif. Saw text appear on her comms gauntlet.

SIF: I HAVE HIS LOCATION.

TRIX: WHERE?

SIF: THE CENTRE FOR ASTRONOMICAL SCIENCE AND ORBITAL DYNAMICS. TOP FLOOR.

CASOD was next to New York University. It was a kilometre high. Though it wasn't to be outdone by the New Empire State Building, coming in at 1.5 kilometres.

TRIX: SEND THAT INFORMATION TO GRIFF. REN NEEDS TO STOP HIM.

SIF: AND IF HE CAN'T?

TRIX: WE RAILGUN THE DICKHEAD.

Sif sent an encrypted message to Griff. It was displayed on the Fox's HUD.

'Commodore, you ready to say hello to an old friend?' Griff said.

Ren activated his plasma bayonet. He couldn't wait to rearrange Crohl with it since killing him had to be a last resort. That was fine by Ren. A clean cut with a plasma blade cauterised wounds. Ren planned on severing Crohl's limbs, then using them to beat his face black.

Crohl's coordinates appeared on Ren's HUD.

'Take me as close as you can, Quartermaster.'

'Hysi, Commodore. Be ready to drop. That flight-suit will take you the rest of the way, no problems.'

Griff disabled one of the last two interceptors going after Trix, then hit the others with light plasma bursts.

"Follow me," those shots said. "I could be on my way to blowing up lower Manhattan. You don't know."

Trix saw the Fox fly towards Crohl. Sif had found him by sweeping the city for Crohl's exact message. She couldn't have done it unless she'd been plugged into the Exile ship at the time. She just hoped she was right. If an AI could hope.

The Valkyrie sat helplessly as the Exile interceptor continued carving away Manhattan's skyline. Tens of thousands must've died already. Trix felt familiar coldness wash over her. She'd been in this situation before. Paris had been training for this moment. Now her task was even easier. She didn't want to stop the interceptor from flying. She just needed to disable the weapons.

Trix left the gunner's seat. Crohl could eject her at any time if Sif wasn't plugged in.

The Valkyrie swung herself out of the cockpit. Attached to the hull with her utility cannon. Walked along the right wing. Cannons were doing all the work. If Trix shut them off, the ship couldn't do any more harm. Except for the nuclear warhead.

Each wing had three big cannons. Corrachs pertained to the school of thought that bigger was always better. No exceptions. It was ironic that none of them were taller than five foot three. Trix hugged the wing. Careful not to place herself on the flaps. Losing fingers wasn't something she wanted in her immediate future.

The cannons were attached to the wings by hardpoints. Hardpoints typically held external payloads like missiles or warheads. However, they were useful for mounting cannons because they enabled weapons to be swapped depending on the situation. This made Trix's job slightly easier than a completely rigid structure, but not by much.

Once Crohl was taken care of — if he was taken care of — Sif could release the cannons from the gunner's console. Until that happened, Trix had to make do with sabotage. She pressed her hand against the hardpoint pylon to alter its density. Fired bullets at point-blanc, bypassing the shields, before it could revert. The casing broke. A mess of thick wires lay beneath. Trix holstered her gun. Drew her bowie knife.

The Exile interceptor banked sharply around a skyscraper to shoot its support beams. It began tipping. Trix saw people trying to break safety glass so they could escape. She hacked through the wires. One of the cannons went dead. Only five more to go.

And the UNSC corvettes were back on her tail.

'Griff, I need assistance.'

'Just had to make a stop, captain,' Griff said. The Fox punched a hole through the corvettes by performing a downward barrel-roll which created a plasma storm against their shields. Dancing on the thrusters, Griff snapped the Fox upwards. He charged the railgun as minimally as possible. It released several bursts. Boom, there went the last interceptor. And two corvettes. There were still eight left.

The Exile ship's shields were at 49%.

Trix didn't have much time before the nuke annihilated everything in a 4km radius.

But she wasn't the only one with problems.

7

The Terrorist & The Pirate

Renier von Gerdac scraped the sky.

His backdrop was explosive light refracted through dark glass, textured by bursting neon punctuated with plasma.

Perhaps it was his upper-class childhood, but there was something to destruction's sound which was akin to ecstasy. Shattering glass — or in Ren's case, crystal — had always made him feel like anything could happen, good or bad. It was life's carefree, anarchic possibilities distilled into sound.

As Ren flew, those bizarre psychoanalytic life commentaries were background noise. Like the screaming. Gramyriapedes roaring. He could hear it all above the city. He wasn't paying close attention to it. His thoughts were occupied by the malfunctioning neural transmitter in Trix's flight-suit. His right arm worked sporadically. If at all. He had grenades in the belt compartment. His rifle was strapped to his back. Extra magazines were in the thighs.

He'd have to hold his gun in his left hand to be safe. Holding it in his right could mean the inability to shoot at the opportune moment.

The pirate was approaching the tower where Dheizir Crohl was supposedly located. The Centre for Astronomical Science and Orbital Dynamics was predominately a place where university students could study space flight's nuances, and improve upon current designs. Top performing students were allowed to take part in experiments aboard the UNSS.

Ren was less than 200m away from one of the top floor windows. CASOD was a triad of spires interlinked with skybridges. Vertical gardens filled the centre. They were a space for students and teachers to relax amid the city without having to leave the building. There were few telescopes on Earth. The amount of objects in orbit made them next to useless. Space-telescopes were preferred.

Some of CASOD's lower levels were showing activity. Or at the very least, they had their lights on. The top floor was darker than a buried coffin. Ren flew around the north facing spire. Into the garden centrepiece. Landed on a walkway lined with flower beds. Ran for a glass door.

There was no point in trying to be quiet. The flight-suit would give him away. The door opened to him. He thought he'd have to crash through. Sleeping computer terminals emitted dull, pulsing lights. An interior breakroom had dishes left out. A mug of half-drunk coffee was cold on the countertop.

Ren heard movement from down the hall. Walked forward, gun raised. His plasma bayonet penetrated the darkness. It hummed like a panther growling. Ren had thought he was going to die aboard Crohl's dreadnought. Now, with only one full arm, almost certainly outnumbered, definitely outgunned, he knew death was likelier than any other scenario. He was surprised to realise the thought unsettled him. He gripped his gun tighter. Ren came to the hallway's end. There was a room. Its door was ajar. A makeshift desk had been set up in the corner. Corrachian military hardware was hooked into a computer terminal.

Simulator software showed a screen that said AUTOPILOT ENGAGED. A breath. Ren heard it just before it would've been too late. He activated his suit's forward thrusters. A shotgun blast tore through his shields. Into his flight-suit. He felt metal enter his good arm. His thrusters went so fast he nearly crashed into the glass. He turned.

Dheizir Crohl had been hiding in the shadows with a sawn-off shotgun. His shadow seemed larger. Almost oni sized. Ren's eyes flitted around the room. His HUD showed no other life signs.

Crohl was alone.

'Crohl,' Ren said. He hadn't even noticed that his gun had lowered a couple of inches.

'Hello, Gerdac. Why haven't you shot me yet?'

Ren remembered his weapon. Raised it.

'These buildings full of scholars. All the equipment. The research. It's invaluable. The uplink directly to the UNSS. We wouldn't have been able to manipulate their scanners so delicately without it. Yet, the security is almost non-existent. Whereas a hotel or apartment block filled with rich residents is likely to be almost as secure as the Hole. It's funny, even now, what your people deem most precious.'

'Why haven't you killed me?' Ren said. Crohl wasn't wearing a mech-suit. Only standard battle-armour. His helmet covered half his face. But it was him. Ren could see those eyes whenever he closed his own. Ren could end it right now. He could crash into Crohl with his thrusters. Mortally wound him with his bayonet. He didn't want to tamper with the simulator equipment. That could arm the warhead.

'Because my mission is being accomplished without killing you. And I lied about not wanting to look into your eyes as you died, Ren. Somehow you and that infernal Valkyrie, the white-haired demon, tracked me here. You even found from where I was broadcasting. So, yes, I would like to look into your eyes. I might learn something from them. You clearly have boundless wisdom. Even if you are lacking your right arm.'

'How did you know?'

'Ah, it is comforting to see your talents aren't as godlike as they first appear.'

'Where are your men? Your backup? It can't just be you.'

'If you want something done right, it is better to do it yourself. The others served their purpose and left. To tell you Raursioc's honest truth, I didn't expect you to find me. Not that it matters. I wouldn't let my white hair fool you. Age has no bearing on a corrach's strength.'

Ren tried squeezing his gun's trigger. He couldn't remember how. His muscles had forgotten. His bones locked in their joints. How did it go again? To pull a trigger? After all these years part of Ren was still afraid of Dheizir Crohl.

'Now,' Crohl said. Half his face contorted into a smile. 'Since I want to see your eyes, we'll have to remove your helmet.'

Crohl charged at Ren with speed that shouldn't have been possible for someone so short. But that was just it. Crohl wasn't short. He had to be six foot three at least. All without a mech-suit. The surprise was almost enough to make Ren freeze. He used his thrusters to skirt around Crohl. Thrust his bayonet.

Crohl sidestepped. Raised his shotgun. Ren begged the neural transmitter to move his right arm up. It worked. Albeit too slowly. Ren's bionic arm knocked Crohl's shotgun to the ceiling. It fired. The spray shore off the top of Ren's helmet. There went the suit's neural transmitting capabilities. His right arm was reduced to a stiff piece of metal.

How is this possible? Ren thought.

'Ren,' it was Trix in his ear. 'I need control of this interceptor now.'

Ren kept his thrusters going until he entered the hallway. Crohl fired his shotgun again. Ren took cover behind a wall. Killing Crohl wasn't an option. He'd have some kind of failsafe. Ren was sure about that. Even if Crohl hadn't mentioned his death impacting the game's rules. That'd be the fine print. Too fine to see among all the chaos.

Commodore Renier von Gerdac was going to lose.

'I'm a little busy at the moment.'

And he wasn't the only one.

8
Touchdown?

It was the finest pass Jets Stadium had ever seen.

Not to mention the most important.

A perfect spiral. The ball flew across the sky like a chariot pulled by gods. It hit the power-up ring dead centre. It was infused with golden light. Cole of Orix watched its trajectory. If the commentators hadn't abandoned their posts, they would've called it one of the greatest passes in smashball's glorious history. The crowd would've been breathless. They nearly were, in fact, but that was due to all the screaming.

Cole's pass was what every fan hoped to see at least once in their lifetime when the klaxon was about to sound, signalling game over. It was so divine that an atheist would've praised the Lord without any sarcasm or jesting. Now all Kit of Aros had to do was catch it.

Due to the power-up ring's placement, Kit had to run to the field's halfway point to catch the ball. He was so focused on receiving that he hadn't noticed only three gramyriapede heads were now above ground.

Rumbling came from beneath.

Cole of Orix noticed. He started running from the end-zone. The ground was rising in a ridge.

'Yo, fool. You've got company coming from down under.'

'Yeah, mate. Just gotta make this catch.'

The ground rose underneath Kit. Then strange things started happening. Shield walls popped into existence. Obstacles shot from the turf. The tunnelling was interfering with the field altering terrain. That didn't stop Kit. Nor did it stop Cole who was running behind him. All of this took place over eight seconds. Time slowed when the fate of thousands rested on your shoulders. Perhaps Father Time was sympathetic. Maybe he just wanted to see the action in high speed.

A wall appeared in front of Kit. This was to stop receivers making a beeline to the end-zone. Kit jumped over it. Walls appeared on either side of him. He started wall-running. The ball was just overhead. He jumped. Arms outstretched. Cole vaulted over the obstacles in his way. Kit was going to need help.

Activating his thrusters, Kit shot into the air. A 50-metre chasm swallowed a chunk of the field behind him. Cole was now running along a gramyriapede's arched back. Kit was right in front of its mouth. He was being pulled in. His thrusters were about to fail. They'd been used too much. And they couldn't counteract the drag. Kit's hands closed around the ball.

Functioning speakers around the stadium played a triumphant chorus, signalling that a power-up had been activated.

Kyra activated her platform on the stadium roof. So did Kimie. They guided themselves towards the gramyriapedes. For this to work, Larry's Kids had to be facing them.

Cole reached the edge of the gramyriapede's mouth in time to see Kit inhaled. Though the oni actually charged inwards at the last second.

The gramyriapede hadn't noticed Cole's presence on its head. He was a single plankton brushing against a whale.

'Kit, you still with us?' said Cole.

There were a few crushing moments of radio silence.

'I'm not dinner just yet, mate. But I'm fucking closer than I'd like to be. I'm just behind its first row of teeth. Gotta wait until this thing exhales,' Kit said.

'Hold on, man.'

Then the gramyriapede began diving. Cole nearly slipped off its back. He grabbed a thick piece of carapace. If the gramyriapede — let's call this one Jake — went underground, Kit would enter its fathomless abyss along with masses of dirt.

'Kyra, Kit's inside the gramyriapede's mouth. We need to get him outta there.'

'These platforms aren't exactly fast. I won't be able to reach you in time,' said Kyra.

Kimie messaged Kyra through a comms channel between their platforms. Kyra connected it to her helmet so Kimie could hear everyone else speak.

'I'm closer. I can try.'

Without waiting for confirmation, Kimie moved her platform towards Jake's mouth.

'Don't come too close. This thing's gonna exhale at any second. I can feel it. My thrusters are more fucked than a triple booked pornstar though. I'll never be able to clear its mouth.'

'If you get out, I can shoot you,' Kimie said.

'At least by me a drink first.'

'I'll use the air cannons. They'll knock you out of the way.'

Jake began exhaling.

'Alright, let's give her a crack then. Cole, you still with us?'

'Always, baby.'

'I'm gonna need your help to reach the roof.'

'If the roof's still there.'

'What'd you mean *if it's still there?*'

'It's starting to come down.'

'Perfect.'

'Jump, now!' Kimie said.

Kit pushed off the teeth he'd wedged himself between. He was grateful these bastards didn't have tongues. He cleared the chasm propelled by the force of Jake's exhalation. Only problem was, now he was headed for the ground with Jake approaching behind him.

A concussive blast hit Kit in the torso. Son of a bitch. It was strong. Smashball players took more of a beating than he thought. He copped a second hit. Kit was flung towards where the stands had been. They were a crumpled mess. Like a giant had picked up half the stadium and scrunched it in his hand.

Kit narrowly avoided impalement on one of Jake's pincers.

Cole jumped off Jake's head. Activated his thrusters. Cole smacked into Kit. Reversed thrusters. They smashed into one of the field's only parts that hadn't been overturned. They ripped up the grass. Stained their armour with dirt.

Kit was still holding the smashball.

'Fool, you can let that thing go.'

'Are you kidding? This is the game winning ball.'

'We haven't won anything yet.'

'Not with that attitude, mate,' Kit said, holding the ball out to Cole.

Cole smacked it away. Gave Kit the finger. Kit's face went wide beneath his helmet. He wasn't looking at Cole.

Kit: 'Hey, Gladiator. Look out.'

Jake arched upwards instead of diving. He was headed for Kimie's platform. She freaked out. She wasn't ready to drive her platform into Jake's mouth. How would she escape?

Kyra was firing her air cannons as this was happening. She doubted whether the gramyriapedes could feel anything, but they were all she had.

'Oh, fuck. Still, better than nothing.'

Two gramyriapedes were angling for her from either side now. Not good. Together they'd destroy her platform, not choke on it. The platform was circular. Its central command console only five metres in diameter. The whole platform was 25 metres in total. This was to accommodate power-up functionality.

Below, Jake hit Kimie's platform. His aim wasn't great. He didn't seem to have any eyes. The force knocked Kimie away from her console. The official had jumped ship on the roof. Jake swung back again. Kimie was holding the railing.

Kyra saw this from the corner of her eye.

'Kimie, you have to let go.'

That name clicked in Cole and Kit's minds. They'd thought she looked familiar. Kimie "Crackshot" Tsukakoshi was easily in the top ten technicians of any Earthen smashball team. She never missed a shot with an air cannon. Her accuracy rate was so lethal it could've jumped off the stats page and pierced your skull. Her club team was the Miyazaki Ronin. Her national team was the United States of America Patriots, as she'd been born in the USA. And her planet team was the Earthen Gladiators.

'Yo, Crackshot. We got you.'

Kimie didn't let go. She clambered back onto the platform.

She knew she had a better chance of landing in Jake's mouth than on the field if she fell. Kimie shoved the platform's control to go left and down. That way she'd be close to the edge of Jake's mouth instead of in the middle. She took a running start. Jumped.

Kyra leaped off her own platform as two gramyriapedes closed in.

The fourth was headed for the other end of the stadium.

Cole and Kit were running across the torn-up field to catch Kimie.

Kyra turned to look at the gramyriapedes devouring her platform. One moved out of the way at the last second as if they were playing a game of chicken. The other swallowed Kyra's platform whole. Kyra hoped the pressurised air canisters would rupture, sending shrapnel into the gramyriapede's soft, interior flesh. Nothing appeared to be happening.

That wasn't true. Something insane was happening everywhere you looked in Jets Stadium. The problem was that none of those insane things were helping the Oni Three.

It looked like everything they'd done had been for nothing.

They were going to need a miracle. A hero.

Maybe a Valkyrie in battered armour.

But the Oni Three weren't cooked yet.

Nuh ah, baby. Nuh ah.

9

Not My First Rodeo

Trix had disabled the cannons on the Exile interceptor's right wing.

Seemingly endless UNSC ships were coming for backup. Griff kept smacking them down. Ejected pilots shot into the air with the frequency of fireworks on Independence Day. Not the one Americans celebrated. The new Independence Day which was celebrated by the entire Earth. It commemorated winning the Plague War. It was ironic that it also marked the start of being bent over by the zireans. But, hey. Nothing was perfect.

Trix couldn't believe the UNSS hadn't fired up the OTS. Then she realised her dumb luck. The UNSS was in Earth's orbit. It took 92 minutes to complete a full rotation. It must've just passed by as they turned up. Though it had thrusters and could essentially function as an enormous spaceship. But positioning it directly above Manhattan wouldn't be an easy feat.

Crohl knew, was Trix's first thought. He'd waited for the opportune moment to release his gramyriapedes so they couldn't be squashed by the OTS. He'd hacked in to the UNSS. It made sense. Still, his careful planning meant Trix wouldn't be blown out of the sky. That was a small comfort.

Continual reinforcements made it smaller all the time.

'Captain, if we keep going like this, there'll be no buildings left to save.'

Trix knew Griff was right. But she couldn't help Ren until she disabled the last of the Exile ship's weapons. If it was on autopilot — which, due to its flight path's patterned nature, Trix assumed it was — then taking the weapons offline would cause it to fly around harmlessly. Save for its nuclear warhead. Sif had scanned its shields. They were holding steady at around 38 per cent.

'Just let me disable the weapons,' Trix said to Griff.

She had to reach the left wing. Trix detached her utility cannon. Crawled across the cockpit. The Exile ship was approaching the tallest building in Manhattan's skyline: the New Empire State Building. Its original form had been preserved as a silhouette inside the new structure.

The Exile interceptor filled its sides with plasma. Trix heard metal wane under the stress. It was going to come down. The damage from its fall would be cataclysmic.

The Valkyrie crossed the cockpit. She was about to reattach her utility cannon when the ship accelerated. Its remaining weapons went into overdrive until the familiar hiss of overheated cannons reached the machina's ears. The NESB started falling at an angle. Trix slipped down the left wing. She went to fire her utility cannon. She was too late. The ship was moving too fast. She didn't even have time to make gravity throw her in the cockpit.

Trix fell towards the NESB's tumbling cross section. She could see the inside of offices, apartments, and hallways. Great electrical tubes and water pipes spewed their contents into the early morning. The New Empire State Building was a behemoth. Its head had been severed. Now its innards were laid bare for all to see as it bled onto the city that'd sustained it.

Cowering people filled the rooms that were still stuck to the rest of the building. They must've been too afraid to leave. Probably thought they were safe. The rooms closest to the support beams were filled with melted corpses.

Come over here, children. Look what happens when you're hit with a ship's plasma round. See the way solids become liquids, and everything fuses together. Sometimes the victim survives in this deformed state for hours before critical organs fail.

Trix moved into a skydiving position. She had a way out of this. But it would mean Griff abandoning his post for a moment. There were currently four UNSC corvettes trying to destroy the Exile ship. More would be arriving shortly. Ones with heat seeking missiles. Ones that would rush the interceptor with no thought of personal safety. The death toll would've been in the tens of thousands now, surely approaching the hundreds.

Counting the smashball game's casualties, they'd surpassed even that.

Trix adjusted gravity so she'd land on the NESB's exterior windows. They were smooth all the way along. Once she hit them, she could slide down until Griff extracted her. Provided none of the panes shattered or she wasn't atomised by a corvette.

The only reason she'd survived thus far was because of the Exile ship's bubble-shield. It'd protected Trix from several mortal wounds while she'd been disabling the cannons. She was grateful, but every blast she was saved from brought Manhattan closer to nuclear annihilation.

'Griff, I need you to get me back on that ship,' said Trix as she slid down the NESB's windows.

'I don't have time to stop. Sif sent me your position. You're gonna have to jump, captain.'

'Hmm,' Trix said. She was avoiding broken windows like a smashball receiver weaving around guards, headed for the end-zone.

'Think one of the UNSC ships is going to reach us first,' Sif said. 'Your three o'clock. Incoming.'

Trix had to make a decision. Was she going to try a gravity assisted jump to escape the line of fire? Too risky. Not enough chance of success. Besides, that'd put her away from the building. If she was inside, they couldn't shoot her without killing civilians. Trix drew her pistol. Massacred the trigger. Eighteen bullets left the chamber. They cracked the glass in front of her. But it wasn't enough to break it.

The Valkyrie jumped enough for her boots to leave the glass then slammed downwards. The glass cracked as the corvette flew overhead. It held its fire.

A topsy-turvy living room awaited Trix when she broke through the window. A man and a woman had been crushed against the wall by their own bed. It'd burst them like a giant, metal flyswatter.

The building continued tipping. Extraction was never going to work if she was inside. Trix felt a tremendous sense of déjà vu. The Dragon Spire's collapse. That'd been years ago. No, it had only been a week. How the world had changed.

Through a mixture of sliding and running, Trix reached the door to the living room.

Instead of looking like an inner-city apartment for wealthy individuals, the room was akin to a magical rabbit hole. One where a girl with golden hair might find herself tumbling towards a mysterious world. A clock fell off the wall. It was an antique. Analogue. It spun. Fell through an open doorway.

Another bedroom maybe.

'Captain, I can grab you without losing any time.'

'How?'

'Jump out the window to your right. Get as far away from the building as you can.'

Trix didn't question how Griff knew the room's schematics. She assumed Sif had sent them. Reloaded her pistol. Broke through the window.

The Fox wasn't anywhere to be seen.

A black shape came from underneath the crumbling building. Trix would've known its thrusters' roar anywhere. Even though Griff had upgraded them, they possessed the same, snarling growl they always had.

Griff was flying the Fox inverted with the cargo bay floor open. Trix was falling right into it. Only two corvettes had followed Daddy Blue. The others were assaulting the Exile ship. Its shields had dropped to 19 per cent. If only the UNSS had any idea what they were doing. Fuck them for not communicating.

Trix hit the cargo bay roof. Griff closed the floor. Barrel-rolled. He was level again. He brought down plasma rain on the UNSS corvettes attacking the Exile ship. One of the corvettes following Griff had been destroyed by the falling building.

'Huntress,' it was Ren. He sounded horrible. He wasn't on his death bed, but he was making it. Tucking in the sheets nice and neat. 'Help.'

'On my way,' she said. 'Griff, I need you—'

'Hysi, already know what you're gonna say, and I'm on it.'

Griff disabled the corvettes attacking the Exile ship. Their pilots ejected. Griff blasted the Fox's engines past hypersonic to high-hypersonic. It was so fast the ship may as well have teleported the two and a half kilometres to the CASOD building.

'Whoa, easy,' Griff said, slamming on every brake the Fox had. Performing a 180 barrel-roll. The ship was stationary for one second. Griff's manoeuvre brought Trix so close to

CASOD's windows that they'd blown inwards. She used her utility cannon to grip one of the support beams.

Griff dropped the Fox a couple of levels so he didn't fry Trix with the thrusters. In another second, he was back in the fray, fighting to keep the Exile ship airborne.

Griff had an inkling of Trix's plan. He knew she wanted the nuclear warhead armed.

But not until the opportune moment.

10
Renier von Gerdac's Prestige

Biological enhancements, it seemed, were not restricted to gramyriapedes.

Strife Squad had seen two loads of boxes aboard the dreadnought. One had been destroyed by a helmet full of grenades constructed by Commodore Gerdac. Trix had incorrectly assumed that they would've contained similar gramyriapede samples.

They'd actually been tailored for corrachs. A growth serum that increased muscle strength and bone density, lowered heartrate, and stimulated growth. It fundamentally changed corrachs' biological makeup.

And Ren Gerdac was fighting what he assumed was the finished product.

Crohl wasn't as powerful as a machina, though he was a fearsome opponent. Strong as his wits were sharp. Crohl knew the corrachs couldn't win a war against the rest of the galaxy as they were. Reliant on mech-suits to give them a fighting chance against the Milky Way's toughest militaries.

They had to become something more.

Like Garth Roche had sought to create saviours in machinas, Dheizir Crohl wanted to turn all of Raursioc into his own superweapons. Corrachs the size of onis with enhanced reflexes. Another addition he planned on making was a serum that uncaged the brain's aggression centres. He wanted Raursioc to return to the savage, icy warzone it'd been in past millennia, even though he'd never been around to see it as such.

But, by changing corrachs so drastically, altering them from the base level, he failed to see the soldiers who would fight in his glorious war would no longer be corrachs. Just roided out freaks who resembled a once proud race. A race who'd believed in honour above all else.

Crohl could see this twisted future everywhere he looked.

However, there was no clearer window to his perfect world than Ren Gerdac's eyes. Crohl's shotgun had revealed them by shearing off his helmet. The pirate was cunning. Crohl remembered why he'd sent him to the Hole. Even half an arm down, Ren Gerdac was proving to be a knife between the ribs.

Ren struggled to stay conscious. All that kept his eyes open was knowing that closing them meant seeing darkness forever. In his scuffle with Crohl, he'd knocked the auto-pilot controls. Called for Trix to help. He had to remember how to speak. Every part of his brain was busy remembering how to fight. How to stay alive.

Ren had only scored one good hit on Crohl. And it hadn't even been *on* him. Ren's plasma bayonet had skewered Crohl's sawn-off, frying its internal electronics. Crohl discarded it. Not before Ren drew his rifle. He was going to need it.

Their fight had taken them back through the hallway from whence Ren came. Now they duked it out on the walkway leading to the vertical garden. Ren had to take Crohl over the edge. He didn't care if his flight-suit's thrusters wouldn't take him to safety. He just wanted to end it.

Pain and hatred had become the only things of which Ren was consciously aware. His left shoulder throbbed. Every movement made shotgun shells grind into his nerves. The tearing sensation was like someone had pushed him to a grindstone which kept accelerating.

Ren crashed into Crohl with his thrusters' full force. Crohl dug his heels onto the metal. It was no good. He kept sliding. Ren fired nine shots from his rifle. Point-blanc into the armour covering Crohl's sternum. He didn't know if they hit flesh. Didn't think Crohl would have the decency to let him check.

Dheizir Crohl was pinned against the railing. Ren tried firing his rifle again. Crohl gave him a shove. Wrenched the rifle from Ren's hand. That wasn't difficult. Ren doubted he could've choked a mouse to death the way he was feeling. If it wasn't for the flight-suit, he would've been dead the second Crohl had laid eyes on him.

Ren swatted Crohl using his right arm's deadweight. The rifle skidded along the walkway. Disappeared into the central garden.

Something about the loss of his rifle slapped Ren across the face. He began thinking differently. He'd been trying to survive before. Now he knew how he was going to kill Crohl. Trix said she was coming. He didn't know if that was true. But at least he had something to try besides prolonging his imminent death, the ramifications of which no longer mattered. This was about killing Crohl. Hang the consequences.

Let's see how much you love misdirection now, you traitorous cur.

Ren needed some time. Not much. Maybe a couple of seconds. Crohl was fast thanks to his enhancements. Not as fast as a flight-suit, though. Ren steeled himself. Head-butted Crohl on the bridge of his nose with what remained of his helmet. Ren saw stars. They were made brighter by the explosions happening before him. An irrelevant thought entered his mind.

There is no destruction. Only creation.

Then it was gone.

Crohl's grip slackened. That was all Ren needed. He used his strafing thrusters to launch himself down the walkway. Into the central garden. His left arm hollered for rest. Pleaded like a POW for mercy. Screamed worse than a wounded child. Ren ignored it.

He scooped up his rifle. Positioned himself behind a corner in the garden. Exited the flight-suit. It could be controlled with no one inside it. No complex actions were possible. Ren didn't need anything fancy. He just needed it to move. Fast. He limped to the triad's southwestern side. Crohl would be able to see him crouching with his rifle held at crotch level.

That was what Ren wanted.

Dheizir Crohl's mighty steps shook the walkway. To Ren's delight, he saw blood coming from Crohl's chest. His weary face lit up like a child's on Christmas morning. It was the best present for which he could've hoped.

Cheers, Santa. You jolly, fat bastard. You did alright.

Ren fired incompetent shots. He wanted Crohl to think he was more hopeless than he really was.

'You're weak,' was all Crohl said. He was in no mood to monologue. He wanted to tear Ren's neck open then strum his vocal chords while he was still alive. He wanted to see if he could play a song on them. One of loss. One of sorrow. One of his own perverted victory.

'Maybe,' Ren wheezed. He had to be ready to evade. 'But not stupid.'

Crohl lunged. He was slower than before. Ren's bullets must've had some effect. Ren fired blindly. The recoil was stronger than his muscles. He felt something in his shoulder tear. A ligament perhaps. Maybe tendons. His muscles. Probably all three.

Ren pressed his gauntlet to his face as he dove. He had to use his nose since his hand was out of commission. The flight-suit thrusters engaged with force that was used to push it above transonic speeds.

The metal husk slammed into Crohl's back. The Exile had heard it power up and had been halfway through turning around. His armour dented severely. Blood spurted from the hole in his chest. Crohl gasped. Hit a wall covered in roses. Thorns embedded themselves into his face's exposed, leathery skin. The wall broke. Crohl stopped himself from going over the edge using his right arm. His left had been broken by the flight-suit.

Ren watched as the flight-suit continued moving. It hooked

Crohl's legs. Forced him over the railing. Its thrusters pushed it off the edge. To the city below. It'd done its job. Ren didn't need it anymore.

Crohl was hanging on by one hand. Ren dragged himself to Crohl's position.

Let's see him try and hold on after I shoot his fingers off.

The last thing Ren expected was for Crohl to haul himself up, one handed.

That's exactly what the mutated corrach did.

Dheizir Crohl flung himself upwards. He landed back in the central garden. He was hunched over. Back at the height he would've been had he not injected himself with who knew how many drugs.

Ren didn't have the strength to fire his rifle. He was out of options. Crohl staggered towards Ren. He was smiling. He felt as if this was no more than a setback. Ren noticed one of Crohl's feet had been twisted inside his armour. It was sticking out to the left. Crohl dragged it across the floor.

'I taught you too well,' Crohl said.

'Fuck you.'

A single note cut through the air. Crohl's left arm left his body. It was caught by someone standing behind him. He was spun around with a shove then bitch-slapped with the back of his severed hand. A straight kick to his chest wound dropped his arse on the ground.

Beatrix Westwood stood in Crohl's place. Her sword slicked with blood. Her white pony-tail stuck out of her helmet like a knight's plumage. Though any who'd been saved by Trix of Zilvia could attest, she was way better than any knight in shining armour.

'All yours,' she said to Ren. She sheathed her sword. Ran down the walkway, still holding Crohl's arm. Trix was curious to know how Crohl had become almost as big as Kit, though she had an inkling. Andy Tozier had said Crohl was looking into biological enhancements. He never specified what kinds. And she'd only seen one lab on the entire dreadnought.

Ren flicked open his rifle's plasma bayonet. He couldn't stand anymore. He belly-crawled to Crohl. Due to how Crohl's spine had been deformed, his body curled upwards. Like the way a spider's did upon death. Ren brought his plasma bayonet over Crohl's face. All he had to do was let himself fall. Let his body rest. Give in to the fatigue. Instead, Ren moved his bayonet to Crohl's severed arm. Blood was pouring out in a pool. The NYU students who used the CASOD gardens for biology practicals always thought a pond would do nicely. One made of blood wasn't what they'd had in mind.

Ren stemmed the bleeding with his bayonet. He also did a hack job on Crohl's stomach to stop the blood flow.

Dheizir tried speaking. He could only breathe loudly. Ren guessed he was in shock. Commodore Renier von Gerdac tried thinking of a fuck you to the old man. In the movies, all heroes had a great line with which to land the killing blow.

But this wasn't a movie. And Ren sure wasn't a hero.

He slumped to the floor. He could hear the sounds of chaos unravelling Manhattan as he lay on his back. Stars behind Ren's eyes turned to darkness. He looked at his shoulder. It was bleeding worse than before without the flight-suit.

Ren Gerdac passed out next to Dheizir Crohl.

He could've sworn that the world's sounds turned to cheering. The kind that happened at a smashball game, after the underdogs made an incredible comeback.

What an odd thing to think.

11

Bad Breakfast

Crackshot Kimie fell.

Kyra reached the front row seats, or what was left of them.

Cole and Kit were coming up on Kimie. Kit jumped. Cole grabbed him by the legs and spun him around.

Kit was launched through the air, narrowly avoiding Jake's underbelly. It occurred to Kit that the gramyriapedes didn't really have underbellies. They looked the same all the way around. He sailed past Kimie. Grabbed the back of her armour. They continued hurtling towards the ruined stands together.

Most of the stadium was empty now. Those who remained wanted to stay. They were filming the event. Hoped to go viral. The chances of them being gramyriapede food were higher.

Kit swivelled his body mid-air. His back hit a collapsed row of seats. His weight broke them even further. He was holding Kimie in his arms.

'Thanks for catching me,' she said.

'Can't let one of the best players on Earth die, can I?'

'Oni Three, regroup at Kit's position,' said Kyra.

Cole began running around the collapsed part of the field.

Jake decided not to eat Kimie's platform after all. His right pincer broke it in two. The air canisters inside exploded. Both platform halves careened through the stadium. One crashed ten rows up from Kit. The other hit the stadium's crumbling roof.

Kyra reached Kit before Cole.

'You've gotta get outta here, mate' Kit said to Kimie.

Kyra: 'He's right.'

'Alright, I'm not arguing again,' said Kimie. 'Good luck.' She started making her way back towards the other end of the stadium.

'Any chance of season tickets?' Kit called after her.

Kyra whacked him on the back of his helmet.

'Actually, that would be pretty cool,' she shrugged.

Cole vaulted over the barrier. The Oni Three were together again.

'So—' Cole started saying when one of the gramyriapedes let out a deafening shriek. It started flailing. It was the one that'd eaten Kyra's platform. Parts of its carapace bulged. Shrapnel came from its mouth along with torrents of sludgy blood.

'Its teeth must've pierced the platform.'

'I'd say it did. Those fuckers are sharp,' Kit said. He gestured to a gash on his chest plate. 'Nearly tore me open.'

'Reckon it's dead?' said Cole.

The flailing gramyriapede turned to the Oni Three.

'You know when you've eaten too much, and have slightly more than ten pints in ten minutes?' Kit said.

'Oh fuck,' said Cole. His voice betrayed no alarm. If anything, he was exasperated. Like he'd made a lazy realisation, and knew he'd have to move.

The Oni Three leapt back onto the field as a deluge of biblical proportions surged from the gramyriapede's mouth. Kit knew that being hit by any of it would make the gash on his chest look like a papercut. He'd read up on gramyriapedes using *Monsters & Other Beasts*. Their stomach acid was akin to anghenfilic acid. And he'd seen enough of that hit Mair Ultima to know it didn't leave much of a person to bury. Hell, it didn't leave much of buildings to repair.

Kyra looked back on the downpour. Liquefied people were mixed with mud, metal, and who knew what else. The gramyriapede couldn't keep its head fixed in one position for long. It reeled back to the others. Burrowed into the ground.

'You were the one who called for us to regroup, so I'm assuming you have a plan?' Kit said. The trio were booking it to the "safe" end of the stadium. They reached it in about eight seconds.

Kyra was about to speak when the vomiting gramyriapede appeared behind them. The Oni Three took a good look at its mouth. Its teeth were shattered. Some had eroded. Cole whipped out his SMG.

'What you got, huh? WHAT YOU GOT?'

Kit and Kyra drew their shotguns. They fired into the gramyriapede's mouth while backpedalling. Maybe Crohl had fitted these bastards with rocket launchers. They didn't know. Better to keep their distance.

The gramyriapede slumped onto the ground. It undoubtedly would've without the Oni Three's bullets. But that's not how Cole would tell it later. If he lived to tell it, that was.

'So, Kyra, plan, yeah?' said Kit.

'I was gonna say we should use more of the platforms, but

the power-up rings are all gone, and we don't have the ball.'

'The rest of the stadium's gone to shit. There's a good chance the security protocols are disabled. We could probably move em by giving em a push.'

'Fool, I don't think my thrusters can carry me to the roof.'

'Elevator?' Kit shrugged. The other gramyriapedes were coming towards them. The Oni Three started running.

'Kit, Cole, Kyra,' it was Trix. 'You need to leave the stadium.'

Cole: 'You kidding me? We just killed one gramyriapede. We have three more to go.'

'I'll take care of them.'

Kit: 'How're you gonna do that, mate?'

'I'm going to nuke them.'

Kyra: 'Figuratively or literally?'

'Leave,' Trix repeated.

'We can't outrun a nuclear blast, Trix.'

'Then I'd better not miss.'

Trix ended her transmission.

'Let's say she does miss. Someone's gonna have to help her get back on target,' said Kyra.

'I was thinking the same thing, baby.'

'So, we really are going to the elevator?' Kit said.

'And if it doesn't work, we're gonna have to climb. Haha,' Cole slapped Kit on the back.

Here it is, folks. This is the moment we've all been waiting for.

Sure is, Bob. Strife Squad has been down from the beginning but they're really clawing their way back.

I think they might have a chance, Dick.

You said it, Bob. Those Exiles are clever, but using gramyriapedes in your line up, it's unsporting.

Not as unsporting as all those casualties. We trust all of you watching around the world have gotten your money's worth.

Now, Bob, can Beatrix Westwood bring it home?

It's the question on all our minds, Dick. She sure is pulling a risky gambit. A stratagem, you might say.

I'll tell you what I will say. I haven't seen anything this risky since the galactic championship of 2768.

And I'm just going to throw this out there; we may never see something like this again.

I couldn't agree more.

12

Nuke In The Hole

Trix of Zilvia sheathed her sword and ran down the walkway, still holding Crohl's arm.

Ren was dying. There was no doubt. Trix had heard his heart struggling to pump blood. Ren's shoulder looked like it'd been mauled by a savage beast. Fleshy flaps stuck out of his busted armour like a grotesque flower dehiscing. Ren hadn't even been wearing her flight-suit. She didn't need to know exactly what happened to know she'd never see it again.

When Griff had dropped her off, she'd come to the exact room Crohl had been stationed. His command console was useless without him. But Trix didn't need all of Dheizir Crohl. Just a piece. Trix ripped the glove off Crohl's severed hand as she ran.

Biometric security systems were sensitive. If the hand wasn't warm, then it wouldn't register a match. This prevented people from hacking off other people's body parts and freezing them for later. More sophisticated systems required a pulse. No pulse, no entry. No dice, hombre.

Trix arrived in Crohl's makeshift headquarters. She could see the ship's "vitals" on the screen. Its shields were at nine per cent. She slapped Crohl's hand on the override panel. It looked as though the console wouldn't register Crohl's handprint. Maybe this had been another one of Dheizir's misdirection ploys.

ZUGROCH EILTODH (*access granted*)

the console said. Trix didn't have time to sift through the controls. She plugged in Sif. The AI recalled the Exile ship. It was headed straight for them. Trix picked up the console which had one yoke attached to it. A basic rig. Not capable of anything extravagant. She considered carrying out her plan from the relative safety of CASOD's top floor. However, if something went wrong, she'd unlikely be able to fix it remotely. Better to do the driving herself. She broke the rig over one knee, after altering its density, so no one else could use it.

'Griff, I need you guarding that ship.'

'What'd you think I'm doing? It's not like there's a smashball game to watch, because Crohl fucking ruined it.'

The Exile ship was upon Trix in less than two seconds. And it was bringing a whole lot of heat in tow. Trix had input a set of commands before smashing the control console. The ship would fly past the window on its side, cockpit facing her.

Trix had to time it just right.

She saw the ship bank. It was starting to come around. The UNSC had brought destroyer corvettes with them. Their guns were slow to fire but packed a wallop. Griff was picking them off. But he wasn't doing it fast enough. He couldn't. He had to keep the Fox from blowing up as well. A lesser pilot would've died ten ships ago.

Out of left field, Trix wondered if Griff's reflexes were even better than hers.

Trix ran at the window. Jumped. Gravity altered so she'd fall straight into the gunner's seat.

Her gambit paid off.

The Exile ship scooped her up. Trix grabbed the yoke. Punched the thrusters to supersonic. The G-Forces nearly made her blackout. The shields were at seven per cent. In a perfect world, she would've had time to sever the connection between the shields dropping and the nuclear warhead activating. The world was far from perfect.

Shields at three per cent.

Trix contacted the Oni Three. Told them to leave the stadium. She knew they probably wouldn't listen. In fact, they certainly wouldn't listen. That was why she had to get this right.

Gramyriapedes were theoretically resilient to radiation. Biologists had discovered similarities between gramyriapedes and cockroaches. Larry was firsthand evidence that the species was indeed radiation resistant. Trix guessed Larry's Kids would be too. There was no reason for Crohl to change that genetic trait. It would've been too troublesome.

If anything, Crohl's meddling would've strengthened their resilience. That was good. Trix hypothesised that a nuclear explosion inside a gramyriapede would be insulated by its hide. With any luck, the exterior carapace would hold the body together, not letting any toxicity escape. It was like a living safe zone for detonation. Then all the authorities would have to do was dispose of the irradiated carcass.

Make no mistake, the exo-skeleton might survive, but the insides would be incinerated.

The next problem Trix had considered was how to kill all four gramyriapedes. She'd been working on it since they appeared on television. Kept coming back to the way they'd emerged from the field. In a braided cord.

The huntress hypothesised that the four gramyriapedes were actually connected to a single body which remained beneath the surface. The gramyriapedes themselves were like fingers with mouths. Conjoined gramyriapedes were documented as a rare occurrence in *Monsters & Other Beasts*. And considering the radiation levels to which the eggs would've been exposed, the chances of birth irregularities rose exponentially.

A nuclear explosion should kill them, Trix thought. The blast will spread through its entire body.

If her hypothesis was incorrect, then she'd still kill one gramyriapede. And without the stress of having to prevent a nuke being dropped in Times Square, killing the others would be easy. Well, easier than trying to defeat them with shotguns.

Shields at two per cent.

Trix circled the stadium. Larry's Kids weren't paying her any attention. She needed a clear shot at one of their mouths or she was fucked. There was too much fallen debris around the stadium's edge. Clipping any of it at high speed would be disastrous.

Now she was grateful that she hadn't disabled all the Exile ship's weapons. She fired at the remaining gramyriapedes with the left wing's cannons. Could hear the screams. Trix thought they were sorry. They were only children, after all.

Gramyriapedes didn't normally go and massacre people. Their nutrients came from the soil. Dheizir Crohl had ruined their natural instincts for his own sadistic agenda. Trix hated him for that. While gramyriapedes were often erroneously classified as monsters, she didn't think of them that way. Just because they were gargantuan and could swallow a small town

(Fenwick came to mind)

didn't mean they'd do so for kicks.

Actually, Trix hated Dheizir Crohl for many reasons. She hoped Ren hadn't killed him. She wanted the bastard to rot. But she wanted to hit him a few more times before that happened.

One of the gramyriapedes rose to the stadium's height. Faced her. She was taken aback. She didn't want to know how far they stretched underground.

'Maybe a nuclear blast won't be enough,' she said.

It was too late to wonder. She had a gramyriapede's attention, now all she—

Her HUD warned her that the ship's shields were at zero per cent. Lights all over the gunner's console blared red. Alarms sounded. A countdown began. Trix had a pretty good idea what it was for.

Then a blast hit her left wing. Another hit her right thrusters. She was going down. And what was worse, she was going to miss the gramyriapede's mouth. Yvach would've laughed his arse off had he been present.

'Not even I could miss a target that big, machina,' Trix heard Yvach say in her head. And this was coming from the corrach who said he couldn't crash into a mountain range because his aim wasn't that good.

Trix fought for control of the ship which was flying low over the stadium roof — the part of it that hadn't collapsed. There was nothing else for it. No other contingency plan. She couldn't eject. Not even that would save her. Someone spoke over the comms. She couldn't make it out. It sounded as though the Oni Three were asking Griff to shoot something.

The Valkyrie plugged Sif into the console to try and deactivate the warhead.

Sif: 'We need biometric confirmation. And we don't have Crohl's hand anymore. Even if we did, it'd be too cold to use.'

The Exile ship started spiralling. Trix had failed too often of late for her liking. First the people of Fenwick, then Paris, and now Manhattan. Not to mention all the corrachs who lost their lives on Raursioc. That hadn't even been Trix's fault. Just at the moment she felt like it was.

No. While she was still alive, there was still a chance.

Until you are dead, victory is a possibility, Minerva Granger had often said.

While you breathe, Felix Westwood would tell her as they sparred, *while your heart beats in your chest like the fiercest battle-drum, nothing is over until you say it is. You hold that power within you, Beatrix. And none other than Death himself can take it away. You must fight. I cannot promise you will emerge victorious. But I can promise that you shan't die wondering. Now, get up. Stand and show me your strength.*

Trix knew Felix was right. The world appeared to move in slow motion. Her heart was beating 200 times a minute. Trix would kill herself shifting gravity to move the ship if necessary. Mireleth had told her she could draw magic from the world's energy. Magic generally wasn't as thick in big cities as it was where nature ruled. But it was worth a shot. Trix was about to leave her seat when the ship suddenly gained altitude.

Then it was pushed forward.

'We got you, baby,' Cole laughed over comms.

The talking Trix hadn't properly heard over comms *had*

been the Oni Three asking Griff to shoot something: them.

As it turned out, the elevator still worked, and the Oni Three had reached the roof. They could see the Exile ship coming down. They had to put it in the gramyriapede's mouth. Their kinetic blasts would do the trick. The problem was absorbing their required energy. It was the one drawback of oni powers. They couldn't use any offensive ones until they'd absorbed energy from their barriers.

Joining forces, as they'd done outside Crohl's dreadnought, the Oni Three created a single barrier to absorb a charge from the Fox's railgun. Griff only hit them with just over half strength. He didn't want to be responsible for killing three of the Valkyrie's closest friends.

Charged up, the onis prepared to hit the Exile ship with a concussive blast. They were aware that their magic might set off the warhead. But they didn't have any other option.

They hit the Exile ship at an angle as it passed. It was still spiralling, but now it was on a collision course with the gramyriapede's abyssal rising mouth.

The Oni Three fell back to the roof. Felt faint. Cole slumped to his knees.

Kit: 'I thought nothing stopped the Cole Train, mate?'

'I'm just pulling into the station, man,' Cole said. He stood. Kyra leaned on him. Kit got down on his haunches. Something was wrong. Why hadn't Trix ejected yet?

'Captain, get outta that ship,' Griff said. He was engaged in aerial acrobatics high above the stadium. Unlike flying in space, flying within the atmosphere possessed certain limitations of which Griff wasn't fond. The suddenness of his movements had to be reduced. The ship was warning him that too much stress was being placed on the hull. And that was *with* his strengthening upgrades.

Trix didn't want to leave until the last possible second. She still had control over one wing flap and one thruster. That was enough to keep the ship on course.

The Valkyrie saw the gramyriapede's maw close in. She

held.

'Trix,' said Kit and Sif simultaneously.

'Eat shit.'

The Valkyrie pulled the ejection lever. Shot high above Jets Stadium. If any UNSC ships were keeping a lock on her, she knew that she was a sitting duck. The chair had all kinds of distress lights on it. Crohl must've disabled the ones on the pilot's chair before launching it into the North Atlantic.

The Valkyrie dove off her seat. Towards the Oni Three.

She looked at the Exile ship. It'd disappeared into the gramyriapede's mouth. It thrashed back and forth like a madman's whip.

Its body came down past the Gladiator's end-zone. The roof split in two. It reversed. Crushed the stadium exterior. Again. Smacked into its fellow siblings. Cries of pain and confusion. Like a toddler with a stomach ache who couldn't communicate their feelings.

The whipping gramyriapede dove for the ground. Its whole body rippled. Gore erupted from its mouth. More erupted from the remaining gramyriapedes. Immense heat followed. They continued squirming before falling silent. Their gargantuan bodies shook the Earth. Trenches formed where they lay.

There were no more pained roars. Aside from the ships flying overhead, the world became quiet. Compared to what it'd been only moments ago, it may as well have been a graveyard.

Looking at the corpses littered around the stadium, then back to Manhattan's destruction, that description was morbidly appropriate.

Trix slowed gravity as much as her exhausted body allowed and hit the stadium roof. She and the Oni Three didn't exchange words. Cole led the way back to the elevator. The whole stadium was unstable. And none of them felt like reaching the ground floor via a 200 metre plunge.

'We need to help Griff,' Trix said as they stepped inside the service elevator. Before anyone could reply, she mentally cursed herself for being so stupid. Crohl's hand on the override panel had stopped a lot of non-critical functions. Trix wondered if the backdoor he'd placed in the UNSS comms was one of them.

'Sif, connect me to the UNSS.'

'Standing by.'

A connection was established.

'This is Trix of Zilvia. We surrender. Allow our ship to land and we will fly to the UNSS under your escort.'

She almost expected a *"we don't negotiate with terrorists"* message to play.

'All ships, stand down. Fugitives have surrendered. You are to escort them to the UNSS. All threats reported to be neutralised.'

Trix knew that voice. It was Bronte. Trix retracted her helmet. It'd been stifling.

'Sif, is Bronte an AI?'

'I think so.'

'That explains the way she was talking, and why we couldn't see her when we established the video feed.'

Kyra: 'Strange that she agreed to let us aboard the UNSS after all that's happened. Some of the cameras around the stadium must've continued rolling. Maybe people saw what we were doing?'

Trix: 'Hmm.'

Cole: 'Man, that move was insane. Now I know why they kept you Valkyries separate from us at the academy. Y'all are crazy.'

Kit: 'We did right a ship by being hit in the faces with railgun fire, mate. Let's not forget that.'

'Where's Ren?' Kyra said.

'He was fighting Crohl. Did a pretty good job of busting himself up. If he's alive, he'll be barely breathing.'

'Think the UNSS will let us make a stop?'

'If we're lucky.'

'What else would you call what just happened?' Kit said.

He'd retracted his helmet too. 'Anyone got a ticket for the galactic lottery?'

The machinas laughed.

They'd won against all odds. It wasn't much of a victory. Over a hundred thousand people had perished between the Stadium and Manhattan. Many more would've died if it hadn't been for Strife Squad's actions.

Each of them had armies of skeletons in their closets. The hard part wasn't surviving the fight. The hard part was surviving the victory. Hearing screams when all was silent. Seeing death in every shadow. Each smile stalked by guilt. How dare you be happy when so many died?

That was a question every soldier had to answer differently. No singular solution satisfied all warriors, or all sins.

As the machinas walked, they knew that now was the time for politics. The assigning of blame. If Yvach hadn't been successful, if Crohl had died, or had yet another trick up his sleeve, they were all going to jail.

Emergency crews were mobilised to the stadium, and to Manhattan. Quarantine crews headed to bag the gramyriapedes in freighters, then dump them on the galaxy's outer edge.

Griff landed the Fox outside the stadium. Nary a scratch. Griff truly was better than anyone Strife Squad had ever seen.

The machinas entered. UNSC corvettes kept their biggest guns ready to fire in case the Fox tried escaping. They weren't allowed permission to stop at CASOD. Instead, one of the UNSC ships was diverted to its top floor to collect Crohl and Ren.

With everyone on board, Griff ascended to the stars once more.

Strife Squad were grimly aware they could be ascending for the last time. In the Hole, flying would be a distant memory until it turned into naught but a dream.

If they were lucky enough to have a break from nightmares.

CONSEQUENCES
LOCATION: Crohl's Dreadnought, Sea of Bones

1

Yvach Aodun couldn't reach Trix.

He'd heard that suspected terrorists, namely the machina known as Trix of Zilvia, had been taken into custody. It looked like he'd have to visit the UNSS. Or at the very least, have someone come to him. That'd be better.

For the moment, Yvach was too buggered to go anywhere.

Yvach and a renegade Mountain King unit had taken Crohl's dreadnought. It'd been one of the hardest fights in Yvach's life. He was sitting in a lab aboard the dreadnought. Dreadful experiments had taken place. Corrachs in glass tubes had experienced grotesque, malformed growth spurts. Many of them had hunched backs. Others had bones growing outside their skin. There was one victim whose organs had pushed so hard against his ribs that they'd exploded.

These experiments didn't help with the case. But the gramyriapede tissue, jata, that did the trick. It looked like the next phase of Crohl's plan was to turn corrach skin into bulletproof gramyriapede carapaces.

All of this still wasn't enough. Especially not to free Vidal Laigalt or expunge Trix. Yvach held his hand to his head. He'd suffered, as corrachs called it, a nasty scrape. Anyone else would've said the right part of his scalp had busted open. It was bandaged now. Even with pain medication it throbbed continuously. Yvach could've taken a stronger dose, but he didn't have any stimulant loaded drugs, and he needed to be alert.

He reckoned his head wound was better than his left hand's missing middle finger. It'd been crushed by an Exile's mech-suit boot. Yvach had amputated it himself using Raursiocan whiskey as both anaesthetic and disinfectant.

To say this fight had taken it out of him wouldn't be right. It had taken pieces *off* him.

One of Yvach's friends, Tourach Grevaggs, entered the lab. All Exiles aboard the ship had been detained or killed. It'd taken hours to sweep the whole dreadnought. The Mountain Kings had their own AIs working to crack Crohl's computers. The Exiles hadn't had the sense, or maybe the orders, to wipe the data drives. But the files were heavily encrypted. Yvach watched his comrades take samples from the glass tubes. Some of the "contents" were still showing vital signs. Whatever they were, they were alive. Yvach hoped they stayed asleep.

Tourach stood beside Yvach. They spoke in Corrachian to each other.

'What news, Tourach?'

'We've cracked their files.'

'Anything we can use? Need I remind you, it's not only our brother Vidal, or sister Trix, depending on us. If this venture proves to be for naught, then we'll be Exiles, same as these tarclabers.'

'You best come and see it for yourself, old friend.'

'You are older.'

'By one year.'

'And let's not forget that.'

Yvach walked with Tourach out of the lab. Through the dreadnought's halls. There would be no clean up. No disposal of bodies. Exiles didn't deserve such ceremonious rites. If Tourach had found useful evidence, Yvach would notify the Grand Corrachian Council, Raursioc's leaders. They would decide the appropriate punishment for the Ghirsioc Raithexils.

Not a single one of Yvach's men had died in the assault. Though there'd been grievous injuries. It didn't look like anyone would die in the aftermath. Honourable corrachs were too resilient for such nonsense. They simply didn't have the time.

Yvach was led to another room. This one was full of computer terminals. Mountain Kings were clustered around them.

'Dherr Aodun,' they all said as they performed the corrachian salute. Dherr was a formal term with a variety of different meanings and variations. In battle, or during a mission, Dherr essentially meant High Commander, or Master Chief. On Raursioc, in times of peace, Dherr meant Lord Ruler. Female corrachs — there was no word for "woman" in Corrachian, all corrachs were just called corrachs — were referred to by the feminine, Dherrine. The meanings, however, remained the same.

'Steady, brothers. What have you found?'

'Look,' Tourach said. He entered commands on the console. Vidal Laigalt appeared on the screens. He was giving a speech at an event on the Bastion. Tourach entered another command. Vidal Laigalt again. This time offering words of advice for the Grand Corrachian Council. More commands were entered. More speeches were shown. Dheizir Crohl had every one of Vidal's speeches in his databases.

'With all these recordings, Crohl could warp Vidal's voice to say almost anything.'

'That explains how he framed Vidal for the gramyriapedes on Earth,' said Yvach. That was a bold gamble on Crohl's part, sticking Vidal for the blame when he was locked up on the Bastion. But people believed anything with enough fear.

'And that's not all.'

Another recording played. This time it had no visual. Garbled noises were followed by a voice that Yvach knew well. It was Trix of Zilvia.

'M'fiak, this was when she met him. This was how he framed her.'

'This is what we need to stop Crohl. The necessary voice algorithms are fragmented on this database. They can be deciphered in the hands of better analysts.'

'Crohl's crimes have affected the galaxy. He won't be answering to us. He'll have to answer to the Consortium. I expect Roger Hobbes will be part of the panel, and so will Rohark Cregalt.'

Rohark Cregalt was a member of the Grand Corrachian Council. Whenever a Raursiocan representative was required, the council would take turns. Previously, Dherrine Arhadh Liavassach had spoken on behalf of the Corrachian home world.

'Orders, then, old friend?'

'Inform Raursioc we've found evidence against the wanted terrorist known as Dheizir Crohl. Trix will have to hold out a few more hours. We need to be certain before we do anything.'

Yvach left the terminal room. He was in command. It wouldn't be fitting for him to return to his ship just yet. Instead, he went to interrogate some of the imprisoned Ice Exiles. Maybe he could get them talking.

If not, well, his right hand could still form a fist.

And he wanted to hit something.

2
Jailbirds
LOCATION: UNSS, Solar System

The UNSS cells were nicer than the one on Crohl's dreadnought.

Strife Squad were separated since no one wanted the machinas to facilitate an escape. They were also in maximum security. That meant magic dampeners and forearm cuffs, even within the cell. Their weapons had been confiscated, though they still wore their armour. None aboard the UNSS were keen to try making machinas strip.

The only person who wasn't detained in maximum security, but found himself inside a regular holding cell, was Griffauron Raivad. His zirean blood unfortunately leant him no magical abilities. Though sometimes he was capable of mild telekinesis. Stirring spoons without touching them, partial levitation, and other mundane tasks.

He talked incessantly over the hours he was detained. Eventually the UNSS guards activated a soundproof barrier in front of his cell for peace and quiet. Griffauron Raivad was not one to exercise his right to remain silent.

Other planets, like Raursioc, didn't have that right. A refusal to talk was taken as an admission of guilt. If you talked and were found to be lying, then you were exiled. If you weren't a Raursiocan citizen, you could find yourself sent to the Rei'ner Ghlain, the Realm of Glass.

In the days before interplanetary travel, exiled corrachs lived out their banishment on the hostile island continent which surrounded Raursioc's southern pole. Arcus storm clouds brewed overhead almost constantly. And there was little liveable land, just ice sheets far as the eye could see. The only land that existed was a craggy mountain range full of loose rocks and sparse vegetation.

Fearsome monsters called the Realm of Glass home. The only civilisation there was a prison built into the southernmost mountains. And an elite dojo for corrachian warlocks. They believed the Realm of Glass held strong magical significance.

It was coming up on six hours since Strife Squad had been imprisoned.

Ren Gerdac had no idea. He was in the UNSS hospital alongside Dheizir Crohl. When they'd been found, Crohl was bludgeoning Ren to death with his fists. He'd been sedated. Both of them were now unconscious. Crohl was strapped to the bed in cuffs. His situation critical. Ren was faring better. According to the doctors, both of them would live. They expected Ren to wake up soon. They didn't know what to expect with Crohl. He was a genetic anomaly. A mutated freak.

Both men were kept under close surveillance.

Ren regained consciousness as the seven-hour mark approached. He was groggy. In no position to give testimony.

The rest of Strife Squad, however, were able. Each of them was questioned individually. How they came to be in Ren Gerdac's employ. Why they were travelling with Trix of Zilvia, and all the rest. None of them had prior marks on their records save for Griff's dishonourable discharge.

They'd discussed what to say as they'd flown to the UNSS. It was decided that they would mostly tell the truth. Cid Tyler's illegal upgrades would be omitted, even though, after inspecting the Fox, the UNSS would see nothing about it was legal except the landing gear.

Noctius Saberil's involvement was also omitted. Trix had no desire to anger the Broker. It wasn't a matter of friendship. They weren't friends. All they had was mutual respect. Trix didn't want to piss him off. She'd made enemies out of a Kalarikian Warlord, a Djurelian Slaver, and a Noble Zirean Family only a month ago. Her quota for new enemies was filled for the next decade. Adding Noctius Saberil would be throwing a grenade into the pot. People who crossed him disappeared. None knew where they went.

Finally, to solidify their stories, Strife Squad made it sound as though their mission had always been to bring down the Ice Exiles.

It was difficult to tell if the UNSS officials who interrogated them believed what Strife Squad had to say, but none of them had been tortured yet. That was a good sign.

The eighth captive hour drew to a close. The UNSS received a direct call from the Grand Corrachian Council. Apparently they had something the UNSS needed to see.

It was during the fourteenth hour that Strife Squad was finally released from their cells. They were taken to a press room. Only, instead of press, Roger Hobbes, Luanu Mieshe, Ronald T. Duckworth, and Oroya Niil were present. There was a man Trix had never met in Vidal Laigalt's place, though she knew of him. Rohark Cregalt.

Strife Squad took their seats. They were still cuffed. Ren was in a wheelchair, hooked up to IV drips. Everything about him drooped. His normally full, curly moustache sagged on his face like roadkill left in the sun too long. Armed guards and mechs lined the walls.

Trix spoke before anyone could call the room to order.

'How come you aren't all dead? You were at the smashball game. And the Consortium box is right in the centre. You would've been the first to die.'

'Yes, glad we didn't have to waste time with all the typical ceremonial tripe. Straight to business,' Ron Duckworth said. He was sitting on a raised stage behind a desk with the other dignitaries. 'We didn't die, Ms Westwood, because we were privately evacuated after we opened the game.'

Luanu's eyes widened. 'Ronald, considering what has happened, it would not do to abandon procedure. These crimes are serious.'

'We're the Consortium Council, Luanu. Everything we deal with is serious. You don't need to remind me.'

'If you were evacuated, how come everyone else wasn't, mate?' Kit said.

Bronte's voice came over a speaker. 'As a precaution, pending the validation of Trix of Zilvia's terrorist attack warning, important council members were removed from the stadium's vicinity.'

'So you could've saved all those people. You condemned them to die. Why would you do that?' Kyra said.

Bronte: 'Kyra of Drion, you are here to be questioned, not the other way around.'

'She's a lot of fun,' Sif said to Trix through her earpiece. Trix couldn't reply. She cracked a wry smile instead.

Luanu: 'Postponing the game would've meant refunding 400,000 tickets, not to mention premium access televised content. It was not a viable option. The threat which you phoned in was not deemed to be serious enough to cancel the event. We believed it could be stopped. You never mentioned the emergence of gramyriapedes.'

'You definitely would've believed us if we had,' Cole said.

'We would've been forced to consider the threat with a greater degree of severity,' said Bronte.

'Haha, hold up now. Just wait a minute, baby. My bullshit sense is tingling.'

'I would thank the lot of you to show respect for this situation, and for the Consortium,' Roger Hobbes said. His hair was in a respectable part. Five o'clock shadow shaded his cheeks. He sat on the opposite end of the desk from Duckworth.

'The main reason the stadium was not evacuated was because we didn't want to indulge the public's thoughts of war with the corrachs, or induce further hatred. There have been countless attacks on corrachs all over the globe, and in human colonies among the stars, since the attack on Paris. We've tried to downplay them because war is not something we desire. The last war we had did not end well.' Roger's eyes flitted to Luanu, who as always, looked comfortably smug.

'Right, so how come Vidal Laigalt isn't here? Still suspicious of him?' Griff said. His cuffs were standard. Just around the wrists. He took off his hat. Scratched his head. His blue hair was wild. Griff needed a shower. All of Strife Squad did.

Ronald: 'Vidal Laigalt went through vigorous examinations on the Bastion. It was determined that he was innocent of all crimes. But we had to let people believe he was still in for questioning. We had received death threats against him. It was for his own protection.'

'Is that why you're here?' Griff pointed to Rohark.

'Jata,' Rohark said. Griff was expecting something more. Rohark remained silent.

Oroya Niil, always a mediator, spoke next.

'Rohark is here to represent Raursioc in light of the atrocity that took place in their Frost Gardens. An atrocity for which you, Renier von Gerdac, were blamed.'

Ren lifted his head. He looked fucked out of his mind on drugs. His face was worse than after Rosamund Galbrand had beaten him bloody.

'You say blamed. Not guilty. This must mean that you know I played no part in that base act.'

Oroya looked to Rohark. He had a beard braided thicker than metal cords. Beads hung off the end. Each one represented a victory either in battle or in politics. In place of beads, corrachs could wear conventional medals. All of them had the necessary scarification, though. Smooth skin was deemed one of the ugliest aesthetic traits a person could possess among corrachs. Scars, whether they were decorative, or earned in battle, were like having eight-pack abs or big boobs on Earth.

'Earlier this morning, by your world's time, former Corrachian Colonel, Yvach Aodun, led an unsanctioned mission into Sea of Bones space with Mountain King military property. At these coordinates,' Rohark gestured with his hands. A hologram appeared in front of Strife Squad. 'He and his squadron discovered an immobilised, unmarked dreadnought. Upon taking the dreadnought, they learned that it belonged to the Ghirsioc Raithexils. Until now, they had specialised in the illegal trade of exotic and dangerous animals as well as countless allegations of theft, murder, and rape. He and his exiled clan are an utter disgrace to our people. Voice modulation software was uncovered by Aodun's men. Further examination revealed its algorithm to be present in all recordings related to the terrorist attacks.'

Kit went to say something. Rohark's powerful voice steamrolled him into silence.

'In addition, gramyriapede tissue was found in labs where the Exiles were mutating corrachs. All those who were detained on the dreadnought now face Raursiocan law, and have been transported to the Rei'ner Ghlain. They were in our system, so they are our responsibility. They will long for their days of exile.'

'In that case, you know we're innocent, and Crohl's guilty. I'd call that a job well done,' Kit held out his arms. 'Now how about unlocking these? My balls have been itching for the last five hours.'

'Son, I find these tedious rituals to be every bit as tiresome as you do. But another comment like that and we'll have to charge you with contempt,' Ron Duckworth said.

Kit lowered his arms. 'Thanks for the warning, mate.'

Oroya: 'This evidence alone was not able to clear any of you.

A sweep of CASOD towers revealed a command station that used a downgraded version of the voice modulation software aboard the dreadnought. Dheizir Crohl's hand was taken for prints when he was brought to the UNSS hospital. It matched the command console's biometrics. We now know he's the owner of the dreadnought and at least an accomplice to everything that happened on board.'

'This doesn't explain why you were suddenly happy to accept our surrender when Bronte made it clear we would be shot down with impunity,' Trix said.

'Bronte is an experimental AI. She's made to try and resolve conflict. Her aggression was an unforeseen dilemma,' Roger Hobbes said. He looked tired. No doubt he'd been up since the attack doing press and helping direct aid where it was needed most.

'That being said, it was partially thanks to Bronte that your surrender was accepted,' said Ron.

'My calculations showed that with the footage of the Oni Three battling the gramyriapedes, and the backup cameras on CASOD towers monitoring Trix, people would be enraged to see you mistreated, or killed, despite your machina genetics. The video of Cole of Orix and Kit of Aros performing a pass in Jets Stadium has been viewed over two billion times in the past 14 hours.'

'Further witness questioning also revealed the testimony of Kimie Tsukakoshi. She confirmed that you were trying to kill the gramyriapedes.'

Cole smiled. 'Haha, so we're getting a reward, right?'

Luanu's lips became thinner than a bulimic's waistline. 'Your *reward*, Mr Cole, is that you are not going to prison, as you do not have a criminal history. However, the same cannot be said for Renier von Gerdac.'

'Ren was an instrumental part of this operation. If it hadn't been for him, we would've never known Crohl was on Earth. And we couldn't have immobilised Crohl's dreadnought,' said Trix.

'This all ties in to the mystical confession Crohl supposedly gave you over your comms devices, does it?' Luanu said.

Sif had recorded Crohl's taunts as he'd spoken. However, upon playback, they were garbled. Encrypted to the point of being broken. Crohl's confession was useless unless he decided to wake up from his drug induced coma and repeat it for the council's benefit.

'At this point, we don't doubt that Crohl is guilty. But that doesn't change the fact that Ren is wanted for crimes prior to these felonies,' said Ron. He was scrolling through information on the desk in front of him. 'Grand Theft Stellar, extortion, murder, possession of illegal goods, selling of illegal goods, impersonating a Bastion officer, impersonating a cleric of the Catholic Church, drug smuggling, and the list goes on. I'd keep reading, only by now you should understand that his help in this matter cannot absolve him of his past crimes.'

'It only took me to be unconscious and missing an arm for you to finally catch me. I'm amazed by the proficiency of your law enforcing efforts.' Ren was too tired to speak with any alarm. He was so drugged he was barely aware of what was happening.

'Renier von Gerdac, this council declares that you are guilty of the aforementioned crimes. By the power vested in us by our people's governments, we sentence you to jail. Twenty years in Bastion Maximum Security with parole possible after ten on good behaviour,' Oroya said.

Trix noted that Oroya seemed regretful.

'If you choose to name your accomplices, we can offer you a reduced sentence.'

'I don't know who you're talking about.'

'This offer will not be made to you again, Mr Gerdac. Lead us to your accomplices, and your sentence will be halved.'

'A captain always goes down with his ship,' Ren said. His eyes were watering. He looked gaunt. Frail. A warmed-up corpse hunched in his wheelchair. 'And I'm a commodore.'

'This man is too drugged to be sentenced. Criminal or not, I won't be sending any citizen of mine to prison in ill health.' Roger nodded to a guard who moved to push Ren out of the room. 'All in favour of postponing Renier von Gerdac's sentencing.'

To Strife Squad's surprise, everyone voted in favour. Ron looked reluctant. That was only because postponement meant having to sit through this again.

Roger gave Luanu an interesting look. The machinas heard her whisper. 'He's a citizen of mine, too,' Luanu said. She touched the tips of her ears absently.

Strife Squad stood as Ren left the room. They weren't sure if they called Ren Gerdac a friend. They didn't know if he was a good man. But they were sure of two counts: Renier von Gerdac wasn't their enemy, nor was he bad. Like most people, he was somewhere in between.

Ren looked back at them with glimmering eyes. He wasn't going to the Hole again. That thought gave him greater comfort than a whore's bosom. There was a chance he could be broken out of Bastion Maximum Security.

He held on to it.

3

Strife Squad sat.

'Now the most important issue has been resolved, we come to your ship, Ms Westwood,' Roger said.

'What about it?'

'You are not licensed to have the calibre of plasma cannons, nor the railgun currently fitted to the hull. As for the thruster modifications, they aren't regulation. Since they're potentially hazardous, they'll have to be removed.'

'The weapons, Chairman, are certainly hazardous,' Luanu pointed out. She was that one kid in class who had their nose buried so far up the teacher's arse you could see it when the teacher did roll call, right at the back of their tongue.

Ronald: 'That's an obvious statement. And since they out manoeuvred all the ships that were sent after them, I think we can agree that they're safe. The problem is that they destroyed UNSS and UNSC property.'

'We already explained why we had to do that. If Crohl hadn't blocked your comms, we could've made your ships to lay off,' Trix said.

'Syor Raivad,' Oroya said. Syor meant mister in zirean. 'You said in your testimony that you were the one who upgraded Trix of Zilvia's ship, which was a Fox Transport, corvette class cruiser.'

'Hysi.'

Oroya cast a look to Roger Hobbes. Leaned back in her chair.

Strange, Trix thought.

'Unless Rohark has anything to add, I believe this hearing is over.'

Rohark — who'd been still as a statue for most of the hearing — looked like he was searching for the right words.

'Yvach Aodun has given the highest praise of Beatrix Westwood. And, indeed, she is an honorary citizen of Raursioc. I see no reason to punish her, or her companions, for the crimes of a tarclaber like Dheizir Crohl. On behalf of Raursioc's people, I will not press charges against you.'

Trix: 'You honour me, Dherr Cregalt.'

'It is you who have honoured us by doing what was right, even when it could've ended in your damnation.'

'Those in favour of releasing the accused,' Oroya said.

Everyone's hands raised except for Luanu. 'I would not have you off so easily. This is your second galactic offense, Ms Westwood. Let's not aim for a third. You may not find yourself so lucky again.'

The Consortium Council was escorted from the press room by six armed guards. Roger Hobbes remained.

'I think we've left these cuffs on long enough, don't you?' he said. Hobbes motioned for the guards to unlock them.

Strife Squad didn't make a show by flexing or stretching. They acted like it was no big deal. Like they could've escaped at any time if they'd wanted.

Roger stood in front of the desk. Arms folded. Looking at the ground.

'You may leave us,' Roger said to the guards. They were perplexed by the order, but obeyed without question. Once they were gone, Roger spoke again. 'Strife Squad and Ultima Company. What are they?'

Trix remembered Kit telling her those names in Desert Star Engines. How did Roger know about them?

Kit: 'A little fun I had repainting the Fox, mate. Beatrix's ship, I mean. A badass name to call ourselves. We hadn't made it official or anything. Just a joke, really.'

'What did you paint on my ship?' Trix said. She still hadn't seen it from the top, with the logos on the wings.

'You know, those skull designs I told you about for a crack team meant to save the galaxy? They wouldn't make bad smashball club names now that I think of it.'

Hobbes: 'You must understand, I can't let any of you off without repercussions of some sort. But I see no reason those repercussions have to be severe.'

Kyra thought about making a joke. Now wasn't the right time. This had to be the worst loss of life outside war in centuries.

'Syor Raivad, what little footage we captured of *the Fox* shows that it handles unlike any other known ship.'

'The C.A.F. would've had those designs years ago if they'd allowed me to keep experimenting. But oh no, not with taxpayer money. Not with military hardware. Not with a blindfold so it's more of a challenge.'

'Easy, Daddy Blue,' Cole clapped Griff on the back. The zirean settled down.

'How about you work for the UNSC aboard this station? I can't offer you an actual title, nor a military rank. What I can offer you is the chance to be a hands-on consultant for the upgrading of our fleet, and a "guest" instructor to our new pilots. Of course, you would also be first to test pilot all new ships we build. Like an independent contractor. What do you say?'

'I suspect I don't have a choice, so, hysi, Chairman Hobbes. You've got yourself the best pilot you've ever seen. I fron you just want to keep an eye on me. And make sure no one else has my designs.'

Roger smiled. Relaxed. His tranquillity was impressive considering the dangerous company he kept.

'As for you, machinas. You've all shown yourselves to possess impressive skills. I expect they're due to the training you received on Mair Ultima.'

The machinas remained silent.

'I would like to offer you the chance for Strife Squad to become a reality. A covert specialist team serving Earth.'

The Oni Three instinctually differed to Trix for comment.

Trix: 'I'm not someone to be owned. And I don't like involvement with military affairs.'

'We wouldn't own you. Just contract you, like we plan to contract Syor Raivad. You would be part of this squad too, Griff.'

'Hysi. Damn right I would.'

'Depending on your answer, I can call a secondary hearing. Any outcome whereupon at least one Consortium member or guest panellist dissents can be retried.'

'Are you threatening me, President Hobbes?'

'Never, Ms Westwood. I owe you my daughter's life. She sends her thanks, by the way.'

'She's welcome,' Trix said. She didn't really have a choice. Had to accept Roger's offer. Maybe it would be a way to clear her conscience. She couldn't see it, but she could feel it. What was once fresh had become grimy. Grease slicked. Blood stained. Trix didn't beat herself up. That was a waste of time. It was also a job already filled by her nightmares.

'I accept on these conditions. I will be the captain. I will pick my team. And you will provide me with whatever jurisdiction I need to complete the missions assigned to me. You will also give me a licence for the way my ship is currently outfitted. All

of us here will be licenced to carry weapons aboard the
Bastion. And we will be paid for our services. Handsomely. If
you can't agree to my terms, President Hobbes, then you may
as well call a second hearing right now.'

'What about the smashball tickets?' Kit whispered.

Kyra laughed. She couldn't help it. Cole had himself a
chuckle, too.

'We have a deal, Ms Westwood.'

Roger Hobbes stuck his hand out. Trix grabbed it a little tight
to remind the Chairman with whom he was dealing.

'I expect you'll all want your effects back.'

'Unless you want to give us better ones,' Kyra said.

Roger Hobbes issued a command on his comms gauntlet. The
guards who'd presided over the hearing returned to the room.
Strife Squad was escorted out. They were disheartened that
Ren would be going to prison. At least they could visit him in
the Bastion. Possibly break him out if they ever needed his
pirating expertise.

They passed panoramic windows on their way to the hangar
where the Fox was impounded.

Earth was wondrously blemished from the space station.
The scars of canyons, acne of mountains, and blotches of red
desert were all marks of beauty. Signs of life.

Trix had to call Yvach and thank him. She looked to the
machinas on her left. The Oni Three were grinning like school
kids who'd weaselled their way out of detention. Griff was
beaming on her right. You could've sworn that the Xardiassian
Ceirlos had won the galactic tournament.

The Valkyrie had an overwhelming feeling that something
important was beginning.

Every end begets a beginning,
new paths lined with gallows.
It's these you must walk,
burdened by sorrows.
Death is lurking
in the shadows.
Grim he reaps
Darkness he borrows.
He's the Final Finality,
Thief of Tomorrows.

Cuthbert Theroux

EPILOGUE

LOCATION: Yephus, Shivering Dominion

1

Trix of Zilvia's last day off was drawing to a close.

It had been a week since the events of Manhattan. Crohl's public trial had taken place the day before, on Earth Date March 16th. He was unable to worm his way out of a sentence. His inability to trust others with important tasks had been his downfall. Had he not used his biometrics on the dreadnought and had a lackey handle the gramyriapedes, he would've walked free.

Crohl didn't seem to care.

2

An Exile Condemned
Location: UNSS, Solar System

The Valkyrie watched Dheizir's trial with the rest of Strife Squad.

She'd always been a lone wolf. It was her nature. But she was grateful that she could trust others. Crohl might've had a thousand Exiles or more under his command. Trix doubted he had any friends.

To everyone's surprise, Crohl wasn't sentenced to the Hole. Vidal Laigalt, now cleared of all charges, made a strong case as to why Dheizir Crohl should be imprisoned for life in the Realm of Glass. Crohl's greatest insult, Vidal claimed, was his tarnishing of Raursioc's honour. Thus it fell to those on Raursioc to condemn him.

Since no one truly knew what happened in the Hole, Vidal wanted to ensure maximum punishment for Crohl's crimes. And that would be a certainty in the Realm of Glass.

The Earthen jury agreed wholeheartedly. The more Crohl was punished, the better, they reckoned. Though no one had actually used those precise words.

Trix was uneasy about the decision. The Realm of Glass was a fortress shrouded in mystery, but it wasn't the Hole. Crohl could be broken out. Hadn't Yvach said there were whispers on Raursioc about corrachs being loyal to Crohl's cause? Perhaps Vidal was one of them.

Crohl's tranquillity didn't sit well with the Valkyrie. She wanted to put a .44 bullet through his crotch and let the pain linger before splitting his skull.

Crohl was asked to give one final statement.

'Bhias   siaren   nihr'nals   gniom'akte,   siett   siaren fehlmith'akte.'

These were more than acts of terrorism, they were acts of misdirection.

His words silenced the courtroom like a guillotine. Dheizir Crohl spoke no more.

He only smiled.

3

Trix remembered Crohl's words with haunting clarity.

She took a draught of her beer. Kit was by the grill. Steaks thick as concrete slabs and bacon strips like duvet covers were over the fire. Griff was tossing around a smashball with Cole and Kyra. The onis were taking it easy on him.

Strife Squad was in the mountains, on Yephus. On the very same plateau Trix had visited a month ago with Yvach, Dai, and Iglessia. Dai's mother's grave was still there. Peaceful among the whistling range. Caressed by cool breezes. Trix had invited Yvach to join her. Due to his actions on the Exile dreadnought, he had to go through lengthy debriefings. He promised he'd make the next one, if only to give Kit the bird with his bionic middle finger.

Kit had wanted to go back to Australia, but everyone else agreed it'd be better to give Earth a wide berth. Though thanks to Crackshot Kimie, they'd all been treated to box seats during the Miyazaki Ronin's first game of the season. Kimie had even said that the Oni Three would be great players. Unfortunately, current rules banned machinas as they were considered to be constantly on "performance enhancing drugs."

The ESA had debated whether the smashball season should be continued. It did, under the proviso that 100 per cent of profits from North American teams went to repair Manhattan, and Jets Stadium. A memorial was to be built in its place. Another stadium would be built later, if at all. International smashball teams pledged 75 percent of their profits to fund the repairs.

So far, it was proving to be the best smashball season yet. People were coming together like never before. Stadiums were packed night after night. It would be years before Manhattan got back on its feet, and decades until the wounds of loss healed. But humanity had made a start. And thankfully, it was a good one.

However, racial tensions between corrachs and humans continued simmering. Prejudice grew stronger. A once proud friendship had been marred. It was too soon to know how deep the wounds ran.

Trix smiled as Kyra tackled Griff to the ground, knocking his cap off. Kit doubled over with mirth, spatula in hand.

The Valkyrie wondered whether or not Ren would've been present if he hadn't gone to jail.

4

Pirate's Life
Location: UNSS, Solar System

Ren's trial was held privately, after Dheizir Crohl's.

The commodore was recovering well thanks to top notch medical attention. The Consortium promised he would receive his own cell on the Bastion and be allowed private yard time. They offered him one more chance to give up the Dread Phantoms. He refused.

Strife Squad was allowed to say their farewells in private.

'You would make a good pirate, huntress,' Ren said.

'Take care of yourself, commodore.'

'Speak to Eosar while you still can. You're in need of payment.'

'But you're going to prison.'

'I don't believe me walking away from this was ever part of the deal. Wording, huntress, is paramount when dealing with pirates. Remember that. I may see you again soon.'

'I wouldn't call twenty years *soon*.'

Ren shrugged. 'The problem with imprisoning a man is that anything can happen before his sentence ends, even if that sentence is life.'

5

Trix mulled over Ren's last words while she looked at the mountains.

He'd been joyful and morose as he spoke to everyone. His prison sentence granted him the opportunity for early release, maybe a breakout. Of course, the same went for Dheizir Crohl.

Per Ren's request, Strife Squad saw Eosar aboard the Dread Phantoms' galleon. Eosar was the new leader until Ren returned. Each of Strife Squad was paid 15,000 orits for their trouble, and for saving Ren.

The only reason the Dread Phantoms still had so much money was because Eosar had agreed to be bought by the Red Wolves. Luc Reno had given him an offer he couldn't refuse.

Once Strife Squad had been paid, the Dread Phantoms returned to Thyria.

That was when Strife Squad made for Yephus. Trix had wired Cid Tyler payment for the ship she destroyed on the way. Cid sent her a message telling her to "get fucked, but come again any time." Trix thought it must've been an Australian thing.

'Beatrix, are you gonna sit there and drink all the beer by yourself?' Kit said.

'I paid for this beer. I can drink it all if I want.'

'Long as you leave room for dinner.' Kit called to Cole, Kyra, and Griff. 'Come on, you bloody galahs, food's ready.'

Strife Squad used the Fox's loading ramp as a table. Kit started divvying up the feast he'd been preparing for the past hour. Everyone ate and drank hearty, for after the food, they were going their separate ways.

Over dinner they talked about adventures, both recent and long ago. Mostly, they ate in silence, happy to be in each other's company. When they finished, Kit kicked back with his umpteenth drink of the night while Trix, Cole, Kyra, and Griff cleaned up. Griff had a shuttle on loan from the UNSS. The Oni Three would be leaving Yephus on Cole's ship to seek another job. They were confident that whatever came next would be nothing compared to what they'd experienced with Trix of Zilvia.

'Guess this is it. For now, anyway,' Kyra said as she sat on the plateau's edge. She was barefoot. Wearing a dress. It was a jarring sight if you'd only ever seen her in battle-armour.

'We make a hell of a team,' said Cole. He put his arm around Kyra.

Trix wove her fingers in Kit's. They didn't kiss.

'Only because the rest of us can pick up your slack, mate,' Kit said.

'You couldn't pick up my slack, fool, if you know what I mean.'

Kyra chortled. 'If you love your penis so much, why don't you marry it?'

'I think that'd be incest,' said Kit, spitting his beer out with laughter.

Griff: 'Hysi. But who would wear the dress?'

'Hey, Daddy Blue. I thought you were on my side.'

'Not if you're marrying your penis. That's where I draw the line.'

Trix: 'Alright. I think we get it.'

'I got it just before,' Kyra winked. She and Cole high-fived.

Trix shook her head with a smile.

Cole: 'We better be going. Got some promising leads for work on Dark's Hide now that it's not in so many pieces.'

Everyone stood.

Kyra and Trix hugged. 'It was nice seeing you again, Trix.'

'Likewise. Don't let those two give you any trouble.'

'Hah, I'm the one who gives them trouble. Thanks for your help. I hate to think what would've happened if you hadn't been with us.'

'If you're talking about the gramyriapede, you three warmed it up for me.'

'You know what I mean.'

'I do. Farewell, Kyra.'

'Same to you, Trix.'

Cole held his arms open wide. A cheesy grin spread across his face.

'Bring it in, baby.'

Trix hugged Cole. He smelled like smoked wood.

'Look after yourself, Cole Train.'

'There it is, haha. See you later, Trix.'

Cole moved on to Griff who was farewelling Kyra.

'Daddy Blue,' Cole said, bringing Griff in for a hug-high-five. 'You're the craziest fool I've ever met, and that's some stiff competition. I believe you know the runners up,' Cole jerked his thumb towards the other machinas.

'Bright stars and clear skies, mufy rami.'

'We still good for that smashball pool?'

'As long as you're okay with losing.'

'I'll hold you to that.'

Kit walked to Griff. He'd bought casual clothes before leaving Earth. He was rocking straight leg jeans, sneaker boots, and a plain white cotton t-shirt that was stretched beyond belief over his brawn.

'I wouldn't be worried about Cole's smashball bets. He's rubbish.'

'Fool, you just pick the teams with the coolest names.'

'*Used to.* I'm smarter now.'

Griff: 'I'd hate to see what you were like before. Did you even know how to read?'

Kyra: 'Only takeaway menus.'

Kit: 'Alright, everyone's had their fun now.'

'Hysi, I better go. Long trip back to Earth. Don't want to be late for my new job. I haven't been this excited since I was working on the Fox. Take care of her, Trix.'

'As long as you take care of yourself. You're the only person who knows how to fix it now if it breaks.'

'Hysi. Don't worry, I won't upgrade Earth's ships to be as good as yours. They won't be as impressive no matter what I do without me at the helm anyway.'

Griff turned to leave. Trix tapped him on the shoulder. He turned around. Trix gave him a hug.

'You really are the best pilot I've ever seen,' she said as they parted.

'You say that like I needed validation,' Griff winked. 'Oh, Sif?'

'I'm here.'

'You can be my co-pilot anytime.'

'If you're so lucky to have me.'

Griff laughed. He waved one last time. Performed a zirean bow. He walked onto his shuttle. The thrusters powered up. Griffauron Fulum Raivad took to the skies. Then space.

The machinas were left alone on the plateau. Trix felt like she was forgetting something.

The prism, she thought. The past week had been so hectic that it'd completely slipped her mind.

'Wait here,' Trix said to the Oni Three. Cole raised an eyebrow at Kyra. But he obeyed. His instincts were hopeless to deny a Valkyrie. Especially when she was a friend.

Those particular instincts failed to kick in for Kit. He followed Trix into the Fox.

'What part of wait didn't you understand?' Trix said. There was no anger in her voice. In fact, there was almost playfulness. A tone Trix rarely took. It surprised even her.

Kit grabbed her around the waist. Kissed her.

'And what was that?'

'A farewell and a thank you all in one. How'd you like it?'

'No complaints,' Trix said. She altered gravity. Floated to Kit's lips. He leaned in to kiss her again. Trix moved upwards at the last second. Kissed him on the forehead.

To add insult to injury, Trix floated out of the cargo bay. Landed in front of Cole and Kyra.

'I need you to have a look at this,' Trix said, holding out the Uldarian prism. Cole and Kyra's hands went to their medallions. Both of them vibrated.

Kyra: 'It's Uldarian. A data drive, perhaps?'

Trix: 'That's what Sif and I think. It appears to show more of a vision, or a recording, with each machina who touches it. I was the first. Dai of Thyria, the spectre who helped save Iglessia Vialle, was the second.'

'Then yours truly,' Kit said.

'What does it show?'

'See for yourself.'

Cole and Kyra grabbed the prism together. Their eyes snapped to slits, then went wide as moons. Their irises came alive. Golden nebulas spinning around their white pupils. They returned to normal in a couple of seconds. Their mouths had fallen open. Kyra gave the prism back to Trix.

Cole: 'It was like being there. I didn't just see things, I—'

Kyra: 'Felt them.'

'Yeah. All these ships in No Man's Land. You know it's there because of the Transfer. And it started powering up.'

'But then you're inside someone's head, getting a POV. They turn away before you can see what comes out. Looks like they're running through a ship.'

'Anything else?' Trix said.

'No, it cuts out. But we saw crewmen. They were definitely Uldarians. Though they looked more gold than black.'

'Maybe nothing was coming out of the Transfer. Maybe they were the ones turning it on, trying to escape,' Kit said.

'Man, this could mean anything,' said Cole. His eyes were still fixed on the prism.

'Is that what you were talking about during our hearing?'

Kyra said. 'Strife Squad, a team for saving the galaxy. You think we're going to fight whatever killed the Uldarians?'

Kit: 'Nah, mate. We're gonna win.'

'Fuck yeah, baby,' Cole laughed. 'You know we are. Trix, this shit ever happens for real, you can count us in. The Oni Three have got your back.'

'To the end,' Kit said, taking this opportunity to use the Oni Academy motto.

Trix: 'It'll be a sad day for the galaxy if we're their last hope.'

Kyra: 'Hey, we were made as a last hope. Way I see it, there's no one more qualified than us.'

Trix thought of Yvach, Griff, and Ren. None of them machinas. All of them qualified.

'Hmm,' the Valkyrie nodded.

There was silence among the machinas, though it wasn't uncomfortable. In fact, it remained unbroken. The Oni Three embraced Trix one last time. Entered Cole's ship. The vertical takeoff thrusters engaged.

Cole's ship was of zirean design. It'd been payment for a job well done nearly two decades prior. Trix watched the onis go.

Alone on the plateau, the Valkyrie looked over the mountains.

6

Hours later, Trix of Zilvia was sitting in the Fox's pilot's chair, dressed in her battle-armour.

She was amused by the thruster settings Griff had written by the controls. There was SLIGHT, LOW, MEDIUM, HIGH, VALKYRIE, and above all of those was a scrap of duct tape with DADDY BLUE scrawled across it.

'Where are we going?' Sif said.

Trix touched her Valkyrie medallion. Her latest adventure hardly seemed real.

She wasn't ready to begin a search for Garth Roche yet. Balthioul had left a bad taste in her mouth. She needed to purge it with a successful hunt.

'Somewhere with monsters.'

'Oh, yes. That's specific.'

Trix powered up the Fox. Its roar was harmonious. The sound of endless possibility. Wherever Trix wanted to go, she could.

In a galaxy full of so many choices you could find yourself stuck in the same place, always trying to choose between them. Trix recalled her conversation with Garth Roche. He said thoughts came into people's heads. They weren't born there. If that was the case, Trix trusted she'd end up wherever she was supposed to be.

The Fox took to the sky. Trix flew to the divide of night and day. Darkness and Light. Mireleth's poem came to her mind. It related to the Uldarian prism's vision. She knew it did. Up to space now. She hadn't tried Griff's upgrades yet.

The Valkyrie made the Fox do six instantaneous barrel-rolls while performing a one-eighty. She continued flying this way a little longer, high in Yephus' orbit. Trix thought about those who lost their lives because of Crohl. She said a silent prayer for them. Not to any god in particular. It was more like a gentle plea to the universe.

Then she went to hyperspace. Headed for the Shivering Dominion Transfer.

Monsters lay beyond.

And so did adventure.

Written over 58 days
Brisbane, Queensland, Australia

Please enjoy this sneak preview of the prologue from *A Clash of Demons: A Machina Novel Starring Beatrix Westwood by Aleks Canard.*

LOCATION: Dark's Hide, Dying Star Nexus
EARTH DATE: May 1st, 2799

Nightshade's music lured everyone into a trance.

Time became meaningless within its darkened walls punctuated by neon colours, flavoured with ecstasy and rife with carnal pleasures. It was an unorthodox duchy. Then again, its ruler was far from royalty.

Nadira Vega surveyed her personal wonderland from a raised VIP platform. She wore no crown, graced no throne, but she was the Duchess. Daquarius Farosi had been killed months ago. He had never so much as showed his face if he could help it. And people thought that made him powerful.

Power was an illusion if maintaining it meant staying hidden. Nadira wanted everyone to know she was here, yet none could touch her. That was power.

Dark's Hide was a duchy of few rules. One rule, specifically.

Don't fuck with Nadira.

Since she had rebuilt it following Anrok Iclon's botched attack, Dark's Hide prospered now more than ever. Nadira had inherited Daquarius Farosi's client list and expanded it considerably. Nadira's wares supplied gangs across the galaxy. Personally, she didn't care for weapons. Nadira Vega was interested in artefacts. Rare ones. Ones of magic.

More so than precious relics, Nadira valued information. Her increased wealth allowed her spy network to expand to places that were previously concealed in shadow.

Rasud Sinnad was a priority target. He was a mysterious medcanol who had secrets like misers had money. Nadira had known of him for some time, though it wasn't until he played a part in seeing Iglessia Vialle ascend to Xardiassant's throne did she become curious. Nadira suspected he was playing a game of long odds. The longest of cons.

What his end goal was, she couldn't say. And his past, well, there wasn't one. He just appeared fully formed. No matter, Nadira had other ventures to pursue. One was close.

Her comms gauntlet flashed once. It was indistinguishable amid Nightshade's strobing lights. Nadira looked at her gauntlet. Her perpetual smirk broke into a smile. One that could turn rivers to ice. A fox would look as cunning as a doe next to her.

The Duchess slinked her way off the VIP platform, through the crowds, to her office. No longer did Dark's Hide's guards wear matching uniforms. They blended into the criminal filth who called Dark's Hide home like grunge in an alley.

Besides, Nadira knew how to handle herself. Her dresses revealed plenty of her curvaceous body. This was done intentionally, both to distract and to deceive. Anyone would assume she couldn't possibly be packing any weapons when so much of her was on display. They would be wrong. Nadira had a dagger strapped to each thigh. They were made of mithril, a rare metal thought by many to be fictitious. In truth, mithril was crafted from copper antimony and copper arsenic. Both these compounds were scarcely found, save for areas around active volcanoes.

Nuallar was rich with it, though few dared journey to its wastelands anymore.

Mithril was favoured by mages due to it lightness and enchantment retainment. Though preferred as armour, only a fool would turn down a mithril blade. While not overly useful for swordplay, their edge retention was unheard of.

Unlike other metals such as obsidian, mithril could be crafted paper thin if the blacksmith was skilled enough. This meant people could die from cuts that were invisible to the eye.

Nadira reached the office that formerly belonged to Daquarius Farosi. Entered. Once there had been an aquarium filled with deadly fish and aquatic oddities. Nadira had it transformed into a garden. Her personal haven from the metal that was Dark's Hide.

Through the garden, past flowerbeds, oak trees, and a babbling brook, Nadira came to a yew nestled behind a hedge. She stroked its bark. The trunk opened, revealing an elevator with plush leather seats and dim lighting made to simulate candles. Nadira entered. She was taken to her emporium on Dark's Hide's fourth level.

When she arrived, her zirean assistant, Dahos Mardulen, had tea waiting on a silver platter. The leaves were from the djurel home world of Djiemlur. They were naturally sweet and afforded the drinker a minor high. The crockery was zirean. Antique. From the Age of Arrows.

'My thanks, Dahos.'

'The pleasure is mine, my lady.'

Nadira drank the tea in one go. It was smooth as a djurel's fur.

'I hear it has been found.'

'Por wyrs,

(*of course*)

I would not have alerted you for a trivial matter.'

'And,' Nadira walked to her terminal. Any common thug would see her as another pretty woman with too much money. Anyone who knew the first thing about fighting could tell she knew how to handle herself. It was in the way she flowed, not walked. 'Where is it?'

'Your sources only speak in murmurs about where it lies.'

'Where, Dahos?'

'The Rose Vale System, on Zilvia.'

Nadira's smirk flatlined. Zilvia was a queer place drenched in magic so heavy that technology tended to fail more than work. It was a place of many kingdoms, often referred to as a planet out of time. Its wilds were deadly, and that wasn't just because of the monsters. Strange things lurked on Zilvia. Why, it was almost stranger than Mair Ultima.

'It's high time I called in the favour I am owed.'

There was but one person who could retrieve what Nadira wanted.

And her name was Beatrix Westwood.

If you liked this story, prepare to join Dante Quintrell on the second part of his grand adventure.

The Tales of Dante Quintrell

Chapter II

Celestial Twins

Aleks Canard

Made in the USA
Las Vegas, NV
07 May 2024

89619263R00308